The Perfect Play

Goodnight Steve McQueen

The Perfect Play

LOUISE WENER

WILLIAM MORROW
An Imprint of HarperCollins*Publishers*

Originally published under the title *The Big Blind*

This book was originally published in Great Britain in 2003 by Hodder and Stoughton, a division of Hodder Headline, under the title *The Big Blind*.

THE PERFECT PLAY. Copyright © 2003 by Louise Wener. All rights reserved. Printed in the United States of America. No part of this book may be used or reproduced in any manner whatsoever without written permission except in the case of brief quotations embodied in critical articles and reviews. For information address HarperCollins Publishers Inc., 10 East 53rd Street, New York, NY 10022.

HarperCollins books may be purchased for educational, business, or sales promotional use. For information please write: Special Markets Department, HarperCollins Publishers Inc., 10 East 53rd Street, New York, NY 10022.

FIRST U.S. EDITION

Printed on acid-free paper

Library of Congress Cataloging-in-Publication Data has been applied for.

ISBN 0-06-058547-1

04 05 06 07 08 RRD 10 9 8 7 6 5 4 3 2 1

For my big brother, Geoff.

Thanks to High Stakes Publishing at
www.highstakes.co.uk for permission to quote from
The Education of a Poker Player by
Herbert O Yardley.

PROLOGUE

The thing Big Louie wanted more than anything else in the whole world was a garden. He wanted a neat lawn surrounded by evergreen shrubs and flower beds, and a pair of fruit trees that grew fat, sour apples and plums. He wanted chrysanthemums and violets and bright yellow lupins, and a bed of wild crocuses that would bloom in the very same spot each spring. Most of all, he wanted a small wooden bench to sit on. A place where he could take in the sun, sip a glass of iced tea and look at what a fine garden he'd made.

This desire to have a garden consumed most of Big Louie's day, and at night he'd sometimes lie awake for hours wondering about the type of watering can he might use to feed his plants. If he was feeling especially optimistic he'd plan on building an elaborate sprinkler system with hoses and a remote control. He liked to imagine the sound it would make. He thought it might go 'shoosh, shoosh' or 'whiputt, whiputt'; or perhaps it would be the expensive kind that spun around in circles and sputtered and spat like a lazy steam engine. Perhaps he would employ an extra gardener to help him one day. But only in the autumn. Someone to help him rake up all the leaves.

Big Louie undressed slowly and climbed into his cotton pyjamas. He brushed his teeth three times. He combed his hair, lifted a fresh pair of earplugs out of their paper wrappers, and sat down on the edge of his bed to think. After a good five minutes of rubbing at his temples and tugging at his eyebrows, he leaned over, reached between his mattress and his quilted headboard and pulled out a frayed canvas bag with plastic buckles. Inside that bag was everything he had left in the world: a gold-plated watch left to him by his grandfather and twenty thousand pounds in hard cash. Thick bunches of twenties held together with elastic bands; wads of crumpled tenners knotted with twine; torn five-pound notes fixed together with thin strips of yellowing sticky tape; and, right at the bottom, a handful of loose coins that rubbed against each other like seashells and wore small holes in the corners of his bag.

There were times in Big Louie's life when he had owned far larger bags than this – with plenty more money in them – but for the moment he tried to be content with what he had. Given the right set of circumstances, a person could turn twenty thousand pounds into a small fortune overnight. All Louie needed was someone who could play it for him. Someone good. Someone he could trust.

Big Louie wrapped up his precious bankroll and packed it safely away. He lowered the mattress, tucked in the brushed nylon sheets and rocked forwards to help lever himself off the bed. He'd gained close to eleven stone since he'd stopped going outside, and it was quite an effort to prise his substantial bulk from the soft suck of his cotton mattress. Once safely on his feet, he fetched himself a cup of warm water and shuffled over to the window, as he did every single night before he went to sleep. He placed his fingers on the metal latch, worked its pin free from the rusty iron frame and stood still, waiting for his pulse to quicken.

It didn't take long. By the time he felt the first rush of air flapping at his cheeks, his heart rate was already up to 105. The further he opened the window, the harder his heart thumped inside his chest and, with his head spinning and his palms oozing salty bubbles of sweat, he snatched the window towards him and closed it tightly shut. He had what he wanted. Even though it was only the second day of March, Big Louie's nose was so sensitive that it could already detect the first notes of spring greenness in the air. Before too long the trees would start to bud, the leaves would spread outwards towards his window, and the view from his tower block would slowly begin to soften.

Content that the seasons were finally on the move again, Big Louie fixed his earplugs with cotton wool and drifted off to sleep without tossing or turning or bothering himself about watering cans once. He dreamt about the next evening's card game and the bowl of tuna salad he had waiting in his fridge. He dreamt about the man who was coming over to build him a window box at the end of the week and about the kinds of flowers he might choose to put in it. And, as he always did, he dreamt about finding the perfect card player to win his match for him. A genius. A magician. The kind who has a special type of gift.

1

Do you remember the card game Top Trumps? I was brilliant at Top Trumps. King of the whole school. I was almost as good at Top Trumps as I was at marbles, and no one could touch me for marbles, not even the boys.

I must have played close to a thousand games while I was in junior school, but my all-time greatest victory was against Gary Martin Washbrook in the winter of 1979. Gary was a spectacularly unsavoury character. He had boss eyes and bad breath and a pet rat called Hooligan that lived in the lining of his Pac-a-Mac. His favourite trick was creeping up behind you in the playground, waving Hooligan's lumpy belly in front of your face, and demanding that you hand over all your pocket money and sandwiches. It was the same story when it came to winning at marbles. With a modicum of skill, a hefty dose of intimidation and the help of one scabrous, flea-infected rodent, Gary Washbrook had earned himself the second-largest marble collection in the school.

It was my life's ambition to win it from him.

The day it happened had begun much like any other. I'd spent the morning constructing a wonky snowflake out of tinsel and wire coat hangers and planned to spend a most satisfactory lunch hour counting my marbles, eating my fish-finger sandwiches and rereading my *Children's Encyclopaedia of Truly Amazing Facts*. I was very keen on amazing facts when I was a kid. I wasn't too hot on the Partridge Family or the middle names of the Bay City Rollers, but if ever you needed to know the speed of something, or the height of something, or the length of time it would take an earthworm to crawl across the Mojave Desert (sixteen years, two months and twenty-seven days, in case you were wondering) I was definitely the person to ask.

It was a bitterly cold afternoon. The lunch bell had just rung and I was about to make a start on chapter eleven – 'Weird Things You'd Never Expect to Happen in a Million Years' – when I noticed Gary Washbrook heading towards me with his pet rat peeping out of his jumper.

At first I thought he was planning to hit me in the head and steal my sandwiches, but it turned out he had something altogether different in mind. He glanced down at my packed lunch, announced that he didn't much care for fish fingers and shoved Hooligan's whiskery face back into his sleeve. Content that he had my full attention, he reached into the nether regions of his sports bag, heaved out his entire marble collection and dumped it at my feet with a deeply satisfying clatter. I couldn't take my eyes off it. If I concentrate I can still see it now: a red felt bag, brimming with clusters of multi-coloured globes that spun the winter sunlight like they were diamonds.

'Oi, Four-eyes,' he said, loosening the string at the top of his bag so I could see farther inside. 'I've decided to break me no girls rule. One day only. All or nothing. You up for it, or are you chicken?'

This was very odd indeed. I'd been trying to engineer a game with Gary for months now, but he'd always claimed I wasn't worth playing on account of my gingerness and my chronic asthma. I knew right away that someone had dared him. I knew right away there was every chance that he'd cheat. I didn't hesitate. Not for a second.

After lengthy debate – and a brief reappearance from Hooligan – we agreed this match should settle the score once and for all. We'd play on the drain behind the dinner-hut wall for the next hour, and whoever was ahead at the final lunch bell would be the undisputed champion. This was big news. There was a small crowd gathering as we knelt down to pitch our opening shots, and by the time we reached the climax of our game there must have been close to thirty people watching us play. Skinny girls that smelt of Charlie and wee, shivering in their fingerless gloves; boys that smelt of linseed oil and mud, tightening their parka hoods against the wind; and me and Gary Washbrook, crouched at the edge of a rusty iron storm drain with our legs turning purple from the cold.

There were 147 marbles on the drain by then. Green ones, blue ones, twisters and Frenchies, and a gold-flecked Chinese oriental that I was absolutely desperate not to lose. I didn't let it show, though. Not for a moment. I'd already missed a couple of shots on purpose to gain his confidence, and with five minutes left before the final bell I offered him the chance to go all-in. One last shot, I said. If I made the hit I took every marble on the drain and everything that was left in his red felt bag. If I messed it up he walked away with a collection it had taken me close to three and a half years to build.

He couldn't resist it. Greed took hold of him like a fever, and he pushed his remaining marbles towards the drain without a second thought. He didn't even bother fetching Hooligan out of his pocket in an attempt to put me off. He never thought I'd make it: not in a million years.

Even by my standards, I played the shot beautifully. I lifted the final marble out of my lunch box, paused for a moment to build up the tension in the crowd, and rolled it slowly between my index finger and thumb. This was my secret weapon. The sheep's eye. A chunk of glass so pitted and hard and misshapen it was impossible to imagine that it had once been as smooth and as spherical as a pea.

The crowd fell silent. Gary slapped his pocket to stop his rat from coughing and I shifted slightly on the cracked asphalt to squeeze some blood back into my frozen knees. I nodded to indicate that I was ready. I rolled up the sleeves of my duffel coat, took a short blast on my sky-blue asthma inhaler, and pitched the sheep's eye at the epicentre of the drain with all my strength. It was perfect. A direct hit. The sheep's eye flew out of my fingers like a pond stone, splitting his cobalt kingfisher clean in two, before ricocheting into the dinner-hut wall with the force of a stray sniper bullet. And then something magical happened. The sheep's eye exploded. It floated in midair for the briefest moment, before shattering into a powder so fine and golden and pale you could almost believe it was true: that glass really was made out of sand.

As is often the way with such things, my victory was cruelly short lived. When he'd finished gasping at the audacity of my final shot, Gary screwed up his face and began to wail like a smacked girl. His eyes awash with tears, he somehow managed to convince one of the teachers that I'd stolen his marbles, instead of winning them from him fair and square. In an act of brutal unfairness – which haunts me to this day – my own marbles were confiscated, Gary was given a tissue and a bag of toffees, and I was banned from the end-of-year disco and sent home early, with a cautionary letter to my mum. I never gave it to her. I shredded it into tiny pieces, pushed them through the tight metal grille on the storm drain, and watched for a good while until I was sure they'd all floated away.

Aware that I'd arouse suspicion if I went home early, I packed up my encyclopaedias and logarithm tables and set off towards the centre of town. I spent the last hours of daylight kicking around the bus shelter, calculating the speed of falling sleet and wandering around on the pier. I grew up in Brighton, fairly close to the seafront, and I liked to spend as much free time as possible watching the sailing boats, and playing on the fruit machines in the arcade. I'd learnt how to read the wheels on a couple of the older machines, and on a good afternoon I could win enough money to buy fish bits and a couple of pickled gherkins. I liked to suck the vinegar out of the gherkins and watch the waves come in: especially when the weather was bad. My dad once told me that every seventh wave was an extra-big one, and I liked to count them and make notes in my rough book to see whether it was true.

That afternoon I sucked gherkins and counted waves until my lips had set hard from the vinegar and my cheeks had frozen solid from the wind. I stared out over the jetties, listened for the clatter of the dodgems on the pier, and decided not to tell anyone about what had happened to me at school. My mum would only worry that I'd got myself into trouble; my stepfather would tut through his teeth and shake his head; and my stepbrothers would say the only reason I'd won the marble game in the first place was because my fingers were too long for my hands.

The only person who would have understood was my dad. He'd have realised how important it was for me to win, and he'd have appreciated the way I'd tricked my opponent into thinking I was a worse player than I really was. He'd have recognised the injustice of it all. He'd have mock-punched me on the chin, stroked the end of his scratchy beard and said something useful like: 'That's the way it goes, Audrey. Genius is always misunderstood.'

2

'Come on, Brain-box, why don't you try getting up. It's a beautiful day outside.'

'I'm not getting up. I'm having a midlife crisis.'

'How can you be having a midlife crisis? You're only thirty-two.'

'I know, but I could be dead by the time I'm sixty, in which case I'm already well behind the game.'

'Is this because it's your birthday next month?'

'No.'

'Well, what then?'

'I can't tell you. You'll get upset.'

'No I won't.'

'You will.'

'*Audrey?*'

'OK, I'll tell you, but don't blame me if you get upset.'

My boyfriend Joe is upset with me and it's all his own fault. He shouldn't have made me tell him about my latent sexual attraction to Bono. I'm not even sure how it started. It sort of crept up on me. One minute I was watching an old U2 concert on MTV, the next I was experiencing a distinct frisson of sexual excitement as Bono launched into the second verse of 'Beautiful Day'. At first I was a little disgusted with myself, sort of the way you feel when you realise you're getting turned on by late-night cable pornography, but after a while I found myself being happily swept along. I didn't even mind when he dragged an eighteen-year-old girl out of the audience and started crooning to her and kissing her on the neck. In fact,

I rather liked it. I sort of wanted to be her. By the end of the song I'd even found myself humming along to 'Elevation' and admiring the Edge's tidy hat. It's a very bad sign and I should probably be much more worried about it than I am, but, to be fair, admiring the Edge's hat and fantasising about Bono is only number three on the list of things that have brought about my premature midlife crisis. I like to think the other two are much more substantial.

'You don't understand nu metal?'

'No.'

'And this is the reason you're upset?'

'Yes. It confuses me. I don't get it. It's definitely my point of departure.'

'What's a point of departure?'

'It's the cultural movement that marks your separation from your youth. It's the thing that dates you, the thing that displaces you from all the generations that follow.'

Joe shakes his head and looks around for his gardening boots.

'It's like this,' I say, getting into my stride. 'For our parents it was punk. For their parents it was the Rolling Stones. For me it's the guy from Slipknot that keeps rabbit foetuses in a jar and inhales the smell onstage so he can puke up over his fans mid-gig.'

'Right,' says Joe, tightening his laces and pulling on his fisherman's jumper. 'Let me get this straight. You're sexually attracted to a balding Irish pop star, and you're confused by a man who wears a leather face mask and keeps rotting rabbit foetuses in a jar?'

'Yes.'

'These are the reasons you're sat in bed with a pillow-case draped over your head and your duvet pulled up over your chin?'

'Yes. Well, no,' I say, backtracking slightly. 'It's not just that.'

* * *

'Look, it was *only* a suggestion.'

'I know, but it gave me the fear. The idea of us moving to the countryside gives me the fear.'

'Why?'

'Well,' I say, 'I would have thought that was obvious. No restaurants, no cinemas, no art galleries, no lesbians, no Asians, no Starbucks, no takeaways, no pickle shops and no theatres.'

'When was the last time you went to the theatre?'

'1987, but that's not the point. The point is I could if I wanted to.'

'And we don't even know any lesbians.'

'We know Pete.'

'He's not a lesbian.'

'I know, but he's half Jewish and if we moved to the countryside he wouldn't be able to work for you or come and visit us any more.'

'Why not?'

'Because the village would organise a pogrom. And imagine what they'd do to Lorna. An unmarried mother. They'd probably stone her to death or something. It would be like that scene in *Deliverance* when the hillbillies come out of the woods with their hunting knives and bugger Burt Reynolds.'

'They didn't bugger Burt Reynolds.'

'Well who did they bugger, then? They definitely buggered someone.'

Joe stands up and folds his arms, signalling that the conversation is over.

'What about morris dancers?' I say, trying to pull him back in. 'You can't tell me they don't give you the creeps. Grown men dressed in flouncy blouses, dancing round maypoles and shaking jingly bells at each other. It's not natural. It's upsetting. It's perverse.'

'Are you going to keep that bed sheet over your head all day?'

'No.'

'Why are you still holding it up, then?'

'I've got a chin spot with two heads on it and I don't want you to see.'

'Too late,' he says, heading for the door. 'I saw it before you woke up.'

'Shit,' I say, letting go of the duvet. 'How am I going to get Bono to sleep with me now?'

Joe goes out to the garden and I wander into the kitchen to make us both some coffee. I fill the espresso machine, open a giant jar of pickled gherkins and watch Joe through the window while he works. Our garden is tiny, about the size of a large beach towel, but Joe's turned it into a miniature oasis since we moved in. There's a tall bamboo curtain that blocks out the line of the council flats; a wooden pergola that he'll have finished by the end of today and, dotted around on the gravel, a jumble of clay pots filled with maples and date palms; and a dozen glossy evergreens whose names I can never remember.

Joe knows the names of all of them. He's been a professional gardener for the last six years and he's got that whole green-fingers thing totally sorted out. He's even managed to pass some of it on to me. Before we met I couldn't keep a house plant alive for longer than a couple of weeks, but I've got a cactus in the bathroom that I've managed not to kill for almost a year now. If it manages to survive another winter, I'm thinking of getting something a bit more complicated: like a pet goldfish, or a cat.

I take a cup of hot coffee out to Joe, and sit on the step watching him, while he cuts fresh lengths of wood for the pergola. It's cold this morning, the remnants of winter hanging in the crisp March air, and I pull my jacket tight round my shoulders to keep warm. As usual, he's not using any plans or instructions, and from what I can see he doesn't seem to be measuring anything either. It used to really bother me. I never do anything without planning it meticulously first, and the idea that Joe could put up a shelf or build a fence without working it all out in advance used to drive me to distraction. I like it now, though. I like the way he can take a pile of bricks and driftwood and sharp metal pins, and turn them into something substantial before my eyes. Joe's like that. He has a way of bringing order to things.

Joe and I met five years ago at a seventies fancy dress party and we've been together pretty much ever since. It was the kind of party that was filled with gatecrashers and dope-heads and students dressed in second-hand Jefferson Airplane T-shirts, and I remember feeling distinctly out of place. I was still working as a waitress at the time and I'd been on the late shift, so I hadn't had time to go home and change my clothes. I had sweat marks under my arms and a ketchup stain on my left lapel and an invite from one of the bar staff at the restaurant folded into the pocket of my jeans.

As soon as the taxi dropped me off, I wished I hadn't let it drive away. I spent the first twenty minutes searching around for someone that I recognised; the next hour talking to an anorexic eighteen-year-old about macrobiotic dieting and shoes; and out of desperation I'd grabbed a bottle of Blue Nun and hidden myself away in a corner, next to the lava lamps and the pile of seventies games.

I was just wondering at what age you become too old to enjoy parties where you have to queue up for the toilet and fish crushed cigarette butts out of your wineglass when I felt someone tap me on the shoulder. It was Joe. He was wearing a black shirt and a white *Saturday Night Fever* suit and his first words to me were: 'What's it to be, then, Top Trumps or marbles?'

I couldn't believe my luck.

'Your choice,' I said, tossing a couple of peanuts into my mouth and offering him some of my wine. 'I'll beat you at both of them anyway.'

'You reckon?' he said, fixing me with a shambolic smile.

'Absolutely. No question about it.'

'Right then,' he said, rubbing his hands together. 'Let's have a bet on it. How's about we say two quid on the marbles, double or nothing on the cards?'

'I'm not sure,' I said, 'I don't really like to gamble.'

'No problem. Just a friendly, then.'

'OK,' I said, 'just a friendly.'

'Well, *that* wasn't very friendly.'

'Sorry, I should have told you. I was a bit of a demon at Top Trumps when I was a kid.'

'So, I've been hustled then, have I?'

'What do you mean? I let you keep your money.'

'Yeah, but you could have let me win one hand. You didn't have to win every single racing car in the deck.'

'Sorry,' I said, raking up the cards and packing them back into their plastic case. 'I couldn't help it. I memorised all the winning statistics before we started.'

'What, just now? Before we started playing?'

'Well, you know. I can memorise numbers pretty quickly. I only have to look at them a couple of times.'

He grinned at me and shook his head.

'So, what else were you good at when you were at school? Apart from cheating unsuspecting boys out of their Top Trumps cards.'

'I don't know. Maths, I suppose. Do you know which day of the week you were born on?'

'Yes,' he said, 'I think it was a—'

'Wait, don't tell me. I'll work it out. What's your date of birth?'

'July twenty-seventh 1967.'

I thought for a moment and then I said: 'Thursday. You were definitely born on a Thursday.'

'Wow, you're right. How do you know that?'

'It's not difficult,' I said, shrugging gently. 'There's an equation you can use.'

I scribbled the formula on to the back of an old till receipt and showed Joe how I'd worked it out.

'And you did all that in a few seconds?' he said, staring down at the complex tangle of figures and algebra. 'You made all those calculations without having to write any of it down?'

'Yes. It's just practice really. My dad taught me how to do it when I was little. I've got quicker over the years.'

'What did your dad do? Was he a mathematician or something?'

'Sort of,' I said, fiddling with the end of my sleeve. 'He was a science teacher.'

'Was?'

'He left home when I was still at school. I'm not really sure what he does now.'

'You're not in touch with him?'

'No,' I said. 'I haven't seen him in a good while.'

We spent the rest of the evening playing cards, working out which day of the week most of Joe's friends were born on, and getting steadily drunk in a corner. I learnt that his favourite album was *Rain Dogs* by Tom Waits; that he'd trained as a lawyer before giving it all up to become a landscape gardener; and that he'd just split up with his girlfriend of six and a half years. He learnt that I was better at asking questions than I was at answering them, and that I didn't like to talk about myself unless I was pushed.

'Well, I'm sort of in between jobs at the moment.'

'You're unemployed?'

'No, not exactly. I'm waitressing. It's just for a little while. Just until I get myself back on my feet.'

To his eternal credit, he didn't ask me to elaborate. He nodded gently, filled our paper cups with more wine and dealt out a final hand of Top Trumps.

'OK then,' I said pulling a five-pound note out of my pocket and laying it on top of his peanuts. 'Maybe we should have a bet on it after all.'

'I thought you didn't gamble?'

'I don't, usually,' I said, smiling at him a little longer than was necessary, 'but the thing is, it's not really gambling if you know you're going to win.'

'Not feeling any better, then?' says Joe, kicking the mud off his boots and joining me on the step.

'Not much. How can you tell?'

'Well, that's the third pickled gherkin you've eaten straight from the jar while simultaneously digging your ear out with a hair grip. I've learnt to read the signs.'

'It's nothing,' I say, pushing the hair grip deeper into my ear and searching about for a nice piece of wax. 'I'm just a bit fed up, that's all.'

'Come on,' he says, 'what's really bothering you? It can't just be Slipknot and the rabbits.'

'No,' I say, staring into the garden. 'It's not.'

'Well, what then?' he says, putting his arm round me. 'Did your stepfather ring up again?'

I shrug my shoulders and offer Joe a slice of pickled cucumber.

'Come on,' he says, screwing his face up and trying not to inhale the vinegar fumes. 'Tell me what he said. Was he still on about having this memorial thing for your mum?'

I frown and nod into my pickles.

'Stay there a minute,' he says, standing up and heading for the kitchen. 'I think I'd better open you another jar.'

3

Next week will be the seventeenth anniversary of my mother's death, and for some reason my stepfather, Frank, has decided he wants to mark the occasion with a remembrance party. He wants the whole family to be there. He wants us to bring pictures and mementoes and witty anecdotes, and sit around telling cosy stories about my mother while we eat slices of buttered malt loaf, and drink wine from his once-a-year sherry glasses. This is typical of Frank. The idea will have come to him on a whim while he was listening to one of his favourite albums – *Ten of the Best Spring Hymns Ever* – and instead of sleeping on it he will have decided to ring up everybody he knows there and then. A week or so later, a small light bulb will have gone off in his head and he'll have remembered that it might be polite to call me.

It's not the act of remembering her that bothers me so much, it's more the fact that he wants us to do it now. The first anniversary of her death came and went unmarked. As did the fifth and the tenth. On the twelfth I called Frank to tell him that the rose bush where they'd scattered my mother's ashes was looking a bit sorry for itself and he confessed that he'd forgotten to keep up the maintenance payments to the cemetery.

That's when I decided to take Joe with me. We'd only been together a few weeks by then, but as soon as I told him about the rose bush, he offered to drive down to Brighton with me and take a look at it. We sat down on the cold metal bench that overlooks the memorial garden and Joe squeezed my hand and promised he'd have the rose plant looking as good as new in no time. He was as good as his word. Two months and three visits later and a withered, near-naked stump had doubled in size and sprouted white, waxy blooms that smelt of summer and sunlight and freshly ironed clothes. She would have liked them. Roses were always her favourite flower.

'So, when is it then?' says Joe, handing me a glass of water, so I don't get dehydrated from all the gherkins.

'Next Saturday,' I say, fishing about for an extra-large one. 'You don't have to come with me, I won't mind.'

'Don't be stupid. Of course I'll come with you. It's about time I met them all anyway.'

'I don't see why,' I say. 'We've only been together five years. I hadn't planned on inflicting my step family on you for at least another four.'

'It doesn't have to be that bad. Why don't we make a weekend of it? We could stay over on Saturday night. In a bed and breakfast or something.'

'I don't know,' I say. 'To be honest, I just want to do my duty and get it over with. Visit the cemetery, drink a cup of milky tea, eat a Wagon Wheel and a sardine sandwich and come straight home.'

'You're sure?'

'Yes,' I say, putting the lid back on the pickle jar and screwing it tightly shut. 'I hate the seaside in the winter. It's depressing.'

Joe goes back outside and I head into the bedroom to look for some pictures of my mum. There's a box on top of the wardrobe filled with papers and old photographs, and I drag it out from underneath my well-worn rucksack and wipe off some of the dust. Most of it is junk from my travels: a wooden Buddha with its nose chipped off; a length of silk cloth from one of the night markets in Chiang Mai; a bag of fake gemstones that I was conned into buying by a peculiarly persuasive elephant keeper in Rajasthan; and a bunch of grubby guidebooks, hostel cards and creased-up museum tickets from halfway around the world.

I clear a path to the bottom of the box and my stomach tightens as I lift out my photo album. I still find pictures of my mum difficult to look at, even this one of her paddling up to her ankles and laughing as the waves splash over her knees. Her eyelids are half closed from the sun. You can smell the salt in her nostrils and the cocoa butter on her sunburnt arms, and if you concentrate you can hear the screams from the roller-coaster that have made her twist her head to one side.

In the next picture the water is up over her shoulders. She's waving at someone, her long fingers splayed out high above the surf, but from the way the shot is framed it's hard to tell how far away from the beach she is. It's unlikely she was more than a few feet offshore, but it looks like she could have been miles away. Adrift in the middle of an ocean.

And, overlapping it all, hovering over the images like a ghostly Polaroid, is the way that she looked when she was ill. Her wide cheeks brutally thinned with pain; the skin on her hands turned grey and papery and old; and the bones in her arms that looked like they might crack in two with no small scrap of flesh left to cushion them.

I try hard not to picture it, but somehow I can always see the expression she had in the last weeks of her life. Her whole being overwhelmed with chaos; her eyes fighting a running battle with their fear. And, in the final days, a new and unreadable expression that I took to be the complete absence of hope. Even as a fifteen-year-old I could tell that the world had stopped making sense to her. It had long since stopped making any kind of sense to me.

There's something else that's strange about these photographs as well. Many of them have been cut clean in half. The moment I realised that my father wasn't coming home for the funeral, I took out a pair of nail scissors and cut him out of every single frame. I did it very neatly. I took a ruler, marked a dotted line with a soft lead pencil and cut along the centre of each print with a single snip. I wish I hadn't done it now, but at the time it felt like the right thing to do. It was my only way of punishing him: my one opportunity to return his slight.

So now there are two people missing from these photographs: my mother before she got sick, and my father before he left home.

I close up the photo album and dig around in the box to see what else I can find. Some pictures of my mum in her nurse's uniform before she gave up work; some shots of my twin stepbrothers doing one of their shows; a handful of my old school reports folded into their original brown paper envelopes; and, tucked underneath them, a thin sheaf of discoloured newspaper clippings, their edges curling inwards and upwards like a plate of leftover buffet sandwiches.

The clippings are from our local paper, the *Argus*. The first headline reads: 'Brighton Girl Passes Maths A-level at the Age of Fourteen' and the second reads: 'Maths Prodigy Expelled from School after Repeated Arrests for Shoplifting'. Both articles are illustrated with a small photograph – each badly smudged from a decade's worth of greasy fingerprints – and I lift them out of the box to take a closer look. The first shows me in my school uniform, adjusting my glasses and holding my exam certificate out to the camera; the second shows me in torn jeans and a Meat Is Murder T-shirt, smoking an unfiltered Gauloise outside the magistrates' court. I look like I've aged about ten years between the two photographs, but if you examine them closely you can see that the expression on my face is exactly the same. I can still remember what I was thinking. That perhaps, by some miracle, my dad would see one of these photographs, and be so proud or alarmed or disappointed that he might change his mind and come back for me.

*   *   *

'So, what do you think?' says Joe, dragging me out into the garden. 'Do you like it?'

'Yes,' I say, thumping the side of the pergola and marvelling at how steady it is. 'It's really . . . *nice*.'

'Not too suburban?'

'No,' I say, 'not at all. It's quite arty really. Especially with those crazy green clips sticking out all over the place.'

'They're for attaching the clematis. I haven't put it in yet.'

'Oh, I see.'

'It'll be great, though. It'll provide tons of shade in the summer.'

'Well,' I say, 'all we have to do now is find a way to stop the drunks from sticking their penises through the hedge, and we'll be laughing.'

'Penises?'

'Yes. I told you. Last summer some homeless man stuck his penis through the hedge while I was sunbathing and peed all over the decking.'

'You're kidding?'

'No. He made a big stain over by the bamboo and I had to sand it all off and revarnish.'

Joe looks disappointed. He's about to say that we wouldn't get tramps sticking their penises through our hedge if we sold up and moved to the countryside, but he thinks better of it.

'Did you find any pictures of your mum?' he says, still straining to pick out the wee patch.

'Yes,' I say, showing him the photograph of her swimming. 'I found a really good one.'

Joe lifts the print from my hands and takes a while to look it over.

'She looks really happy, doesn't she?' he says, rubbing the back of my neck.

21

'Yes,' I say, 'I think she was.'

'Who was she waving to? Was it you?'

'I'm not sure. It could have been. But from the expression on her face, I'd say it was probably my dad.'

4

'Jesus, I can't feel my face. I thought you said you didn't like the seaside in the winter.'

'I know. But look at those waves. They're fantastic, aren't they? All churned up like that.'

'Audrey, it's sleeting. Let's just go and get something to eat.'

We've arrived in Brighton an hour and a half early for the memorial party (on account of me making us leave the house at ten o'clock in the morning) and we're ankle deep in sand and damp shingle: watching the waves. Joe thinks I made us leave early because I've got an irrational fear of being late – which I have – but the real reason was so I could get a good look at the sea.

'What are you doing?'

'Counting.'

'Why?'

'To see if every seventh wave is an extra-big one.'

'And is it?'

'No. Of course not.'

'Come on, I'm starving. Let's go and get some fish and chips somewhere.'

'What about seafood?' I say, shouting at him through the wind. 'There's a stall over by the pier. We could get cockles or something.'

'No way,' he says, shivering and pulling his coat round him. 'Nothing pickled, nothing that's not already dead, and nothing that makes its own brine.'

I can't understand his reluctance. There's almost no type of seafood that I don't like. There used to be an old-fashioned café next to the station that my dad would sometimes take me to as a special treat, and it sold every type of seafood you can imagine. Cups of fat yellow mussels sprinkled with pepper; whelks that you had to pick out of their shells with a pin; chunks of bony eel soaked in ladlefuls of bright pea-green liquor; and, best of all, plates of gritty oysters that wriggled in their shells and slipped down your throat like warm salt jellies.

I lick my lips and go to work on Joe.

'What about oysters?' I say, hoping the aphrodisiac angle might swing it. 'They're great. They're supposed to give you the horn.'

'And this is useful to me *how*, exactly?' says Joe, wiping some icy drizzle off his face. 'Given that we're outside. On a beach. In the middle of March.'

'Good point. But you never know. If you eat enough of them, it might last until we get home.'

'No way,' he says. 'No deal.'

'Come on. You get to put your own Tabasco sauce on and everything.'

'OK,' he says, clearly tempted by the Tabasco sauce option, 'but only if we can go to the Grand Hotel for tea and buns afterwards.'

'Excellent,' I say. 'You're on.'

'I feel sick.'

'You shouldn't have eaten so many. You're supposed to savour them, not shovel them out with a wooden fork and swallow them all in one go.'

'How do you know? You've never even eaten them before.'

'Yes, but I think I might be developing a taste for them. They're not nearly as bad as I thought.'

'I need to use the bathroom,' I say, trying not to burp. 'Go ahead and order without me. I may be some time.'

24

I leave Joe in the tearooms waiting for a five-pound pot of Earl Grey and a plateful of toasted teacakes, and set off past the pensioners to find the loos. My nerves are beginning to get the better of me. It's not the oysters that have made me feel sick – it's the thought of seeing my stepbrothers and Frank. I still speak to them on the phone from time to time, but we haven't been in the same room together for years. Not since I came back from travelling round Asia for the last time. Not since I started going out with Joe.

I can feel myself regressing as the minutes count down to seeing them. The capable me is morphing into the awkward, wheezy kid that spilt food down the front of her T-shirt, and knocked lamps off coffee tables every time she came into a room; the kid that was made to eat her dinner with a soup spoon every time she got taken out to a restaurant. It's not that I'm clumsy, in fact I'm peculiarly dextrous, but for some reason they always seem to bring out the worst in me.

It isn't that Frank's a bad person, it's just that after my mum died he never really knew how to handle me. I didn't make it any easier for him. I left open tampon packets scattered around the bathroom because I knew it would make him feel uncomfortable. I shaved my legs with his razors until they were blunt and choked with soap. I filled the house with scooter boys that smelt of hormones and Paco Raban, and had tepid sex with them on the bunk bed in my boxroom, just so I could see the look on Frank's face when I dragged them down for breakfast in the mornings.

I drank a lot, stopped studying, attempted – unsuccessfully – to grow marijuana in the potting shed next to Frank's broad beans, and existed for the best part of three years on a diet of Mars bars, smoked tofu sausages and rice. The low point came when I removed the circuit board from our TV set during the 1982 World Cup final between Italy and West Germany. It took the twins half the afternoon to dredge it out of the fish pond and, one way or another, the TV was never quite the same after that.

'You know in films?' I say, sitting back down next to Joe.
  'Yes?'
'Why do they always splash their faces with cold water at times of high anxiety?'
'Not sure. Maybe it makes them feel better.'
'Well,' I say, 'it doesn't. I tried it in the loos just now and all it did was smudge my mascara and wash the concealer off my double-headed chin spot.'
'I don't know what you're worried about. You can't even see it.'
'Yes you can. And look, the tap went mad while I was washing my hands and splashed soapy water down the front of my jacket. So now I'm going to have to turn up looking like a bag lady, and everyone will nudge each other and say I told you so.'
'You look fine,' he says, trying to reassure me. 'At least the sea air has brought some colour to your cheeks.'
'That's the nausea,' I say, reaching over for my toasted teacake.
'I mean it,' he says, running his hand over my cheek. 'You look great.'
'Not sad?'
'No.'
'Not like a bag lady?'
'No. Nothing like a bag lady.'
'What about someone who keeps a lot of cats and eats Whiskas for dinner when she hasn't got time to go to the shops?'
'Definitely not,' he says. 'You look like more of a Felix kind of a girl to me.'
'Thanks very much,' I say.
'You're very welcome.'

                    *   *   *

'So, who's going to be there exactly?' says Joe, tucking into his second scone.

'Frank and his sister Margi. Assorted cousins. A sprinkling of people from the local church and, of course, my retarded twin stepbrothers.'

'The magicians?'

'Yes,' I say. 'The magicians.'

'What are they called again?' says Joe, clearly amused by my having members of the Magic Circle in the family.

'Larry and Paul,' I say, pouring some milk into my tea. 'Otherwise known as the Great Stupendos. They'll probably come in their outfits and spend the whole afternoon doing tricks.'

'Will there be doves?' says Joe, trying hard not to snigger.

'Yes,' I say. 'There will doubtless be doves. And I don't know why you're laughing. It's not funny.'

'I know. But come on, you've got to admit, your lot are pretty weird.'

'They are not my *lot*,' I say, lowering my head towards the table. 'They're my step family.'

'Right, sorry. I didn't mean it.'

'Yeah, well you'd better be careful what you say. I haven't even told you the worst of it yet.'

'What do you mean?' he says, looking slightly nervous.

'Well,' I say, leaning over the jammy tablecloth and dropping my voice to a whisper, 'the twins live in a . . . *bungalow*.'

Joe shudders and takes a long sip of his tea.

'Yeuch,' he says. 'A house with no top on it. That gives me the creeps.'

'I know,' I say. 'I thought that would get to you.'

5

'Of course, I'm looking for a bungalow of my own now. It doesn't do to be climbing up stairs at my age.'

Joe is sat next to Frank's sister Margi and he's already looking a bit the worse for wear. He's staring at the booze trolley like a man who wishes he'd never learnt to drive, and he's nodding his head back and forth, like someone's emptied it and filled it full of sand.

'It was lovely up at the cemetery though, wasn't it? Wasn't it lovely up at the cemetery?'

Joe nods and casts a longing glance at Frank's whisky glass.

'It was right nice when the sun came out. Like she was smiling down on us all. Don't you think so?'

'Yes,' says Joe, doing the heavy nod again. 'It was a nice moment.'

Silence.

'So, what are you doing with yourself these days, Audrey? It's been so long since we've all seen you. Are you still going on your travels about the place?'

'No. I stopped backpacking a few years ago. I'm a bit more settled now.'

'Well, that's good, isn't it? Isn't it good, Frank? That our Audrey's more settled. We wouldn't want her getting into trouble again, would we?'

'Margi, that was a long time ago. Let's not be dragging it all up now.'

'Well, I was only saying. I was only saying it was nice to see her settled.'

More silence.

The talk turns briefly to the stain on my jacket ('She was always the clumsy one, was Audrey'), the spot on my chin ('It looks like a carbuncle, does that') and moves swiftly on to what a waste it was that I didn't grow up to be Brighton's answer to Stephen Hawking.

'I mean, you were such a clever girl, weren't you? I'm not saying I'd like to see you crippled and in a wheelchair, Audrey, but it must be some comfort to him, mustn't it? Knowing he understands everything in the universe.'

Everybody nods in agreement.

'Of course, I think he's got a nice little voice. He sounds friendly, doesn't he? Like ET if he could speak.'

'ET *could* speak.'

'Could he?'

'Yes. Don't you remember? He said, "ET phone home."'

'Did he sound anything like Stephen Hawking?'

'No,' I say. 'Nothing at all.'

The afternoon grinds on for another hour or so – Frank in particular is very subdued – and just when I'm about to burst apart with the tension, my stepbrothers announce that they're going to perform some of their tricks. I never thought I'd be happy to hear them say it. Their magic shows were the bane of my life. Every other weekend they'd dress me up in a colander and a cooking apron, introduce me as their 'unglamorous assistant', and spend the whole afternoon pretending to saw my head in half with a whisk.

'Come on, Audrey,' says Larry, hitching up his nylon trousers and straightening his bow tie, 'let's see if you can still remember how to do it.'

'Are you sure?' I say. 'You don't want to do it by yourselves?'

'No,' they say, in unison, beckoning me over and handing

me an apron. 'It'll be fun, just like old times. Someone get a colander from the kitchen.'

'What for?'

'For your hat.'

Before I have time to protest Larry is lowering the colander on to my head and saying: 'Ladies and gentlemen, may we proudly present the Great Stupendos and, for one day only, Audrey, our unglamorous assistant.'

Everybody claps and Margi says, '*Unglamorous* assistant, fancy that.'

For the next half-hour I dart about, handing them their wands and shouting 'hey presto' at appropriate moments, and they make a big show of putting my head inside a velvet-lined box that smells of BO and pretending to cut it off with a cheese grater.

The routines are much the same as they always were. Their patter is still woeful – it's no wonder they earn most of their money dressing up as clowns and making balloon animals at children's parties – but some of their illusions look almost convincing from a distance. They can do that one-legged levitation trick that David Blaine does on the television; some pretty good stuff with a trio of metal rings and string; and, after another round of hankies, silk scarves and plastic flowers, they break open a brand new deck of cards.

This is my favourite bit. I was always better at the sleight-of-hand stuff than they were and I'm hoping it might still piss them off. I can do it all: palming, false cuts, card culling, base dealing, and, on a good day, with a bit of practice, I can even do a perfect Faro shuffle. It took me four months to master. Four months in my bedroom, working hour after hour on a deck of cards that felt as pliable as lead. Until my thumbs were red raw and covered in cuts, and my fingertips were peppered with crimson blood blisters.

The instant I had it nailed I rushed downstairs to show

Larry and Paul what I'd done. They watched in awe as I split the deck into identical halves and riffled them together in startling symmetry. They didn't speak to me for a week after that. I've a feeling they might never have spoken to me again if they hadn't driven themselves near insane trying to work out how to do it for themselves.

'You've still got the knack, then?' says Larry, watching me produce yet another ace from the bottom of a recently shuffled deck.

'Yes,' I say. 'I guess it's like riding a bike.'

'Well,' says Paul, testily, 'either that, or your fingers are still too long for your hands.'

That does it. Maybe I should ask them if they've found the time to 'come out' yet. Maybe I should report them to the RSPB for mistreatment of doves. Maybe I should take the colander off my head and creep outside for a quick smoke while no one's looking.

I rest up against a damp wall in the driveway and savour the head-rush from an unfamiliar cigarette. My head spins as I inhale the bitter mist of nicotine, and I glance back at the house, wondering whether anyone, apart from Joe, has noticed that I've gone. I can't believe how little they've all changed. Larry and Paul still finish each other's sentences and dress like mirror images of one another, and Frank still taps the side of his rocket-shaped barometer – twice – every time he walks past it in the hall. He even sits in the same chair that he always did; a beige leather recliner with mismatched cushions, its headboard stained black from years of contact with the layers of oily Brylcreem in his hair. No one else was ever allowed to sit in that chair. Apart from my mother and the church, I sometimes think it was the nearest he ever came to really loving something.

*   *   *

'Are you alright, Audrey?'

'Yes,' I say, a little startled to see Frank peering round the back door, 'really, I'm fine.'

'I didn't know you still smoked,' he says, closing the door and fidgeting with the buttons on his sports coat.

'I don't Frank, not usually. I bought them on the way down here. I thought it might turn out to be a bit . . .'

'Difficult?'

'Well, yes. You know, stressful at least.'

'You must still miss her,' he says, rubbing the back of his neck.

'Well,' I say, 'I'm sure we all do.'

Frank wants to talk. He indicates the plastic patio set next to the pond and the two of us crunch across the wet gravel and sit down.

'What is it?' I say, wondering if he might be ill. 'There's nothing wrong, is there?'

He pauses for a moment and then he says:

'Audrey, this is quite difficult for me to say, so I'll just come right out with it.'

I tighten the grip on my cigarette. This isn't like Frank – he's not the confessional type.

'I'm glad you came today,' he says, picking a speck of lint off his trousers. 'It's been a long time.'

I shrug and wave some smoke out of my eyes.

'I've never said this to you before,' he continues, quietly, 'but I sometimes think . . . well, I sometimes think we didn't give you as much as you might have needed while you were growing up.'

I feel a lump rising in my throat. Like I might cry.

'It's OK,' I say. 'You did what you could. It wasn't easy for any of us.'

'Well,' he says, clearly feeling uncomfortable, 'I'm glad you seem more settled these days. Joe seems like a good chap.'

'He is,' I say, 'he is.'

Frank pauses and takes a sip of his whisky.

'He told me you were doing some tutoring now.'

'Yes, private lessons. I've been doing it for a couple of years. I do some bookkeeping as well. For Joe, and a few of the local businesses.'

'He said you might go back and finish your degree course this year, that you might do a teaching qualification.'

'I've been thinking about it,' I say, fiddling with my bracelet. 'But I haven't made my mind up yet. I'm pretty out of touch with degree-level mathematics, and anyway, I'm not sure if I want to get—'

'Tied down?'

'Yes,' I say. 'I suppose that might be it.'

Frank takes a moment to think this through.

'You're a lot like your dad, you know,' he says, clinking the ice cubes in his drink. 'Two peas in a pod.'

'How do you mean?' I say, pulling my cardigan round my shoulders to keep warm.

'Well,' he says, puffing his chest like a pigeon and draining the rest of his drink, 'he was always looking for something better, wasn't he? A drifter; one of those romantic types.'

I can't make any sense of this. I can't help feeling that I'm being criticised in some way.

'I'm not sure what you mean,' I say, carefully. 'I'm not sure there's anything romantic about being an addict. And he threw it all away, didn't he? He lost everything.'

'Your mother, you mean?'

'Yes,' I say, looking at the floor. 'Well, we all did.'

Frank sits still for a time, turning things over in his mind. He seems distracted, like he wishes he were somewhere else.

'This is for you,' he says, clearing his throat suddenly, and pulling a creased envelope out of his pocket. 'I should have passed it on to you some time ago. I hope you won't think too badly of me.'

'What is it?' I say, taking it from his hand.

'It's something that your dad sent for you. After we stopped him coming to the funeral.'

This last part he forces out, like he's expelling something raw and distasteful. And my breath literally freezes in my throat.

'You *stopped* him coming?' I say, as soon as my lips start working again.

'Yes,' he says, lowering his shoulders and letting go of the weight of it. 'It's what your mother would have wanted. For you to be stable. To be left alone to get on with things. No more interruptions.'

'I don't understand. I thought you didn't even know where he was.'

'He contacted us once. Just before your mother went. He wanted to see her, I think.'

'And you didn't let him?'

'She was too weak by then,' he says, staring at his empty glass. 'It would only have upset her.'

'That's not true,' I say, suddenly welling up. 'She would have wanted to see him. I know she would.'

Frank takes out his hanky, licks it, and begins to scrub at a stubborn clump of moss on top of the table. He waits until he's shifted it before he speaks.

'Yes,' he says, 'I've thought about it on many occasions over the years, and I sometimes think it might have been the wrong thing to do.'

I don't know what to say. My cigarette has burnt down to a short glowing stub and I'm wondering why I can't feel it burning my hand.

'Why are you telling me this now?' I say, desperately trying to read the answer in his face.

'I was waiting to see you settled,' he says, briskly. 'Margi and I thought it was best to wait.'

And just like that he changes everything: flips my life

over like an egg timer and sets it draining in the opposite direction.

The two of us collect our thoughts for a moment – avoiding eye contact and fidgeting with our drinks – then Frank smooths out the creases in his trousers, and quietly motions to leave. He hesitates, hoping that I'm about to say something more, and when he realises that I'm not he taps me stiffly on the shoulder and walks away. I listen to him crunch across the gravel – attempting to regain his composure by taking deep, regular strides – and I hear him rest for a moment when he reaches the safety of the back door. I don't return his gaze. I wait until he goes inside and take a second to slow my breathing before prising open the grubby corners of the envelope.

There's no letter inside. Not even a card. Just a small shiny matchbook – perfect and unused – with a neat line of script scored under the flap in bright blue ink.

Chin up, my little genius, it says. *One day you'll understand this was probably for the best.*

With my love to you always, Dad x.

6

It's two o'clock in the morning, and despite the bottle and a half of wine I drank when we got home last night I still haven't been able to fall asleep. Joe is flat out beside me – dreaming and twitching and smiling in his sleep – and I'm staring at the cracks in the ceiling, and listening to the flutter of the second hand as it skids across the face of our alarm clock. Occasionally Joe stirs and turns over. Every once in a while he opens his eyes.

'You still awake?'

'Yes. Go back to sleep.'

'Still thinking about your dad?'

'Yes,' I say, 'I'm thinking about the last time I saw him.'

The last time I saw my father I had thick metal braces on my teeth and my favourite food – inadvisably – was crisps. It was the second day of April – the afternoon of my tenth birthday – and things had already got off to a fairly dismal start. Frank had bought me a sewing kit instead of the *Amazing Factual Guide to Astronomy* that I'd asked him for, and the twins had secretly scoffed all the butter icing off the top of my space shuttle cake. To make matters worse, Frank had arranged for the five of us to go to a magic show as a special treat, and I'd had to spend the whole morning fending off surprise wand attacks from my evil stepbrothers.

We were almost through the door when the phone began to trill in the hallway. My mum finished buttoning her coat before she answered – I think she was half hoping that it would stop – and I could tell right away that it was my dad.

It was obvious from the way she was touching her hair. She patted it and plumped it and pulled at the stubborn layers of her fringe, and I noticed her check the line of her plum-coloured lipstick in the mirror.

I could tell he was asking whether he could see me, because she was scolding him and saying that we'd already made plans. She was saying it was typical of him to leave things to the last minute, and that it was too late for us to change our arrangements now. And then her voice softened. Her words loosened at the back of her throat and I watched the colour drain from her face. She'd changed her mind. I would be allowed to see him after all.

My mother and Frank exchanged a few choice words and the five of us piled into the car and drove off towards the seafront. I picked him out from a hundred yards away. Six feet tall, with hair the colour of coal, smoking a hand-rolled cigarette in his thin leather coat. He wore that coat every day; even in the depths of winter. I used to think he wore it so much because it made him look a little bit like a film star; now I realise it was because it was the only one he had.

Frank kept the engine running, and I scrambled out of the car and ran towards my father as fast as I could.

'Hello, Ginger-nut,' he said, rubbing his hand through my hair, 'how's the teeth?'

'Almost done,' I said, baring my braces at him with a grin.

'And the marble championships?'

'Um . . . bit of a long story.'

'Right,' he said, winking at me. 'You can tell me later.'

And then he looked over at my mother. She'd wound down her window as far as it would go and she was staring at him sadly, like he was a broken and dearly loved shoe.

'We'll pick her up at four o'clock,' she said, evenly. 'Please don't be late.'

Their eyes locked for a moment, and I think she would

have said something more had Frank not reached over and wound up the window for her. The car pulled away and the two of us watched in silence as it picked its way along the length of seafront. Until neither one of us could make it out any more.

'So, Ginger-nut,' he said, bending down and mock-punching me on the chin, 'what do you want to do first?'

'What's the choices?' I said, knowing full well what he'd say.

'Well,' he said, counting out the options on his fingers, 'there's dodgems, the aquarium, ice cream, cockles, or a giant plate of special birthday oysters.'

I shrugged, as if none of this was particularly appealing. I knew he didn't have the money to buy cockles or birthday oysters, and from what Frank had said on the way down here I wasn't sure he could afford to ride on the dodgems either.

'Thing is,' I said, running my tongue round my teeth as if I might have rogue crumbs stuck in my braces, 'I'm already pretty full up from birthday cake and crisps, and it's a bit cold for ice cream today.'

'Well then,' he said, as if he'd just had the most brilliant idea. 'How's about we go for a nice long walk along the front? Blow away the cobwebs. What do you say?'

And off we went.

We spent the next hour strolling up and down the beach; feeding pebbles to the hungry green waves and stopping here and there for cups of boiling tea when it got too cold. Usually when we took one of our walks together my dad would tell me something about the moon or the tides or the peculiar and interesting properties of sub-atomic particles and π, but on this occasion he seemed unusually thoughtful and reserved. I was half hoping that he'd tell my favourite story – the one about the astonishing twenty-thousand-mile, pole-to-pole migration of the Arctic tern; but even though I prompted him – on more than one occasion – he didn't seem unduly bothered about telling it to me again. He had far more important things on his mind.

'So, how is it living at Frank's house?' he said, when we'd stopped for our second cup of tea.

'It's OK,' I said, not wanting to let him know how bad it was. 'It's a bit like being French.'

'French?'

'Yes. Because most of the time I don't understand what anyone is saying.'

'You mean you feel foreign?' he said, smiling at me and warming his hands on his tea.

'Yes,' I said, swirling my polystyrene cup to get at the sticky sediment of my hot chocolate. 'The twins are always on about stamp collecting and magic tricks and Frank's always on about some chap called the Holy Ghost. And the thing is, I don't even know who he is.'

'Who do you think he is?'

'Not sure,' I said, running through the options in my head. 'He can't be a real ghost, because everyone knows they don't exist. On balance, I think it's probably someone he knows from work.'

After he'd finished laughing, he put down his cup, folded his arms and fixed me with his most serious stare.

'Audrey, you do understand that they're getting married though, don't you? That Frank is going to be marrying your mum?'

'Yes,' I said dolefully. 'I know.'

We both paused for a moment to let this sink in.

'Listen,' he said, pushing my anorak hood off my forehead and brushing my hair out of my eyes, 'there's something I need to ask you. Does your mum seem happy? Does she seem happier now than she was?'

'I don't know,' I said, wondering what he was getting at.

'Well,' he said, 'does she cry at all? Does she look sad sometimes, like she used to when I didn't come home?'

'No,' I said, honestly. 'She doesn't cry at all.'

I wanted to say that she didn't laugh very much either and that she'd spent ages patting her hair when he'd called, but I didn't. I used to wonder if it would have made a difference if I had.

The two of us spent our last half-hour together sitting in an empty café, sharing a packet of shortbread biscuits and betting on the speed of falling raindrops. This was a familiar game. Each of us would select a fat tear of water at the top of the window and bet on which one would be first to reach the bottom of the pane. He shook his head when I got the first four guesses right, and I noticed how tightly his skin pulled across his cheekbones when he smiled. He looked gaunt. And worn out. He had circles under his eyes the colour of winter puddles, and I wanted to ask him if he was sick. Most of all, I wanted to know what he'd said to my mum on the phone: the thing that had drained all the colour out of her face.

'Did your mum tell you I was planning on going away for a while?' he said, handing me my winnings in shortbread biscuits.

'No,' I said, worrying that the biscuits were all he had left for his dinner. 'She didn't say anything.'

'Well,' he said, cautiously, 'I've been thinking it might be time for me to make a fresh start. I don't think there's much point in my staying in Brighton. Not now your mum is . . . well, not now that she's getting married again.'

'Where will you go?' I said, slipping my hand into his and waiting for a reassuring squeeze.

'I was thinking I might go back to America for a while,' he said, gazing out over at the pier. 'Maybe you could come and visit me there one day.'

'I'd like that,' I said.

'Here,' he said, reaching into his pocket. 'It's not much of

40

a birthday present, I'm afraid, but I remembered how much you like them.'

He opened his hand and I stared down at the shiny casino matchbook with the words Taj Mahal embossed across the front in silver letters. He used to bring them back for me every time he took one of his trips to Las Vegas or Atlantic City, and I had dozens of them stashed away in a shoebox under my bed. Treasured glossy rectangles from Sands and Dunes and Binion's Horseshoe Casino, which smelt of gunpowder and glamour and a brand-new world far away from this one. Sometimes he'd bring home bags of sweets as well. Piles of exotic confectionery like Hershey bars and Oreo cookies and Reeses peanut butter cups; and packets of shocking-pink bubble gum that came in fat, juicy bricks, instead of those thin strips that tasted of petrol, and ran out of flavour the moment you put them in your mouth. I used to ration them, one piece a day until they'd all run out. And then I'd collect up all the empty wrappers and store them in a sealed plastic bag, sniffing them from time to time: just to remind me what they tasted like.

I held on to the matchbook for as long as I dared, turning it over in my hand and thinking how nice it would look with all my others, then I stiffened and handed it back to him.

'You keep it,' I said, stoically. 'Give it to me next time.'

He understood. He nodded and tucked it back into his leather coat, patting the side of his pocket just to let me know it was safe.

'So, Audrey,' he said, reaching over and clutching tight hold of my hand. 'Did I ever tell you the story about the twenty-thousand-mile migration of the Arctic tern?'

'I'm not sure,' I said, smiling and pretending not to know what he was talking about.

'Well,' he said, 'it's most peculiar and interesting. Some time just before the start of winter, this tiny bird that weighs no more than a bag of sugar somehow begins to notice the days are starting to shorten . . .'

It's almost 4 a.m. and I'm still wide awake. My head aches, my legs are stiff from lying scrunched up in a ball for half the night, and I finally give in to my insomnia and get up. I pad into the kitchen, drink a cup of cold cranberry juice and search around in my bag for the casino matchbook. I take it back to bed, prop it up next to the alarm clock and stare at the neat loops of my father's handwriting, illuminated in the soft yellow glow of the Roman numerals. It's the same matchbook that I handed back to him that day at the beach. All this time I'd assumed he still had it and, as long as he did, there was a small chance that he might still come home.

Him sending it back to me was his way of saying that he never was.

7

'Here, have some more of the twice-cooked pork.'

'Yeah, or the honey chilli fish.'

'I can't even finish my noodles.'

'More noodles? Have some of mine.'

'There's more sake if you want it. What about some more sake?'

It's Sunday afternoon, Joe is working and I'm sharing a Chinese takeaway with my best friends Lorna and Pete. Pete works part time for Joe – on the days when he's not redrafting his epic science fiction film script – and Lorna and I have known each other since we were at school. Everyone is trying their hardest to make me feel better.

'I'm alright. Honestly. I don't feel that bad about it.'

The two of them glance over at each other, then quickly back at me.

'I don't get it,' says Pete, making a hole in his won ton and filling it with a puddle of soya sauce. 'What kind of a man stops someone coming to his own wife's funeral?'

'Ex-wife,' says Lorna, indicating that this is crucially different.

'Well, yes,' says Pete solemnly, 'but even so.'

Lorna tops up my sake and I lift a snow pea out of my rice with the points of my plastic chopsticks.

'It's strange that he never called you, though, isn't it? Not even a letter. Not once in all this time.'

'Maybe he's dead.'

'*Pete.*'

'Sorry. I was only saying.'

I shift uncomfortably in my seat.

'It's not his fault. If Frank told him that it was what my mother wanted, he would have respected her wishes.'

'Even if it meant giving up contact with you?'

'I don't know,' I say, quietly. 'By all accounts he was in a pretty sorry state by then. Perhaps he believed them . . . that I was better off without him.'

'Well, I think it's really sad,' says Lorna. 'I wonder where he is now? I wonder what he's doing?'

'Losing his money somewhere, probably,' I say, topping my glass up with more sake.

'You think he's still gambling?'

'Yes,' I say. 'If he's still alive, I think he probably is.'

The two of them make coffee and clear away the lunch plates, and I slouch on Lorna's sofa; flicking through her cable channels and watching a bit of a programme called *Dogs with Jobs*.

'Sorry,' she says, bringing over some biscuits and sitting next to me. 'We didn't mean to make you feel worse.'

'It's alright,' I say. 'You were only trying to help.'

'So, what do you want to do now? Do you think you might try and find him?'

I shrug my shoulders.

'I don't know. I'm not really sure where I'd start.'

'What does Joe think?'

'He thinks it's a bad idea. He thinks it's unlikely I'd be able to trace him now anyway.'

'Where was he when they last heard from him?'

'The States, I think. But who knows, he could be any-where.'

'Well,' she says, putting her arm round my shoulder and giving it a reassuring squeeze, 'perhaps Joe's right. If he'd wanted to get in touch with you he'd have done it by now, wouldn't he? And it's not like he was the world's number-one dad or anything. Or number-one husband for that matter. He did treat your mum pretty badly.'

'I know,' I say. 'You're probably right. The best thing I can do is forget about it.'

Lorna looks at me carefully. Like she thinks I should leave well alone but knows full well that I won't.

'Hey,' she says, attempting to cheer me up. 'What do you fancy doing for your birthday next month?'

'I don't know. I'm not sure I want to do anything much.'

'Come on, we should do something special. To help you with your midlife crisis.'

'My what?'

'Joe told me,' she says, fighting back a smile. 'He said you'd developed a curious Bono obsession and he wanted to know if it was serious.'

'You're kidding? What did he say?'

'He said, "Erm, Lorna, you know Bono." And I said yeah, what of him, and he said, "Do you think he's attractive at all?" And obviously I said no, he's a repugnant little gnome, and Joe thought for a while and said: "Right. It's just that Audrey seems to think he's good looking or something."'

I start to laugh. I can't help myself.

'I can't believe he told you that.'

'Yeah, he was taking it really seriously. I think he was quite worried about it.'

'Worried about what?'

'I don't know. Maybe he thinks you're getting bored with him or something.'

'Did he say that?'

'No. But you know what men are like. They need a lot of reassuring.'

'Do they?' I say, feeling a little uncomfortable.

'Absolutely,' she says. 'It's well known.'

*　　*　　*

'You know what worries me about getting old?' she suddenly says, out of nowhere.

'No, what?'

'Those adverts for Tena Lady.'

'What's Tena Lady?'

'Those incontinence pads that you have to start wearing in your fifties because you've just started pissing your pants when you laugh.'

'I'm going to start pissing my pants when I laugh?'

'Why do they always put those ads on when I've got no booze in the house? Just after Meg's gone to bed and I'm feeling vulnerable.'

'Wait, go back a bit. I'm going to start pissing my pants when I *laugh*?'

'Only if you have kids,' she says licking the cream out of a Bourbon.

'Right,' I say, 'that makes me feel a lot more like coming off the pill.'

'The thing is,' she says, seriously, 'I think they should start making Tena Chappie as well.'

'Tena Chappie?' says Pete, coming in with the coffee, 'what's that?'

'Incontinence pads for blokes. Think about it Pete, you're bound to get a bit of leakage when your prostrate starts to go, and the thing is, it would definitely make me feel better if they made Tena Chappie as well as Tena Lady.'

'Prost*ate*,' says Pete, adjusting his trouser zip. 'Prost*rate* is when you're lying down. Hey Audrey, is it me or is that basset hound in the hat working as an emergency lighthouse keeper?'

'You're looking better.'

'Yes,' I say. 'The guys really cheered me up.'

'How were they?'

'You know. The usual. Pete followed Lorna around like a

lovesick puppy all afternoon while Lorna stabbed him in the heart, just for fun.'

Joe smiles and hands me a glass of wine.

'Frank called,' he says, putting his arm round me.

'Did he?' I say, pulling away.

'He wanted to know how you were.'

'That's considerate of him.'

'Well . . . I said you'd give him a ring. Maybe some time in the week.'

I nod and take a sip of my wine. The mere mention of Frank's name is making my skin itch and I start fidgeting with the metal clasp on my necklace.

'Listen. If you decide to look for him, you know that I'll help, don't you?'

'Yes,' I say. 'I know you will.'

'I'm just saying that it might be difficult. You don't even know which country he's in.'

'No,' I say, digging my fingernails into my neck. 'You're probably right. Lorna said exactly the same thing.'

'But you still want to try?'

I do. From the moment I saw his handwriting on that tiny matchbook it's all I've been able to think about. I keep wondering if things might have been different. If Frank had let him see my mum before she died. If he'd just summoned up the strength to come to the funeral. If I'd told him that I didn't care what kind of state he was in, that I loved him anyway, because he was my dad.

Joe seems to know what I'm thinking but he hesitates a moment before he speaks.

'It wasn't up to you,' he says, pulling my hands away from my neck. 'You were a child. It was up to him.'

Joe starts on some pasta sauce for dinner and I hang about in the kitchen, getting quietly drunk and watching him cook. He tosses garlic, fresh tomatoes and olive oil into a pan – in no particular order – and even though I'm still full from the Chinese, I can already tell it's going to taste great.

'Hey,' he says, pouring some red wine on to the tomatoes and watching them sizzle, 'I forgot to tell you, I had a really weird phone call on my mobile this weekend.'

'Who from?' I say, fighting the urge to make him measure out the pasta and add some anchovies to the sauce.

'Some guy. Said he'd got my number out of the Yellow Pages, wanted to know if I fitted window boxes.'

'Window boxes? You're listed as a landscape gardener, aren't you?'

'Yes, but he said he wanted someone good. Someone who could design something extra special.'

'What did you say?'

'I said I'd pop over later in the week. I felt sorry for him. He lives in one of those grotty tower blocks behind King's Cross station. And here's the strange part, he doesn't go outside.'

'What, never?'

'No, he's agoraphobic or something.'

'Wow,' I say, inhaling the garlicky fumes from the pan. 'He's going to need a pretty amazing window box then, isn't he?'

'Yes,' says Joe, pulling me towards him and offering me a spoonful of sauce. 'I suppose he is.'

8

'Who did he murder?'

'One of his students.'

'Why?'

'Well, it's a little bit complicated, but Pythagoras believed in the concept of perfect numbers. He believed these perfect numbers could explain why everything in the universe is the way that it is.'

'Yeah, so?'

'Well, one of his students suggested that this might not be the case. He came up with a new theory. The theory of irrational numbers.'

'What's irrational?'

'Well, you know when your mum took you to the super-market last week?'

'Yeah.'

'And she forgot to put her shoes on and refused to buy you the bumper case of David Beckham Pepsi that you wanted?'

'Yeah.'

'Even though she'll probably end up buying you a single can of Pepsi every day anyway, and it'll end up costing her a whole lot more?'

'Yeah.'

'Well, that's irrational. It doesn't make sense. There's no logic to it.'

'Cool. I'm going to tell my mum she's irrational.'

'Anyway,' I say, getting back to the point, 'pi is an irra-tional number because its decimal places go on for ever and ever without resolving or forming any kind of pattern. A professor at the University of Tokyo has calculated pi to six billion decimal places, and still there's nothing logical or regular about it.'

'Six billion. That's quite a lot.'

'Yes,' I say. 'It certainly is.'

'And this whole pi thing drove Pythagoras mad and made him want to kill this bloke?'

'Yes.'

'Excellent. How did he do it?'

'He had him drowned.'

'Like a sick puppy?'

'Yes, I guess you could say that.'

'Did he hold his head under, or did he tie him up in a sack with a brick in it?'

'Um. Not sure. Which would you like it to be?'

'The brick thing . . . no, wait, the holding his head under the water thing.'

'OK then, that's probably the way it happened.'

'Cool. Did he struggle?'

'Yes.'

'Did his eyes pop out of his head?'

'Very possibly.'

'Brilliant. What was his name?'

'Hippasus.'

'Bit of a shit name.'

'Well, what would you like him to be called?'

'Dunno. There's a kid at school called Keith and I wouldn't mind drowning him.'

'Good. That's very nice. Let's call him Keith then, shall we?'

'Wicked.'

'Anyway, the thing is, numbers were so important to the philosophers of ancient Greece that people sometimes killed each other because of them. The early Christians even had the first libraries burnt to the ground and all the maths books destroyed because they were so afraid of what numbers might tell them.'

'So it wasn't just blokes in togas sitting around on their arses, plotting ways to ruin my life with homework?'

'No. It was violence and murder and secret sects and drowning and war and lots of stabbing.'

'A bit like the Mafia?'

'In a manner of speaking, yes.'

'Cool.'

'So you'll try and have some of this algebra homework done for me when I come round again next week?'

'Yeah. I'll have a think about it. Do you fancy a can of David Beckham Pepsi?'

'OK then, why not?'

It's 3.30 on a Thursday afternoon and I'm drinking cola and listening to Slipknot with one of my numerically challenged maths pupils, Ryan. I've been teaching Ryan for a little over a year now and he's possibly the worst student I've ever had. If I had any sense I'd abandon him to a sorry life of idiocy, innumeracy and incompetence, but I feel a certain compunction to help him through his GCSE. That's why I've decided to cut a deal with him. He's promised to get his head down and at least attempt a pass grade and I've promised that, if he makes it, I'll teach him the rudiments of building an atomic bomb. Given that weapons-grade uranium is notoriously hard to come by, I figure there's not too much cause for concern.

'Audrey?'

'Yes Ryan.'

'If you didn't have uranium, could you maybe use Semtex?'

'No.'

'You're sure?'

'Completely.'

'Even if you had lots and lots?'

'No. Not even if you had lots and lots.'

'Audrey?'

'Yes Ryan.'

'How far away is Afghanistan?'

'Um, why do you want to know?'

'No reason.'

I leave Ryan's flat just after four and make my way into the early evening rush hour. It's been a busy week. I've prepared half-yearly accounts for three different businesses, and I've taken on half a dozen new pupils from the local comprehensive school. It's a bit like catching nits. Once word gets round that a few of the parents have hired a private tutor for their kids, all the others have to make sure they get one as well. Still, it's good to be busy. It stops me obsessing about my dad.

It's taken me a while to settle down after my visit to Frank's house at the weekend but I'm gradually beginning to feel better. I've decided Joe's right and that I should probably leave well alone. At least for the time being.

After some consideration, I decided to put the matchbox away. I packed it into a shoebox, tied it up with three layers of Sellotape and hid it in the cupboard under the stairs. I've been very good about looking at it and so far I've only crept down there to dig it out once. Well, twice, but the second time Joe caught me before I'd burrowed past the shears and I had to pretend I was looking for moth balls.

Even so, I still think I'm doing pretty well. It's not like I've been studying missing person's sites on the Internet, or looking up the numbers of private detectives in the Yellow Pages. It's not like I've been having surreal dreams involving Frank, my dad, a giant roulette wheel, and Joe dressed in a suit of shiny poker chips, in which he looks disturbingly like Tom Selleck in *Magnum PI*. In fact, I'm feeling quite balanced about the whole episode. Very calm. More settled than ever. If I believed in the concept of closure, which I don't, I'm fairly sure this is exactly what it would feel like.

Except for the stubborn patch of eczema that's broken out on my left elbow. And the fact that Joe caught me arranging my peas into prime numbers while we were eating our dinner last night.

'Hey. It's me. Where are you?'

'I've been giving a maths lesson. I've just finished up.'

'What's that noise? You'll have to speak up, I can hardly hear you.'

'It's the car stereo.'

'What are you listening to?'

'Um . . . Slipknot. Ryan lent it to me.'

'I see. Look, I was wondering if you could do me a quick favour. Are you anywhere near King's Cross?'

'Not far away. Why?'

'I was wondering if you'd mind calling in on that window-box guy for me.'

'Me? What for?'

'Because I'm tied up at the garden centre and he's already phoned four times today to make sure I was coming. He sounds a bit desperate.'

'Joe, I don't know . . .'

'Look, all you have to do is go over and find out what he wants. I wouldn't ask, but I can't get away for another couple of hours at least.'

'Can't Pete go?'

'No, he's out on another job.'

'Well, what shall I tell him? What if he wants some suggestions?'

'Just ask him what sort of colours he likes. That'll probably be enough for now.'

'Can't you ask him over the phone?'

'No. He's got some crazy idea about measuring the window space and gauging the light and knowing where it's all going to be.'

'I don't know, Joe. It sounds a bit complicated . . .'

'Please. It would really help me out. I'll feel bad if I have to put him off again.'

'OK then,' I say, turning off the Slipknot CD and reaching for my notebook. 'You'd better give me his address.'

Window-box Man lives in a concrete sixties tower block the colour of putty and rain clouds. It's sandwiched between an industrial estate and an artery of disused rail track, clogged up with shopping trolleys, bicycle wheels and weeds.

There is no possibility on earth that a person could chance upon a place like this. If, by some fluke, you were to take a wrong turn behind the railway terminal and point your car towards the opening of his cul-de-sac, you'd reverse out as quickly as you could. No one comes here to sightsee. No one comes here to shop at the local supermarket, or take tea in the local greasy spoon, and no one in their right mind comes to sell their services as a landscape gardener. The only people that come here are the ones who can't afford to live anywhere else; and the odd architect who wants to make his peace with God.

There are three tower blocks in all. Their name plates have rusted away amid the graffiti and the flaking concrete, and I have no way of telling which one is which. I wind up the windows, triple-lock the car doors and look around for someone to ask. There's a woman the colour of a ripe tangerine making her way into a derelict-looking tanning salon and a teenage boy selling knock-off cigarettes next to a pair of broken swings, but I decide the off-licence with the iron bars across its window is probably my best bet.

The man behind the counter shakes his head.

'You don't know which one is Widnes?'

'No.'

'You're sure?'

'Yes.'

'Who are you looking for? Who is it you're after?'

A middle-aged woman buying a pouch of tobacco and a three-litre bottle of cider is intensely keen to know my business.

'I'm looking for Widnes Tower,' I say. 'Do you know which one it is?'

'Who is it you're after?' she says, again.

'Mr Bloom. Do you know him?'

'Who?'

'Bloom. Louie Bloom.'

The woman shakes her head and holds out her plastic bag for another bottle.

'She means the fat man,' says a voice behind me. It's the kid who was outside selling cigarettes.

'Mr Bloom?' I say, walking over to him. 'Do you know what block he's in?'

The kid points to the second building from the left.

'What do you want with him?' says the cider woman conspiratorially. 'Murdered someone, has he?'

'Er, no, not as far as I know. I've got an appointment with him, that's all.'

'Social worker, are you?'

I think about explaining but I just say, 'Yes, something like that.'

'He doesn't go out,' says the cider woman. 'He's been shut up inside that flat for years.'

'Yes,' I say, 'I heard he was agoraphobic.'

'Oh,' she says, a little disappointed. 'I thought he was American.'

'How fat is he, d'you reckon?' says the cigarette kid, helping himself to a packet of Rizla.

'Who knows?' says the cider woman, scratching her

moles. 'We've barely laid eyes on him since he moved in.'

At this point, the man behind the counter – who hasn't so much as grunted since I first asked him for directions – glances up from his copy of the *Daily Sport*.

'Fat enough to stink,' he says, gravely. 'Fat enough to stink.'

9

The lift smells bad: a pungent mix of alcohol and stale piss with a dash of sour milk thrown in for good measure. I hold my breath. I squeeze my nose, take shallow gulps of air through my mouth and listen to the squeal from the metal ropes as we rattle up the narrow concrete shaft. Cigarette Kid has come along for the ride. He's keen to show me where the 'fat smelly weirdo man' lives, and I get the impression he sometimes comes up here to spy on him when he's got nothing better to do – which is probably quite often.

The lift shudders to a halt at the fifteenth floor. It bounces slightly as it comes to a stop and the doors take an age to grind apart. They open halfway, close, open, then close again: like an old person struggling to sit up. Cigarette Kid is clearly used to this, and as the doors squeeze together for the third time he reaches out with his foot and forces them apart.

'This way,' he says, nodding left. 'Fatty lives right at the end.'

We stop outside a door that looks significantly dirtier than all the rest. The paintwork is pared down to the bare wood and the narrow casement window is splattered with a stubborn layer of rain dirt and grease. I find myself peering through the reinforced glass instead of looking around for a bell. The kid has obviously picked up on my reticence because he says, 'What's wrong? Changed your mind now, have you?'

I suppose the sensible thing to do at this point would be to turn round and walk away. In fact I'm just about to chase after Cigarette Kid and shout for him to hold the lift when I notice that this particular flat has an entryphone. I decide to press the buzzer. Just to see what his voice sounds like. It's a good minute before there's any answer.

'Who's there? Who is it?'

He has a loud voice. Deep, gruff and breathless around the edges with a light Southern American twang.

'Hello, my name's Audrey. I've come about your window box.'

'You were supposed to be a man,' he says, clearly disappointed.

'Yes, I'm sorry. He couldn't make it. I'm, um . . . his assistant.'

'You any good with window boxes?'

'Well, yes, I think I can probably sort something out for you.'

The voice sighs as if this is just another of the thousand and one things that have gone wrong in his day, and he pushes the buzzer to let me in.

'Make yourself at home,' he says, through the intercom. 'I've got to go back to the bathroom. I'm constipated like you wouldn't believe.'

Just as I'm deciding what to do he says: 'Make your mind up, lady, it's cold. And be sure to close the door up after you.'

My first worry is that the flat is going to smell. It doesn't. It's quite possibly the cleanest flat I've ever seen. Each stick of cheap melamine furniture is polished to within an inch of its life and there isn't a magazine, plate, book or gaudy china ornament out of place.

It's warm inside, which lends the air a slight mustiness, but the overwhelming scent is of wood polish, floor cleaner and plants. There are plants everywhere: a pair of succulent rubber plants on the bookshelf; a money tree on the scratched wooden coffee table in the middle of the room; a fruit-bearing orange tree on the serving hatch that leads through to the galley kitchen; and, taking pride of place on his mock mahogany sideboard, a tall china vase filled with tulips, yellow roses and a soft white cloud of gypsophila.

The carpet has a dozen bald patches where the floorboards are beginning to show through, but it's clearly just been freshly hoovered and brushed. It's quite dark inside. The other tower blocks shut out most of the light and there's only one window in the room. I walk over and peer out through the years-old grime but there's not much to see. A narrow balcony runs the length of one wall and, far below, the tips of a scrawny beech tree struggle upwards towards the window. If I squint hard – and balance on my toes – I can just see round the edge of the next-door block. A triangular portion of London stretches towards the horizon like a blunted arrow, and a couple of aeroplanes queue up in the distance, waiting to land. It's not much, but it gives some small sense of there being a world outside.

'Admiring the view, huh?'

I've been so busy snooping that I didn't hear Window-box Man enter the room. He's a giant. The kind Hans Christian Andersen has restless dreams about when he's eaten too much cheese. He's seven foot tall with eyes the size of golf balls and a foot-wide face that dangles with fat. At a guess, I'd say he weighs close to thirty stone.

He lumbers towards me, smiles, and makes a laborious detour to the kitchen. He's wearing a multi-coloured Hawaiian shirt the size of a tablecloth, tan sweat pants held up with a yard of taut elastic, and a pair of pristine running shoes that appear trapped under his oedematous ankles. He has a New York Knicks cap squeezed on to his voluminous head and a dainty butter knife clutched tightly in his plate-sized hand. I'm trying hard not to stare, but I've a feeling my mouth has fallen open. Quite widely.

'Mind if I eat before we start talking plants?' he says, genially.

'No,' I say, quite relieved that his opening words weren't 'fee-fi-fo-fum'. 'Go ahead.'

'You wanna sandwich?' he says, lifting a packet of meat out of his fridge and piling a mound of it on top of his bread. 'It's no trouble.'

'Um, no thanks. I already had lunch.'

'You think I should be taking more roughage?'

'I'm sorry?'

'For my constipation. Do you think I should be taking more roughage? Maybe I should order myself another bottle of Colon Blow. Hottest chilli sauce on the planet. Guaranteed to clear the tubes no matter how many hard-boiled eggs you've eaten for breakfast. Recommended by four out of five proctologists. Whaddya think?'

'Well, I don't know,' I say, feeling slightly queasy. 'Have you tried bran flakes or something?'

'No good. Backs me up even worse. Maybe I should have some pickles. Do pickles count as roughage? Whaddya think?'

He's not waiting for an answer. He lifts a white paper bag out of his fridge, unwraps two torpedo-sized cucumbers and leans back to sniff them with a satisfied sigh.

'Best pickles in the world,' he says, turning to me and smacking his lips. 'A friend of mine brings them up from his delicatessen in Golders Green. You wanna try one?'

'Pickles?' I say, trying hard not to lick my lips.

'Sure. They're cured in garlic, sugar, brine and a touch of dill vinegar. Try one. It ain't gonna kill you.'

'OK,' I say, tentatively. 'Maybe just a very small slice.'

By the time I've polished off my second half of cucumber, Window-box Man is obviously quite impressed. He makes it clear that he likes a girl who knows the value of a good pickle and that he can't be doing with a woman who's overly picky about her food.

'Big Louie,' he says, wiping his mouth with a serviette and holding out his sausage-meat hand. 'Pleased to make your acquaintance.'

'Audrey,' I say, staring up at him, 'Audrey Ungar. Pleased to meet you too.'

He peers at me quizzically for a moment, like he's about to say something more.

'Is something wrong?' I say, wondering if I've spilt pickle juice down my T-shirt.

'No,' he says, massaging his dough-coloured jowls. 'Ungar's a pretty unusual name, that's all.'

'Is it?' I say, wondering whether it would be rude to ask for more pickle.

'Sure,' he says, nodding his head sagely, 'it's distinctive. Has a nice ring to it. A real pedigree. You know, a certain class.'

10

I'm quite keen to get on with discussing the window box but Big Louie clearly has other plans. He finishes his sandwich, shifts his gigantic bulk to the edge of the sofa and wheezes as he heaves himself upright. The coffee table provides some temporary ballast as he scoops up the used plates and serviettes and carries them gingerly to the kitchen. He starts to wash up. He dabs soap on to the sandwich plates and scrubs at them with a scourer for a good minute and a half. He rinses, dries, polishes and stacks; then changes his mind and repeats the process all over again.

A pool of garlicky vinegar has collected on the counter where he broke open the pickle bag, and he scrubs at that with a cloth and a dollop of bleach. He hums distractedly while he's doing it: 'My Way' by Frank Sinatra, then the opening bars of Gershwin's 'Rhapsody in Blue'. His humming builds in intensity as he wipes, polishes and cleans, and he times the crescendo of his performance to coincide with his most important task of all: cleaning his hands.

'OCD,' he says, scrubbing at his fingers with a nail brush. 'Have to get everything real clean.'

'Right,' I say, shifting in my seat. 'I see.'

'I'm obsessive compulsive. As well as being agoraphobic. Did your boss tell you that? Did he tell you I don't go out of the apartment?'

'Well, he's not exactly my boss, he's my boyfriend. But yes, he did mention that you were agoraphobic.'

'How d'you like him?'

'Pardon?'

'Your boyfriend. How d'you like him?'

'Well, um, he's fine. I like him very much.'

'That's good,' he says, nodding at me briskly. 'It's good that you like him. I was married once. Biggest mistake I ever made. Seven and three-quarter years and there wasn't a single day that she didn't aggravate me.'

'Right, I see. What was wrong with her?'

'What was right with her?' he says, grimacing and lifting his bulging eyes skyward. 'When I met her she was the spitting image of Angie Dickinson. Two years after we got hitched, she was heavier than I am now.'

I try to look sympathetic.

'Stuffed her fat face with cookies,' he continues. 'Morning, noon and night. Even when we were in bed together. Can you believe it? I'm trying to get my hand up her negligee to have myself a little squeeze of her bosoms, pardon my French, and she's stuffing her fat face with Twinkies and chocolate-chip cup cakes. I'm telling you, Audrey Ungar, don't get married. As soon as you buy the ring they got you by the balls.'

'Well ... um ... what if you're not the one buying the ring?'

'In that case,' he says, waving his freshly scrubbed butter knife at me, 'make sure he gets you a decent-size stone. That ways you can always sell it when he cheats on you with a woman half your age.'

'Right. Good. Maybe we should move on to your window box now.'

'Sure. Let me show you where I want it.'

'What *colours* do I like?'

'Yes. I thought we could start off with the colours?'

'I thought you knew something about plants. You don't know the first goddam thing about them, do you?'

'No, I'm sorry. I'm afraid I don't.'

'Great. That's just great. Do you know how long it's taken

me to get someone to come up here? Have you any idea how long it's been? Six months. *Six* months it's taken me. Half the gardeners I called gave me the brush-off over the phone, the other half took one look at the building and didn't even bother riding up in the elevator.'

'Yes,' I say. 'I nearly didn't come up either.'

'The ones that do make it up here,' he says, getting into his stride, 'take one look at the state of me and bolt for the door like someone's about to stuff a boiled zucchini up their ass. What is it with English people? It's like they never saw an overweight person before.'

'Well, you are quite . . . large.'

'Of course I'm large. What the fuck? I've been locked up in this shit-show of an apartment for two years straight. What else am I gonna do? All I got to do all day is shit, shave, beat off and eat. Pardon my French. You don't even have any good TV over here. I thought you were meant to have good TV. What is it with the English? Even your soap operas are depressing.'

Big Louie looks sad. He slumps down on his armchair, spilling his fatty curtains over the purple Dralon and crushing the faded tassels with his sleeves.

'It's not too much to ask, is it?' he says, morosely. 'One lousy window box. One lousy window box to tide me over until I can get the garden.'

'The garden?'

'Sure,' he says, brightening slightly. 'One of these days I'm going to have the finest, widest, greenest garden in the whole of the state of New Jersey.'

'I thought you didn't go out.'

He looks at me like I'm clearly a moron.

'That's because I don't have a garden, idiot. If I had a garden I'd go out all the time.'

'Mr Bloom?'

'Yes.'

'Would you like a cup of tea?'

'Sure. Why the hell not? Make it with lemon, though. I gotta cut back on my cholesterol.'

Over lemon tea and a box of cinnamon Pop Tarts, Big Louie tells me a little about his life. He grew up in San Antonio, Texas, and moved out East to Jersey when he was twelve. His parents owned a clapboard house by the shore, and while he missed his winter camping trips into the desert, he quickly fell in love with the ocean.

In his teens he won a scholarship to the prestigious Rutgers College, and he describes these as his happiest days. He's vague about what kind of job he did after he left, but he tells me that it involved a lot of travelling. He met his wife in a hotel lobby in Atlantic City – where she was working as an overnight receptionist – and liked her right away on account of her big bosoms and her cute English accent. By the time she'd fixed up a twenty per cent discount on his room and arranged for his early afternoon wake-up call he was already contemplating marriage.

For a brief time they were blissfully happy. They hired Elvis costumes and married in the Graceland Wedding Chapel in Las Vegas, and his new wife gave up her hotel receptionist job to travel with him and support his flourishing career.

It didn't last. One way or another she grew fat and sour and aggravating and Big Louie's business began to suffer under the strain. A little over two years ago he went broke overnight. Big Louie lost everything he had. His house, his 1959 Coupe de Ville Cadillac and his beloved wire-haired dachshund: Little Louie.

'How come you lost your dog?'

'Ungrateful mutt wouldn't eat the economy dog chow I was feeding him. Only ate premium. I swear that damn dog was punishing me. Wasting away before my very eyes. Would have served him right if I'd taken him to the local pound to be euthanised.'

'Did you?'

'No. He chased after a French poodle while I was fixing some cardboard into the heel of my moccasins, and never came back.'

'I see. That's very sad.'

'Yes it is.'

Shortly after losing Little Louie, Big Louie was forced to bid a harrowing farewell to his wife. She choked to death on a cup cake the day after they moved into their trailer park; and even though Big Louie did everything in his powers to save her, his efforts were tragically in vain.

'It was horrible,' he says, shaking his soggy jowls from side to side. 'I was trying to perform the Heimlich manoeuvre but I couldn't get my arms around her. I tried punching her in the gut but there was too much fat. I'm telling you, Audrey, it was heart wrenching. *Heart wrenching*. The way her lips turned blue and her tongue lolled out her gasping mouth. And the noise she made. Jeez, I can still hear it now. A rasping, or was it more of a gagging . . . maybe it was more like a tickly cough. Anyway,' he says, rubbing his hands together, 'at least she died happy, God rest her soul – cup cakes were always her favourite.'

After that, he was down to almost nothing. He pawned his grandfather's gold watch to pay for her funeral, but it cost him a lot more than it should have, on account of her needing an oversized coffin. A couple of weeks later, just as he was contemplating buying a gun and ending it all, a small miracle stepped up to save him. It turned out his wife had left him something in her will. Five hundred dollars in Nestlé stocks and the deeds to a one-bedroom apartment in London that had once belonged to her late mother.

For a day or two, Big Louie thought all his prayers had

been answered. He stopped mourning his dog, gave up his plans to buy a gun, and made arrangements to fly to London and sell the apartment right away. He'd pay off his crippling debts, buy himself some brand-new moccasins and, with a bit of luck, he might even start up his failed business all over again. It was then that he discovered how much the flat was worth. The sale would barely keep him in leather moccasins, let alone cover what he owed.

Depressed as he was, Big Louie took this news on the chin. With the overeating and the OCD kicking in hard, he thought a fresh start in a new country might be just what he needed. He packed his bags, booked his flight and decided to head for England right away.

On a bitter winter's morning, Big Louie began his last real journey. He boarded a flight to London, ate three airline dinners, drank five miniature Bourbons, and snoozed his way across the cold Atlantic. As the plane skimmed over the ragged edge of Ireland and started its descent, he turned and pressed his face up to the frozen window. A patch-work of shabby towns and snow-covered fields stretched out before him, and he wondered whether he might not have made a mistake. He tightened his expandable seat belt, washed his hands with an anti-bacterial wipe-cloth and said a small prayer as the wheels touched down on the tarmac. Once through Heathrow airport, he consoled himself with a king-sized Snickers, squeezed himself on to an over-stuffed Tube train and carved his way under the city and onwards into King's Cross.

The journey had sapped the last of his strength. By the time he arrived at Widnes Tower, he was cold, broken, penniless and defeated, and he took one look at the rail yard, the tower blocks and the concrete walls covered in poorly drawn graffiti, and something inside of him snapped.

At that precise moment he vowed that he'd never leave the confines of this apartment. Not until he could afford something much better. He'd live in this cheap mismatched box, with its paper-thin walls and its sweaty plastic furniture, until he could finance his life's long dream. A house with a screen door and a front porch and a deep wide lawn with immaculate and freshly watered flower beds. He'd dust his late mother-in-law's china ornaments every day – bull terriers and kittens dressed as cowboys and Sioux Indians – and keep his environment spotless and sanitary until he could buy his way out.

He hopes he might leave any day now. He won't tell me how he's going to do it, but he assures me he has a failsafe plan.

'I can't tell you about it.'

'Why not?'

'We only just met.'

'But I'd like to know. I'm interested.'

'Maybe I'll tell you next time. We'll just have to see how it goes.'

'Next time?'

'Sure. You still gotta build my window box, don't you?'

'Me?'

'Who else?'

'Well, I'll send my boyfriend over next time. He knows everything there is to know about plants.'

'No.'

'No?'

'No. I got to know you now. I want you to do it.'

'But I thought you said I was an idiot.'

'Yeah, well. I sort of like you. Maybe it's your red hair or something. It suits you.'

'Thanks. That's very nice of you to say.'

'Yeah, well, don't get carried away. It's not like you're Rita Hayworth or nothing.'

'No. Right. Obviously not.'

*   *   *

After that Big Louie informs me that he has things to be getting along with – I assume it's something important to do with germs and floor polish – so I collect my coat and get ready to leave.

'You got e-mail?'

'Yes.'

'Then I'll mail you. I'll send you a list of what I want and you'll bring it me next time.'

'You've got a computer?'

'Sure. You think I'm stupid just coz I'm fat?'

'No, of course not . . . I just . . . I don't know, they're quite expensive, that's all.'

'Yeah, well. I got funds.'

'OK. That's fine then. You send me your list and I'll bring over the . . . um . . . mud and stuff next time.'

'I want the good bulbs, though. I don't want any of that cheap shit you get delivered via the Internet.'

'No. I promise. I'll get Joe to pick out the best plants he has.'

'Someone's cooking pot roast,' he says, as I prise open the front door.

'Sorry?'

'Downstairs. Can't you smell it? Someone's cooking brisket.'

I shake my head. Big Louie shrugs and lumbers into the middle of the living room and I open the door just wide enough to slip out. He tells me not to open it fully because it makes his palms sweat, and I do my best to keep the aperture as narrow as possible.

'I'll see you next week, then?'

'OK. Next week.'

'Definitely?'

'Definitely.'

'You're not gonna not call me or nothing?'

'No. I promise. I'll call.'

'OK then.'
'OK.'

I walk the fifty yards to the lift and as I rattle back down to the ground I notice something sweet mixed in with the sourness of the stale urine: the scent of stewing meat. Big Louie was right. Someone in the building is cooking brisket.

11

'You did it on purpose.'

'I didn't.'

'You did. You thought you'd send me to the bleakest, meanest, most run-down inner-city tower block in the whole of London, just so you could convince me to move to the countryside with you.'

'That's not true. Don't be ridiculous. I'd never have sent you out there if I'd realised it was going to be that bad.'

'You had the address.'

'Yes, but Pete was the one who looked it up on the *A to Z*. He said it looked OK. Didn't you?'

'Don't bring *me* into it.'

'Well you did. You said it was right next to the station.'

'It *is*.'

'Yes,' I say, 'but it's in a back road. A cul-de-sac in fact. It's a war zone. It's full of middle-aged, bleach-blonde alcoholic women and violent-looking street gangs with knives.'

'*Knives?*'

'Well, stolen cigarettes.'

'Look, I'm sorry. I promise, I'll never ask you to go on another job for me again.'

'It's too late now.'

'What do you mean?'

'I've got to go back again next week.'

'Why?'

'The giant wants me to finish the job.'

I'm having an early evening drink with Joe and Pete and neither of them is taking my giant story seriously.

'I'm just saying that he couldn't have weighed forty-five stone. It's simply not feasible.'

'He does. At least.'

'How heavy was the fattest person that ever lived? What was his name?'

'Robert Wadlow.'

'No,' I say, 'he was the tallest. The fattest was Robert Earl Hughes.'

'How do you know that?'

'I used to read *The Guinness Book of Records* when I was a kid.'

'You still do,' says Joe, tucking into some beer nuts.

'Yes. OK. I still do. Occasionally. But you have to keep up to date. There've been a lot of changes over the years.'

'How does he survive, then?' says Pete, sceptically.

'Who?'

'Your giant. How does he get food and stuff?'

'He has it delivered, I suppose.'

'How does he get the money?'

'I don't know. He has enough to eat well and buy a computer and he's got enough cleaning fluids to stock a decent-sized hypermarket . . . but I'm not really sure. He wouldn't say.'

'Perhaps he's a terrorist.'

'I don't think so, Pete.'

'He might be some kind of international criminal. You never know. Maybe he makes his money from gun smuggling.'

'He doesn't.'

'How can you be sure?'

'Well, he seems . . . nice.'

'He has a pickle fetish,' says Joe, shaking his head. 'This is how she judges people. If they like pickled food they must be alright.'

'But I'm telling you, they were amazing pickles. I must remember to find out where he got them the next time I go over there.'

'Hold on. You're not seriously thinking about going back?'

'Why not?'

'It's not safe.'

'It's safer in the countryside then, is it?' I say, eyeing Joe suspiciously.

'Well, yes. Now you come to mention it, it is.'

This is it. This is the moment I've been waiting for.

'Joe?'

'Yes?'

'Have you ever seen a film called *The Wicker Man*?'

'No, I don't think I have.'

'Right. What time does the video shop close?'

'Jesus.'

'Exactly.'

'That's not very nice.'

'No, it's not, is it? How would you like it? How would you like it if a bunch of bare-chested pagans tied you up in a giant wicker toaster and burnt you alive at the top of a windswept tarn? That's what could happen to us if we moved to the countryside.'

'You think so?'

'Yes. If it can happen to Edward Woodward, the Equalizer, no less, then it could definitely happen to you and me.'

'But it was on a remote Scottish island. A mull. In the Outer Hebrides.'

'Yes, well, that's how it starts. You say you only want to move as far as Hemel Hempstead but the next thing you know we'll be wearing fish skins and living on some god-forsaken loch, being chased through the purple heather by a gang of bare-breasted devil worshippers.'

'Men or women?'

'What difference does it make?'

'Quite a lot actually.'

'Men then.'

'You're sure?'

'Positive.'

'Not women?'

'No.'

'Look, I just think it would be nice, that's all.'

'What?' I say, incredulously. 'What would be nice about it?'

'Well, we could have a proper garden for one thing. And we could afford to go on a decent holiday. We could sell this flat, put some money in the bank, get a place with an extra bedroom maybe.'

'What do we need an extra bedroom for?'

Joe makes a face.

'Seriously. It's not like we ever have anyone over to stay. Whenever Pete gets chucked out by one of his girlfriends he sleeps on the sofa.'

'Well . . . perhaps . . . you know . . . we might want kids one day. We'll need an extra bedroom then.'

'Hmmmm. Joe?'

'Yes.'

'Have you ever heard of a product called Tena Lady?'

Joe is sulking in the bath with a beer and a magazine about hardy annuals, and I'm taking late-night phone advice from Lorna.

'You told him that you don't want children?'

'No. Not exactly. I just told him I didn't feel ready yet.'

'You should do it. I think it's a good idea.'

'You do?'

'Why not? Having Meg was the best thing I've ever done.'

'Right. This from the woman who tells me I'm going to be incontinent by the time I'm fifty and moans about her three-foot stomach envelope every time we go shopping together.'

'We don't go shopping together.'

'I know. That's because I can't stand shopping with other people, but if we did, you would.'

'Don't forget the baggy fanny.'

'Pardon me?'

'The baggy fanny. It's never the same afterwards.'

'*See.* You see what I'm talking about?'

'It doesn't matter though, because you can always have it tightened up later on.'

'Can you?'

'Yes. There's an operation you can have. They can shorten your labia as well.'

'Why would anyone want their labia shortened?'

'You know . . . if they're a bit *dangly*.'

'Dangly?'

'Yes. If they hang down past your pubes. Some women are paying to get them shortened.'

'Which women?'

'Californians.'

'Fuck me.'

'I know. Can you imagine? Can you imagine having the kind of life where the only thing you had to worry about of a morning was the length of your labia?'

'No,' I say. 'I don't think I can.'

'Seriously though, you should definitely think about it.'

'Having my labia shortened?'

'No. Moving to the countryside and having children with Joe. What's so great about living in London anyway? Cities are only good if you've got lots of money.'

'That's not true,' I say. 'It's the complete opposite, in fact. At least if you're poor in the city you have the comfort of being surrounded by other poor people.'

'Being surrounded by poor people is a *comfort* to you?'

'Yes. I like to be able to look out of my window and see other downtrodden human beings battling with their carrier bags and their existential angst. If I lived in the countryside all I'd see would be trees. And grass. And diseased sheep. And large-breasted pagans rushing round windswept tarns with flaming torches.'

'Audrey?'

'Yes.'

'Have you been watching *The Wicker Man* again?'

'No. Absolutely not.'

'Look,' she says, firmly, 'I just don't think you should be letting this whole thing with your dad get in the way of your relationship with Joe.'

'What are you talking about? Where did that come from? What's my dad got to do with *The Wicker Man*?'

'Nothing. It's Joe. He says you've been acting funny all week.'

'Acting funny? Like what?'

'He said he caught you hiding in the cupboard under the stairs with a camping torch in your hand.'

'I was looking for moth balls.'

'And he says you've been counting your dinner peas again.'

'That's not true.'

'OK. But I don't want you freaking out and dashing off to South-East Asia with your rucksack like you did the last time.'

'The last time what?' I say, scratching at the eczema patch on my elbow.

'The last time things got on top of you. Like the time you dropped out of your degree course and went to live on a beach in Ko Samui for six months.'

'Don't be ridiculous. I'm not going to run off to Ko Samui.'

'Why not?'

'It's horrible. I'd be more likely to go to Ko Phi Phi.'

*   *   *

'How was your bath?'
    'Fine.'
'How was the magazine on hardy annuals?'
'Very illuminating.'
'There was enough hot water then?'
'Yes.'
'You didn't run out halfway through?'
'No.'
'The Imperial Leather lathered up OK?'
'It lathered up fine.'
'Joe?'
'What?'
'Have you ever thought my labia were too long for my pubes?'

12

For some reason all the talk about pubes and labial pref-
erences ended up giving both of us the horn, and after a
brief bout of post-bath sex and a promise that I'll stop
counting my dinner peas, Joe and I have arrived at a new
understanding. I've agreed to visit Hemel Hempstead (or
similar) at the weekend (just to look), and he's agreed to
help me navigate the plethora of missing-person sites on the
Internet when he gets home from work this evening. We've
both agreed that hiring *Magnum PI* would be pointless –
given that he's fictional and lives in Hawaii – and Joe has
agreed to ask a lawyer friend of his if he knows anything
about tracing missing relatives.

Lorna thinks I should call Frank and ask him if he has
any more details about my father's last known whereabouts,
but I'm having trouble gearing up to it. I can't face the
disapproval in his voice when I tell him that I'm thinking
of looking for my dad, and I can't face him saying that
it's a bad idea for me to turn my life upside down again.
Which it is.

Over the years I've developed a nasty habit of turning my
life upside down at the least provocation. I'm a complete
control freak about doing it. These two qualities may, at first
glance, appear to be mutually exclusive, but to my way of
thinking they couldn't be more synergistic. There's no point
in turning your life upside down unless you're going to do
it in an orderly fashion, and there's nothing like a savage
restructuring of your daily life to make you feel more at
peace with the world.

I'm not talking about cleaning the oven, getting a new haircut or plucking the hairs out round your nipples, satisfying as these activities can be – I'm talking about far-reaching, irrigating change. Every five years, since the age of eighteen, I've diligently spring-cleaned and rebooted my life. Changed jobs, moved home, travelled to a new continent and, on occasion, finished and begun a new relationship. I'm acutely methodical about doing it. I never leave a job – even a menial one – without having a new one to go on to, and I never leave a boyfriend without remembering to pack all my CDs in alphabetical order first. If I'm planning a trip, then I make sure I have precisely the right amount of money to survive for six months in relative comfort (calculated on a day-by-day, pro rata, biweekly, unforeseen-emergency basis) and, unlike most wistful, hippy, 'go where the vibe takes me' travellers, I never leave home without a blow-by-blow, month-by-month itinerary, and a medical kit containing tiger balm, smallpox vaccine and a decade's worth of calamine lotion and Imodium.

According to Lorna, who watches a lot of Oprah Winfrey while she's cooking dinner for Meg, this is classic behaviour for someone like me: a person who fears abandonment and craves order. I'm so fearful of things falling apart that I seek to destroy them before they have an opportunity to collapse beneath me: which they undoubtedly will – at some stage.

I abandon relationships just as they're reaching their succulent peak, leave jobs just as I'm being handed a measure of responsibility, and desert my studies moments before I have the sudden urge to rediscover shoplifting and get myself expelled all over again. Or at least I used to. Until I met Joe.

These days I have a more stationary response to pressure. I spend happy hours reciting the Periodic Table backwards in my head whenever I'm feeling anxious or depressed, and there's nothing more likely to lull me into a deep and dreamless sleep than a crafty bit of adding up and taking away. Half-yearly accounts are emotional balm to me. Facts and figures and algebraic calculations are the way I lure sense out of a random universe. And, in the moments when I can't, I've got Joe. The one person who's made me feel content to sit still. The one person I've ever met who seems halfway at ease with life's unpredictability.

'You said you'd stay in and look through missing-person sites with me.'

'I know,' says Joe, apologetically, 'I'm really sorry. Pete's coming over in a while. He'll help you look.'

'Why have you got to work tonight? It's dark. How can you plant things in the dark?'

'I'm not planting anything. I'm going over the design details for the ornamental lake. It's a big job.'

'I thought you said it was ornamental.'

'Yes. But it's *big* ornamental. The garden's almost seven acres. I'm sorry, I'll be back by nine.'

'OK. But Pete better not be bringing his film script over with him this time.'

'He won't, I promise.'

'How do you know?'

'I asked him not to.'

'I don't get it. What's the problem? Why don't you believe in aliens?'

'I do, theoretically. I just don't think it's likely they'd be green.'

'Why not?'

'Well, things that are green usually signify the presence of chlorophyll. Are you suggesting that your aliens are half plant?'

'Maybe.'

'I thought they came from a planet that was made of ice.'

'Hmmm . . . perhaps I should make them albino then.'

'Albino?'

'So they blend in with their wintry landscape.'

Pete has turned up with the seventy-fifth draft of his untitled science fiction epic (*Alphaville* meets *Them!* meets *Blade Runner* meets *Planet of the Apes*) and he's taken exception to my views on alien life forms.

'So, given the size of the universe, you *do* think the existence of life in other galaxies is a possibility?'

'Yes. But the fact that your cousin Adrian woke up with a sore anus on a camping trip to Arizona doesn't prove that aliens have landed in the desert.'

'I told you his dream about the oily proboscis that looked like a nose?'

'Yes.'

'And that a tube of KY jelly was missing from his washbag when he woke up in the morning?'

'Yes.'

'And that he was camping near to Area 51?'

'Yes.'

'And you still don't believe he was visited by aliens hell-bent on researching the human anatomy?'

'No. I think it's far more likely that he had haemorrhoids. Your cousin Adrian probably doesn't eat enough fruit. Now, are you going to help me look through this pile of missing-person websites or not?'

Pete makes himself comfortable in an armchair, muttering lines of alien dialogue to himself and crossing things out with a Biro, while I scroll through the Internet looking at sites with names like People Search, Missing.org and Traceline. I try basic searches that cover phone listings, e-mail and inclusion on the electoral roll but, as I'd expected, they don't turn up anything much.

I try some American search engines and my dad's name,

Harry Ungar, brings up thirteen phone listings from the White Pages. Once I've eliminated the Ungarmans, the Ungarlichts and the Harry Ungar Juniors I'm only left with three names. A cross-check on Who/where.com reveals their ages: Harry Ungar from Ocean Parkway in Brooklyn turns out to be seventy-three, while Harry Ungar from Rockaway turns out to be twenty-four. Harry Ungar from Savannah, Georgia, is the right age, late fifties, but his middle initial is M. My father's middle initial is B.

There are plenty of organisations that offer to perform detailed searches for money and I think briefly about shelling out the $59.95 on my credit card, but I'm not sure it would do any good. They all ask for social security numbers and information about last known addresses, but given that my dad made his living – if you can call it that – from playing cards, I'm not sure he'd have any tax, employment or social security records to search.

He could be living in a wooden hut in Alaska for all I know. Or a cave in the Australian outback. A part of me thinks that he might be as close as London or Brighton and a part of me thinks he might very well be dead. Traceline suggests checking death, probate and marriage indexes if the electoral roll doesn't turn up anything; and if all else fails, they suggest putting a missing-person advert in a national newspaper. I decide that a newspaper advert might be a good idea. At least it'll make me feel like I'm doing something.

Pete's bored and wants to chat. He wants to tell me all about his unrequited love for Lorna (the details of which I've heard a thousand times) and all about his latest bonkers conspiracy theory. Something to do with sightings of unmarked black helicopters over Nevada and the ascendancy of a top-secret new world order. He's just about to hijack my computer and log me on to www.conspiracyworld.com when I'm rescued by the arrival of new e-mail. It's a message from the giant.

He's written out a list of plants that he wants for his window box and I ask Pete to take a quick look.

'Lavender, lotus vine, rose moss, impatiens and geraniums. Cool, good choices. Especially in the shade.'

'Well, he doesn't get much sunlight. The other tower blocks cut most of it out.'

'Right, these will be no problem then. They're pretty low maintenance as well. What's "hold'em" mean, do you think?'

'*Hold'em?*'

'Yeah, look, his e-mail address is biglouie@hold'em.com.'

I hadn't noticed. I lean over and take a closer look.

'I'm not sure,' I say, scratching at the eczema on my elbow. 'It could mean Texas Hold'Em, I suppose.'

'What's that?'

'Um . . . poker. It's a type of poker game. There's loads of different variations.'

'Are there?'

'Yeah. You know, there's Hold'Em, Stud, Omaha, Hi-lo, Pai Gow . . . um . . . well anyway, there's lots.'

'Right,' says Pete, nodding at me quizzically. 'Your dad played a lot of poker, didn't he?'

'Yes,' I say. 'He did.'

'So maybe that's your best bet.'

'How do you mean?'

'Well,' says Pete, crossing out another line in his script, 'there's bound to be loads of gambling sites on the Internet, aren't there? Especially poker ones. Maybe you should try posting on a couple of those. Someone might remember having played with him. You never know.'

Typical. Just when you're thinking that someone's lost to the fairies, they come up with a brilliant idea.

13

There's a fold-away table in the kitchen with six men sitting around it playing cards. No one seems to mind that I'm here. I'm curled up on the floor, reading a book about deadly snakes and scorpions, enjoying the heat and the chatter. The room smells of cigar smoke, spilt beer and melted cheese, but I don't care too much because it's warm. The kitchen is the only room in the house that stays warm all through the night in winter, and it means I can take off my shoes.

From my vantage point next to the oven I have an unobscured view of the action. My dad is sat at the head of the table, spinning anecdotes and gesticulating with his neat hands, and the other men are laughing generously and nodding their heads. I know four of the other faces well. They turn up on the first Friday of every month (on the weekends my mum works her night shifts) and stay until the early hours of Saturday morning. The one in the wire-rimmed spectacles is Mr Santos – head of chemistry at my father's school – and the one who smells of broccoli is our doctor. The other two are next-door neighbours of no particular note, but tonight there's a face that I've never seen before. Mr Santos says he met him in the pub on his way over here, and he introduces himself to everyone as Jimmy.

Jimmy has crooked teeth, the kind that get pieces of food trapped between them if you don't pay strict attention to your dental hygiene, and they stick out in all directions, filling his mouth. He's wearing a plaid sports jacket and a colourful tie, and when he concentrates his lips purse together into a plump, girlish 'O' shape.

The other men have begun to tease him. He's shaking his head and saying that he's never played poker before and that he wasn't aware they'd be playing the game for money. I listen to them argue a little longer, soaking up the heat from the hot-water boiler and reading about the most poisonous scorpion in the world; and all of a sudden my dad leans over and pats the top of my head.

'Ginger-nut,' he says, casually, 'tell Jimmy here what wins.'

I don't want to catch sight of Jimmy's crazy teeth again, so I keep my eyes fixed firmly on my book while I recite the answer.

'Straight flush, four of a kind, full house, flush, straight, three of a kind, two pairs, one pair, highest card.'

'See, Jimmy,' says my dad, grinning proudly. 'If a nine-year-old can learn, it can't be so hard, can it?'

Jimmy supposes that it can't.

'Here we go then,' says Dr Broccoli, shuffling the pack and loosening his shoulders. 'Each matchstick's worth fifty pence. Who's in?'

The cards come down on to the table, hand after hand, minute after minute, in a gentle, repetitive rhythm. The voices become less boisterous as the hours wear on and the back-slapping and the teasing gradually subside. Someone says, 'Jimmy's definitely bluffing,' and it turns out Jimmy wasn't bluffing at all. Someone says Jimmy's got 'aces full of queens' and it turns out he had nothing but a 'lousy pair of twos'. Someone says it looks like Jimmy's played this game before, and Jimmy frowns like a liar and swears on his mother's life it's not true.

The men are quieter now, staring at their cards and puffing gently on their panatella cigars, and I'm busy studying the diamond pattern on the kitchen floor. There's an oily silver-fish snaking its way across the lino, and I reach out and bash it hard with the heel of my shoe. When I lift it up there's nothing left but a blob of grey slime, and just as I'm about to scrape it up with a piece of tissue Jimmy shoots me a loony-toothed smile.

I'm a little embarrassed that Jimmy's caught me bashing silverfish, so I turn away and busy myself with what's going on underneath the table. I concentrate on the dozen shoes and the dozen feet and the movements each of them is making on the floor. Dr Broccoli's feet are tapping on the lino, hard and fast, like he's hitting drum pedals, and my dad's shoes occasionally swoosh from side to side. Jimmy's feet never move. His legs are perfectly still: rooted to the lino like pot plants. He's wearing black brogues tied with brown laces, and his socks are thin and tan coloured like a woman's. At first I think Jimmy's socks are made of old tights, but when he bends down every now and then to hitch them up I can see they're made of something shiny, like silk.

I watch feet and bash silverfish a while longer, but somewhere around ten o'clock the heat and the smoke get the better of me, and I fall asleep. When I wake, some time around midnight, I'm wrapped in a tartan car blanket with a settee cushion propped underneath my head. The next-door neighbours have gone home to their wives and there are three people left in the game: my dad, Dr Broccoli and Jimmy. Mr Santos looks like he lost all his matchsticks hours ago, but he's sticking around anyhow, just to watch.

Jimmy is dealing. He's whipping the deck together like a croupier, and each time he lays out a hand he takes a sip from his tall glass of milk. The other men have Scotch and warm beer parked next to their ashtrays, and they all look tired and drawn, whereas Jimmy still looks patient and alert.

Mr Santos shakes his head as Jimmy rakes in yet another pot and my dad pushes his index finger deeper into the crease of his forehead. Jimmy holds out his hands. 'What can I tell you?' he says, spraying a thin mist of spittle through his crazy teeth. 'Beginner's luck.'

The game drifts on for another half an hour or so, until

Dr Broccoli throws in his cards and stands up. He shakes everyone's hand cordially. He stares at Mr Santos, points over to Jimmy and says, 'Next time, William, leave this one in the pub.' He tries to sound jovial about it, but I can tell by his clipped voice that he's serious. 'Don't invite him again,' he's saying. 'This is a casual game between friends. Jimmy Silk Socks isn't welcome here.'

With Dr Broccoli cleaned out, Jimmy and my dad play one on one for a while – my dad calls this playing 'heads up' – until Jimmy says it's time he was getting along. My dad is chewing his lips because he'd quite like the opportunity to win some of his money back, but Jimmy is stretching his arms above his head and calling time. My dad shrugs, converts a pile of skinny matchsticks into money and hands over a thin sheaf of five-pound notes. He doesn't get out of his chair or offer to show Jimmy Silk Socks to the door. Mr Santos mouths 'Sorry' as they stand up to leave, and my dad waves his hand in front of his face: slowly, like he's batting away flies.

I offer to help tidy away the empty plates and glasses, but my dad knocks back the last of his whisky and shakes his head. He says it's high time that I was in bed and that my mum would be furious if she found out I was up this late. He walks me upstairs, and because it's cold in the bedroom I scramble under the covers without taking off my clothes.

'Sorry about the beginner's luck,' I say, as he bends down to tuck me in.

'No such thing,' he says wearily. 'That man Jimmy was just a better player than the rest of us, that's all.'

'But he said it was the first time he'd ever played.'

'Yes, he did didn't he?'

'He made you all think he was a bad player. But it turns out he was good all along.'

My dad frowns at me like I'm a little too sharp for my own good and folds in the corners of my blanket.

'I didn't like him much anyway,' I say, turning over and burrowing into my pillow.

'How come?' says my dad, standing up.

'His shoelaces were the wrong colour for his shoes and he was wearing women's socks.'

'Women's socks?'

'Yes. They were made of silk or something. And his feet never moved.'

'His *feet*?'

'Yes. Sometimes when you made a bet your feet swished to the side and Mr Santos's feet were tapping all the time.'

'And Jimmy's feet?'

'Like I said, they never moved.'

'Never?'

I think for a moment to see if this is true.

'Only when he won,' I say, finally. 'Just before he won he tugged his socks.'

'Every time?'

'No,' I say, yawning gently. 'Not every time. Just the times when Mr Santos said Jimmy had aces or a full house and it turned out he only had twos.'

'He pulls up his socks when he bluffs?'

'Yes,' I say. 'That's what he does.'

'Well done, Ginger-nut,' says my dad, cheering up all of a sudden. 'That's very useful to know. We'll tell your mum you were in bed by ten thirty then, shall we? How does that sound?'

'That sounds fine.'

I'm up and out of bed as soon as I hear my mum's key in the latch, and eggs are cooking on the stove by the time I get downstairs. She looks worn out. She wears her lids low over her eyes like sagging blinds, and the strain of a long night at the hospital is ground into her pale skin like dirt.

I sit at the table feeling nervous and queasy, wondering

if I'll be able to manage the egg. After a night shift at the hospital my mum often likes to spill out her bag of miseries and sad stories while we eat. The beautiful baby that died from an asthma attack (a warning that I should always carry my inhaler); the young woman that died choking on chicken bones (a warning that I should always chew up my food); and the endless stories of imbecile doctors who screwed up their patients' medication and operations and crippled them or killed them stone dead. She tells her stories with a hushed voice, touching wood every now and then to ward off bad luck for the three of us, and throwing salt over her shoulder when she spills a few grains on the kitchen table.

I ready myself for a stream of ghoulish tales, but this morning she doesn't have too much to say. Just a teenager that should have been wearing a seat belt when his car crashed into a brick wall and smashed his head to bits, and a description of the new hospital administrator who paid a visit to the ward at the end of her shift.

'How was your game?' she says, half-heartedly, spooning some egg white into her mouth.

'Good,' says my dad, rubbing her shoulders. 'Didn't go on too late.'

'Lose much?' she says, like she doesn't care much one way or the other.

'A little,' says my dad. 'Just a little.'

We eat the rest of our breakfast in silence and I notice how loud the buttering of toast and the stirring of tea can sound when nobody has anything to say. When my dad finally breaks the silence, his words sound sharp and intrusive; like the hiss of a freshly boiled kettle.

'I thought I might go for a quick drink this afternoon,' he says, briskly. 'That's if you don't mind.'

My mum yawns and begins collecting up the breakfast plates. She says she'll be asleep by lunch-time anyway, and even though no one asks I say I've got plenty to be getting along with down at the pier.

'Who are you going drinking with?' she says, standing up and straightening her skirt.

'Jimmy,' he says, casually. 'He's an old friend of William's. Played cards with us last night and I think he might become a regular in the game.'

'Oh,' she says sleepily. 'That's nice. What does he do?'

'What does he do? He . . . er, he imports socks.'

'Socks?'

'Yes, silk ones. From Italy.'

My dad winks at me to keep the secret – like he always does when he has something to hide – but this time I feel a little uncomfortable and my face begins to itch down one side. I can't work out why my dad would want to see this Jimmy man again. I didn't like the way he counted out his winnings last night – licking his fingers and turning over the banknotes one by one – and I'm still not happy about him wearing brown laces on his black leather shoes.

'So,' says my dad, clearly eager to change the subject, 'what's the name of your new boss?'

'Oh,' my mum says, pulling distractedly at her fringe, 'the hospital administrator? Didn't I tell you? His name is Frank.'

14

Here is my suspicion about Big Louie. I think he may have been a card player like my dad. I might be reading too much into his hold'em e-mail address, but other things have been bothering me as well. The fact that he met his wife in Atlantic City. The fact that he went bankrupt overnight. The fact that he set up home on the outskirts of Las Vegas, and the way he was so taken with my surname when we met.

It could mean that Ungar was the name of his school-teacher, or the name of a boyhood friend or favourite aunt. Ungar may have been the name that swung on a scratched enamel shop sign outside his local delicatessen, or it may just have reminded him of someone else.

'Your name?'

'Yes. Why were you so taken with my name?'

Big Louie takes the brown paper bag I'm holding and sniffs at it gently, while he thinks.

'Well,' he says, 'it's a good name. It's old fashioned. Makes me think of Audrey Hepburn or somethin'.'

'No,' I say, reminding him. 'It wasn't the Audrey bit that you liked.'

'Wasn't it?'

'No. It was the Ungar bit.'

'The Ungar bit?'

'Yes.'

I hadn't planned on visiting Big Louie quite so soon – Joe hasn't even picked out his plants yet – but I had to find out if I was right. There are four and a half million poker sites on the Internet and I had no idea of the best place to start. There are chat rooms, forums, dozens of online casinos, and pages of tournament lists, statistics and players' tips. I tried cross-referencing my father's name, just to see what would come up, but all I could find were links to a player called Stu Ungar: three times World Series champion of poker, no limit Hold'Em master, now dead.

By all accounts he was an astonishing player. They called him the Kamikaze Kid on account of his wild and fearless playing style, and he won his first World Series bracelet at the age of twenty-four. He had a photographic memory – he could memorise the card order of three successive packs – and the kind of talent that most players fantasise about all their lives.

As I read through some of the details of Stu Ungar's life – his brilliance at the card table and his addiction to the narcotics that eventually killed him – I remembered my dad having mentioned his name the year before he left. He was having another of his arguments with my mum and I was sitting in a corner, scratching my cheeks and watching them fight. The rows started soon after Jimmy came round that first time, and they were almost always about gambling or money. My mum wanted to know how it was possible. For a fully grown man with a wife and a child to waste his money on a foolish game of luck.

He always gave the same answer. He'd ask her whether she'd heard of the chess player, Bobby Fischer, and she'd shrug her shoulders resignedly and say she had. His voice would rise and tighten as he laid out his argument, but he maintained he was correct right up until the moment he left.

To my father's way of thinking, the best poker players – legends like Stu Ungar, Doyle Brunson and Johnny Moss – were as talented as any grand master of chess. To him, poker was a unique form of gambling. It bore no relation to the whims of the slot machines or the spin of a wheel or the wild luck of betting on dice. To the uninitiated, it might appear simplistic or childish but, to those who understood it, it was a game of intellect and skill.

As far as my mother was concerned, this was further evidence of her husband's inexorable delusion and decline, and I imagine Frank was telling her much the same thing. I imagine him wheedling his way into her affections at this point, with his grocery-shop flowers and his Sunday morning visits to church, and I suspect she might already have decided to leave my father by then. For my own part, I've always rather liked the chess analogy. I'm not sure I could stand it if I thought my father had left us for something as insubstantial as a game of chance.

'Sure,' says Big Louie, quizzically, 'Stu Ungar. That's exactly who I was thinking of. You know who he is?'

'Yes,' I say, unwrapping a packet of cream-filled truffles. 'He was a poker player. Perhaps the best there ever was.'

'No perhaps about it,' says Big Louie, narrowing his golf-ball eyes at me. 'That kid was a genius. A one-off. How come you heard of him?'

'My father used to play. It was a good while ago now . . .'

'Amateur?'

'To begin with. Then he . . . you know . . . decided to try and make a living at it.'

'Lose much, did he?' says Louie, noticing the look on my face.

'Yes,' I say. 'You could say that.'

'Well,' he says, sniffing at the chocolates through their white cardboard box and rubbing a hand over his porous jowls. 'That beats the lot. A woman who can pick out a grade-A cucumber *and* knows a thing or two about poker. Where have you been all my life?'

'So I'm right, then?' I say, wondering how far to push him. 'You played poker back in the States.'

'Now and then.'

'Now and then?'

'On and off.'

'On and off?'

'Like I say. Now and then. On and off. Here and there. You're pretty nosy for a girl, you know. It's not very attractive. Has anyone ever told you that?'

'How do you like your truffles?' I say, trying a different approach.

'Well, sure,' he says, 'they're fine.'

'And the pickles?'

'Not bad at all.'

'And you still want me to put this window box together for you? You still want me to pick out the best plants and bulbs?'

Big Louie flattens his face into a frowning wad of fat to let me know he doesn't appreciate being messed around.

'So tell me, then.' I say, getting slightly agitated. 'I'm interested, that's all. I'd just like to know.'

'Know what?'

'The best place to search for a missing card player. The best chat rooms, web forums and casinos. You know, the best places to look.'

He calms down a little when he realises I'm not about to pry further into his recent past, and sinks back into his armchair to think.

'This is about your dad, then?' he says dolefully. 'I take it that it's him you're trying to find.'

'Yes,' I say. 'I'm not sure if it'll do any good but something happened to me recently that makes me think I might like to try.'

'What happened?' he says, eager to hear all the details.

'Well, you know, family stuff,' I say, clamming up.

'Fine,' he says, popping a truffle into his mouth. 'If you don't want my help, don't tell me. Maybe he doesn't want anything to do with you anyway. Maybe that's why he left in the first place. Maybe a ginger-headed, smart-alec, nosy-arsed kid ain't something he's missing in his life right now.'

'Louie?'

'Yes.'

'You're a very mean person.'

'Yes,' he says, smiling to himself, 'I know.'

I tell him a little about my father's history and the manner in which he left, and he yawns and nods like it's a story he's heard a thousand times before.

'Sounds like he wasn't much of a card player, if you ask me,' he says, rolling a violet cream round his mouth.

'Well, I don't know,' I say. 'He won sometimes. I mean I think he was OK.'

'You see,' he says, cagily, leaning towards me, 'anyone can be good when they're winning. The real skill is knowing how to lose.'

'I don't understand. What is there to know about losing?'

'Everything,' says Louie, solemnly. 'You got to know how to handle it. You got to know how to quit when you're down and walk away. You've got to be able to draw a line under your losses and digest them, otherwise it'll chew up on your insides like vermin. Curl right round your intestines, chewing and chewing and chewing away. Until it worms its way right through your soul.'

He sounds like a man who knows well of what he speaks.

'Anyway,' he says, changing the subject and shifting uneasily in his seat, 'I can recommend a few websites and magazines that you might want to look at, but if you're serious about finding him, you're best off heading out to some of the tournaments. The World Series maybe.'

'In Las Vegas?'

'Yup. They fly in from every corner of the world. Thousands of them. Every May. Amateurs, pros, hustlers, halfwits, every type of poker player you can imagine. They even have tournaments just for the women. Keeps them busy while they're waiting for their husbands. The ones that don't know how to knit, that is.'

'What about here?' I say, ignoring his comments and offering him another chocolate.

'Don't know,' he says, loosening up a little. 'Never played outside of the US myself. Couldn't see the point. Had friends that spent half their lives chasing card games all over Europe and Asia, but I found all the action I needed without getting on a plane. Besides, I didn't like to leave Little Louie alone any longer than I had to. That dog was my mascot on the road.'

'He went with you when you played?'

'Always. Reno, Atlantic City, Tunica, the gambling boats moored out along the Mississippi. I'm telling you, that dachshund never steered me wrong. Not once. Sniffed out bluffers like a starving man sniffs out a steak.'

'Right. I see. What did he do?'

'Nothing.'

'Nothing?'

'Nope. Was just a certain look he had about him. You had to know him real well to be able to read it.

'Still,' he says, 'I know a few players here that might be able to help you out. Most of them can't play for shit but they know the English scene pretty well.'

'There's a scene?'

'Sure there's a scene. Nothing like as big as it is back home, but that's because you're all fags.'

'Excuse me?'

'The English. Apart from one or two, you're all pussies when it comes to playing cards.'

I lower my head into my hands.

'What about you, then?' he says, wondering what's wrong with me. 'What type of game do you play? Bet it's something dumb like crazy pineapple or Caribbean stud. Women love those kind of Mickey Mouse games.'

'No,' I say, looking up at him. 'I don't actually play.'

'Why the hell not?'

'I don't know. I just thought that, you know, after everything that happened with my dad . . .'

'Sure,' he says, helping himself to the last truffle. 'I get it. You were afraid you might like it too much.'

15

Big Louie watches me chew my nails, staring at me sideways and sizing me up. The whites of his eyes are cream coloured and bloodshot and he's making a laboured clicking sound when he breathes. He seems to suck the trouble right out of me, like a sponge, and I feel tense and fidgety under his gaze. He doesn't speak for a long while. He taps his fingertips on the sides of the chocolate box, rustles the empty pickle packet on the arm of his chair, and dabs at his mouth from time to time with the edge of a freshly ironed handkerchief.

'How old were you when he left?' he says, finally.

'Ten,' I say, taking my fingers out of my mouth.

Big Louie takes this in.

'And you never heard from him once, in all this time?'

'No,' I say. 'Not once.'

'What about the rest of his family? Did he keep in contact with them?'

'His parents are both dead. He has the odd cousin knocking about in Ireland somewhere, but no one he was close to. No siblings either. He was an only child.'

'Like you?'

'Yes. How did you know?'

Big Louie shrugs like it's obvious.

'Well,' he says, sinking further into his sofa, 'what if you didn't like him when you found him?'

'I don't know,' I say. 'I hadn't really thought about it.'

'What if he was a drunk? Or a thief? What if he was super-fat like me?'

'I wouldn't care.'

'Wouldn't you?'

'I don't think so. No.'

'You think it's romantic, I bet. Your dad taking off to make his fortune at the card table.'

I'm annoyed that he's saying much the same thing as Frank, and I answer him a little harshly.

'No. I don't. I don't think it's romantic at all. I think it's insane.'

'I guess you're angry with him, then?' he says calmly.

'Yes,' I say. 'I suppose I am.'

'So maybe he knows that. Maybe he doesn't want you to see what he's turned into. Maybe he doesn't want the shame or the aggravation.'

I shake my head, reach for my jacket and decide that I should probably get going.

'Don't leave yet,' he says, quietly. 'I don't get too many visitors during the day. Why don't you stay a little longer?'

'I have to,' I say. 'I've got things to do.'

'Half an hour,' he says. 'Help me clean up a while before you go. There's something I'd like to show you. Some stuff you might be interested to see.'

I put down my jacket, think for a minute and sit back down on my chair. I don't know what makes me stay – with this mess of a human being, in this claustrophobic box, hovering at the edge of the sky – but something does. I accept a spare pair of rubber gloves – he has bundles of them under the sink – and together we clean the vinegar off the plates and the non-existent chocolate crumbs off the back of the faded settee. When we've finished scrubbing, brushing and cleaning the bleach from our hands, Big Louie points towards a narrow door in the hallway.

'In the cupboard,' he says. 'There's a bunch of photo albums on the first shelf. Go fetch them for me and I'll fix us both a cup of lemon tea.'

*   *   *

The cupboard is stuffed tight like a sausage. Every last inch of space is crammed with papers, photos, playing cards, gambling chips, empty bleach bottles and poker magazines. It's disorganised and dusty and I can sense Big Louie's palms starting to sweat as I peer into the clutter and the gloom. The mere fact that this cupboard exists must keep him up at night; the dirt, the germs, the mould spores, the grime, and the wilful lack of order.

On the top shelf are a pair of photo albums, and I squeeze them out carefully, trying not to disturb any of the other papers and books. A couple of back issues of *Card Player* magazine fall to the floor and I hear Big Louie mutter to himself as a puff of dust shoots out from between their yellowing pages. I bend down and pick them up – carefully so as not to disturb any more dust – and wedge them back in between two hardback books. A biography of Wilt *the Stilt* Chamberlain and a well-thumbed copy of *Super/System*, the seminal book on poker tactics by Doyle Brunson. It has the same cover design as the one my father owned. A little less dog-eared, but otherwise identical.

'You got the albums?' says Louie, with his back to me.

'Yes. Should I bring them over?'

'Give them a little clean first. Use a damp cloth. And some washing-up liquid. And some Mr Sheen wood polish, maybe.'

I wipe down the plastic-coated album covers, douse them with a spritz of wood polish and hand them over to Big Louie. They're broad and heavy, but he handles them like they were newspapers; flipping the covers like loose sheets, and grimacing at the spots of mould on the stiff cardboard pages.

'What do you think?' he says, proudly. 'Pretty handsome devil once, wasn't I?'

I move over behind the sofa and peer down over his bulky shoulders. Smiling out of the faded pages is a finely toned college athlete; a tall, sinewy teenager with a heavy jaw-line and knowing, honey-hazel eyes. He's wearing a white cotton sports vest with crimson trim, and holding a fire-coloured basketball in his outstretched hand. The muscles in his arms are silhouetted by the distant pop of a flashlight, and the veins in his forearm are bulging through his skin from the way he's squeezing his fingers so tightly around the ball.

Underneath this portrait is another photograph of the same sportsman. He's on a basketball court mid-game. He's leaping towards the net like a spring salmon, while the other players writhe, struggle and fight to keep him down. Their hands stretch out, desperately trying to block him, but it's clear beyond doubt that the ball is going in. Next to this picture is a game report from a college newspaper. The headline reads, 'Bloom scores third winning basket of the season, as Scarlet Knights defeat Princeton 75–73.'

'I don't understand,' I say, keeping my eyes fixed on the photographs. 'Is this . . . is this *you*?'

'Yep. That's me. Hard to believe, huh?'

'When? I mean how long ago?'

'I was nineteen. Just started college. Coach reckoned I was gonna go all the way.'

'All the way where?'

'To the NBA. Might even have ended up playing for the Knicks one day. Who knows?'

I stare down at the picture then back at Big Louie, trying to reconcile the handsome, long-limbed athlete with the mountain of saggy flesh slumped in front of me.

'What's wrong?' he says tersely. 'You don't think it's me?'

'No. I do. I mean it's just . . . well . . . you look so different.'

Big Louie looks back at his photo album. He turns the pages carefully, rolling his eyes round his glory days, and slowly drinking them in.

'You know how many guys play college basketball in the US?'

'No,' I say. 'I've no idea.'

'Around half a million. Out of them, maybe fifty make it on to an NBA team each year. Pretty poor odds, wouldn't you say?'

'Ten thousand to one,' I say, immediately.

'Exactly. I had a ten-thousand-to-one shot but I always knew I'd make it. Never a shred of doubt in my mind. My limbs knew which way they were headed before my brain did. Knew the position of every player on that court, every second of the game. Even with my back to them, I knew. Some games, I felt like I could have played just as good with my eyes shut. Like I had a sixth sense or something, you know what I mean?'

His face lights up and he lowers his puffy eyelids at the memory. His lips struggle into a half-smile and he rests his head on the back of his old settee. He sees the crowds at Madison Square Garden and the girls yelling his name from the stands. He sees the New York Knicks vest with his name on it and the NBA trophy in his hands. And then his face darkens. His lips turn downwards and split apart, and a moan eases through his tobacco-stained teeth, like the growl of a wounded animal. His voice is barely audible.

'I never saw it,' he says, quietly, the words wafting over his lips like a breeze. 'I never saw it coming.'

He takes a deep breath and shuts his eyes. He runs his hands slowly across the arms of his chair, before digging his fingers sharply into the fabric.

'It broke me up,' he says with his eyes still closed. 'Broke me up like I was a doll. I thought I was indestructible. You ever thought that, Audrey? That you was indestructible? In the moment before it hit me I thought I was.'

He seems tired after this and he closes the photo album firmly, resting it between his knees and his ample lap. There are a hundred more photographs scattered through its pages – fractions of his life, frozen like ice – but he clearly doesn't want to show me any more.

'Ran into me like a wayward sled,' he says, coldly. 'The driver was dying at the wheel. He's having himself a heart attack, so he presses down hard on the accelerator, coz he knows he's about to die. And if he's going to die, then he wants to die fast. Wants to take people with him, you know what I mean? That car came right out of nowhere. Slams into my pelvis like a freight train and smashes my legs into paste. Snaps my ankles, tibias, fibulas and thigh bones, and I'm spilling blood like a sacrificial goat with its throat slit. I was in a wheelchair for three years. Couldn't even wash or take a piss by myself . . . couldn't even wash or take a piss.'

Big Louie stands up and makes his way towards the hall cupboard. In a small act of defiance he wants to put the photo albums away by himself. I watch as he shuffles along the narrow corridor, and I realise his peculiar gait has as much to do with his ancient injuries as his excessive weight. He slips the albums back on to the shelf and his whole body shudders as he closes the door. He makes his way to the bleach bottle as quickly as he can and scrubs at his fingers so furiously I think they might bleed.

'That's when I started to play cards,' he says, while he scrubs. 'Not right away, you understand, a year or so after the accident. Spent the first year in the hospital moaning and sobbing like a girl. Couldn't stand it. Couldn't stand the fact that it had happened to me. But you know what it's like when you're a kid, right? You still think life's fair. You still think it owes you somethin'.'

The lemon tea has gone cold on the coffee table and I offer to make us both some more.

'Well,' I say, switching on the kettle, 'that's an awful story. It must have been terrible for you. To have been so good at something, then to have it all taken away. It must have been—' I stop mid-sentence. I'm not sure I can find the appropriate words.

'It was a bitch,' he says, sniffing the bleach fumes from his hands. 'But what you gonna do about it? Just when you think you've got it made, life always finds a new way of fucking you up the arse.'

16

'What are you reading?'

'*Country Life.*'

'Why?'

'I'm doing a spot of research. For our trip. I've bought new wellington boots and I've dug my old anorak out of the wardrobe as well.'

'Your green one?'

'Yes. It looks a bit like one of those posh Barbour jackets that everybody wears in the countryside. It's not waxed or anything, but I could always put some hair gel on it to make it shine.'

'Audrey?'

'Yes?'

'We're only going for a pub lunch. We're not going fox-hunting or badger-baiting or anything.'

'I know. But I don't want everyone staring at us like we're "townies". I don't want them thinking that we don't fit in.'

I'm sitting in a country pub drinking pints of rust-coloured ale with Joe, and everyone is staring at me like I'm strange. I'm wearing my old school anorak – which I've coated with two layers of hair gel – my bright green wellingtons – which I've splattered with extra clumps of mud – and I've messed up my hair specially, and tied it in a loose, tangled ponytail. I look like I've spent the morning mucking out horses. Everyone else looks like they've just taken their Range Rovers to be valet-cleaned.

*   *   *

'How come everyone is so well dressed?' I say, blowing some foam off the top of my beer.

'What did you expect?'

'I don't know. But look at them, they're wearing . . . *jumpers.*'

'It's cold out. What else would they be wearing?'

'OK, well, I see what you're saying. But I thought they'd be wearing worse clothes. And I thought there'd be more . . . you know . . . staining.'

'Staining?'

'Yes. You know. Less cleanliness. More . . . *wiffiness.* I thought everyone in the countryside would smell of dog. Still,' I say, glancing around to make sure no one's eavesdropping, 'at least there aren't any loony morris dancers on the loose.'

'Rocket salad with sun-dried tomatoes and seared scallops for the gentleman. And . . . ehem . . . steak-and-ale pie for you, madam.'

'What's wrong now?' says Joe, watching me twist the corners of my napkin.

I keep quiet until the waiter is out of earshot.

'He was turning his nose up at me. For ordering the steak-and-ale pie. He was. Did you hear the way he "ehemmed" me? He thinks I'm common. He thinks I'm common for ordering a meat pie with a puff pastry lid.'

'It wasn't on the menu. They had to dig one out of the freezer. What did you expect?'

'What was I meant to do? I wasn't going to order the roast guinea fowl with a Parmesan beard.'

'Why not?'

'Because we're in a pub. In the countryside. They shouldn't be serving rocket salad, they should be serving gammon steaks and scampi in a basket. And look at the prices. Main courses are twenty pounds. Twenty pounds for a pub lunch. It's an outrage.'

Joe ignores me and tucks into his seared scallops, which look fantastic. I make a start on my steak-and-ale pie and, because I don't want Joe to know how bad it is, I swallow the bits of bone and gristle instead of spitting them out.

'How's the pie?'

'Ummm . . . delicious,' I say, picking a speck of cow skull out of my teeth. 'Very glad I ordered it. How're the scallops?'

'Good. You want to try one?'

'No, no. You're alright. I'm fine.'

'You're sure?'

'Well, maybe just a *small* one.'

After finishing half of Joe's scallops and consoling myself with a chocolate cherry soufflé – there's nothing like a snot-nosed twenty-something waiter calling you 'madam' to put a dampener on your day – we decide to brave the elements and go for a walk. A narrow tow path runs behind the back wall of the pub, and we make our way down to the lock and out along the canal towards the centre of the village.

Our original plan was to drive into Hertfordshire and have lunch in a place called Tring, but we've ended up in a whole other county (Berkshire), in a toy-town village called Cassocks. This is because Joe was driving. And because he refused point blank to use a map. He had this whole 'let's just point the car in a north-westerly direction and see where we end up' thing going on, and I'm not sure this is exactly the type of place he had in mind.

Everything is slightly too perfect. The village green looks like it's been trimmed with nail scissors and the mill pond looks like it's been measured out using a protractor. There's a moss-covered wishing well, a neat hump backed bridge, and a main street lined with thatch-roofed tea shops selling champagne-flavoured marmalade and wicker ducks. The rest of it is just as cloying. The side streets are lined with faux Victorian street lamps and identically sized artificial cobbles, and the whole place looks like it's been built from a kit.

We walk on past the edge of the village and out along a narrow lane, bordered by oak trees and densely meshed hedgerows. The view stretches for miles. Fields of newly sown rape taper off towards the hills, and a sky the colour of wet bread frames the valley like a softly dampened canvas.

'It's beautiful, isn't it?' says Joe, admiringly.

'Yes,' I say, trying to be objective. 'It's very . . . um . . . *hilly*.'

'You don't think it's nice to be out of London? Away from the traffic, and all the crowds?'

I'm not sure that I do. I can see the attraction. On paper. But to me the whole scene just looks sort of bleak. This is the cosy, picture-postcard version of rural England, but the emptiness just makes me feel lonely. I wouldn't mind the odd day trip now and again – as long as I avoided frozen meat pies I'm sure I could have a satisfactory afternoon – but I'm convinced living so far from the city would make me feel sad.

'What's the matter?'

'Hmm . . . oh . . . nothing. Why?'

'You look a bit maudlin. Are you OK?'

'Yes. I'm fine, honestly. Hey, how's about we go back to Cassocks and have a cream tea or something. Buy some knick-knacks in the gift shop. A duck made out of wicker, or some home-made chutney or something?'

'You don't want to see if we can make it to the next village?'

'Well, if you want to . . . how far is it?'

'Another mile or so. The pub landlord said there was an interesting church on the way. Maybe we could take a look around.'

I try not to groan.

'They've got graves that date back as far as the Norman Conquest,' says Joe, trying to entice me. 'And a giant plague pit as well. Could be quite interesting.'

'Hmm,' I say, mulling this over for a moment. 'A plague pit, you say. OK then, why not?'

Joe is strolling round the churchyard with a paring knife in his hand and a plastic carrier bag tucked under his arm. If you didn't know any better you'd think he was up to no good, but he's just busying himself taking cuttings from the plants. If he sees something unusual he'll mutter a complicated phrase in Latin and set about the plant with his opened blade. He dabs root powder on the freshly severed ends, wraps them in moistened cotton wool and, back home, he'll pot them and nurture them into full-size plants.

After Joe's collected up a small pile of cuttings, and I've spent an enjoyable half-hour calculating the life expectancy of the average Norman, we head on past the graveyard towards the next village. The bent, arthritic lanes curve through the valley for another half-mile or so, eventually giving way to a sparse hamlet called Ling's Walden. This is definitely more of what Joe had in mind. There are no fancy tea shops or Michelin-starred gastro-pubs with snotty waiters, just a post office, a regular pub and a small farm shop.

Joe wraps his arm round me and squeezes my shoulder tightly. I can tell what he's thinking. That this is exactly the kind of place he'd like to live. He'd like chickens and a goat and a thriving organic vegetable patch and a biannual visit to the city would suit him fine. He'd toast crumpets in front of the hearth in winter and build a garden that bloomed with wild jasmine and night-scented stock all summer long. He'd earn his money designing gardens for all the Aga-owners in Cassocks, and they'd pay him a fortune to build topiary hedges in the shape of flying mallards and corn-fattened geese. Joe is thinking about the future. About the two of us making a life together. He's thinking about buying a home and starting a family and imagining the names he'd like to give to each one of his children.

I watch his eyes flicker and soak it all up and lay my head close to his neck. Even with his plant cuttings under his arm and his hair stuck flat to his head from the drizzle he still looks unfairly attractive. He's sexy because I know he could exist without me, and because he'd take care of me in a second if I'd ever let him. For a moment I feel safe and at peace with the world. For a second I feel stable and at ease.

And all of a sudden my heart starts to race like a pigeon. And I'm thinking about something completely different. Of coming home to one of these wintry cottages and finding nobody there. No curtains, no possessions, no photos, no people, just a view from a cold gaping window. Of trees and winding lanes, and empty cornfields brittle with frost, and no landmarks anywhere that I recognise.

So I let my mind wander somewhere safe. To a broad Manhattan avenue choked with people, to a Bangkok street market oozing petrol fumes and stuffed with life. To a disused inner-city rail yard, choked up with broken bicycle wheels and grass. And to a filthy, pock-marked tower block that's home to a fairy-tale giant.

17

'He's a freak.'

'He's not.'

'Well he sounds like it to me. He sounds like he might be dangerous or something.'

It's taken us less than an hour to drive back to London, and even though we're stuck in the middle of a mile-long traffic jam at the top of the Holloway Road, I couldn't be happier. I could feel myself starting to relax as soon as we hit the motorway. As soon as the shrubs, fields and skeletal trees gave way to the petrol stations, asphalt and bargain basement Travelodges.

I'm not sure Joe feels quite the same way. His shoulders slumped the moment we hit junction 14 on the M1, and when he spotted the long line of orange tail-lights queuing to get back into central London, his mood blackened measurably. He cursed the truck drivers and the weekend shoppers and the windscreen washers with their buckets of filthy rags; and just because he caught me humming the chorus to 'Downtown' as we drove past Archway tube station, he's decided to give me a hard time about Big Louie.

'He's not dangerous. He's vulnerable.'

'Vulnerable?'

'Yes, in a Danny DeVito kind of way. You know, brittle on the outside, fragile in the middle.'

'Danny DeVito doesn't strike me as being particularly fragile. He strikes me as being rude. And mean spirited.'

'Yes. Well, it's true. He's both of those things, but it's only because he's suffered so much.'

'That's what serial killers say after they get caught boiling people's heads and stuffing them down drains. How do you know he's not going to strike you across the shoulders with an iron bar and boil your head?'

'He doesn't move fast enough. He'd never muster the element of surprise. Plus, he couldn't stand the mess. Or the smell. He's obsessive about sanitation and cleanliness.'

'Obsessive?'

'Yes. He's got that disorder where you have to keep cleaning your hands a million times a day. It's quite upsetting, actually. I think he makes them bleed sometimes. He even has scabs.'

'*Scabs?*'

'Just a couple. On his knuckles and the backs of his thumbs. They're red raw. Livid and flaky, like wind-dried beef.'

Joe flinches and tries not to look too disgusted.

'Well look, I'll get hold of all the stuff you need for the window box and Pete and I'll go round next week to fix it up.'

I bite my tongue before I answer.

'No ... um ... really,' I say, trying to sound casual. 'There's no need.'

'Look, I don't want you going over there on your own any more. I still don't think it's safe.'

'It is. It's fine. And anyway, he trusts me. He really wants me to finish it for him.'

'Well, I'll come with you then. When did you arrange to go back?'

'Thursday.'

'OK. Thursday afternoon. I'll make sure Pete's free to take care of everything else.'

'Evening.'

'Sorry?'

'I'm going in the evening this time. Not the afternoon.'

'What for? How are we going to plant a window box at night?'

'Well,' I say, 'the window box we can do any time. He's not in any real rush. He's waited the best part of a year for it as it is, and mostly he just wants to make sure it's done right.'

'I don't understand,' says Joe, pulling into our turning. 'If we're not going round to fix up the window box, then what are we going round for?'

'Well . . . um . . . I was going to tell you about that.'

'Tell me about what?'

'The lessons.'

'What lessons?'

'With Big Louie.'

'You're going to start teaching him *maths*?'

'No. Not exactly.'

We pull up outside the flat, and even though Joe's switched off the engine it's clear neither one of us is getting out of the car until I've explained.

'It's the other way round,' I say, trying hard not to fidget. 'He's the one who's going to be giving the lessons.'

'To *you*?'

'Yes.'

'Well what's he going to be teaching you about? How to be grossly fat and scared of germs?'

'No,' I say, scratching my eyebrows and wondering why I've waited a day and a half to tell him. 'It's something else. He's going to teach me how to play cards.'

The thing is, it seemed like a perfectly good idea. After a second cup of lemon tea and a slice of home-made buttered pound cake, Big Louie kindly offered to become my personal poker instructor. It turns out that's how he makes his living. He's been doing it ever since he arrived in England. He advertises over the Internet and gradually, through word of mouth, he's built up his very own card school. He has a rotating tutor group of two dozen pupils who each pay him upwards of forty pounds per private lesson. On Fridays they get a chance to test out their newly acquired skills by joining him at his portable card table and playing Texas Hold'Em against one another for money. This is where Big Louie really scores. He lets them win from time to time, just so they keep coming back, but mostly it's a chance to fleece his pupils for extra cash.

When he asked me if I'd ever thought of learning to play I scratched my cheeks with both hands at once. He asked me if I was too scared to try it and I laughed, picked some loose skin out of my fingernails, and suggested that he was being preposterous. I asked him what would happen if one of his students ever got so good that they started beating him back. If they worked out how to bluff him and steal his money; right out from under his nose. This suggestion tickled Big Louie to the point of nausea.

I was a little reluctant at first, but a part of me has always wanted to learn. I'd like to know why my father was so drawn to it. To find out whether it's half as seductive as he said it was. And who knows, learning might even help me to find him. I already know the basic rules and skills and I'm sure I could master the rest of it fairly quickly. That way I could walk into a casino and not look out of place. I could take my seat at the table, stack up my poker chips like a pro, and blend into the background with all the other players.

It's not like I'd be doing it for no good reason. It's not like I'd be doing it out of some romantic fascination with the game. Chances are I'd be rotten at it anyway. Unless I studied the odds and probabilities compulsively. And pored over the subtle nuances night and day. It's not like I have a latent desire to be the best female poker player in the world or anything. It's not like playing Top Trumps or marbles.

It's just that it might be interesting, that's all. To see if I was any good at it; if I still had it in me to master something new. It'd be comforting to think I'd inherited something else from my father. Apart from a head for facts and figures. And the roaming instincts of a restless Arctic tern.

'*Cards?*'

'Yes. Poker in fact. He's offered to give me free poker lessons in return for me fixing up his window box.'

'You're kidding me, right? This is some sort of a joke?'

'No. He . . . er . . . well, it turns out that's how he makes his living. He runs a poker school from his flat. It's quite well thought of, apparently.'

'When did you find all this out?'

'The day before yesterday. He sent me an e-mail about the type of plants he wanted to put in his window box and it had a poker reference in it, so Pete suggested—'

'This is *Pete's* idea?'

'No. It's just that Pete suggested I try and trace my dad via the poker circuit and it turns out Big Louie knows a little bit about it.'

'A little bit?'

'Well . . . quite a lot actually.'

'How much?'

'Um . . . everything.'

Joe looks at me like he's about to implode.

'I know,' I say, glancing at the tendon vibrating in Joe's jaw. 'It's probably a bit unfair of him not to pay us for the plants, but it seemed like quite a good deal. I mean, he *is* a professional. I'd be learning from the best. You can't really put a price on that kind of expertise.'

Joe unclips his seat belt and gets out of the car. He walks towards the house without saying anything more and I follow on behind, carrying three jars of home-made champagne chutney and a hideous wicker duck under my arm. I try to think of something reassuring to say, but I can't think of anything helpful.

I imagine Joe is cursing himself for sending me over to Big

Louie's flat in the first place. I imagine he's blaming himself. He's probably thinking it's a hell of a coincidence that I should run into a professional poker player at this precise moment in my life, but he'll probably put it down to karma or destiny or some such. In an effort to make him feel better I decide a brief debate encompassing chance, coincidence and mathematical probability might be in order.

'Do you know how many Americans play poker?' I say, following him into the house.

'No,' says Joe, like he could care less, 'I don't.'

'Approximately sixty million.'

'Really.'

'Yes,' I say, wondering whether Joe would notice if I threw the wicker duck in the bin. 'That's almost one in four. Except most of them are men. Between the ages of twenty-five and fifty. So, when you think about it, the chances of meeting a North American male between the ages of twenty-five and fifty and him having a working knowledge of poker are statistically quite high. I grant you, the chances of him being a professional with his own poker school in King's Cross narrow the odds somewhat, but even so, it's not as statistically unlikely as you might think.'

Joe pulls out a pile of brown plastic plant pots for his cuttings, thinks better of it and opens a fresh bottle of wine instead.

'The point is, the chances of a person experiencing a life-altering coincidence at one time or another are much higher than you might first imagine. More common ones happen all the time. For instance, that time last week when you were thinking about Lorna and the phone rang and it turned out it was her. Well, those kinds of things happen every day. And mostly people say wow, how amazing, what a coincidence, we must have some sort of psychic connection or something. But in reality that's not the case.'

'I don't think I've got a psychic connection with Lorna,' says Joe, quickly.

'No, well, of course not. But the fact is, the probability of you thinking about one of your close relations or best friends and them calling you up at that precise moment is actually very high indeed. It's much more likely to happen at one time or another than not. I could show you the mathematics if you like.'

I'm about to get out my pencil and continue with a more pertinent example when Joe heads towards me with a glass of wine and indicates for me to sit down.

'Just promise me you'll be careful,' he says, frowning and running his eyes over mine. 'I don't want you getting hurt, that's all.'

'Don't worry about me,' I say firmly, 'I know exactly what I'm doing. I'll be fine.'

18

'The man who invented gambling was bright. The man who invented the poker chip was a genius.'

Big Julie, New York gambler (no relation)

LESSON ONE

'What's that?'

'What's what?'

'That look you got. Like you're constipated or something. I told you before, if you want a swig of my Colon Blow, you only have to ask.'

'I'm not constipated. This is my poker face.'

'Your poker face?'

'Yes. You know. Blank and formless. Loose mouth, relaxed muscles, eyes fixed on some point in the distance, straight ahead.'

'Uh-uh.'

'So nobody can tell what I'm thinking. So no one will be able to guess what cards I've got.'

Big Louie shakes his head like it's going to be a long night. Like it's all going to be much harder work than he'd thought.

'Well,' he says, 'you walk into a card room looking like that, and everyone's going to think you ain't taken a decent dump for a week.'

I'm a bit hurt by this. I spent most of last night in front of the bathroom mirror putting the finishing touches to this face. I even tested it out on Joe. When he asked me if I fancied getting an Indian takeaway for dinner I looked at him blankly and asked if he could tell whether I wanted one or not, just by looking into my eyes. He said, on balance, it was quite likely that I did (given that he's never known me to pass up the offer of a chicken and chick-pea bhuna in all the years he's known me) but, when pressed, he acknowledged that he couldn't be one hundred per cent certain.

'That's because he thought you looked bilious. That's because he was worried about your bowels.'

Big Louie continues to tease me, until I agree to relax my cheek muscles and go back to normal.

'That's better,' he says, poking at my cheek with the end of his finger and wiping any rogue germs off on his shirt. 'You look halfways normal now.'

'Thank you.'

'Don't mention it. And there's something you should know before you go giving yourself a migraine and permanent lockjaw. You ain't going to be needing your poker face for a good while yet.'

'Why not?'

'Too much else to be getting along with. The trouble with you is you think you know it all already, when the truth is you don't know squat.'

'OK,' I say, a little disheartened. 'I'll let you decide where we start.'

'Right,' he says, rubbing his hands together. 'Let's begin.'

Big Louie pulls up a chair and leans towards me across his octagonal card table. He arranges two stacks of poker chips in front of him, ripples his fingers along each column, then weaves them together with one hand.

'OK,' he says. 'First lesson is all about money. How much you got in your pocketbook?'

I reach into my handbag and pull out what I have. Six pounds seventy-five in loose coins and thirty pounds split between a twenty-pound note and two fives.

'Well, the coins we don't need to worry about. You might as well put them away. The five-pound notes too. We'll just look at the twenty.'

I lift up the twenty-pound note and place it in the middle of the table.

'OK. Now, what could you buy with this money?'

'Well, not very much, really. Three point seven chicken and chick-pea bhunas. Four-fifths of a hardback atlas. Nine-tenths of a second-class day return to Brighton, or two-thirds of a tank of petrol for my car.'

Big Louie huffs and sighs, like I've chosen spectacularly bad examples, and takes the twenty-pound note from my hand. He reaches into a carved wooden box, pulls out a twenty-dollar poker chip and slides it across the table towards me.

'Supposing I swap you your twenty for this poker chip,' he says. 'What could you buy with this chip?'

'Well, nothing. I mean I couldn't use it in a shop.'

'So it's not worth anything, then?'

'No. I didn't say that. At the end of the night I could swap it back for money. So essentially the poker chip is worth the same as the cash.'

'It could buy you things?'

'Yes.'

'Curries and petrol and shit like that?'

'Yes. Exactly. It could buy me the same stuff.'

'Wrong answer.'

For a minute I think Big Louie is still aggravated by my less than inspired shopping choices, but I'm not sure that's his only objection. He picks up my twenty-pound note, holds it over his ashtray and reaches into the breast pocket of his Hawaiian shirt for a lighter.

'What are you doing?' I say, watching him spark up a yellow-tongued flame.

He doesn't answer. He moves the flame towards the edge of the twenty-pound note and sets it alight. He holds it by a corner while the Queen's face buckles and burns, until all that's left is a crumble of ebony-coloured ashes.

'Now what's it worth?' he says, folding his arms and frowning at me. 'What could you buy with it now?'

'Nothing,' I say, staring at the remains of my petrol money. 'It's not worth anything at all.'

'Right answer. See? You been here all of five minutes, and already you learned something. In fact, you probably learned just about the most important poker lesson there is.'

'I don't understand,' I say, wondering what he means. 'Are you trying to say my money's not worth anything?'

Big Louie stares at me like I'm a moron.

'I'm not saying it ain't worth anything. I'm just saying you got to learn to disregard it a little. When you play poker you want to look at money like it's an instrument; learn to use your chips like they were tools. The second you lift up a poker chip and start thinking about what it could buy you, you're sunk. Finished. There's no way you're coming back from that.'

I nod my head sagely, like I know what he means.

'Now then,' he says, standing up, 'I'm gonna go make myself a sandwich. In the meantime I want you to stare long and hard into this ashtray and consider two things. The value of what you just lost and the value of what you just learned. I'm pretty sure you'll find you're still ahead.'

Big Louie begins the laborious buttering, layering and cleaning process in the kitchen, and I stare into the ashtray just like he told me to. This isn't how I'd expected the lessons to start. I thought we'd get right down to it and play a couple of hands. I even brought a half-smoked cigar with me. I was going to stick it in the corner of my mouth and smoke it like a cheroot; chewing on the damp end and rolling it round my mouth, with my eyes narrow and steely, just like Clint Eastwood's. I was going to impress Big Louie with my inordinately dextrous card-handling skills and run a few bluffs by him when he was least expecting it. And – of course – I was going to pay strict attention to the way he handled his socks. You can tell a lot about a poker player by the way he handles his socks.

Big Louie glances over to make sure I'm still staring into the ashtray and hobbles back to the table with his three-storey club sandwich. His legs are playing him up quite badly this evening and steadying his bulk on the edge of a hard-backed dining chair clearly takes a great deal of effort. Once settled, he enjoys his sandwich for a while – chewing on the spicy salami and picking a sliver of lettuce out of his teeth – and when he's finished he pushes his plate away and leaves it right where it is. This surprises me. I'd expected him to clean it up straight away, but for the moment at least he seems content to leave it be.

'In the old days they used to play with dollar bills,' he says, riffling the chips in front of him and making them click-clack against one another with his fingers. 'So the value of what you were betting with was always on your mind. The idea of the chip is to make you forget what you're playing with. That ways you can stop worrying about what each bet is costing you and get right on with thinking about your strategy.'

I nod my head, wondering if it would be alright to stop staring into the ashtray yet.

'When you look at your chips,' he says, turning a blue one over in his hand, 'I don't want you to think of them as currency. I want you to imagine them as your weapons. The tools you're gonna use to defeat your opponent. Perhaps he's the kind of guy that raises the pot fifty dollars and thinks about the mortgage repayment he's gotta make next week. Perhaps when you go for the deep reach and pull out a thousand-dollar stack it makes his heart pound and his palms start to sweat. That's because he's thinking about what every chip is worth to him. But you know different. You know it's not about the money. It's about power. If you keep that in mind, you're already halfways to having him beat.'

I nod, indicating that I'm just the type of person to put

my opponent under pressure by making a casual thousand-dollar bet.

'That's not to say it ain't going to eat you up if you lose it,' says Louie, flicking another chip towards me. 'Truth is it's gonna hurt like hell. Getting back to your hotel room with a twenty-thousand-dollar bank roll reduced to a tangle of elastic bands, just because you made one dumb mistake. Because you lost concentration for a second. Because you played all night long and you hadn't slept for a week, and your eyes could barely pick out which suit you were holding any more. But these are the things you think about afterwards,' he says, gravely. 'You never think about them while you're at the table.'

I mull this over for a moment, turning the poker chip over in my hand and trying to make some sense out of what he's just said.

'OK,' I say, looking up at him, 'I see what you're saying. You've got to imagine that once you've swapped your money for chips, then it's gone already. You've got to accept that it might be lost.'

'No,' he says, sharply. 'That's not right at all. If you imagine it gone then it will be. If you let go of it in your head, then you'll let go of it just as easy at the table. Your chips are a measure of how well you're playing. The marker of your success. And you want to be a success, don't you?'

'Yes,' I say. 'I do.'

He looks at me like he's still not convinced.

'Well, I'm telling you,' he says, with certainty, 'right now you don't have it in you. You sit down at a poker table with me and make a play for fifty dollars and I'd know in a second what you had in your hand. There's no way in the world you'd be able to hide it. I'd sniff it out of you in a second. You know what your problem is, don't you?' he says, noticing his dirty plate all of a sudden, and grimacing at it.

'Um . . . no,' I say. 'What is it?'

'Well,' he says, picking up the plate with his fingertips and shuffling towards the kitchen, 'you got the same problem everyone has when they're just starting out. Right now, you're still in love with the money. What you gotta do is fall in love with the game.'

19

'He burnt your petrol money?'

'Yes.'

'With a lighter?'

'Yes. He set fire to it right in front of my eyes.'

'So you didn't play any games yet? You didn't beat him, or win any of his chips?'

'No. He didn't even deal out the cards. I didn't get a chance to smoke my cheroot or anything.'

Joe starts to laugh. I'm not sure what's amusing him most. The thought of me with a chewed-up cigar butt between my teeth, or the fact that I've just wasted two hours in a damp ex-council flat, watching a grossly fat agoraphobic man set fire to my money.

'So, what did he think of your poker face? Did he think it was the right sort of look?'

'He thought I looked a bit unwell. Constipated. Like I needed more roughage.'

This tickles Joe even more, and he offers to go to the kitchen and make me a giant bowl of raisin bran.

'No,' I say, 'that's OK. I had a sip of Big Louie's Colon Blow before I left.'

'Colon Blow?'

'Yes. It's the hottest chilli sauce on the planet. He sort of dared me.'

'How was it?' says Joe, noticing my swollen lips.

'Hmmm, you know. Not that bad.'

'Really?'

'Yeah. Hot, but I've definitely tasted worse.'

'It didn't burn your mouth and make your lips swell up like you'd just had three pounds of collagen injected into them, then?'

'No,' I say, running my tongue around my mouth and moistening the chilli-induced blisters. 'Not at all. My lips always look like this.'

'Do you want some Vaseline to put on them?'

'Yes please.'

Joe smirks and heads off to the bathroom cabinet.

I must say, Joe is taking this whole poker lesson thing much better than I'd imagined. When I first mentioned it to him in the car I thought he was going to start an almighty row, but he seems exceptionally mellow about it today. He probably thinks I'm going to get fed up with it. Especially now Big Louie's started setting fire to my petty cash. He couldn't be more wrong though, because the truth is I'm already quite taken with it.

It seemed a little strange at first, but I've become increasingly impressed by Big Louie's highly individual teaching technique. In fact, I've begun to look at him in a whole new light. We've only just started, but I can already tell that he's passionate about the game. It was obvious from the metre of his voice and the way he forgot about his dirty plate while we were talking. When he spoke, he was clear, distinct and unhesitating, and for a while I almost forgot about his physical condition. He wasn't a fat, half-crippled man with a catarrh-filled chest the size of a beer barrel, he was an enthusiast, an expert in his field. He was a man with thirty years of knowledge wrapped up in his red-raw fingertips, expressing it with his own peculiar brand of eloquence. It makes me wonder how good he was. How much money he must have won and lost over the years.

I spend the next few minutes merging the scant facts of Big Louie's life with a bag of half-remembered stories from my dad. I lie back on the sofa, light up my cheroot and conjure up an imaginary world for my tutor. I picture him first as a college student, flat out on his hospital bed. His muscles withered on his bones like autumn fruits; his youth ripped out from under him like a magician's tablecloth. I see him moaning and cursing and throwing things at his nurse, while his brain begins to ferment from lack of use.

Years later, I see him at a neon-lit poker table, shuffling a tower of poker chips in his hands. His limbs have forgotten what it feels like to be warmed by the sun, but his brain has sharpened well inside his misshapen body. By now he's playing for the World Series title in Las Vegas: the most prestigious poker tournament in the world. He's battled through the ranks to the final table, demolishing his opponents one by one. His dachshund is fast asleep at his feet – whiskers twitching violently as he dreams – and each time a new player is eliminated, Big Louie bends down to pat his wiry rump.

The game struggles on into the small hours but by 2 a.m. it's head to head. The casino staff carry out the prize money and spread it across the green baize table – like they do when there are only two competitors left in the game – and all of a sudden it's real. It's not chips any more, it's cash. A cool million laid out right in front of them; in piles of crisp green dollar bills.

And Big Louie is still there. Knowing that if his body can absorb the impact of a wayward Pontiac, then his mind can absorb the pressures of any game. His opponent is sweating meat through his pores and Big Louie is shivering from the chill. So I wonder why he cracked. And I wonder how he went broke and lost it all. And I wonder why the smoke from this cheroot is making my lips feel so much worse.

'Audrey?'
  'Yup.'
  'Are you sure that cigar's not a bit strong for you?'

'Grghahah, what makes you say that?'

'Well, you look slightly green.'

'Grghahah . . . ahah . . . ahaha . . . ehem. No . . . euurgh . . . ehem . . . noo . . . it's fine.'

'Shall I get you a glass of water?'

I nod, gasp, pull a wet piece of tobacco out of my teeth, and start scrabbling around for my asthma inhaler.

'I'll take that as a yes, then.'

20

'I do not believe in luck. Only in the immutable law of averages.'

Herbert O. Yardley, *The Education of a Poker Player*

LESSON TWO

'What are you wearing?'

'It's my new coat. Don't you like it?'

'It looks like you mashed up a bunch of roadkill and had your grandmother knit it together with spoons.'

'It's fake fur. It was in the sale. I thought it looked good.'

'How much did you pay for it? Wait . . . don't answer that question. Whatever it was you been had.'

'Two hundred and fifty pounds,' I say, defiantly. 'Feel it. It's really warm. It's a classic design. It'll probably last me for years.'

Big Louie rubs his hand over one of the sleeves, tuts loudly and announces that he's never felt such a cheap piece of cloth in his life.

'It's a schmutter,' he says, shaking his head. 'It'll fall apart in a week. Besides, it doesn't even suit you. Makes you look sort of wide around the hips.'

I grimace, slump on to the sofa and dig around in his sweet jar for a lump of butterscotch.

'What's wrong with you now?'

'Nothing.'

'What? You're so sensitive that you're gonna sulk all morning, just coz I said I don't like your squirrel-fur jacket?'

'No. Of course I'm not.'

'How come you got that look, then?'

'What look?'

'Like you been slapped round the head with a fish.'

'Well,' I say, picking some toffee off my teeth, 'I couldn't really afford it. I only bought it in the first place as an exercise.'

'In what?'

'I've been thinking about what you said about money last week. All that stuff about the top poker players not really caring about it one way or the other. I thought I'd try spending more than I could afford for once. You know, just to see how it would make me feel.'

'How *did* it make you feel?'

'Pretty good to begin with. It was quite a buzz, in fact. The shop assistant was giving me one of those looks like I was too scruffy to be shopping in such an expensive shop. So I marched over to the coat rail, picked out this jacket and paid for it in cash, without even trying it on. She was pretty impressed, I can tell you.'

'I see. And how d'you feel now?'

'Well,' I say, quietly. 'Not that good.'

'How come?'

'Turns out it's not a very nice jacket.'

Big Louie takes pity on me and fixes us both a strong cup of coffee. When he's sure that I'm feeling better he clears away the cups, leaves them in the sink to soak for a while, and invites me to sit back down at the card table for lesson two.

'Lesson two,' he says, shaking his jowls at me. 'You're an idiot. I ought to call up your boyfriend right now and tell him exactly what kind of an idiot he's dating.'

'Well,' I say, slightly taken aback, 'I don't think that's entirely fai—'

'You made a classic beginner's mistake,' he says, waving his finger at me. 'Right there in the clothes store. With your pocket full of cash and your cheap squirrel jacket.'

'Look, I thought we'd already established that it's *not* made of squirrel. Anyway, I don't understand. I thought you said I had to develop a more blasé attitude to money if I wanted to become a good poker player.'

'When did I say that? At what point did I say you was meant to come over all blasé and start buying crap you couldn't afford? At what point did I say you had to get above yourself and let your ego dictate the way you played . . . I mean *shopped*.'

'You did. Last time I saw you. You said the pros all walk around tipping cocktail waitresses with hundred-dollar bills, just for bringing them a glass of club soda. You said that, one way or another, they live the high life no matter how much or how little they've got in their pockets.'

Big Louie scratches his head. Hard, like he has a particularly persistent nit burrowing into his skull.

'And why do you think that is? How come they walk around tipping waitresses too much and driving fast cars and ordering themselves private jets, just so they can get to the next poker game on time?'

'Well, I'm not sure. Maybe they're all millionaires. Maybe they're a bit . . . you know . . . wild. Perhaps they're all nuts or something.'

'You'd like that, I bet,' he says, wryly. 'A bunch of hell-raising wildcats running around on helium, living for the moment, not caring if the sun comes up the next day or not.'

'Well –'

'You think it's like the movies, I bet. You think they're all good looking too, no doubt.'

'No. *Are they?*'

'What do *you* think?' he says, prodding the fat tyre round his stomach.

'Anyway,' he continues, sourly, 'great poker isn't about being reckless, it's about being fearless, which is a whole other thing. Underneath all the bluff and machismo, there's something real, something solid. A core of discipline, patience and logic, stricter than someone like you could ever imagine.'

'Well,' I say, a little defensively, 'that's not entirely true. If you knew me better you wouldn't be saying that. Because I'm really a very disciplined pers—'

'It's all about control,' he repeats, pointing his finger at me. 'You got to be able to stand back from a situation and judge it rationally. You can't let emotion dictate the way you play. That's why women are so lousy at it. Card table's no place for romantics, Ungar. Poker is a realist's game.'

I'm about to raise my voice to object, but Big Louie has already moved on.

'The great poker player is a well-honed mental athlete. A thinker. Do you see what I'm saying? He ways up the precise odds of every hand before he bets, responds to the smallest gesture his opponent makes. He calculates the probability of hitting his winning cards in a heartbeat, reads people quicker than most folks read the TV guide. He's not engaged in some senseless gamble. He plays a game of calculated risk.'

'OK,' I say, 'I think I get it. You're saying that poker is something like a chess game. That it's a game of intellect, like bridge. Not a game of blind luck like craps or roulette.'

'Well, as usual, you're jumping way ahead of yourself,' he says, flicking a loose chip at me. 'What you doing? Repeating some shit your dad used to say to you, I bet.'

I don't say anything. I'm embarrassed about how easily he's read me.

'And poker is a game of luck sometimes. At least in the short term it is. You might run bad six, seven or eight games in a row, get nothing in your hand but sevens and twos. You might sit down with an orthodontist from Ohio who's only ever played against his mother-in-law and other orthodontists, and he'll get served up aces hand over hand.'

'So someone as good as you could still be beaten by a novice?'

132

'It ain't likely, no, but it could happen. If that's the way the wind's blowing, then the worst kind of out-of-town sucker can get lucky every once in a while and take you down. The point is, it wouldn't last. In the end, over time, a player's superior skill will always see him through the rough spots. The best ones know that. They know that if they drop ten thousand one night, they'll make it up the next night, or the next. That's how come they got the strength to get up and walk away when they're running bad. There's no rush. No hurry. Life is one long poker hand to the pro.'

'OK,' I say, carefully. 'But what if they didn't walk away one time? What if they'd been running bad for weeks on end and this time they didn't walk away? What if a player made a huge bet and lost everything he had?'

'Well,' he says, running a palm across his dampening forehead, 'in that case you'd just go fix yourself a loan. From a friend maybe, or another card player. Someone you'd played with, and hung out with, and trusted like a brother your entire adult life. The kind of guy you'd introduce to your wife, and not worry about leaving them alone together. In your own house, with your best whisky and your faithful dog. The kind of guy who wouldn't rip your guts out through your throat and stamp around in the mess like a rabid coyote.'

Big Louie is so irate all of a sudden that he starts to hiccup uncontrollably. He grabs a butter knife from the Formica sideboard and pulls it sharply towards him, as if he plans to burst his escaping hiccups like fairground balloons. Moments before the butter knife reaches his chest, his hand makes a swift change of direction, and he rams it hard into the side of the card table. It rests there, swaying in the splintered wood for a moment, before cluttering unceremoniously to the floor. His face is perfectly still all the while – steady, formless, composed – but his skin has turned the colour of soured wine. And if eyes could emit sound, then Big Louie's would surely be roaring.

'I'm sorry,' he says, after a while. 'I don't know what came over me.'

'That's OK,' I say, trying hard not to think about serial killers and boiled heads. 'I didn't mean to upset you. Perhaps we should call it a day. I'll come back tomorrow or something.'

He shrugs and rubs his temples and I'm almost at the door before he finds the strength to speak again.

'Over there,' he says. 'On the night stand. I wrote down some websites you might want to look at. And I picked out some poker magazines. You know, if you were still thinking about placing a missing-person advertisement for your dad.'

I walk over to the table and pick up Big Louie's notes. A concise list of websites and chat rooms, and a couple of online card rooms where I can practise my basic poker skills.

'Thanks,' I say, turning round to look at him. 'That's really good of you.'

'No sweat,' he says, trying hard to raise a smile. 'Let me know how you get along.'

I'm almost through the door when he calls out to me one more time.

'Hey,' he says, 'I meant to ask you. What you gonna do about that crappy squirrel coat you bought?'

'I'm not sure. Take it back to the shop, I suppose.'

'Good,' he says, like he's happy to hear it. 'Just you make sure that you do.'

I climb into the lift feeling a little dazed, and search through my handbag for my purse. Stuffed between the credit cards and the banknotes is a compartment where I keep all my old receipts. I have dozens of them. Neatly indexed and folded, jammed in between a pile of used Tube tickets that I somehow can't get around to throwing away. Some of the receipts date back over a year. Petrol receipts, bar receipts, a present that I bought for Lorna's daughter, Meg, and the receipt for a watch that I bought for Joe on his thirty-second birthday. And, nestled right at the back, my father's matchbook that I've carried with me since that afternoon at Frank's.

As you might imagine, it's a fat and inelegant purse, full of zips, buttons, clips and unnecessary pockets, but I like the fact that I can find what I need at a moment's notice. I locate the receipt for my fake fur jacket and move it deftly to the front of the pile. Turns out buying it wasn't much of a risk after all. Like I said to Big Louie when I arrived, I'm far more disciplined than he realises.

21

It's a strange sensation, but whenever I'm up in that tower block for longer than an hour or so I seem to forget all about the outside world. An odd pallor comes over me, and all I can see is that one room, with its sticky plants and its woodchip walls and its lurid, cracked lino floor. I'm glad to be down. The air inside Big Louie's flat has grown thicker and staler since my last visit, and once I'm safely out of the lift my lungs suck in the city air like it's pure alpine oxygen.

There's no one around, so I stand still for a moment, enjoying the breeze on my face and staring up at the pale fissures in the winter cloud. It was completely overcast when I left to drive over here, but I can just make out the watery March sunlight struggling to find a route through.

A few miles to the west, a plane is snaking its way through the frozen crystals and the bundles of airborne steam. The growl of its engines reaches me a second or so after I see it, and my eyes follow the lazy white vapour trail as it arcs its way high over the city.

I've loved aeroplanes for as long as I can remember. Ever since my dad took me to Heathrow airport for my seventh birthday to watch Concorde and the 747s taking off. We sat on the concrete viewing platform for the whole afternoon; guessing where each of the planes was coming from or going to, and discussing the major principles of aerodynamics and supersonic flight. We chatted about updraught, downdraught, lift, thrust and drag, and after a lunch of hamburgers and cold vanilla milk shakes he demonstrated Bernoulli's principle of flight with the remains of my McDonald's burger wrapper.

He smoothed out the greasy yellow sheet, held it in front of his lips (horizontal to the ground) and blew hard across the top of it, like he was trying to put out a birthday candle. The sheet rose gently as the air pressure lowered above it, and I nodded sagely and picked up my binoculars.

Concorde had pierced the skyline far in the distance. You could pick it out from miles away, on account of its distinctive shape, and I smiled as I watched it swoop into view. It was utterly different from all the rest, cutting through the air like a razor blade, its shoulders gently arched in an arrogant shrug. We drove home as soon as we'd watched it touch down and shaken the engine noise out of our shattered eardrums. On the way back I fell asleep quickly and easily, with my burger wrapper still clutched in my hand. Dreaming of flying at twice the speed of sound, content that another of the world's mysteries had been solved.

A mile or so further on, the plane banks sharply and tilts its wings eastward towards the river. Its curved belly glints in the sunlight and I try to work out what model it is from the position of its engines. I push my head backwards as it passes overhead and follow the stiff lines of the tower block up towards Big Louie's window sill. He's opened up the window just a crack, allowing a thin stream of fresh air to dilute the fug. I wonder if he can see the aeroplane from where he is. If he's standing there watching it, just like me.

22

Joe is working in the garden when I get home, digging around in the weeds and fixing extra clips on to the pergola. He's definitely got the right idea. The sun has won its battle with the rain clouds – taking the edge off the cold – and for Big Louie's sake, I feel like I should be spending the afternoon outside. There's no doubt about it. Now is the perfect opportunity. Today's the day we teach Lorna how to run.

'Where are we going?'

'To Lorna's house,' I say, handing Joe a clean shirt and a pair of Nikes.

'What for?'

'I've just told you. We're going to teach Lorna how to run.'

'How come she doesn't know how already?'

'She does. It's just that she looks a bit like a donkey while she's doing it. We both do.'

'I don't understand,' says Joe, grinning at me. 'Are you trying to say that Lorna runs like a girl?'

'Um . . . yes.'

'Well,' he says, wiping some dirt on to the side of his jeans, 'it seems to me, and excuse me if I'm stating the obvious here, that Lorna *is* a girl. So what's the problem?'

I resist the urge to fill Joe's Nikes up with earthworms and mud.

'It's Meg's sports day,' I say, grimacing at him. 'All the parents have to compete in their own hundred-metre sprint, and Lorna wants to make up for the lack of a handsome dad stroke husband figure by winning the race and not looking like too much of an idiot.'

'Right. I see. And when is this sports day exactly?'

'July.'

'That's *four* months away.'

'Well,' I say, dragging him towards the door, 'that's as maybe. But these things can take a lot longer than you think.'

'You'd better make sure you call Pete, then. He won't want to miss out on this.'

'I'm not doing it.'

'Come on, you have to. You said you wanted me to help.'

'Yes, exactly. I wanted *you* to help, not *them*.'

Joe and Pete shuffle their feet uncomfortably and kindly offer to go to the pub while the two of us get on with things.

'No,' I say, firmly. 'It's no good just the two of us. We're both as bad as each other. You need Joe to help you. He's a really good sprinter, he used to run for his school.'

'Did you?' she says, looking at him expectantly.

Joe attempts – unsuccessfully – to look bashful, and slaps his non-existent beer belly like he knows it's hard to believe.

'OK,' says Lorna, pulling an old pair of trainers out from under the sofa. 'We've got two hours before Meg gets back. Let's make this quick.'

It doesn't start well. Lorna crouches at the top of the road in her baggy sweat pants and a long-sleeved T-shirt and Pete doubles up with mirth as she starts towards him. She glares at him hard, which probably turns him on even more, but Joe shouts at her to take no notice. He's very patient with her. He explains that she's slouching her shoulders and moving her arms all wrong, and after forty-five minutes of gentle coaching he has her body working in something approaching symmetry. I spend the next half-hour shouting encouragement and joining in with the odd lap to keep warm, while Pete kindly offers to hold on to the stopwatch. That way he gets to stand at the finish line and watch the two of us bouncing towards him.

'Audrey?'

'Yep.'

'You know this running thing?'

'Yeah.'

'Well, have you ever thought that you and Lorna might be better at it if you stopped wearing bras?'

Joe takes Lorna back to the top of the road for her final lap and this time he runs alongside her. He instructs her to lengthen her stride and keep on the balls of her feet, and she begins to look almost graceful. Less like a flat-footed giraffe and more like the kind of woman who used to captain the school sports team in her teens.

'What do you think then?' she says, bounding over the finishing line and holding her arms aloft. 'Do I still look like Big Bird off of *Sesame Street*?'

'No. You were much better that time,' says Joe, going over to congratulate her. 'I told you you'd get the hang of it, didn't I? You should have done more sports at school. I bet you'd have been great at netball or something.'

'Do you think so?' she says, breathlessly, leaning on Joe's shoulder and digging about in her sweat pants for a cigarette. 'I mean, I always thought it was a bit of a stupid game. You weren't even allowed to move about with the ball. Maybe I'd have been good at it, though. If those cows that picked the team had ever given me a chance.'

'Maybe they were lesbians.'

'Excuse me?'

'The girls that didn't pick you for the team. Maybe the

reason they didn't like you. Because they were lesbians.'

Lorna smiles and blows a thin coil of cigarette smoke through her lips.

'Yeah, Pete. Now I come to think about it, you might be right. Maybe one or two of them were lesbians.'

'Really?' says Pete, heading over with the stopwatch. 'How could you tell?'

'Hmmm,' says Lorna, shrugging and wiping her face on the bottom of her T-shirt. 'I don't know, it was something to do with the showers, I suppose.'

'Go on . . .'

'The way they used to stare at you when you were soaping yourself up.'

'Yes. *And?*'

'The way they used to let their towels fall down and stand in front of you, stark naked and glistening with water droplets, while you were getting dressed.'

'Anything else? At all?'

'Um . . . yeah. Their hairy legs, handlebar moustaches, short hair and clumpy work boots. They were usually a dead give-away.'

'Cheers Lorna. Thanks a lot. Now I've got an erection and I'm thinking about the Village People.'

23

'How are the poker lessons going?'

'Good, I think. We haven't actually played any games yet. Big Louie's just been guiding me through some of the general principles.'

'Like what?'

'Well, the fact that poker's a game of discipline. That it's more about expertise than it is about luck.'

'The first time she went over there, he set fire to her twenty-pound note,' says Joe, shaking his head sceptically.

'Really?' says Lorna. 'What on earth for?'

'He was . . . um . . . trying to teach me some stuff about the value of money. I'm not sure I understand it all yet.'

Lorna and Joe exchange a brief look, which bothers me slightly, and Pete jumps in with a few words of advice.

'What's your poker name?'

'My what?'

'Your poker name. All the top players have got cool names, haven't they? Do you want me to try and think of one for you? I'm really good at that kind of thing.'

'Sure,' I say. 'Why not?'

Pete starts thinking about it straight away, but I notice that Joe and Lorna have already begun talking about something else. I can't hear exactly what it is that they're saying – Pete keeps elbowing me in the ribs and asking me what kind of image I'm going for – but I presume Joe's just giving her some more tips on her running style.

'What about that dealer in *The Cincinnati Kid*? She was called Lady Fingers. Perhaps you could use that.'

'Not sure,' I say, shaking my head. 'Sounds a bit, you know, gynaecological or something.'

'Hmm,' says Pete, smiling to himself. 'I hadn't thought about it like that.'

Joe and Lorna finish their conversation and join in with a few suggestions of their own, but I'm not sure either of them is taking my poker name very seriously.

'Joe's right,' says Lorna, stretching her arms above her head. 'He's probably some kind of a pervert. Why else would he invite women over to his creepy flat and spend hours telling them sob stories about his life?'

'He's not a pervert. He's a good teacher. And he enjoys the company.'

'Do you think he'd fit on to a pair of bathroom scales?' says Pete, excitedly. 'I mean, would he be able to stand on a set without breaking them?'

'Look, I don't know. He probably hasn't weighed himself in years.'

'Maybe we should tell the local newspaper. There might be a story in it. The fattest, maddest, creepiest man in King's Cross. A true-life story. You know the sort of thing.'

I can feel my skin starting to prickle. I'm not sure I like everyone talking about Big Louie as if he's some kind of a freak.

'Who else does he have coming over there?' says Pete, getting into his stride. 'You want to be careful. They might be weirdos as well.'

'Exactly,' says Lorna, tapping the ash off the end of her cigarette. 'Gamblers are a pretty dodgy bunch of people.'

The room goes quiet.

'Sorry. I didn't mean your dad or anything. I wasn't trying to suggest . . .'

Everyone starts to fidget, so I pull Big Louie's list out of my pocket in an attempt to persuade them of his good intentions.

'Look,' I say, holding it up. 'He gave me this. A list of the best poker sites and gambling chat rooms on the Web. It must have taken him ages to sort through them all.'

Pete takes the list from my hand, a little too quickly, and for a moment I almost feel like slapping him.

'That makes sense,' he says, studying it warily. 'There's a bunch of online card rooms here as well. He's probably on a cut. He probably gets a fee for every new sucker he gets hooked on the game.'

I snatch the list back from Pete, and watch Joe and Lorna exchange another brief glance. Joe sighs and leans forward on his elbows, and he's just about to say something more when the door bell rings. It's Meg.

Meg bundles through the door like a mini-tornado, throwing off her denim jacket, and scattering shoes, cake and half-deflated balloon animals in her wake. She's been to a birthday party – another of the parents has brought her home – and she's dressed up in her favourite jeans and a Britney Spears T-shirt, with a paper fairy's hat scrunched up on her head.

'Did you have a good time, sweetheart?'

'It was OK,' she says, lifting her shoulders in an exaggerated shrug.

'Was there a magician?'

'Yep.'

'Was he good?'

'No. He was rubbish. His tricks were rubbish and his balloon dogs looked like chickens. And his breath stinked.'

'Well, did he do anything good? Did he make anything disappear?'

'He pretended to cut off Sarah Whitaker's head,' she says, thinking about it with relish. 'That was quite good.'

'Did he put it in a velvet box that smelt of BO?'

'Yes,' she says, frowning at me. 'How do you know?'

'Ah,' I say, 'all magicians have velvet boxes that smell of BO.'

Meg nods at me like she thinks that's probably true and pushes her fairy hat out of her eyes.

'Can I have a tuna sandwich?'

'Didn't you have anything to eat at the party?'

'They only had egg.'

'I see.'

'And sausage rolls.'

'And what else?'

Meg remembers her piece of birthday cake and picks the soggy portion off the floor.

'It's got currants in it,' she says, screwing her face up.

'I can see that,' says Lorna, taking it out of her hand and trying a bit. 'It's not bad, though. Do you mind if I eat it?'

'Can Joe have some?'

'Yes. Of course he can.'

Lorna breaks off a piece and Meg makes a big show of handing it over. Joe eats it like it's the best thing he's ever tasted.

'Mmm,' he says, pointing out the currants. 'Dead-fly cake. Delicious.'

Meg giggles and asks Joe whether he'd like to look at her painting. He tells her that he most certainly would.

From where I'm sitting it's pretty hard to tell what it's a painting of, but Joe seems to work it out right away. He knows the pink bit is the sky and the yellow bit is a boat and that the three-legged dinosaur-shaped thing is meant to be Lorna.

'Do you like her necklace?' says Meg, pointing to a red line round the dinosaur's leg.

'Yes,' says Joe. 'She looks very pretty.'

The pair of them chat away about powder paints, balloon dogs and the size of Sarah Whitaker's fat head, until Lorna comes back from the kitchen with Meg's tuna sandwich.

She sits down next to the pair of them, ruffling Meg's hair and mouthing a quick thank-you to Joe for keeping her occupied.

'Hey, Meg,' says Pete, making a half-hearted attempt to join in. 'How many Pokémon cards have you got now? Must be hundreds, eh?'

Meg looks at him like he's an idiot.

'I don't collect Pokémon cards any more,' she says, sighing like it's obvious. 'Nobody does. They're boring.'

'What about Harry Potter?' says Joe. 'I bet you like him now, don't you?'

Meg's face lights up and she goes into a long rant about Hogwarts and the Bloody Baron while Joe throws in the odd line of clarification for the rest of us. I don't know how he does it. There's no reason why he should know about any of this stuff, and I wonder how he's managed to pick it up.

Pete is becoming increasingly agitated. He looks at the three of them – Meg sat on Joe's lap eating her sandwich, Lorna glowing and still slightly sweaty from her run – and announces that he's going to do the washing up. He picks up the teacups and the coffee mugs and heads into the kitchen to sulk. I decide to follow him.

'I'll wash, you wipe,' I say, giving his shoulder a quick squeeze.

'OK,' he says, perching himself on the draining board so I can get on with doing both. 'Good idea.'

'Hey,' he says, handing me the washing-up liquid. 'Am I mad to still fancy her or what? I mean, she's never going to fancy me back, is she? Not in a million years.'

I don't bother answering him. We both know the answer to this question.

'And look at the three of them in there. All cosy on the sofa like that. Like he's her dad or something. What's he playing at?'

'Pete, settle down. He's just being friendly, that's all. Meg likes him. She doesn't have many male role models. It's good that she gets on with Joe.'

'So you're fine about it, then? About your boyfriend cosying up to your best friend and your best friend's kid?'

'Come off it. You're being ridiculous. You're just feeling left out.'

'It doesn't bother you at all?'

'No.'

'Not even a bit?'

'I just said so, didn't I? I'm not bothered.'

Pete stares at me from the draining board, and starts pushing his glasses up and down the length of his nose.

'Audrey?'

'Yes.'

'You've washed that mug already.'

'Shit. Have I?'

'Yes,' he says. 'You've done it twice.'

24

The cutlery scrapes hard against the draining board, making my jaw ache and the hairs on my neck stand on end. I'm not sure why she's making such a noise with the washing up, but it's probably got something to do with my dad being out so late. He's out a lot more than he used to be, these days. Ever since he started hanging out with all his new friends, and that idiot man, Jimmy Silk Socks.

Jimmy is round here a lot, with his crazy teeth and his plaid jackets and his girlfriends that never wear any tights. One of them has the ace of hearts tattooed on her ankle and another wears a sickly perfume that smells like cheap talcum powder and Parma violets.

When he's too drunk to go home to his own house, Jimmy goes to sleep on our fold-out sofa. Sometimes he sleeps in his white felt hat, and other times he walks around the house without his shirt on, even though he knows it upsets my mum. One thing he never takes off is his wristwatch. It's fat and gold and weighs down his hand, but it never seems to tell the right time. My dad says that's because Jimmy forgets to wind it. Apparently, time doesn't mean much to a man like Jimmy.

It's been six months since the Friday night card group fell apart – on account of the stakes getting too rich for some people's blood – and these days my dad spends his weekends gambling in the local casinos, or playing poker in a private card room down by the train station. My mum says these places are mostly illegal drinking dens and knocking shops, and I'd like to say that I agree with her, but I'm not entirely sure what a knocking shop is.

To begin with, they only played on Saturday nights and my dad would spend the whole day preparing for his game. He'd sit in his study all afternoon, reading his copy of *Super/System*, and making detailed notes in the margin with the edge of a soft lead pencil. He studied it like a traveller studies a guidebook – finding out the fastest way to get somewhere, picking out all the very best places to go. He'd read those same pages over and over, until his eyes were sore and pink around the edges and his lips were as dry as baked cooking paper. Hour after hour he'd stare at it. Drawing up strange lists and probability charts in his neat hand; immune to the door-slamming and the plate-crashing and the sour metal scrape from the kitchen cutlery.

He wasn't even that bothered about talking to me. On Saturdays we'd often play card games in the afternoons – whist or cribbage or pontoon – but we never seemed to play together any more. Sometimes I'd creep into his room – just to spy on him – but he barely seemed to notice I was there. Once or twice he'd look up and say, 'I think I've cracked it now, Ginger-nut.' But most times he said nothing at all.

She's been sitting at that same window for over an hour, pretending to read passages from her book. She nods her head and purses her lips like she's concentrating, but I haven't seen her turn a page in over ten minutes. Every so often she'll stand up to make herself a cup of tea, but mostly she just boils the kettle and forgets to carry on with making it. The third time she does this, I fetch some milk out of the fridge and finish it off for her myself. As I hand over the steaming teacup, she grabs hold of my wrist and squeezes it so tightly it hurts.

'We *will* be alright, you know,' she says, letting go of my arm. 'I promise you, it'll all be better soon.'

I'm not too sure what she means so I nod, fetch myself a couple of slices of bread and switch on the overhead grill. As the bread darkens, and the kitchen fills with the scent of warming yeast, she smiles to herself and seems a little happier. She goes back to the tissue-thin pages of her Bible – turning the pages carefully from time to time – and I spread a thick layer of cold, creamy butter on my toast.

The next morning my dad comes in bright and early to wake me up. He's still dressed in his overcoat and his Saturday evening clothes and he has a thick layer of stubble poking through his chin, like spider's legs. His breath smells of digested Scotch and nicotine, his jacket smells of nervous sweat and smoke. He has something that he wants to tell me and he hopes that I won't be too upset. It turns out that I'm going to have to walk to school every day this term because, for some reason, he's had to give away our car. I tell him not to worry about it. It's not that far to walk anyway, and to be honest I don't really care about it one way or the other.

As the months slip by and the winter sets in, she stops waiting up for him altogether. She goes to bed with a hot-water bottle and a glass of warm Scotch and milk, and leaves for work without bothering to make sure he's up. The long nights turn into lost weekends, and he's sometimes away from home for days at a time. He's up at the London casinos or staying over at someone else's house, and occasionally – during the holidays – he collects his passport and his navy blue bank book and flies off with Jimmy Silk Socks to Las Vegas. Or Vienna. Or Amsterdam. Or somewhere that I've never even heard of, and have to look up on my inflatable globe.

Most nights I'm not sure if he's coming home or not. One evening he turned up with a tear in his jacket and a bloodstain on his shirt and his arm wrapped in a sling made out of cotton handkerchiefs. He'd been gone without a word for three days. When I finally got round to asking him how he'd hurt himself, he looked at me like it was the strangest kind of a question he'd ever heard.

'To be honest, Ginger-nut,' he said, shaking his head and sinking to the ground, 'I'm not really sure.'

Two months before we moved out for the last time, my dad won a whole pile of money. He turned up with crumpled notes sticking out of his pockets at a dozen different angles, and threw bunches of them into the middle of the sofa, like creased confetti. She tried not to be impressed, but I could tell deep down that she was. Her face lit up at the sight of it, and the little creases around her eyes that sometimes bunched together and filled with make-up melted back into her skin. That afternoon he took us shopping. We took a taxi up to Jimmy's second-hand car garage by the horse track and she picked out a bright red convertible. We drove up and down the seafront for hours. Roaring through the traffic like a hailstorm, with the bitter rush of wind freezing the tops of our ears.

Halfway home, we stopped off at our favourite café and he treated the three of us to a plate of ice-cold oysters. We doused them in lemon, ground powdery white pepper into their flesh, and swallowed them down as quickly as we could. My mum smiled as she tossed back the dozen salty shells, and I watched him study her properly for the first time in months. Her river-coloured eyes and her cold-water skin, and her beautiful, apple-shaped face.

He stared at her hard, until she had to look away, and took tight hold of her hand. He had an important announcement to make. He was thinking about giving up his job for good. This win had been the breakthrough he was looking for: he was going to try to make a go of it professionally.

Her shoulders slumped as he said it, and that was the moment when she began to look like a photocopy of herself. Everything about her visibly dimmed. She cursed herself for being so stupid and broke an oyster shell apart in her bony hand. It was a wonder that he hadn't been sacked already.

It was a wonder we hadn't been thrown out on to the street. It was only because she'd spent the last year crying on Mrs Santos's shoulder that the school had taken pity and kept him on part time. There were bills in the cupboard that dated back to last winter and letters from the bank that she was too scared to read. And – if she sniffed at him hard enough – she could still smell the scent of Parma violets on his skin.

They argued a little longer, their dark voices rising and falling and embarrassing the other customers, until he finally turned his back on her and walked away. We drove home quickly, with the roof pulled up like a pie lid, and the windows wound up tightly against the wind. By the time she stepped out of that car, I could tell she was sick of the sight of it. She stood on the pavement, straightening her skirt and pulling at her fringe, and stared at it like it was coated in rust: wondering how something so perfect could be so easily ruined.

Things happened fairly quickly after that. The job was gone, the bank accounts were empty and the house that I grew up in would soon belong to someone else. Towards the end he'd sometimes creep into my bedroom early in the mornings, and empty my money box of coins. Most times I'd pretend to be asleep, but if I bothered to let him know I was awake he'd always pretend to make a game of it. If it was sunny we'd bet on the colour of passing cars. If it was raining we'd bet on the trajectory of falling raindrops. Double or nothing. Until he'd won it all.

The week before we left, she caught him coming out of my room. Creeping down the hallway with a pile of coins cupped in his fist; scattering a trail of copper pennies on the floor. I had to block up my ears to cut out the sound of their shouting, and two days later we were gone. Mrs Santos picked us up in her car, loaded our belongings into the boot, and helped move us into a bed and breakfast along the seafront. The landlady shook her head when she let us in and her husband carried our things into the hallway. We climbed a stairwell that smelt of reconstituted potato and pork fat, and for a whole week we ate each one of our meals in our room.

The following Monday, a man in a smartly pressed over-coat came to collect us and my mum introduced him to me as Frank.

'We're going to be living with Frank from now on,' she said, zipping up my jacket and packing our suitcases into the boot of his car. 'You'll like it. He has a house with a garden and gas central heating, and you'll have a brand-new bedroom all to yourself.'

I looked at her blankly, unsure what I was supposed to say. I wanted to ask if we could go home and fetch my inflatable globe first, but there didn't seem to be very much time. Frank offered to buy me a new globe, or a Barbie doll perhaps, and I remember that he tried to take hold of my hand. I pulled it away like a circus whip, and he stuck with patting me on the shoulder after that.

'Come on,' said my mum, bundling me into the car. 'You're going to like it at Frank's. He has two boys. Twins. They're only a couple of years older than you, so you'll always have somebody to play with.'

I watched her kiss Frank on the cheek as we got into the car, and I noticed him blush wildly inside his suit. As his flush faded and his car took off carefully along the seafront, she turned round and told it to me over again. Once we got to Frank's house I'd be warm. At Frank's house I'd never feel lonely again. I didn't take much notice. I knew it wasn't me she was trying to convince.

25

Last night something rather disturbing happened. I dreamt I was having sex with Bono and the Edge. A fantastic, filthy, sweaty, dirty shag, on a bed the size of a small Third World country. It started well enough – the Edge was very attentive – and I was just about to orgasm when Bono's hair plugs started coming out in my hands. Bundles of them. Hot and oily and caked with sticky wig glue that smelt of Parma violets and aftershave. I wonder what it all means. I wonder if I should ask Joe what he thinks. Hmm. Maybe not. We've been going through a bit of a dry spell lately – it's been two weeks since our bout of post-bath sex – and it would only upset him if he thought I'd spent the night tossing and turning and getting it on with three-quarters of U2. (I can't be sure, but I've a sneaking suspicion that Larry Mullen Jr was there as well.) I know. It's hopeless. I should probably just kill myself now.

I leave Joe sleeping – it's still early – and make myself a pot of coffee in the kitchen. I can see my morning face reflected in the mirrored tiles by the kettle, and I pull at it and prod it and examine it for signs of ageing while I wait for the water to boil. It doesn't look good. I have lines round my eyes that are months away from turning into fully fledged wrinkles, and a brown patch in the middle of my forehead that won't fade because I've spent too much time in the sun.

I stir two lumps of sugar into my coffee and search around in the cupboard for a jar of pickles. I try not to eat them for breakfast if Joe's up, but I find them particularly delicious first thing in the morning. There's nothing like the violent tang of a salty gherkin to wake up your system, and there's nothing like a sour pickled onion to take the edge off your premature midlife depression.

I munch through the crisp flesh, lick the vinegar juices off my hands, and tug my eyebrows upwards and outwards to see what I'd look like with a face lift. Pretty weird, as it turns out. Not dissimilar to my constipated poker face. I wonder if a dose of Botox would do the trick. Or one of those face exercisers that give your muscles electric shocks. Lorna says I should be drinking more water, but I'm pretty sure that would just make me pee a lot and leave my face looking exactly the same.

This time next week I'll be thirty-three years old. The same age my father was when he took up professional gambling. I'm still not sure what made him do it. He was such a rational man. He'd devoted his life to making sense of the world, to finding out how it operated and behaved. It wasn't like he had a history of being reckless with money, and up until his early thirties he played everything by the book.

He did everything that was expected of him. He had a decent education, a secure job and a wife that he doted on, to begin with. They were an odd mix in some ways – he was a solver, she was a worrier – but they balanced each other with a Newtonian level of symmetry. Her fear of the world was counteracted by his grasp of it, her confusion largely eradicated by his clarity.

I've sometimes wondered if he got bored, if that's the reason he started having affairs. I know part of him craved excitement, abandon and change, but deep down I suspect he always adored her. So I want to ask Big Louie what it feels like. To risk everything. To lose everything. To cast off an entire way of life and embrace another.

I can understand why he enjoyed the challenge of his weekend poker games; I can even understand why he wanted to raise the stakes. What I can't work out is why he became so eager to risk his winnings. It never made any kind of sense. Even on the nights he did well, he'd end up frittering his money away. My mum said he'd leave the poker table with a roll of twenties tucked into his pocket and plough it straight back into a high-stakes game of blackjack or roulette. Or craps. Or a long-lost weekend at the dog track. It's almost like he wanted to destroy himself. Like he chose to split his sanity apart. The urge to gamble spread through his bones like rising damp, and it scared me to watch him lose control. It went against everything he'd taught me. Everything that I considered him to be.

By the time he started taking off to Las Vegas with Jimmy Silk Socks he was already fully lost to the New World. He loved everything there was to love about America. The spread of it, the size of it, the movies, and the food, and the heady, dollar-bill glamour. He loved the ambiance of the roadside diners and jazz clubs, and the cocktail bars that stayed open all through the night. He liked the mountains and the big skies and the dingy downtown poker rooms, and the way no one apologised for themselves.

Most of all he loved the fact that it had no manners. Not the kind that make you treat a person with respect, the kind that keep a person in his place. Vegas was a town where everyone was created equal. Where a second-hand car salesman could don a white fedora and call himself Jimmy Silk Socks, and nobody would think to crease their brow or bat an eyelid. A place where an ordinary man could sit down at the poker table and play a hand of cards with a millionaire or a world champion. Where women wore scarlet lipstick and asked for glacé cherries in their drinks, and, for a moment at least, a secondary school teacher could be a king.

The winter before he left, he called round to Frank's house, to collect me on one of his increasingly sporadic visits. He had a rare twenty-pound note folded up in his hand and he made a point of showing it to me before he tucked it back inside his wallet. As we made our way down towards the seafront, I asked him what it felt like to win. He thought for a long while as we gazed out at the waves and told me it was the purest feeling in all the world. When I asked him what it felt like to lose, he squeezed my hand and told me, 'Much the same.'

My father's birthday is a few weeks after mine. He'll be fifty-eight this year. I wonder what he looks like these days – if he's shrunk much or fattened much, if his eyes are still as brown as they once were. I wonder if he still tucks his thumb underneath his index finger when he's concentrating, or if his voice has become deeper over the years.

I wonder if he's ever thought about calling me: it would be the simplest thing in the world for him to do. Frank still lives in the same house he shared with my mother, and the phone number has always remained the same. In some ways it's easier to imagine that he never thinks about me. My biggest fear is that he thinks about me all the time.

I spend the next half-hour online, looking through the websites that Big Louie recommended and posting missing-person alerts in the poker chat rooms and players' forums. I write my father's name among the poker tips and the endless tales of great hands gone wrong, and leave my e-mail address and mobile phone number for anyone who might care to call. When I've gone through as many as I can, I grab a pencil and a notebook and start drafting a missing-person ad for the newspapers and card magazines. It's difficult to find the right words. There's something about the Internet that feels reassuringly anonymous, but I'm not sure how I'll feel to see my words in print. If, by some miracle, he actually comes across it, it'll be the first piece of communication we've had for over twenty years. I want it to be good. I want it to strike the right note. And for some reason I don't want Joe to see me struggling with it.

'Hey.'
   'Hey.'
'Did you sleep alright?'
'Yeah. Um . . . why d'you ask?'
'No reason,' says Joe, yawning and helping himself to some coffee. 'You were singing in your sleep, that's all.'
'Really? What was I singing?'
'Not sure. It was quite hard to tell. There was a lot of mumbling going on.'
'Mumbling?'
'Yeah. For a while I thought you were doing the chorus to 'Where the Streets Have No Name', but then you started mumbling about someone called Barry, or Reg.'
'Not . . . um . . . Larry and Edge?'
'Yeah. Shit, that's it. Larry and Edge . . . hey, come back here. Where are you going?'
'Bathroom. Sorry. *Yeuch*. Need to take a shower. Can't stop.'

26

I haven't heard from Big Louie for a few days now – he's been ignoring my e-mails since his peculiar outburst with the butter knife – so I've decided to go over to his flat unannounced and surprise him. I've spent all morning down at the garden centre with Joe – picking out plants, bulbs and fresh bags of peat – and I think I've found the perfect combination. It's surprising how much you need to know. There's light soil, loamy soil, chalky, limey and sandy, and it's all to do with particle size and texture. Some plants are liable to change the colour of their petals depending on the combination of minerals in the ground, and it's imperative that you find the right balance. You also need slug pellets, water-retaining granules, a brace of different fertilisers and plant foods and, most importantly, you need to find the right type of watering can.

'What type of watering can does he want?'
  'I'm not sure. What's the difference?'
  'Well, metal or plastic. Short spout or long. One that holds lots of water so he doesn't have to keep going back to his taps, or a small one that'll be easy to hold over the balcony.'
  'Right. Long spout, lots of water, green plastic, fixed sprinkler. No . . . wait. Long spout, small amount of water, detachable sprinkler.'
  'Plastic or metal?'
  'Metal.'
  'You're sure?'
  'Positive. Unless he'd prefer a green one.'
  'A green one, then?'

'OK, why not?'

Pete is being especially useful this morning. He's lent me a book called *Window Boxes of the Rich and Famous*, and even though the pictures are just artists' impressions of what the window boxes may have looked like, I still think Big Louie would like to see it. I've half an idea to make his window box look like Greta Garbo's – on account of his studious aversion to the outside world – but Pete doesn't think it's a very good idea.

'It doesn't have any lobelia or lavender in it. Your giant said he definitely wanted lavender.'

'I know. But look at those white roses. They're beautiful, don't you think?'

'They'd need a lot of taking care of. Pruning, dead-heading, thinning, that sort of thing.'

'OK then,' I say, reluctantly. 'Let's just make do with what we've got.'

Joe helps me load everything into the boot of the car, before offering one last time to come with me. He knows I'm feeling a bit down, on account of no one replying to my newspaper ad or my poker-site postings yet, but he recognises that I want to do this by myself.

'Are you sure you're going to need all this stuff?'

'Definitely. Louie was very particular.'

'You could make it a lot simpler, you know. You don't really need three different types of soil.'

'Yes. But I want to be safe. I want to make sure I've got every angle covered.'

He sighs gently, knowing that he won't change my mind.

'And you're sure this is the correct-sized box?'

'Certain. I measured the balcony space three times when I first went over.'

'So you know what you're doing?'

'Absolutely. How hard can it be?'

'You know to soak them first?'

160

'Yes, and I'm not supposed to disturb the root ball. I know. I've read it all fifteen times.'

'OK then. But don't get out of the car if there's anyone dodgy hanging around.'

'I won't. I promise.'

'And call me if you need some help carrying it in.'

'Look, I'm telling you, I can do this by myself. It's simple, honestly. I'll be fine.'

The thing is, soil is quite heavy. And watering cans are notoriously difficult to carry underneath your arm. The plants are especially spindly and delicate and I'm paranoid that I'm going to damage them in some way. Thank God for Cigarette Kid. If he hadn't been hanging around selling cartons of knock-off Rothmans to a couple of pregnant teenagers I'm not sure what I'd have done.

Even between the two of us, it takes three trips to the car, and two trips up in the lift, to get it all done. It was decent of him to help me out, though. And it's not like he wanted anything in return. Well, that's not strictly true. He did demand I give him twenty quid if I didn't want him to pour my second bag of peat over the fifteenth-storey railings; but in the end he settled quite happily for seventeen. He even threw in a free packet of Marlboro Lights. Despite my repeated protestations that I'd given up smoking. Which was nice of him. When you think about it.

Big Louie's door is already open. Just a crack. I peer round the edge and into the dimly lit hallway, but predictably he's nowhere to be seen.

'Come on, Ungar. Whaddaya waiting for? Hurry it up, for Chrissakes.'

It's him. Shouting at me from the safety of his bedroom. Demanding that I speed up the load-in and close up the front door as quickly as possible.

'How did you know I was coming?' I say, wiping a drizzle of perspiration off my face. 'How did you know I was bringing the stuff?'

An eye and half a cheek peer round the door frame – like a demented Picasso painting – and he shrugs and rubs his hand over some of his chins. I ask if he heard me arguing with Cigarette Kid.

'Nope,' he says, trying not to look too pleased with himself. 'Knew you was heading up here long before that.'

'How come?'

'Could smell the plants,' he says, matter-of-factly. 'Soon as you loaded them into the elevator.'

I look at him suspiciously, like he's not telling the truth, but I'm half inclined to think that he is.

'Got a highly developed sense of smell,' he says, filling the doorway with the rest of his face. 'From all those years shut away in card rooms and pool halls and casino basements. For years, the only thing I smelt was beer nuts, Budweiser, body odour and cigarettes, and the dog breath from my wife and Little Louie.'

'Your wife had dog breath?'

'Why you askin'? I just told you so, didn't I?'

'Yes. You did.'

'Anyway,' he says, his eyes scanning me anxiously as I close the front door, 'my sense of smell was pretty limited back then. I was OK at picking out sweat, beer and dog breath, but I wasn't too good with anything subtle. Wife thought it was because of the accident, thought it did something to my brain. Ruined my sense of taste as well. That's how come I like pickled food and chilli sauce so much. For ten years they were about the only things I could really taste.'

'So what happened?' I say, laying down some of the plants. 'How did you get it back?'

'Was pretty weird,' he says, lowering his voice at the strangeness of it all. 'I was playing cards with a bunch of truck drivers over in Carson and we'd been going at it for sixteen hours straight. A few of the guys were pretty spent by then, so someone had the bright idea to raise the shutters and let in a little air. I didn't think too much of it. Wasn't even sure what time of day it was, whether it was midday or the middle of the night. Anyways, the shutters flew up like a kite, the window burst open, and the room filled up with fat yellow sunlight.

'For a moment the glare of it hurt my eyes: blinded me, like I was Dracula or somethin'. And then the smell hit me. It was a fine smell. Light and subtle, lots of complex notes in it. A mixture of cactus, bursage and Ponderosa pine, all mixed in with a top note of the sea.'

'The sea?'

'I know,' he says, holding his hands aloft. 'That was the weirdest part. Imagine smellin' the ocean in the middle of the damned desert.'

'How did it smell?'

'Good. Really good. Cold and salty and fresh. Like fish scales and ozone and ice. Anyway,' he says, smiling at the memory, 'this damned scent was only around for a moment or so, but it was the sweetest thing I ever breathed in my life. Breeze must have carried it right across the Mojave and in off the top of Mount Charleston. It had the whole world wrapped up inside of it. California oranges, English roses, Virginia bluebells, Caribbean palms, wheat fields and cherry blossom and bamboo and limes and a whole load of other cool shit as well. You name it, that scent had a little bit of it. Even had a slice of raw mountain snow.

'Anyhow,' he says, rubbing his head at the wonder of it, and sitting himself down, 'everything changed after that. My nose was so keen to get another sniff of this honeysuckle sea scent, that all of a sudden it could smell ripened cheese through two foot of solid steel. I could smell my wife coming from the top of the street. Smell foliage from three rooms away.'

'Wow,' I say, wondering whether to believe him or not. 'That's incredible. What about your sense of taste?'

'Sure, came right back along with it. Why do you think I'm so fat? Once my tongue started working again I was done for. Could chew my way through an all-you-can-eat buffet, end to end in thirty minutes flat.'

'Well,' I say, coming over to join him, 'it must have been good, though. To have your sense of smell restored after all those years?'

'Nope,' says Big Louie, miserably. 'It was a bad thing. Was part of what . . . you know . . . part of what ruined me.'

'Why? I don't understand.'

'Stopped me concentrating. That one sniff of Ponderosa pine did it for me. It reacquainted my senses with the outside world. After that my nose was always on the lookout for it. Under poker chips, behind beer glasses, in the trail of some skinny hooker's cheap perfume. Part of me wasn't paying attention any more. One of my senses was always somewhere else.'

'And that's a bad thing?'

'Sure it's a bad thing. You need every sense you got to win. You need your nose to be sniffing the fear out of the bluffers and the confusion out of the suckers, and the torment out of the fellas who can't help do anything else but play. You can't be scouring the air for a blast of seaweed every five minutes. You got to be one hundred per cent focused, all the time. Worst thing was, I couldn't stop myself,' he says, lowering his head onto his chest. 'It was such a beautiful smell. I knew I wouldn't rest till I smelt it again.'

Big Louie shakes his jowls slowly. He picks up the small plastic watering can, tilts it on its side and smiles at it like it were a living thing.

164

'So why didn't you go looking for it? Go on holiday. To the seashore. Or somewhere green?'

He answers but he doesn't look me in the eye.

'Wife tried to get me to take a break,' he says wearily, 'but I never would. She said it was like I'd been institutionalised or somethin'. Reckoned card rooms were the only place where I felt at home.'

'Is that true?'

'Maybe,' he says, lifting his shoulders morosely. 'I mean, I always knew where I stood in a card room. I knew the names of all the players; their characteristics, their weaknesses, their addictions: everything about a person that I needed to know. I could tell exactly what kind of a man he was from the way he played his very first hand. Same way as I could always tell which way a basketball player was gonna run, right before he picked up the ball.'

A bundle of memories seep into the creases of his face and his lips begin to move up and down. They form words and sentences and phrases that I half recognise, but no sound comes out of his mouth. I leave him in his chair, fussing with his bulbs and narrating his silent stories, and head into the kitchen to boil fresh tea. He looks a bit happier by the time I get back, so I decide to press him a little deeper.

'Mr Bloom?'

'I told you, you can always call me Louie.'

'Right. Louie?'

'Yep.'

'Did you ever . . . I mean, do you think maybe it would be a good idea for you to see someone?'

'Someone like who?'

'Well. I don't know. A counsellor or something. Someone to help you deal with your phobias.'

'A shrink, you mean?'

'Well. Yes. A psychiatrist or something.'

'Seen dozens of them,' he says, blithely. 'They all say exactly the same thing.'

'Really? What do they say?'

He grins at me, like it's obvious.

'Well, Audrey Ungar, they say I'm crazy. They say I'm the craziest, fattest fuck that they've ever seen.'

'Right. I see.'

'Whole thing's a waste of time,' he says, contemptuously. 'They sit you down in front of some wiseass college kid whose balls ain't even dropped yet, and it takes him a whole hour to work out I'm a fuck-up. Play a hand of poker with me for an hour, then I'd show him what was what. Tell more about a man in an hour playing Texas Hold'Em than a shrink could tell you in a thousand hours of therapy.'

'So you never got anywhere? They didn't even help you over the germs?'

'Nope. Halfway through the session I'd start cleaning their couches with an anti-bacterial face-wipe, and right around then they'd usually ask me to leave.'

'Right.'

'And charge me two hundred dollars.'

'I see.'

'Two hundred dollars to tell me that I'm crazy and that I secretly want to bang my own mother. I tell you, Audrey, these guys are sick. Sick friggin' fucks the whole lot of them. 'Scuse my French. Anyways,' he says, slurping his tea noisily and reaching for a biscuit, 'whaddaya wanna do? Sit here all afternoon psychoanalysing me, or help lay out this window box that you've humped halfway across town?'

'The window box.'

'You're sure now?'

'Yes.'

'OK. Let's make a start. Nice choice of watering can, by the way.'

'Good,' I say, 'I'm glad you like it.'

166

27

'The action is everything, more consuming than sex, more immediate than politics; more important always than the acquisition of money, which is never, for the gambler, the true point of the exercise.'

Joan Didion, *The White Album*

Big Louie spreads a thick layer of newspaper down the length of the kitchen table. He overlaps several sheets at once – sticking them together with sticky tape to make sure there are no gaps – and hauls the terracotta window box into the centre. It's a large box. Three foot long from tip to tip, and wide enough to fill his entire balcony. By the time he's positioned it just right, lifted a swollen bag of soil off the floor and slit it open with his hunting knife, he has beads of sweat dribbling down both of his cheeks. His breathing is clotted and heavy and the grating of his lungs is beginning to make me feel uncomfortable.

I suggest he take a moment to rest, but he seems determined to get on. He's keen to take care of things by himself, so I stand at the edge of the table and hand him the plants and bulbs one by one. He takes it slowly, pouring an inch or so of gravel into the box, and smoothing it out carefully with his fingers. Next he moistens the plants, leaving their root balls to soak and soften, while he pours out a thick layer of peat. He curses and snorts and hums to himself while he's doing it, and from time to time he breaks into song. A verse or two of 'Ain't That a Kick in the Head' followed by a chorus of 'Mr Bojangles', when he's got his breath back.

I tell him he has a good voice – low, resonant and treacle thick – and he looks at me like he knows this already.

When he was learning his game – back in the Atlantic City card rooms – he'd sometimes earn extra cash by doing Sinatra impressions for the locals and retirees. That's how he started. Playing the old folks and the 'bennies' (day-trippers) for ten-dollar pots, and tending bars in the casino lounges during the evening.

It wasn't the worst way to make a living, but the constant ring of the slot machines used to bother him. He could never get them out of his head. Even when he was sleeping he heard them: chiming and jangling and jarring round his skull, like metal cups on thick jail house bars.

Just when he thought he could stand it no longer, the clanging inexplicably vanished. He sat down to play in his regular game at the Taj, stared down at his pair of kings, and realised that something was wrong. He couldn't hear the slots any more. All he could hear were the other players. The anxiety in their heartbeats, the fear in their nasal twitches and the sigh in the shuffling of their chips. It was then he knew he'd found his concentration: then that he decided it was time to move on.

By the time he settled in Vegas, Big Louie was playing poker ten hours a day, six days a week, fifty-two weeks of the year. Most nights he played downtown, 'in the joints around Fremont Street', but a couple of times a week he'd cruise up to the Strip and graze on the out-of-towners with the other card sharks. He'd pick them off one by one. The tourists in their shiny nylon jogging suits and the insurance salesmen with their cheap suits and beetroot tans. He could smell their ten-dollar roof racks and their five-year-old Station Wagons and the spittle of their bosses on their backs.

If there was a convention in town, which there always was, he'd spend a happy night separating the delegates from their cash. He'd circle the tables like a hunter and take a seat when he'd selected the easiest prey. The loud ones chain-smoking cigarettes and splashing the pot with their chips; the bold ones ordering bottles of whisky and buying in for twice what they could afford. And the quiet ones, fidgeting with the plastic name tags on their lapels, and gazing up at the chandeliers like they were comets.

Big Louie would sit tight. All night long if he had to. Nursing his cards and a Diet Coca-Cola – in his Hawaiian shirt, moccasins and K-Mart slacks – while his opponents eyeballed him like he was nothing. And one by one, he'd squeeze the juice right out of them. While they raised, folded, checked and reraised, and tried to work out who the sucker was. Perhaps he should have told them what he knew: 'If you're sat at a card table for longer than twenty minutes and you ain't worked out who the sucker is yet, then it's you.'

'There's a strange thing happens when a man starts losing,' he says, smiling at me. 'It's almost like he wants to give it away. Take him down one time too many and something inside of him bursts like a blister. Before you know it, he's raisin' on a pair of threes and going "all in" on ace high. He's too proud or too stupid to admit he's being outplayed and leave the table, and by the time you finished with him, he can't even afford to pay his bar bill when he leaves. Man like that can't believe his own bad luck. Can't believe fate has picked on him hand after hand. And that's his ego talking,' he says, pointing his finger at me. 'Only an egotist favours fortune over odds.'

'Did you ever play in the tournaments?' I say, eagerly, 'The World Series and stuff like that?'

'Sure,' he says, like it's of no particular consequence. 'Played in the World Series every year. Even made it to the final table one time. But the side games were where the real action was. Playing in the no-limit cash games.'

'For what kind of sums?'

'I just told you, didn't I? No limit.'

'At all?'

'Nope. Played games where you needed a hundred-thousand-dollar bank roll just to sit down at the table. Fifty grand riding on the turn of a single card. And let me tell you,' he says, patting down another geranium, 'at that level it's a whole other game. It takes imagination, subtlety, character, as well as all the mechanical skills. You might be able to calculate the pot odds to two decimal places, right there in your head, but at that level so can everyone else. At that level you're always working six steps ahead. You're making judgement calls that would convince anyone who didn't know any better that you were clairvoyant. I'm telling you, Audrey, there's nothing like it. Nothing at all.'

'Because of the money?'

He shakes his head, wondering why I don't get it yet.

'No,' he says, 'because of the risk. For the rush of it. The thrill of making what seems like an impossible, once-in-a-lifetime play and bringing it home. Because somewhere at the margins, no matter how much you know or how much you've studied, the world, the game, it's all chaotic. But every now and then, you walk the perfect line. Make the perfect play. It's like you've gathered up the whole universe in your hands. For a second, it all makes perfect sense.'

He pauses for a moment to catch his breath, rubbing his temples with his hands while his eyes begin to bulge and glaze over.

'And this time you've fooled them all,' he says, pushing his chair back and standing up suddenly. 'This time, you've set it up just right. You've read every tick, every twitch, every breath your opponent makes, and in a split second it all becomes clear. Your brain is drawing on information stored up from a lifetime of hands: you know your opponents better than you know your own wife. Their strengths, their weaknesses, their cowardice, their regrets – but they don't seem to recognise you at all.

'You've advertised three big bluffs in the last three hours

and they can't believe you're not trying to stick it to them over again. But this time you have it,' he says, hyperventilating. 'The stone-cold nuts. And it's beautiful, Audrey, better than sex. You feel content, light headed, free. Like you're screaming down the side of a mountain on a single ski with only your arms held out for balance. For an instant you feel like you're actually living in this world, instead of sitting around on the edge of it waiting to die.'

Big Louie stands behind the window box like a preacher in front of his pulpit. His wet eyes sparkling like marbles, his filthy hands cupped at the side of his head like giant spoons. His barrel chest heaves sluggishly up and down, compressing air like a failing combustion engine and shaking splinters of loose paint from the walls. He stays like this for a long while. Staring into space and spilling dirt from his fingertips to the table, until he realises where he is and comes back down.

'Well. Anyway . . .' he says, taking a deep breath and picking up his trowel again. 'It's one hell of a feeling. It's something that your dad knew all about.'

'How can you be so sure?' I say, gazing up at him.

'He was a gambler wasn't he?'

'Yes.'

'Then he knew.'

28

Big Louie settles back at the table and sniffs the seedlings gently. In the few weeks I've known him I've never seen him look this content. He has dirt ground deep into his fingernails and gravel dust down the front of his tablecloth shirt, but he doesn't seem in the slightest bit bothered. He takes his time. Arranges the plants and seedlings one way, before taking them out and arranging them carefully over again.

I've brought almost everything that he asked for, but Joe has included some finishing touches of his own. An asparagus fern in place of the trailing ivy, and a couple of succulents that thrive well with very little water. Big Louie seems rather taken with them. He tells me that his wife used to grow aloe in their desert garden when he first moved to Las Vegas and recommends rubbing the thick juices on your skin if it gets sunburnt or inflamed. He's truly in the finest of spirits. He can smell the night-scented stock just by handling the bulbs and the honeysuckle months before it thinks of bursting into bloom.

Big Louie turns his head. He glances from me to the balcony then back again, before running his eyes over the finished window box. He breathes in deeply once more and draws his nose through the air. Backwards and forwards, forwards then backwards, sieving the stale room for a taste of the outside world.

'What do you think?' he says, uneasily. 'Not bad for an amateur, huh?'

'No,' I say. 'It looks beautiful. Perfect.'

172

Big Louie clicks his teeth. Perfect is a word he clearly likes.

'You want to put it out there for me?'

'You don't want to do it yourself? It's only a balcony. It's not even like you'd be going outside the flat.'

He shakes his head, tells me that he can't do it, and the old pain flows back into his face like bad blood. I don't push it. He lifts the box off the table, manoeuvres it as if it were made of polystyrene and deposits it in the centre of the living room. He takes it as far as he can go, nods longingly towards the window, and leaves me to get on with it on my own.

It's a struggle. The box is ferociously heavy now that it's filled up with plants and damp soil, and I only just manage it. I open the window, bend my knees and heave the box slowly into place. I call out to Louie to see what he thinks but he's already engrossed in something else.

He's busy in the kitchen. Bleaching and scrubbing his fingers, and scraping away the flesh on his hands.

29

Big Louie has cancelled my poker lessons. Just like that. With no word of warning. He sent me an e-mail at the weekend saying he didn't have time to see me any more and I have to admit I was more than a little hurt. The way I look at it, I've been had. He strung me out just long enough to make sure I'd build the window box for him, and as soon as it was finished he fobbed me off. Like I was nothing. He sat there munching truffles and pickles and super-hot chillies and cast me off without a moment's regret. I hope he gets bleach burns on his fingertips. I hope he chokes on a chocolate cup cake, just like his wife.

After a good hour spent cursing and moaning and fantasising about tracking down Little Louie and having him euthanised, it turns out I had it all wrong. Big Louie is a much busier man than I'd realised. He has many demands on his time. With the World Series of poker coming up in just over a month, some of his more experienced pupils are demanding extra lessons. At least five of them are planning on making the trip over to Vegas at the beginning of May, so he hasn't got time to be bothering with me. And my ineptitude. And our cosy 'little chats'.

On top of that, Big Louie thinks he's found someone special: a player with championship flair. He's been hothousing him every week for the last six months, and if he works on him through the whole of April he might stand a chance of finishing 'in the money'. Last year a twenty-three-year-old British player placed second in the main event, and walked away with a $1.1-million-dollar pot. Who's to say it couldn't happen this year as well? Who's to say it won't be Louie's boy?

I think about reminding him that he once told me all British players were pussies, but I decide now's probably not the time.

Thankfully, all is not lost. After receiving the post-window-box brush-off, I came up with a crafty three-pronged line of attack. I decided to bribe him. With the offer of two matching indoor planters and the book on *Window Boxes of the Rich and Famous* that I forgot to give him the last time I went over to his flat. He really wants to see it. He thinks it might be quite interesting and informative. He'd also quite like some indoor planters. Especially if they have lavender in them. And perhaps a couple of cacti. If I think that would be OK.

Step three was infinitely more subtle. I decided to make him feel sorry for me. I explained that I'd had no word back from my poker-site postings yet (aside from a couple of marriage proposals, and a kind invite to a home game in Queens) and that, all in all, I was still feeling quite down about the whole thing. I told him that learning the game was the nearest thing I had to getting to know my dad. To discovering how his mind worked. To understanding how the game devoured him. To finding out why he never came back.

It took a while – you could almost hear him grimacing in his e-mails – but after half a dozen attempts I finally broke him. He called me nagging, persistent and irritating, and I accused him of trying to rip me off. He told me women should stick to crochet and slot machines, and I told him he was mean minded and sexist. Which he rather liked.

Eventually, we made a gentleman's agreement. Big Louie has agreed to contact some of his old poker buddies back in Las Vegas and put the word out about my missing father, and I've agreed to stop annoying him for the rest of the week and get started on my poker homework. If he considers that I've made a decent enough effort (and likes the planters, cacti, pickles, truffles and gardening books that I've agreed to bring over for him) then he might even let me play a real game. For money. Against his regular Friday-nighters. And this hotshot dynamo kid.

'How much did you spend?'

'I don't know. Not much.'

'You've got twenty-two books in that bag. All about exactly the same thing.'

'Ah. That's where you're wrong. They may, at first glance, appear to be about the same thing, but the truth is, each one is subtly but substantively different.'

'*How to* Play *Texas Hold'em* is different to *How to* Win at *Texas Hold'em*?'

'Yes.'

'*Pot-limit Technique for Beginners* is different from *Tournament Technique for Beginners*?'

'Very.'

'*The Man with $100,000 Breasts* is a seminal guide to poker tactics and strategy?'

'Yes. Well, no. It's more like a collection of gambling stories. But check it out,' I say, handing him the book and flicking it open to the appropriate page. 'Some guys bet this gambler a hundred thousand dollars he wouldn't have a boob job and walk around with double-D implants for a year. And he did it. How mad is that?'

'I'm beginning to wonder,' says Joe, shaking his head.

Joe is not impressed with my poker library, and it's true, I might have been a little over-enthusiastic. Yesterday afternoon I went to a specialist gambling shop on Great Ormond Street and bought myself every teach-yourself-poker manual I could find. I have manuals by all the great tacticians: David Sklansky, Lou Krieger, Mike Caro, Bobby Baldwin, Mason

Malmuth and Herbert O. Yardley. The only one they didn't have was *Super/System* by Doyle Brunson. Apparently it's quite hard to get hold of.

Nevertheless, the salesman said they cover everything I need to know. Psychology, position, bluffing, semi-bluffing, over-cards, check-raising and pot odds. There are essays devoted to hand rankings, probability and slow-playing, and five-hundred-page encyclopaedias devoted to 'tells' – the give-away ticks and nervous mannerisms that indicate the strength (or otherwise) of your opponents' cards.

After a great deal of thought, and some calculated persuasion on the part of the salesman – who suggested that it never hurts to be over-prepared – I decided to buy the whole lot. I'm determined to impress Big Louie when I go over to his flat at the end of the week, and I don't want to have missed out on any angles. I plan to learn it all. To study every nuance and subtlety of the game, until I'm almost as good a poker player as he is.

Buoyed up by my extensive purchases, I decided to splash out on some suitable poker snacks to go with them. Maple syrup, a packet of beef jerky, a box of corn-bread mix, some cookie-dough ice cream and a giant pack of 'home-style' cheesy grits. Just the kind of food you need when you're studying. Exactly the kind of food to keep you sharp.

'You're not concentrating.'
'I am.'
'How come you're not getting it, then?'
'I'm trying.'
'Well try a bit harder.'
'OK, we each get dealt two cards face down?'
'That's right. We each make a bet based on what we think those cards are worth, then the dealer lays out three more cards face up. They call that the flop. After that, each of us bets again.'

'And all the players can use these new cards to complete their hand?'

'Exactly. After that we deal two more cards face up, one at a time, with another round of betting between each. Players make the best five-card hand they can from the first two cards they were dealt and the others face up on the table . . . What? Why are you moaning? What's the matter?'

'It's my stomach.'

'What's wrong with it?'

'I think it was the grits. Are you sure you're supposed to put sugar on them?'

'Yes.'

'It says on the packet that you're supposed to serve them with chicken.'

'Does it?'

'Yes. I think they're meant to be savoury.'

'Not sweet?'

'No.'

'So you're not supposed to put maple syrup on them?'

'Not on the cheese-flavoured ones, no.'

Joe gives up on his poker lesson and heads off to the bathroom, while I stare guiltily at the cheesy mess on my plate. It's most unlike me to screw up a set of cooking instructions – I usually follow them to the letter. It was probably because I was trying to read a book called *Poker Farce and Poker Truth* while I was doing it. And then I became distracted by the man with the $100,000 breasts. And finding out that President Nixon financed his run for the US Congress in 1946 almost entirely out of poker winnings. And discovering that the odds of being dealt a royal flush in five-card stud are precisely 649,739 to 1.

I curl up on the sofa while Joe reacquaints himself with his dinner and the toilet bowl, and surround myself with open books and slabs of beef jerky. To begin with I flick through them randomly, pulling in facts and figures like a child opening sweet jars in a shop. The more my eyes flick over the pages the more rich and complex the game becomes.

The books are written in unfamiliar phrases, and words that I don't recognise or understand. They talk about compulsory bets called 'big blinds' and 'small blinds' and about good hands gone wrong called 'bad beats'. They describe players as tight and passive, or loose and aggressive, and a dozen other combinations I can't quite fathom. They give advice on playing against rich people, nervous people, loud people and old people; even on how to play against men with tattoos. Because poker's not a card game played with people, they say, it's a people game played with cards.

Interestingly enough, in almost five thousand pages of text they don't say anything, not even once, about setting fire to your weekly petrol money.

My favourite books are the ones that concentrate on the mathematics. The percentages and odds calm me down. I like knowing that in eight hours of poker, playing thirty-five hands an hour, I'll be dealt a pair of aces approximately 0.45 per cent of the time. I like knowing that the odds of completing my flush (five cards of the same suit) with one card left to come are approximately four to one. The people-reading skills seem to me to be mostly tips and tendencies, but the number skills are irrefutable and clean. The numbers make some sense out of the whole thing, provide me with a tangible route in.

I go back to the beginning of the first book and fetch myself something to write with. I don't hear Joe coming back from the bathroom. I don't hear him washing up or going to bed. I don't hear him call down and ask me if I'm coming up soon, I stay just exactly where I am. Lips pursed in tight concentration, index finger tucked neatly underneath my thumb. Marking out notes in the margins. And underlining the relevant passages with the edge of a soft lead pencil.

30

'So, let me get this straight. You don't want me to do any algebra this afternoon?'

'No.'

'No percentages or wanky calculus of any kind?'

'That's right.'

'We're gonna play a game instead?'

'Yes.'

'This isn't some kind of a trick, is it? Because my mum plays tricks like this on me all the time.'

'Does she?'

'Yeah. She says for me to come downstairs because she's bought me a new DVD or a David Beckham football shirt, and then it turns out I can't have it until I clean up my room.'

'I see.'

'Or have a bath.'

'Right.'

'Or paint some extra-strength Wart-Eaze on my warts.'

'Well, you have to be careful with those. They can . . . you know, spread or something.'

'I *want* them to spread.'

'Do you?'

'Yeah. I think it would be cool if I was covered in them.'

'OK. Well, I'm not going to make you have a bath or paint your warts. I just think it might be useful if we played a game.'

'Of what?'

'Cards.'

'*Cards?*'

'Yes.'

'Not a computer game?'

'No.'

'Not Doom or Doom 2 or Redneck Rampage?'

'No.'

'What about Duke Nukem?'

'Probably not.'

'No weapons of any kind?'

'None.'

'Not even . . . you know, a small pipe bomb.'

'No.'

'I knew it,' says Ryan, sulkily. 'I knew this would turn out to be some sort of a trick.'

Tomorrow night I play my first game of poker over at Big Louie's house and I've been practising for it as hard as I can. I've read all twenty-two of my books (cover to cover), played hours of mock hands with Lorna and Pete and, after both of them got bored and refused to play with me any more, I switched to playing online at www.paradisepoker.com.

I showed the website to Ryan before I left this afternoon and to my surprise he seemed quite taken with it. He was especially keen on the fact that you can play against people from all over the world, in countries as far away as Russia and the Middle East. It might seem a bit irresponsible of me to teach him how to gamble, but I'm sure it won't do him any harm. I mean, it's not like I haven't got anyone else to play with. It's not like it gave me any pleasure to practise on a kid. It's not like I enjoyed winning all three of his Korn albums off him, it's just that I thought it might help him out with his maths. This time last week he didn't even know what a percentage point was; by the end of our lesson he was calculating pot odds almost as quickly as me.

Joe has steadfastly refused to help me practise. He doesn't

even want to play tonight. It could be that he's still angry over the cheesy-grits incident, or it might be because I screwed up his plans for my birthday.

That's the other thing. This morning I turned thirty-three. I woke up looking decidedly older than I did when I went to bed, and I'm pretty sure my face had fallen a couple of centimetres in my sleep. Joe doesn't agree, but that's only because he refused to look at me from underneath. I told him the only way he'd fully appreciate the gravity of the situation was if I stood on the kitchen stool and he lay on the lino while I peered down on top of him, but for some reason he really didn't want to.

Anyway, the point is I don't want to make a fuss. I don't want to draw attention to my birthday. I know it would have been nice to go out for a meal and see a film; it might even have been nice to have a party. It's not like I didn't appreciate the necklace or the hybrid rose that he's growing especially for me, it's just that I don't want to think about it too much. It's more important that I put the hours in. It's much better that Lorna and Pete come round to drink beer and play cards, and put everything I've learned to the test.

'I don't know why you're so upset. It's not the end of the world.'

'It is.'

'You were just unlucky, that's all.'

'I told you. It's not about luck. It's about skill.'

'Well, maybe you've studied too hard. Maybe you were thinking about it too much.'

'I wasn't. That's not possible. I was thinking about it just exactly enough.'

'Look, come to bed. You only lost a couple of hands, and it's not going to do you any good, is it, sitting down here going over it and over it.'

'I can't sleep now. I'll be up in a minute. I'm just going

to reread the opening chapters of *Pot-limit for Advanced Players*. It won't take me long.'

'Audrey?'

'What?'

'Nothing . . . just . . . happy birthday.'

'What? Yeah, thanks. I won't be too long.'

'I'll leave the light on.'

'Yeah. Leave the light on. I'll definitely be up in a minute.'

31

'You're early.'

'I don't like being late.'

'By a whole hour.'

'I'm sorry. It's a thing I have. I always leave too early when I'm nervous about arriving somewhere on time.'

'What were you nervous about? I only live twenty minutes away.'

'Look, are you going to let me in or not? I can always go and sit in the car if you're not ready.'

'No. What the hell, come on in. I could use a couple of truffles before we start.'

Big Louie buzzes me into his flat and I hand over the bribes we agreed on last time we spoke. A two-pound box of cream-filled chocolates and a dozen pickled cucumbers from his favourite deli.

'What about the planters?'

'I'll bring them next week.'

'Who said you were coming back next week?'

'You did. You said if I played OK and didn't slow up the game, you'd let me come back again next Friday.'

'I said maybe,' says Big Louie, taking the chocolates and opening them. 'I said *maybe* I'd let you come back again next week.'

Big Louie has made a special effort. He's cleaned the flat from top to bottom (twice in the last hour) and dressed up in his favourite shirt. It's Hawaiian, just like the one he usually wears, but this one is coral coloured and crisply ironed. He's laid out a couple of deli trays in the kitchen – cured meats, cheeses, pitta bread and dips – and a crate of beers and lemonade on the sideboard. There's a pot of coffee ready to brew on the stove and bottles of fizzy spring water in the fridge. He's freshly shaven and splashed with lemony cologne, and he's even put plasters on his hands to cover up the scabs. He's also newly coiffed. It's the first time I've seen him without his baseball hat and I'm surprised to see he has a full head of hair. Grey and wavy and expertly combed and parted, like he's just come back from the barber's.

'You look smart,' I say, attempting a compliment.

'You look tired,' he says, grumpily.

'Well, I was up late last night playing cards. We played until one o'clock this morning.'

'Is that so? How much did you manage to lose?'

'What makes you think I lost?'

'Didn't you?'

'Yes,' I say, grudgingly. 'I lost a bit.'

Big Louie chuckles to himself, making the floorboards vibrate under his feet.

'Here,' he says, reaching behind the sofa. 'I got you somethin' that might help. You know. For your birthday or whatever.'

He pulls out a tidy package wrapped up in two layers of yesterday's newspaper, and tied with hairy green string.

'It's not like you deserve a present or nothin',' he says, fidgeting with his plasters and looking embarrassed. 'Just thought you might appreciate it, is all. I got two of 'em anyway. So it's not like it cost me anythin'.'

I can't help but be touched when I see what it is.

'Wow. A copy of *Super/System*. I've been trying to get hold of one of these everywhere.'

'Yeah, well, they're pretty hard to find. But like I said, I got two of 'em so it's no sweat. And you're thirty-three, aintcha? I figured you could do with cheering up. It's all downhill for a woman after the age of thirty. It's pretty much over, don't you think? I mean, you don't look too bad right now, but you got to know you're on the slide. On the turn, right? No disrespect.'

Big Louie holds up his hands, like the truth can't be helped, and I change the subject before he decides to insult me some more.

'Hey,' I say, putting the book into my bag, 'how's the window box looking?'

'Good,' he says, beaming at me. 'You wanna see it?'

Big Louie retreats to the safety of the kitchen while I squeeze open the window and let in a blast of early April.

'You've been watering it,' I say, looking at the newly damp-ened soil. 'That's good. You've been opening the window and watering it.'

'Yeah, well. I don't want the roots to dry out. A sniff of fresh air every once in a while ain't gonna kill me.'

'That's fantastic,' I say, turning round to face him. 'It's an achievement. Real progress. Why don't you come over here now and look at how well it's doing.'

He taps his fingers on the cabinets, cross that I'm pushing him, and eager for me to close the window back up.

'Sorry,' I say, adjusting the latch. 'That was stupid of me. I didn't mean to make you feel uncomfortable.'

'Yeah, well, one thing at a time. One thing at a time.'

'I had a few enquiries about your dad,' he says, waiting until I've sat back down again.

'You're kidding?' I say, staring up at him. 'Why didn't you let me know?'

'Well, nothing concrete yet. A few fellas think they might have played with him, that's all. What with his name being Ungar and everything.'

'Well, when? When did they say they'd played with him? Recently? In the last year? Is he in Las Vegas? Is that where

186

they're from? Is that where they said they saw him? Is he in London? Is he here?'

'Slow down. Slow down. A couple of people wanted to know if you had a picture of him is all. Something they could maybe show around.'

'Well, who are these guys?' I say, searching around for my asthma inhaler and taking a quick blast. 'Did they say he looked OK? Was he still playing cards? Was he healthy? Was he eating? Was he alright?'

'Like I said,' says Big Louie, getting irritated, 'someone who knows someone who knows someone who knows someone *maybe* thinks he knows someone who might have played with him. Could be bullshit as far as I know. Probably thought I was asking after Stu.'

My skin starts itching like it's been dipped in nettle juice and I try not to get too angry with him.

'Well, how do I find out? Can you give me their addresses? Can I phone them or e-mail them or visit them or something?'

'Look, they're not the kind of guys who like to be given the third degree. You have to take it slow with these guys. Let me have a picture of him and I'll scan it and send it over. Somebody might remember him from an old picture.'

'I don't have any pictures,' I say, clawing urgently at my cheeks. 'I don't have any pictures of my dad.'

'What do you mean? Everyone has pictures of their dad, even me.'

'I don't,' I say, feeling violently ashamed all of a sudden. 'I tore them all up.'

'Why would you go and do a thing like that?'

'I don't know. I mean, I was angry. When he didn't come back.'

'From where?'

'Because he didn't come back when my mum died. He didn't come back for her funeral.'

'She'd remarried by then, right?'

'Yes.'

'So what did you expect?'

His question takes the wind out of me and I'm not quite sure what to say.

'Look,' he says, realising that he might have upset me, 'maybe someone else has got a picture of him. Maybe your mum kept one somewhere or somethin'.'

'No. They were our photo albums that I cut up.'

'You went through all of them?'

'Yes.'

'You're sure now?'

'Yes, I think so. Unless Frank kept some pictures back.'

'Frank?'

'Her second husband.'

'Well, there you go then. That's what you should do. Maybe you should try asking him.'

There are a thousand other questions I want to ask, but the door bell rings and Louie shrugs his heavy shoulders.

'Make yourself useful and go let them in,' he says, dragging himself up and lumbering across the room. 'And remember what I told you. Don't slow up the game. Don't ask too many questions, and for Chrissakes try to look like you know what you're doing.'

'I will. Don't worry. I won't show you up.'

'And another thing,' he says, like it's doubly important. 'Don't get involved in a showdown with the guy in the brown leather jacket. It's not worth it. You hear me? That guy'll steal from you every single time.'

32

It's five minutes to midnight, I'm down fifty pounds, and I'm involved in my first proper showdown of the evening – with the guy in the brown leather jacket. It's taken me a while to get the hang of things, but I can't remember when I've enjoyed an evening more. It's completely different from playing against Joe and Lorna. Everything is far subtler and more complex. I feel like I'm back in the playground, shooting marbles on the storm drain with Gary Washbrook. I feel like I'm a kid on the pier again, watching the arcade slots spinning round and round and knowing precisely where each of them are going to stop. The only dampener on the whole evening is my poker name. I was hoping I'd get a much better poker name.

'Who are you going to be? Has Lou told you who you're going to be yet?'

A weasel-faced chemist named Sidney is topping up my drink with lemonade.

'Because we all have to have one, you know. We all have a poker name at the table.'

'Well,' I say, watching him fill my glass up until it almost overflows, 'I didn't realise. Perhaps I'll try and think of one for next time.'

'No good. No good. You ought to think of one now. Hadn't she, Louie, she'd better think of one straight away? Tell her, Lou. Tell her who she's going to be.'

Big Louie looks at Sidney like he's had just about enough of him and raises his plate-sized hands in mock despair.

'There's no one left, Sid,' he says. 'There's nobody left for her to be.'

'What about Joey Bishop? No one's been Joey Bishop yet.'

'I thought the Chinese chef was Joey Bishop,' says an Asian kid with Walkman headphones on his ears.

Big Louie nods in agreement.

'Yeah, he was. But come to think of it, he hasn't been back for a while. Not since Dean Martin cleaned him out last month. Audrey, sit down, you're gonna be Joey Bishop.'

Everyone at Big Louie's Friday night poker game is named after one of the Rat Pack. Big Louie is Frank Sinatra, the man in the brown leather jacket is Dean Martin, the Asian kid with the Walkman headphones is Peter Lawford and the retired banker with the eyepatch is Sammy Davis Jr – for obvious reasons.

There's one other woman at the table (so much for Big Louie's theory) and she gets to call herself Lauren Bacall – on account of Lauren Bacall coining the term 'Rat Pack' in the first place. Sidney, the lemonade guy, gets to be JFK (after the President), and a gay butcher from Highgate, who specialises in organic sausages, gets to be Marilyn Monroe. The last two aren't strictly Rat Pack, but it sort of fits in with the general theme.

'I don't think it's fair,' I say, hissing at Big Louie as we sit down.

'Why not?'

'Well, no one's even heard of Joey Bishop. He's the one that no one remembers. No one even knows what he did.'

'So?'

'So, if I've got a crap name I'm already at a distinct disadvantage. It's obvious Sammy, Dean or Marilyn are going to win. Why can't I be Bugsy Siegel or something? I think I'd make a good Bugsy Siegel.'

'You do?'

'Yes, or Ava Gardner or Jackie Kennedy or . . . ooh, wait, what about Humphrey Bogart? Why can't I be Humphrey Bogart?'

'Because I just told you, you're Joey Bishop. Now sit down and drink your lemonade.'

Lauren Bacall leans over and tells me that Roy, an amateur kick-boxer from Luton, is usually Humphrey Bogart, and that he's off this week with an inner ear infection. Which is making quite a lot of pus. And isn't responding to antibiotics. Big Louie tells her to shush.

'You girls finished bickering about your names yet?'

'Yes.'

'You ready to play cards?'

'Yes.'

'You're sure now?'

'We're sure.'

'Right. Let's get this summit started.'

There's plenty of good-natured banter as we sit down to play. Everyone drinks beer, eats crisps and gossips about Humphrey Bogart and his infected ear, and a few of them chew over some of last week's winning hands. The unlikely flush that Marilyn found on the 'river' card, and the big pot Dean Martin won by 'slow playing' aces. I nod and smile and try to look confused – like I don't understand what they're talking about – and they smile archly at one another like it's pay day.

Sammy Davis Jr doesn't say much. He has a nasty cough and should probably have stayed at home, but his wife wanted him out of the house. His wife says the Friday night card game is the only time she gets any peace. To catch up on her soaps. And speak to her friends. And give herself a mud pack and pedicure.

Dean Martin reckons Sammy's wife is having an affair.

191

That's why she wants him out of the house. Sammy Davis Jr doesn't think so. He says it's more likely that she's plucking the hairs out of her moles and waxing the dark roots off her top lip. By all accounts, Sammy's wife can grow a better moustache than he can.

Lauren Bacall shifts uneasily in her seat. She takes out her compact, lowers her eyes and checks her reflection in the powder-specked mirror. Sammy Davis Jr starts to laugh. And cough. He laughs and coughs and moans about the cold spring weather we're having, and spits up a glob of phlegm the size of a sugar lump. He asks the table if they want to see it and everyone politely declines. Except for Peter Lawford. Who seems oddly fascinated.

They ask me a lot of questions. Their enquiries seem fairly innocent to begin with – where do I come from, what do I do for a living, do I prefer salt beef to ham or am I vegetarian – but they soon become nosier and more intrusive. Do I have a boyfriend? What does he do? Which is my favourite London casino? For a while I think they're asking questions just to be friendly, but I soon realise they're trying to sound me out. They want to know how much money I have. If I'm rich or poor, flush or broke, if I can afford to lose to them or not.

JFK wants to know how far he can push me, so he makes a few crass jokes about women making lousy poker players and asks me if it's my time of the month. Lauren Bacall tells him he's a shit-head and starts fiddling with her 'lucky' rings, but I can tell a part of her is wondering whether I'll answer or not.

I don't rise to it. I shake my head slowly like he hasn't bothered me, and then I do something that surprises everyone. I riffle my chips together like an expert. Two neat towers shuffled into one; cleanly, coolly, in perfect symmetry. Like a poker pro who's been doing it for years. Like a poker pro who's sat at a thousand poker tables for a thousand hours and doesn't even know that he's doing it. And just like that

I'm ahead. I've sown a seed of doubt in their minds. Up until now they've presumed I'm a novice, but now they're not so sure. It means they'll all be watching me more closely, but it also means I have the advantage. They don't know what to make of me, and I plan to keep it that way.

For the first hour I don't do anything much. I fold almost every hand I'm dealt and concentrate on watching the other players. The second hour I start to play better and my patience begins to pay off. I pick up some good cards, make some astute judgements and swell my coffers by almost twenty pounds. The table can see I'm being careful and only backing good cards, but they don't push me around too much. The third hour is much less productive. I'm dealt a ragbag of bad hands – sevens and twos, tens and threes – and out of a mixture of boredom and impatience, I suddenly decide to make a stand. Fifty pounds. A big bet. The biggest single bet of the night.

Big Louie huffs and puffs. He shifts in his chair, making it creak under his bulk, and shoots me a critical glance. I look round the table nervously, waiting to see what the others will do. Every one of them folds. Except for Dean Martin – the man in the brown leather jacket.

'What are you doing?'
'A victory dance.'
'You look like you've got Parkinson's disease or somethin'. Sit yourself down for Chrissakes.'

The game's over, everyone's gone home, and I'm scooting round the room like an overexcited teenager: spilling my surplus adrenalin like milk.

'Louie, please, you've got to let me enjoy this for a moment. Did you see what I did? Did you see how well I bluffed him? It was amazing. He had no idea. I played him like an out-of-tune banjo.'

Big Louie looks disappointed in me.

'Only good thing you did all night was riffle your chips like that. Confused everybody. Made them think you were some kind of an expert.'

'I know,' I say, getting my breath back and standing still for a moment. 'I thought that would surprise them.'

'How come you can do it? Did your dad teach you?'

'No. It's just a thing I have. I'm good with my hands. I can shuffle cards pretty well too.'

'Yeah, well, I can see how you might,' he says, staring at my hands. 'You've got pretty long fingers. For a girl.'

I don't bother answering him back. I'm too excited to be cross.

'Anyway, you played like shit tonight. I thought I told you to play carefully. To watch and learn.'

'I did. I mean, I was. I added up the pot odds, and investment odds, and the percentages of every single hand. But in the end I got—'

'Bored?'

'Yes. Well. Maybe. I mean, I just wanted to take a chance. I almost didn't care if I lost or not. It felt sort of—'

'Liberating?'

'Yes. That's exactly it. It was liberating.'

Big Louie starts tidying away the plates.

'That's a dangerous mindset to get into. I told you before, you got to be patient. You were lucky tonight, that's all. It's only because it was your first time. Any other time he'd have called you. Any other time you'd have lost it all.'

My face falls a little and Big Louie registers my disappointment.

'You got to learn to pace yourself,' he says, pulling off his plasters and screwing them into a tight ball. 'I'm telling you now, he won't let you walk all over him like that again.'

'Does that mean I can come back next week?' I say, realising what he's just said.

'Yep,' he says, grudgingly. 'I guess so.'

33

I toss and turn through most of the night, feeling fidgety, aggravated and hot. Joe and I had an almighty row when I came in – about me staying out so late – and now I'm having nightmares about the way I played.

In my dreams I'm at a poker table in Las Vegas, gambling for everything I have. My relationship, my home, my money, my friends; even the clothes on my back. Dean Martin is playing against me. Not the man in the brown leather jacket, but the real Dean Martin; the one with the hooded eyes and the raven-coloured hair and the bottle of Bourbon in his hand. Frank Sinatra is sitting next to him, all louche and hard and immaculately dressed, and Bugsy Siegel is sitting there as well.

The three of them are laughing at me, joking and teasing and whispering to one another, and I'm becoming increasingly confused and impatient. My brain doesn't seem to be working right. It won't do the simplest of sums. I know the odds of making my hand on the next card are a dispiriting ten to one, but for some reason I still want to bet it. I run my fingers over my chin while I think and it feels coarse and stubbly, like my dad's. Eventually I pick up all my chips – a pile twice the length of my arm – and hear myself saying: 'Raise you all-in. I raise you everything I own.'

'What's wrong? Wake up. Are you alright?'

Joe shakes me awake like a box of coins and tells me I've been crying out in my sleep. My first thought is that I've been having sex with Bono and the Edge again, but that doesn't appear to be the case. I have sweat dripping down my cheeks and tears in the corners of my eyes and Joe says I've been shouting about river cards and singing the chorus to 'My Way'.

He fetches me a glass of water from the bathroom while I catch my breath, and gradually it begins to come back to me. Last night I made a fifty-pound bet. In the space of a second. I could have lost it all, just like that. I wasn't even thinking about what it was worth. All I was thinking about was the thrill of it. The way it made my blood fill my veins and my breath rise in my chest, and my heart beat that little bit faster.

'Are you alright?'

'Yes,' I say. 'And I'm sorry.'

'About what?' he says, stiffly.

'About last night. About staying out so late. About switching off my mobile phone and waking you up when I came in, and almost losing all of our money.'

'I thought you won?'

'I did. But I could have lost it. I could have lost over a hundred pounds.'

Joe looks at me strangely. Like he's not sure he recognises me for a moment.

'I'm sure you knew what you were doing. You never do anything without being sure.'

'Don't I?'

'No,' he says, 'you never do. You're like a barrister or something. You never ask a question you don't know the answer to.'

Joe heads off to the bathroom and leaves me sitting on my own. When he comes back, still damp and warm from his shower, I badly want to go over and hug him. I want to wrap myself up inside his towel and feel the heat from his body on my skin, but I'm pretty sure he'd just push me away. I want to tell him that I'm sorry all over again. For staying out so late and coming in so full of myself, and boring him senseless with my Rat Pack stories. Instead I say:

'What are you doing this afternoon?'

'Nothing much. I'm not working, if that's what you mean.'

'Well how about coming down to Brighton with me? I think it's about time I caught up with Frank.'

Frank's not sure he can help me. He's glad that I've come and he's relieved that I'm still talking to him, but he's not sure he has any pictures.

'Why would he?' says Margi, tersely. 'Why would Frank have kept pictures of your father?'

'No,' I say, turning towards Frank, 'I can understand why you wouldn't. It's just, well . . . I've met someone who might be able to help me find him. It'd be useful if I had a photograph. Perhaps . . . perhaps Mum kept one. Among some of her things.'

Frank looks crestfallen. His pleasure at having me here suddenly deflated like a tyre.

'I don't know,' he says, quietly. 'There might be one or tw—'

'Frank. You don't have to. You don't need to bring this up now.'

'What is it?' I say, looking from Frank to Margi and back again. 'There is one, isn't there? Frank, please . . . do you think you might have one?'

'I might,' he says, heading towards the banister. 'I might have something upstairs.'

Margi opens her mouth to object and Frank bristles and tells her to be quiet. It's the first time I've heard him speak sharply to his sister and it almost shakes me out of my seat. I spill forward, stand up and follow him dutifully to the foot of the stairs.

'Will you be alright for a while?' he says, looking at Joe apologetically.

Joe nods and says that he will.

It's been a long time since I've stood on this landing. The staircase still has a dent where I tried to scratch my initials into it with the edge of my plastic slide rule, and my room has barely been changed. It still has a solar system duvet cover on the bed and perched high up on top of the wardrobe is something I haven't seen in years. My inflatable globe.

'Wow,' I say, picking up the saggy plastic and topping it up with air. 'I can't believe you kept this. Jesus.'

Frank tuts at me for blaspheming and takes the globe from my hand.

'You spent hours with this thing,' he says, shaking his head at me, 'working out where you were going to go. Working out where your dad was. How long it would take you to get there.'

'On foot,' I say, feeling slightly awkward. 'I used to calculate how long it would take me to walk to Nevada.'

'Do you remember the answer?'

'Three hundred and twenty-seven days,' I say, without thinking. 'Assuming I walked eight hours a day at an average speed of 2.24 miles an hour.'

Frank smiles broadly.

'I think that would have tired you out somewhat.'

'Yes,' I say, smiling back at him. 'I suppose it would.'

Frank sits down on the edge of the bed and beckons for me to come over and join him. I know he's going to give me some kind of lecture, some kind of warning about trying to find my dad, but he's taking his time getting round to it.

'You were always an inquisitive child,' he says, fondly. 'Always looking for answers to things.'

'Really?' I say. 'Do you think so?'

'Yes. All the time. Always had your nose in a book.'

'Joe says I never ask a question that I don't know the answer to. He says I'm like a lawyer or something.'

'Well,' says Frank, tugging at the cuffs of his trousers, 'I'm sure that's not true. Just one of the side effects of getting older, I suppose. We all become a little more closed. When we're young we don't seem to mind if a question begets another question. As we get older we look for certainties. For truths. And I'm not sure there are very many of those.'

I fidget with the valve on my globe, wondering what he's getting at.

'Margi seemed a little upset with you,' I say, wondering if they've fallen out with one another.

'Well,' he says, cautiously, 'I think she is. She's unhappy about my not going to church.'

'Since when?'

'Not for a few weeks now,' he says, clearly troubled by saying it out loud. 'Not since . . . not since I last saw you, in fact.'

'Why would you stop going?' I say, turning round to face him. 'You haven't missed a Sunday in twenty years.'

Frank slides his hands back and forth against one another, searching for a way to explain.

'That's the problem,' he says, quietly. 'I'm not sure if it's much more than a habit. Perhaps that's what my life amounts to, Audrey. A series of tics, habits and routines. Your mother definitely thought so. She wished I'd been a little more daring, a little more adventurous, a little bit more . . . like your father.'

'I don't think that's true,' I say, wondering if it is. 'You're being much too hard on yourself.'

Frank sighs and stands up. He bends down, reaches underneath the bed and pulls out a battered yellow shoebox.

'She kept this,' he says. 'I don't think she realised that I knew about it.'

I take the box from his hands and squeeze off its tightly

sealed lid. Packed inside a layer of dusty newspaper are some things that once belonged to my dad. A button from one of his shirts, a driving glove stained black with engine oil, a birthday card signed with all his love and, at the bottom, a battered leather wallet with a broken zip.

'Look inside,' says Frank, steadily. 'Look at the pictures.'

I pull the wallet apart and gingerly reach inside. There are two photographs. One of my parents on their wedding day and one of my father at the beach, waving to someone: his hand held out high above his head.

The picture is folded in half with a crisp crease that runs the length of my father's left arm. On the other side, bent carefully behind him, is Jimmy Silk Socks; in his check jacket and his shiny shoes and his pristine white fedora hat.

'She would have cut him out of the photograph, but she didn't want to damage it,' says Frank, sitting down again. 'She blamed that man for destroying her marriage, but she didn't want to damage any part of your father. She never knew, but I stood on the landing and watched her fold it. She was sitting right where you are now, with that shoebox on her lap and a pair of scissors in her hand, but she couldn't bring herself to cut through it. She loved him so much, it killed her just to put a crease through his arm.'

Frank leans forward and wraps his hands around the tops of his knees. He looks so small. This neat, tall, upright man – in his waistcoat and his stiff collared shirt – folded up like a collapsed seaside deckchair.

'I've always thought of myself as a good person,' he says, quietly. 'Just because I went to church each week. But I wasn't, was I? I kept him away from you. I punished you. Because you reminded me of him. Of all the things I could never give to your mother.'

I can hear that Frank is talking to me, but my mind isn't processing the words. It's already somewhere far away; flooding with memories and stories and detailed images, from every line in my father's suntanned face. It's been years since I've looked at him. His conker-coloured eyes and the ripples in his cheeks and his kind, considered smile. He was already changing at this point. Becoming more fluid and distant. He'd just bought his leather coat and he'd already started going to the casinos every weekend, and this was the year they pulled apart.

'I've been feeling guilty, Audrey. About what I did. About not telling you, not passing on his letter.'

It's Frank. In the distance. Talking. I'm not sure about what.

'But I didn't want to lose you. You were all I had left of your mother. You're beautiful like her and kind like her and I was trying to protect you. At least . . . I hope I was. The twins cared about you too. They always thought of you like a sister.'

For some reason, mention of the twins punctures my thoughts and I look up from my picture for a moment.

'Did they?' I say, looking back down at it. 'They never seemed to like me very much.'

'No, no, you mustn't think that. They certainly did. They were just a little jealous of you, that's all. You were always so much cleverer than them. So much more capable. Do you remember those card tricks you used to do? The fancy shuffles, and the deals where you pulled aces out of the middle of the pack?'

'Yes,' I say. 'That was quite a difficult one. It took me years to learn how to do it.'

'They never forgave you,' he says, grinning at me all of a sudden. 'They still bring it up to this day. Every Christmas. Right before Margi serves up the pudding. Perhaps you might come one year, then you'll see.'

His words trail off and he raises his eyes and I reach round suddenly and give him a hug. I'm not sure which one of us is the more surprised, but I can't bear to see him in so much pain. At first his body is stiff and bent under my arms, but it gradually begins to relax. His shoulders fall and his arms unwind and he slowly begins to hug me back.

'I hope you find him,' he says, after a minute. 'I hope it's not too much of a disappointment after all these years.'

'Yes,' I say, holding on to him. 'I hope so too.'

'And maybe we'll see some more of you. At Easter, or at Christmas perhaps?'

'Yes,' I say. 'I'll try. And I'll give the twins a call some time.'

'Really?' he says, brightly. 'I'm sure they'd like that.'

'Yes,' I say. 'I'd like it too.'

34

Joe and I head for the beach. We spend the next hour walking along the seafront, watching the windsurfers struggle with their sails and listening as the waves crash on to the piles of damp grit and shingle. Neither of us says very much but it feels good just to be outside; with the sun spilling warmth on to our faces and a picture of my mum and dad packed safely into the front pocket of my bag. I'd always suspected that she still loved him after he left, but I never thought about how hard it must have been for Frank. To care and love and live with someone, and know that you'll never be enough for them. To realise a part of them will always be somewhere else.

We reach the start of the burnt-out West Pier and sit down on the pebbles to rest. The remains of its crumpled frame struggle out over the waves, looking skeletal, fragile and weak; like they might collapse into the sea at any minute. I take a handful of pebbles and start to count them. Working out how many there are under my feet; working out how many in the entire beach.

'How do you know if you're enough for someone?' I say, suddenly, wrapping my arm round Joe's waist.

'You're asking *me*?'

'Yes. I mean, how do you know they won't get bored or get sick, or want to leave you for somebody else . . .'

Joe pulls away from my arm and runs his fingers over the back of his neck.

'I don't know,' he says, narrowing his eyes at the waves. 'I don't think you ever do.'

'Never?'

'No. I don't think so. There's no way of being certain.'

With that he leans forward and stands up. He picks up a smooth white pebble and tosses it across the beach into the sea. I watch it skim across the waves, once, twice, three times or more, before it loses its momentum and sinks.

It wasn't the answer I was hoping for, but I suppose it serves me right. I should know better than to ask a question that I don't know the answer to.

35

We make one final stop on the way home, at the casino down by the station; the one where my father used to play. I must have walked past this building a thousand times when I was growing up, but I never felt compelled to go inside. Until now. I'm suddenly desperate to see it.

Joe waits outside in the car and I try to convince the doorman that I'm thinking of joining so he'll let me in to have a quick look around. It isn't what I was expecting. As a kid I'd imagined all casinos were full of tall women in gloves and long dresses, and David Niven lookalikes in dinner jackets and ties. I thought they'd be glamorous and vibrant and abandoned, and that everyone would be drinking champagne and smoking cigars.

This place looks more like a bookie's waiting room. It's dingy and sunless and uptight and bleak, and filled with people having the life sucked right out of them. A few crushed-up pensioners wasting their savings on roulette; a couple of tourists hunched up at the blackjack tables, making minimum bets; and a gang of lonely slot machines, gurgling away in a corner, their bulbs flicking on and off like a chain of broken Christmas-tree lights.

The decor is tired out. It's chintzy and shabby and over-wrought, and after a few minutes the carpets begin to make me feel dizzy. All yellows and oranges with slashes of green, like someone has knitted them out of vomit.

An old lady with grape-coloured nails is searching through her purse for more money. She pulls out a plastic carrier bag, and spends a long time unwrapping it and counting out her five-pound notes. A man in a clip-on bow tie swaps her money for chips and she scatters them around the roulette table like pills. Odds and evens, blacks and reds, making sure to include the birth dates of both her grandchildren.

The betting ends and a bored-looking croupier reaches down to spin the magic ball. All faces are on that tiny ball bearing. Staring at it, mumbling at it, willing it on like a secret.

The wheel gradually slows. The silver ball judders and clicks, and bounces out of one number into another. Black two. No good to anyone. No good to the grape-nailed lady. I watch her for a moment, while her face absorbs the loss, wondering what she'll do next. She shrugs, shakes her head, reaches for her purse, and starts the routine all over again.

At the rear of the casino, up on a raised platform, is what passes for the card room. This is where my father must have played. On a cluster of octagonal tables and hard-backed chairs, separated from the rest of the casino by a low wooden banister. It's hard to imagine him here. In this bowed, soulless place. With the pensioners and the tourists and the croupiers who smell of days-old sweat, and the waitresses with their tight black skirts and grubby tea trays.

It's illegal to drink alcohol while you're at the tables, so everyone is sipping hot tea and Coca-Cola. A few of them are ordering rounds of sandwiches from the bored attendants; white bread filled with thin meat and margarine, like the kind you find in motorway service stations. Almost everyone is smoking. Ivory-coloured sticks, held close to their mumbling lips, while they concentrate and curse and cross their fingers.

I sit at one of the empty card tables and run my eyes over the sunken room. I'd expected to see people smiling and laughing, but no one looks like they're having any fun. They just look depressed and grimly serious, even the odd few who are winning. Perhaps it's the time of day. Perhaps it's more lively at night. Or perhaps it's always like this: grey and hopeless and sullen.

I hang around just long enough to see Grape-nails win twenty pounds, and stop to congratulate her on the way out. She asks me if I have a lucky number, and seems most disappointed when I say that I haven't. I tell her that I'm quite keen on prime numbers, and she looks at me like I'm quite mad. 'What's a prime number?' she says, fiddling away with her plastic bag.

'Well,' I say, 'they're very interesting. It's a number that's only divisible by one and itself. Like two, three, five, seven, eleven or thirteen. The largest primes are over four million digits in length. They're discovering new ones all the time.'

'I see.'

'Of course, I'm not suggesting you bet on one of them. I was only sayin—'

'Seven's good. My granddaughter was born on the seventh. Do you think I should bet on that one again?'

I smile politely, wish her luck, and leave long before the wheel stops spinning.

I sleep most of the way home. I dream about my dad and Frank and a troop of murderous morris dancers and wake up cotton mouthed and disoriented. I spend the rest of the evening in the bedroom; looking at my pictures, preparing a couple of lesson plans, and getting increasingly maudlin.

I check my computer for e-mails but there's still not much to go on. A few people have replied to my missing-person alerts but none of them has much worth following up. I've looked up my dad's old school and left messages on Friends Reunited, but no one seems to have heard from him since he stopped teaching. I've even located the e-mail address for one of Jimmy Silk Sock's ex-girlfriends, but she hasn't heard from either of them in over a decade. Like Frank, she thinks they're probably in America somewhere, but she hasn't got any contacts who could help.

I'm just about to give up and go to bed when a new message flashes up on my screen. It's from Big Louie, and it's highlighted and headlined GOOD NEWS. This might be just what I'm looking for. Exactly what I need to cheer me up.

36

'I still don't see how you could say that was *good* news.'

'I thought you'd be happy about it. Now you get to be Sammy Davis Jr instead.'

'Louie, the man had a heart attack and died.'

'His wife had a moustache. What's the problem? He's probably glad he's dead.'

'I glare at Big Louie through my fringe but he just shrugs at me like I'm being overly sentimental.

'Plus, he had emphysema,' he says, opening the fridge to make a pre-game sandwich. 'Could barely make it over here as it was. Did you see those phlegm balls he was spitting up? All green and gnarly and pitted with blood. Jeez. What kind of a life is that for a person?'

'Some people might say the same about you. Stuck up here in your tower block; all fat and phobic, with no one to talk to. They might say you'd be better off dead.'

'Well, that's a fine way to talk to your friends. A fine way to treat your favourite poker mentor. What's got you so riled up all of a sudden? Don't tell me. It's your boyfriend, right? He's finally come to his senses and started screwing someone else?'

'Nice, Louie. That's very nice. But no, it's not about my boyfriend.'

I reach into my bag, pull out my pictures, and pass them over to my 'poker mentor'. He cleans his hands (obviously) before taking them, and spends a good while looking them over.

'That lady your mom?'

'Yes,' I say. 'It was their wedding day.'

'She's pretty. Looks a bit like you. Same red hair and sad eyes.'

'Sad eyes?'

'Yeah. Bit like Little Louie, right after I'd kicked him up the ass for farting. You kinda look like that all the time.'

'Thanks very much.'

'Don't mention it.'

'This is my dad,' I say, pointing at the beach shot. 'The other man is a friend of his. The one who got him into gambling in the first place.'

Big Louie stares at Jimmy Silk Socks for a long time, running his fingertips gently over the print.

'He always wear this hat? This white pimp's hat that he's got on his head?'

'Yes,' I say. 'How do you know?'

'Looks like the kind of man that likes to wear a hat, that's all. Your dad ever wear one?'

'No.'

'Still have all his hair last time you saw him?'

'Yes.'

'Any distinguishing marks? Boils, birthmarks, false limbs, shit like that?'

'No. Nothing. Except for his arm.'

'What about it?'

'He couldn't straighten it properly. He got into a fist fight and broke it and it never really set right. Only straightens halfway.'

'Bad debt?'

'Yes,' I say, miserably, 'I suppose so.'

Big Louie nods and asks if he can keep hold of the pictures for a while. He promises to send them right back. As soon as he's scanned them into his computer and mailed them out to all of his old contacts.

'So, what did you think of the casino?' he says, packing

my photos into an envelope. 'Did they let you in? Did they let you have a good look around?'

'Yes,' I say, taking off my coat. 'It was pretty much just like you said it would be.'

'Full of miserable people, huh?'

'Yeah. They all looked pretty depressed.'

'You know what the problem is with the English, don't you?'

I have a feeling he's just about to tell me.

'They don't know how to enjoy themselves. Hell, they're too *embarrassed* to enjoy themselves. Come to think of it, you English are embarrassed about pretty much everything. Sex, food, complaining, winning, but mostly, *mostly*, you're embarrassed about money. That's why your casinos are the way they are. They're either run-down dumps full of low-lifes and crooks, or nose-in-the-air joints with shitty dress codes and croupiers who think they're better 'an you.

'Either way, they make you feel like you don't wanna be there. Not like that in Vegas. In Vegas you can sit at a table with stains in your shorts and your belly hanging out, and as long as you got dollars in your pocket that's all that matters.'

'Really? That's good to know.'

'You English are in denial,' he says, unwrapping a couple of juicy pickles. 'You pretend you don't like the stink of money but you're all hell-bent on sniffing it just the same. You're like drug addicts, the lot of you. It's all hidden. Bound up in manners and guilt and accents and etiquette, and rules and class, and shit like that. I'll tell you somethin',' he says, squeezing the edge of a three-decker club sandwich into his mouth, 'it's all bullshit. Class don't mean nothing to a poker player. Class don't mean shit to someone like me.'

'Funny,' I say, watching a bubble of ketchup ooze up over his lips. 'I hadn't noticed.'

'You got to know what you want in this life, Ungar,' he

says, turning round and pointing his pickle at me. 'Ain't no use playing to other people's rules. Don't get nowhere in this world apologising for yourself and letting other people keep you in your place. You got to buck the system, otherwise it'll suck you in and swallow you right up. If you don't take in this life, you don't get. You see what I'm saying?'

Big Louie rambles on. About our lousy weather, our archaic gaming laws, our lousy service and our crummy English teeth. He's in full flow now. He informs me that the English are a nation of pussies and moaners, and he's halfway through telling me how we'd all have been Nazis if it wasn't for the Americans when I finally sense my chance to interrupt.

'Why don't you go back, then?' I say, as he breaks for a bite of his sandwich. 'If you like it so much back in the States, what are you still doing over here?'

Big Louie smiles the widest smile. Like it might swallow up his entire face. He laces his fingers together, wraps them behind the crown of his bulbous head, and lets out a self-satisfied sigh.

'Funny you should say that,' he says, tapping his nose, conspiratorially. 'Things might be about to change around here. Who knows? Maybe I've been shut up inside this dump for long enough.'

Despite repeated attempts, he refuses to be drawn on the matter, and one by one the other Friday-nighters start to arrive. Dean, Marilyn, Lauren and JFK, but this week no Sammy Davis Jr.

On my insistence, Big Louie begins the evening with a short tribute. We drink a toast of gin and Dr Pepper (Sammy's favourite drink) and he talks about Sammy's contribution to the game. Everyone remembers him as being a gracious player. Even though he lost almost every week. And never seemed to know what anyone else was holding. And always screwed it up by saying 'That's it, guys, I've got you over a barrel now', every single time he had something good. Still, at least no one mentions his wife's moustache. Except for Big Louie. Who wants to know whether anyone actually saw it.

After a brief debate and a quick show of hands, it's agreed that I should take over as Sammy Davis Jr. I suggest that we wait a couple of weeks – out of respect – but JFK says it's what he would have wanted. With that settled, we drink a final toast and Big Louie splits open a brand-new deck of cards. Last week he dealt for most of the night, but this time he wants the dealing duties to move round the table. His hands are hurting him – he has more plasters showing than skin – and the first deal of the night falls to me.

I pick up the deck – fresh, stiff and clean out of the cellophane – and execute a perfect riffle shuffle. Big Louie can do it almost as well, but I'm neater and quicker and more precise. I concentrate hard as I do it. Running things over in my mind. This time I won't get bored. This time I won't be so rash. I'll be patient and calculated and logical and calm and I'll make use of everything I've learned. From staying up every night of the week. And rereading every one of my books. Over and over and over again.

'Well?'

'Well what?'

'I'm pretty good. Aren't I? Admit it. I'm not a bad player.'

'You're OK. For a *girl*.'

'Come on, admit it. I played well tonight. Didn't I? I did alright.'

'You weren't so bad,' he says, frowning at me and picking up a wash cloth. 'But if you want me to go over the rights and wrongs of what you did, you might as well make yourself useful. Here, grab yourself a sponge and a bucket. There's a fresh tub of bleach under the sink.'

We clean up the mess together, just the two of us. Scrubbing the surfaces, mopping the floors and grinding away the grease marks on the poker table. I'm not sure which one of us is finding it the more satisfying, especially when Big Louie breaks into a quick rendition of 'New York, New York' and suggests that I join in with him on the chorus.

'You did OK,' he says, pulling off his rubber gloves and scratching at his bloody palms with a wire nail brush. 'When you took Dean Martin down with those trip queens, he was as pissed as I've ever seen him. But you had great cards. You were on a rush. Only an idiot could have screwed up cards like that.'

'Ah, yes, but did you notice how I varied my play? Did you notice how I played tight for an hour then loose for an hour then—'

'Yeah, what d'you take me for? Of course I noticed. You did good. You paid attention. You were patient this time. You didn't over-play your hands.'

'And I watched their faces. Did you see how I watched all their faces?'

'Yup. But I've been meaning to talk to you about that. You might want to think about being more subtle. You're not meant to lean over the table and eyeball them for ten minutes face to face, with your chin in your hands.'

'But it's good, right? It's the right kind of thing to do?'

'Yeah. I guess so. I mean, the rest of the idiots don't know how to concentrate. They just chatter and gossip and eat and get cranky, but they don't realise you got to be paying attention. All the time. Even after you fold. Even when you're not playing the hand, you got to be watching and learning and concentrating. Every second of the game.'

We pack away the last of the plates, and after a quick antibacterial wipe-down Big Louie sighs and says that we're done. And then I ask him the question, the one I've been wanting to ask him all night.

'I don't get it,' I say, peeling off my apron. 'I mean, I could be wrong, but it always seems to me like you're holding back.

Like you know you could win whenever you wanted to, but you don't want to push anyone around.'

'Nope,' says Big Louie, yawning at me, 'I just try to break even. Only seems fair.'

'Why? I thought the idea was to win. You told me, first rule of poker, never give a sucker an even break.'

'But this is the remedial class. No point in screwing up the rookies. I want them to graduate. Wait till they go up to the big game. *Then* I'll start stealing their money off 'em.'

'What do you mean?' I say, buttoning up my coat. 'I thought these were your very best players? I thought everyone was going to the World Series next month, that Dean Martin was the best player you'd ever taught?'

Big Louie lets out a hoot of contempt.

'You're kidding me, right? You thought that was the best I got? Shit, that kid couldn't bluff his own grandma. No, these are the beginners. I thought I'd start you off easy.'

This upsets me more than it should. If I thought about what he was saying I'd be grateful, but I'm not. I'm far too competitive for that.

'But you said I could play in a real game. For real money. Alongside your hotshot freaky kid.'

'You think you're ready?'

'Yes. I do.'

'Two games in the remedial class and a few lucky hands and you think you're ready to dance with the big boys?'

'Why not?'

'Because you'll lose, idiot.'

'How do you know?'

'Because you ain't up to it yet. What? Just coz you read *Super/System* a couple of times and you got a head for math, you think you're gonna turn up on Saturday night and beat 'em? I'm telling you. They'll eat you alive.'

'Saturday night? You mean tomorrow?'

'I'm warning you, Ungar. You don't wanna go there.'

'Why don't you let me try?'

'I mean it. You don't wanna get involved.'

I put my hands in my pockets and sulk. Until he can't stand it any more.

'OK then, big-shot. You got a spare thousand pounds under your mattress?'

'Um . . . one thousand . . . yes. Why not?'

'You'll need at least that much to sit down with us. You think you can handle that kind of action?'

'Um . . . yes?'

'OK. So come then. I ain't gonna stop you. If you want to shoot yourself in the foot go right ahead. One thing though, you gotta make sure—'

'I know. I know. Keep quiet, don't show you up, try to look like I know what I'm doing, and never, under any circumstances, slow up the game.'

'Exactly.'

'So I can come back tomorrow?'

'It's your funeral, Sammy Davis. Your funeral.'

37

Big Louie is right. This is like a funeral. No one is talking, no one's touched the finger buffet, and a man in a black gabardine suit that looks at least two sizes too big for him has just asked if he can pull the curtains closed. His name is Bob and he's a funeral director. He smells of embalming fluid, toothpaste and cigarettes, and he has a thick pad of soap scum wedged at the base of his fingernails. Next to Bob is an overweight Lebanese man called Rabih, and next to him a dirt bike enthusiast called Patrick. He's wearing jeans and leather boots and a T-shirt that says *motherf**ker* on the front, and has reddened skin that's vicious with razor-rash and pock marks.

Next to Patrick is Hamish, the 'resting' actor. It's a cold evening, but he appears to be wearing pyjama bottoms instead of trousers, and he has a pair of open-toed Jesus-creeper sandals falling off his long-toed feet. To his right is a retired bookie, a heavy-set man called Keith Sharp, and next to Big Louie – wearing mirrored sunglasses and a baseball cap – the freaky, hotshot, super-duper talented kid.

As usual, I arrived long before anyone else. I dropped Joe off at Lorna's flat – we were both meant to be going over there for dinner – and drove over here as fast as I could. Louie had kindly agreed to help me out with some advance research before the game, and he took it as slowly as he could.

'OK,' he said, wheezing through the layers of his salt beef sandwich. 'Now Patrick, he likes to play hardball. He'll raise you with nothing, but just when you think he's bluffing he'll lay down the stone-cold nuts. Rabih might like to bust your balls a little. Keith too, but the way I figure it, the more they try to rile you, the more they got something to hide. Just don't let them get inside your head. You'll be dead and buried the moment you do.'

'Right . . . I see.'

'And you know the maximum bet is three hundred pounds, right?'

'Yes. I do.'

'So you're all set, then?'

'I think so.'

'Nervous?'

'A little bit. And Louie?'

'What now?'

'Which one is he? Which one's the hotshot kid?'

'Name's Karl. He'll be wearing dark glasses and a lucky green shirt.'

'Anything else?'

'Yeah. He likes to make balloon animals while he plays. It's a good trick. Puts the other players off. Gets 'em so aggravated they forget what it is they're meant to be doing.'

'That's the door bell,' I said, straightening up suddenly. 'Should I get it?'

'It's your choice. You can leave right now if you want to. I won't think any less of you.'

'Is that possible?'

'Not really, no.'

'Then I'll stay.'

These people are impossible to read. I've done my chip-riffling routine and shown them all my very best shuffle, but no one looks remotely impressed. They don't talk to me or offer me their cigarettes and nobody asks me any questions. I was hoping I'd get to quiz them about the British poker scene and tell them a little bit about my dad, but I'm not sure any of them would be all that interested.

They might not be saying very much, but that doesn't stop them observing everything I do. From underneath their cards, through a soft veil of cigarette smoke, from the corner of a bespectacled eye. Even Big Louie is watching me, because tonight he's actually playing.

He really is brutal to watch. He's reraised by the maximum three hands in a row, and each time the whole table folded. He looks bigger than ever tonight; upright and firm and larger than life, goading the other players with his low, liquorice voice. And it's not because he's nervous. When he calls Bob Dr Death and tells Keith he's got 'shit stripes' in his pants, it's not because he's hiding something – it's because he means it.

He refers to me as 'the idiot' for the first hour and a half of the game. 'What you got, idiot? What you holding, idiot? What's the idiot doing raising with rags?'

It makes me fidget more than I ought to, but in truth I'm not all that upset by what he says. I know he's only doing it to toughen me up; to see whether I can take it and to let me show the others that I can. What was it he said? That you have to see right inside your opponents' souls. That you have to get to know them – their strengths, their weaknesses, their ambitions, their regrets – better than you know your own wife. And so I do. I watch them and study them and sit as tight as I can, and make up a potted history for each and every one of them.

It's an hour and a half later and everything has shifted; none of them scares me any more. I know Bob fantasises about having sex with his corpses before he buries them and that Rabih owes a ton of money to the bank. I know Hamish wants the whole world to love him and that that's the thing that's making him weak. Patrick thinks he's a rebel. His girlfriend likes it when he sends food back in restaurants and he likes to ride his motorbike without a helmet. It makes him feel good, like he's challenging the natural order of things. So he calls every time: even when he suspects other people of holding superior cards. He can't help himself. As long as he lives, he'll always want to try beating aces with tens.

The process of analysing my opponents calms me down and I gradually settle into a pattern. After two hours of watching and concentrating, and obsessive self-control, I finally begin to play them back. I don't think about my cards, I think about theirs. I don't think about the money, I think about winning. Because I know I can beat them. Beyond any reasonable doubt. From the moment I watched those dozen legs swish back and forth across the kitchen lino at my dad's house, I've always known that I could win.

'Don't dwell on it,' says Big Louie, matter-of-factly, 'it'll only make you feel worse.'

'How can you tell me not to dwell on it? How can you sit there and say don't dwell?'

'It was a bad beat, is all. That's what happens. The odds don't always work out the way you expect them to. Sometimes the universe throws you a curve ball. Stop whining and put it down to experience.'

'I didn't have to bet it though, did I? I didn't have to put up everything I had left?'

'Well. No. That was bad. That was definitely the wrong way to go.'

I run my hand over my empty pocket and try to work out what I did wrong. It was all going so well. I won three small pots, one after the other; I even took some money off the Hotshot Kid. And it pissed him off. I know it did. I totally out-played him. I took down his two pairs with three sevens and he never once suspected what I had. And then I saw a chance to finish him off for good, with his aggravating balloon animals and his eighties mirrored sunglasses and his lucky flush that he was never going to fill.

'But I knew he was looking for a flush,' I say, holding my head in my hands. 'I raised him all-in with three kings and he knew I wasn't bluffing. I don't get it. Why would he stay in the hand? Why would he stay in against three kings with a four-to-one shot?'

'Because he's got balls,' says Big Louie, fidgeting in his seat. 'Because he's got courage and instinct; that something extra you'll never have.'

I shake my head. I'm still not buying it.

'I don't know, Louie,' I say, walking towards the window. 'It doesn't make sense. I went over it a thousand times, I covered all the angles. I played that hand exactly like I should.'

'You think so?'

'Yes, I do.'

'You don't think you let him get the better of you? You don't think he out-figured you somewhere along the line?'

'No. I don't see what else I could have done. It's like . . . it's almost like he knew that he was going to win. Like he knew that diamond was coming out on the last card.'

Big Louie doesn't say anything, he just huffs and puffs and begins to wheeze like a steam train.

'Now you're talking like an idiot,' he says, crossly, dragging himself out of his chair. 'I told you, didn't I? Sometimes you'll miss something and get outmanoeuvred. Sometimes the math don't add up. It's always gonna fox you every once in a while; it's how you deal with it when it happens that counts. I told you that the second time we met. The mark of a great player is how he copes with his losses. You got to be able to accept it, learn from it, absorb it; you got to figure the law of averages will be on your side next time.'

'But Louie . . . I lost it all.'

'Yeah, I guess you did.'

'Everything I came with.'

'That's how it goes.'

'One thousand pounds.'

'Yep. One thousand pounds.'

I stand there with my hands in my empty pockets, staring out of the window into the gloom. There's a plane circling high in the distance and a small bonfire burning on a patch of wasteland beyond the station. A raindrop is snaking its way down the window pane and I watch it squirm erratically round the latch and down towards the window box at the bottom.

'Louie, quick, come over here for a second.'

'I'm busy. I got plates to clean.'

'I'm serious. Come over here for a moment.'

'What is it?'

'It's your lavender.'

'What about it?'

'It's budding, Louie. It's starting to bloom.'

He starts slowly, inching across the floor like it's covered in broken glass and he's only got stockings on his feet. He stops three times on the way – once to mop his brow, once to clean his hands, and once for a cup of warm water. It takes him the best part of a minute to reach me.

He opens the window a fraction at a time, wincing as the fresh air swamps his face. And then he sniffs, drawing his nose through the air like a butterfly net, eager to catch the first atoms of purple scent. He rests there just long enough to see it – a small bud of lavender piercing through the woody stem like the edge of a fine glass button. And then he leaves. Turning his head as fast as he can and pulling the window towards him like a shield.

'I'm sorry,' I say, watching him scoot back to the kitchen to clean his cup, 'I shouldn't have asked you to look.'

'No,' he says. 'It's getting easier. It's definitely getting a little easier.'

38

Last night something rather disturbing happened. I dreamt I was having sex with three world-class poker players: Johnny Chan, Amarillo Slim and an Englishman called Barney Boatman. Thankfully, I can't remember too many of the details, but I know we were doing it on a giant green baize card table. In a casino. Being watched by a crowd of old-aged pensioners. Who all had curly, grape-coloured fingernails and chronic emphysema. Some of them were clapping. Some of them were cheering us on. A few of them were making wonky balloon animals while they watched.

'You look tired. Didn't you sleep well?'

'No . . . um . . . I did . . . I just, you know, bad dreams or something.'

'Barry and the Reg?'

'Huh? Oh, no. What are you talking about?'

'Well, who was it this time? Brad Pitt? Russell Crowe?'

'No, see, that upsets me. It upsets me that you would say that. Who in their right mind could find Russell Crowe attractive? He looks like your fat uncle.'

'I don't have a fat uncle.'

'You know what I mean, the kind of uncle who gets drunk at weddings and makes a show of himself. The kind that looks like he has athlete's foot and underpants with skid marks down the middle of them.'

'You've thought about this quite a lot, then?'

'Yes. Lorna fancies Russell Crowe.'

'Does she?'

'What can I tell you? She's sick.'

'So who were you thinking about?'

'Um . . . when?'

'Last night. When you were lying there tossing and turning and sweating and shouting, "All-in, go all-in!"'

'*Yeuch.* Um, Joe?'

'Yes?'

'Have you showered yet?'

'No.'

'Do you mind if I go first?'

I don't know what's wrong with me. This game is taking over my life. I'm thinking about it, talking about it, reading about it, teaching it and dreaming about it every single night. And now it's turning me into something I don't like very much. It's turning me into a liar.

'How much did you win?' says Joe, pouring out a bowl of cornflakes.

'I didn't,' I say, drying my hair off with a towel. 'I, um . . . lost. A bit.'

'How much?'

'Not too much. Just . . . a couple of hundred pounds.'

'You lost *two* hundred pounds? In one night? What the fuck were you thinking?'

'I know, I know. I made a mistake. I went all-in against this freaky balloon-animal kid who was on a flush draw and the thing is . . .'

'Balloon animals? What the hell are you talking about?'

'He makes them while he plays. To distract the other players. He makes rabbits that look like poodles and poodles that look like giraffes and . . .'

'Like Meg's magician?'

'Sorry?'

'Like Meg's magician. She said the magician at her party made balloon dogs that looked like chickens.'

'Yes, well, quite possibly. Anyway, the thing is, the point I was trying to make, is that I was very unlucky.'

'Unlucky?'

'Yes. Supremely.'

'I thought you said it was all about skill?'

'It is. In the long term. But sometimes the odds flip on their head. Sometimes you can't control every aspec— *Shit*.'

'What?'

'Do you think he was a magician?'

'Who?'

'The balloon guy. The guy that stole off me. The dick-head who wound me up all night long and walked away with my one thousand pounds. That's typical. Of all the people it could have been. Of all the people in the world to rip me off, it had to be a frigging magician. All my life, wherever I go, I'm plagued by lunatic magician—'

'A *thousand pounds!*'

'No.'

'That's what you just said.'

'No I didn't.'

'I heard you. You just said one thousand pounds.'

'No . . . I didn't.'

'You did. Audrey, for fuck's sake, how much did you lose last night?'

Joe isn't talking to me any more. I appreciate that he wanted me to stay home and discuss my going to counselling, and I appreciate the way he called up my friends and asked them to come straight over. It's not like I didn't want to talk to Lorna and Pete. It's just that I can see them any time. It's not like I crept out of the house moments before they arrived and sped away in the car, making the wheels screech. It's just that I've got things to do. I've got gambling shops to visit and libraries to tour and I have a very important appointment to keep. With two people I don't visit nearly often enough. My beloved stepbrothers, Larry and Paul.

'Wow, nice bungalow.'

'Do you like it?'

'Yes, it's very . . . *neat*. And, goodness, you guys have a lot of *Men's Health* magazines.'

'Yeah. We love it. All those pictures. Of big men. With super-toned bodies. We've been collecting them for years.'

'Right. Good. I see.'

The two of them glance at one another. They were a little surprised to see me today, but they think they know why I've come. I told them I had something important to ask, and they think they've worked out what it is.

'Audrey?'

'Yup?'

'You know we're both gay, right?'

'Yes.'

'It's not like it's any kind of surprise?'

'No.'

'So . . . well, how long have you known?'

'Pretty much always.'

'Always?'

'Since we were kids, I suppose.'

'What gave it away?'

'You know, there were the odd indicators here and there.'

'Was it because Larry bought *The Sound of Music* sound-track?'

'No.'

'Was it because we used to wait in all night in case the Blue Stratos ad came on the TV?'

'No.'

'Was it because we went to see Take That seventeen times?'

'No.'

'Well what was it then? The spangly trousers? The doves? The brief dalliance with moustaches?'

'Nope. Not really. It's just that neither of you fancied any of the girls at school. Lorna said you once turned down the offer of a double-handed hand-job from Hailey Foster, and right around then I realised you probably preferred boys.'

'Hailey Foster?'

'Yes. You remember, the girl in my chemistry class with the lazy eye. We used to call her Ski Sunday because she could jerk off two boys simultaneously. She sort of looked like she was holding skiing poles. Anyway, no one passed up the offer of one of those double-whammy hand-jobs, they were legendary. If you were lucky enough to be offered, you didn't say no.'

I sit there looking all pleased with myself while Larry and Paul stare at me, open mouthed.

'Audrey?'

'Yup.'

'Why did you never let on? If you knew about us all this time, why did you never say anything?'

'I don't know,' I say, taking a sip of my tea. 'I was too wrapped up in my own stuff, I suppose. Mum going, my dad leaving. I'm sorry. I didn't mean to make you feel bad.'

'You didn't,' says Larry, offering me a Wagon Wheel. 'It was just weird, that's all. We never knew where we stood with you.'

'Why didn't you tell me yourselves? I wouldn't have said anything to Frank or Margi.'

'Are you sure about that?'

'Of course not. There's no way.'

'Not even to pay us back for all those times we made you put a colander on your head?'

'Hmm, well . . . maybe.'

* * *

With everything out in the open, the three of us finally begin to connect. We reminisce about Frank and his broad beans and his hair pomade, and about the way he still refuses to let anyone sit in his favourite leather chair. We talk about my breaking the TV set and about what a swot I was, and all about my obsession with maths and numbers. It seems that Frank was right. It annoyed the twins that people thought I was going to grow up to be some kind of genius, and it frustrated them when I tried to get in on their act and master their tricks. Magic had become their own means of identity and escape, and they humiliated me as a way of keeping it for themselves.

We chat easily for the rest of the evening. We drink more tea, talk fondly about my mum, and after they've shown me pictures of their respective boyfriends I finally get round to explaining the real purpose of my visit. They couldn't be more helpful. They relish the fact that they know more about something than I do, and we spend the next couple of hours swapping information and teaching one another what we know. I can't help wishing I'd got to know them better when we were kids. In the midst of all that loneliness and chaos, it would have been good to think I had brothers. To feel like I had some allies against it all.

'Maybe it's time that you told him,' I say, packing up the books they've given me and loading them into the car.

'We think he knows,' they say, in unison. 'He doesn't want to confront it, that's all.'

'Are you sure? I mean, he seems to be relaxing a bit. He gave me a hug the other day.'

'Did he?'

'Well . . . I hugged him and he hugged me back.'

The twins say that wonders will never cease, but that they don't think Frank's ready for twin homosexual sons just yet.

'OK,' I say, kissing them both goodbye. 'But you'd better be careful. Because if either of you even *think* about putting my head in a colander again . . .'

'Don't worry,' they say. 'We won't have to. We've just hired a brand-new assistant.'

'Right,' I say, smiling back at them. 'And don't tell me. I bet she's somebody really glamorous.'

Joe is fast asleep when I get home. I can tell he's tried to stay awake, because the lights are still on in the bedroom and the radio's still playing beside the bed. I turn off the radio and the lights and creep downstairs as quietly as I can. I grab a pillow and some spare blankets from the airing cupboard, curl up on the sofa, and dive into the books that I've borrowed from the twins. I read and reread them and mark off important sections with my pencil. I study the diagrams, copy the hand positions and crack open a brand-new set of cards.

It takes me a while to get the hang of it. I shuffle them and riffle them and manipulate them again and again, until I feel my fingers beginning to stretch and loosen. And suddenly the stiff-backed cards are flying, like each one is coated with a film of oil. I have control over every single one of them. I can make them go anywhere I want. You'd almost think you were imagining it: you'd almost think it was magic.

I fall asleep hours later, when my hands are too sore to shuffle any more. I have blisters on my palms and playing cards scattered across my chest and my fingernails are broken and badly chipped. My wrists are stiff and my knuckles are aching, but I think I've begun to break the back of it. Tonight I began to learn a new trade. And, if everything goes to plan, by this time next week I'll be a fully qualified *mechanic*.

39

'Hello, Audrey?'

'Yes.'

'This is Lynne Thomas. Ryan's mother.'

'Oh, hello, Lynne. How are you?'

'Highly irrational, according to you. But that's not why I'm calling.'

'Oh. I see.'

'It seems you've been teaching my son a few tricks.'

'Tricks?'

'Gambling tricks.'

'Ah. Well, no, I just . . .'

'Have you or have you not been teaching my son the rudiments of playing poker?'

'Yes, but—'

'Have you or have you not been recommending that he goes online and plays Texas Hold'em on a sight called Paradise Poker?'

'Yes, but—'

'He's lost two hundred pounds.'

'Goodness.'

'Of my money. On my American Express card. And I've got fifteen hundred owing on it as it is.'

'Look, Lynne . . . um . . . Mrs Thomas, I'm very sorry. I only told him to go on the play money tables. I said on no account was he to try gambling for real mon—'

'You do know I could have you arrested, don't you? You do know I could have your licence taken away?'

'Yes, well, I'm not sure it needs to be a police matter. And I don't have a licence as such, it's more like a—'

'That's not the point. The point is, what are you going to do about all the money I've lost? How am I supposed to get it back now?'

'Well, I'm not sure. Perhaps you could get in touch with the website. If you explained what happened they might think about refund—'

'Don't be ridiculous. I'll never get a penny of that money back. How am I going to afford to buy David Beckham Pepsi now? How am I going to afford to buy Ryan his book on euphoniums.'

'Euphoniums? I didn't know Ryan was musical.'

'He's not. Euphoniums is a radioactive material.'

'Ah. You mean *plutonium*.'

'That's what I just said, didn't I?'

'Erm . . . yes. You're right. God, I'm so sorry. I'll get the money back for you right away.'

'You *will*?'

'Yes. Absolutely.'

'Well . . . that's OK then. Because, you have to admit . . . it is all your fault.'

'I know.'

'You did lead him astray.'

'Yes, I did.'

'So you'll sort it all out?'

'Yes, I promise.'

'Good.'

'Good.'

'Still, I'll tell you something for nothing. It's a right funny old website.'

'How so, Mrs Thomas?'

'Well, you can play cards with people from all over the world. Last night Ryan says he played against someone who lives in Kabul.'

'In *Afghanistan*?'

'Yeah. I think so.'

'Mrs Thomas?'

'Yes.'

'Is he . . . is Ryan still playing?'

'No. I told him he wasn't allowed.'

'Good. Good. It's just that . . . I mean I don't want to scare you or anything, but you might just want to make sure.'

'Why?'

'Well. I don't know quite how to put this. But have you ever heard of a game called Duke Nukem?'

By the time I get off the phone with Ryan's mother it's already seven o'clock. I'm due at Big Louie's by half past, and I can't find my car keys anywhere. I've searched the entire flat. Underneath the sofa, at the bottom of the laundry basket; I've even tried looking in the oven. Joe is refusing to help me search. That's because he's still barely talking to me.

It's been a long and difficult week. Joe's been working late every night, Lorna's been leaving messages every day, and even Pete has taken to popping round unannounced and offering me his unique brand of advice. They're all worried about me. They think I'm going to do something stupid; that I've become obsessive, erratic, distant and withdrawn, and that I might be on the edge of some sort of a nervous breakdown.

It hasn't helped that I've been studying so hard. I've been up until midnight almost every night; cutting and culling and crimping and dealing, and learning how to manipulate the deck. I'm good at it. Even better than I thought I would be. Most of the moves are variations on sleight-of-hand tricks that I already knew, and I was surprised at how quickly it all came back to me. I'm pretty sure I'll be able to spot anything underhand at tonight's game, just so long as Balloon Boy gets to deal again. I can't bear the idea that Big Louie's been getting ripped off all this time, but there isn't a shred of doubt in my mind. The twins confirmed all my suspicions. Balloon Boy is a cheat. A fully fledged card-sharp. A 'mechanic'.

As soon as I was sure I had it mastered, I went to the bank and withdrew another chunk of savings from my account. Joe went ballistic when he found out. He even threatened to call up Frank and the twins. Things got so bad that at one point he threatened to cut up my cash card with his shears. I promised him I wasn't going to lose again. I told him I had a failsafe plan. I promised I was going to win back everything I lost, but for some reason he still won't believe me.

'You've hidden them, haven't you?'

'Don't be stupid, of course I haven't.'

'Joe, please. Just tell me where they are.'

He sighs one more time, rubs his hand over his forehead and walks resignedly towards the kitchen.

'The icebox? You buried my car keys in the *icebox*?'

'Pretty good, eh? Bet you'd never have guessed.'

He's trying to make light of it, but I'm not in the mood, and I start hacking at the ice with a fork.

'Don't go over there tonight,' he says, reaching for my arm. 'The pair of us . . . we should talk.'

'I have to,' I say, chipping away at the ice block. 'I have to try and win back what I lost.'

'But it's crazy. You've lost enough money as it is.'

'Look, just let me try and get back what I'm owed. I've been practising hard all week. I'm pretty sure I can do it. I just need to go over there one more time.'

'And then you'll stop?'

'I . . . yes . . . probably.'

'Probably?'

'Well, I mean, I might have to play a couple more games after that. I'll need some extra to pay back Ryan's mum.'

Joe shakes his head and walks away and I stuff my frozen car keys into my pocket.

'What is it you're trying to prove?' he says, staring back at me. 'That you're capable of destroying yourself? Like your dad?'

'That's not fair,' I say, glaring at him.

'Isn't it?'

'No Joe, it's not. I have to go over there tonight. I told you. There's something I need to find out.'

'About what?'

'You wouldn't understand.'

'No,' he says, turning away from me. 'I don't suppose I would.'

40

'You're late.'

'I know. I'm sorry. I had a lot of trouble getting away. Joe didn't want me to come tonight and then the phone rang just as I was leaving and—'

'I told you to get here early, didn't I?'

'Yes.'

'I told you I had something to say.'

'I know. But we can talk after the game. We'll have time after the game, won't we?'

'Yeah . . . I suppose so.'

'Louie?'

'What?'

'Who's dealing tonight?'

'Dealing?'

'The cards. Who's going to be dealing?'

'Why do you care?'

'No reason, I was just wondering. Is it going to be Balloon Boy again?'

'What you so concerned about? You want to deal tonight, is that it?'

'No. I just thought, you know, it might be better if we took turns. Like we did in the last Rat Pack game.'

'You don't like the way he deals?'

'No, it's not that, it's jus—'

'Fine then, we'll take turns. See if I care. See if it makes an ounce of difference to me.'

'There's no need to get upset.'

'Who's getting upset? What the hell make's you think I'm upset?'

Big Louie decides to take the first turn. He's fine for the first dozen hands or so, but I can tell that his fingers are starting to bother him. They're as swollen as I've ever seen them and the sharp edges of the cards keep biting into his raw patches and cuts. Every now and again a card slips out of his fingers and he has to collect them all up and start again. After he messes two hands in a row, Balloon Boy reaches over and offers to take the pack.

'Anyone mind?' he says, lowering his mirrored sunglasses for a moment.

No one does. Especially not me.

For the next half-hour I don't spot anything untoward. He executes perfect shuffles and squeaky-clean deals, and the game proceeds exactly as it should. My play has come on from last week, and I'm slowly beginning to get the measure of them. I play a calculated and careful game. I pocket a hundred pounds from Hamish, another two from Patrick, and I even take some small change off Balloon Boy. Rabih wins a monster hand from Dr Death, which cheers everybody up, and Big Louie relaxes and goes back to pushing everyone around.

And then it starts. Just when everyone's getting comfortable.

The first thing he changes is the way he holds the pack. He uses the classic mechanic's grip: the meat of his palm obscuring the deck, instead of supporting it from underneath. He starts off slowly; dealing off the bottom, putting a crimp in the pack when he offers it up to be cut, and peeking at the top cards when he shuffles. As his confidence grows, he begins to employ some more complicated moves. He starts to stack the deck.

It's a skilful manoeuvre. He begins by collecting up (or culling) the discards from the previous hand and arranging them so he knows their precise order. After that he begins to distribute them through the pack, using a series of complicated shuffles. A good mechanic can place a long series of cards in any order he likes. The idea is to deal a good hand to one or two of the other players and an even better hand to himself. That way there'll be a lot of betting. He doesn't want people to fold, he wants them to stay with him all the way to the last card. Because he always knows what the last card is going to be; it's going to be another club to fill his flush draw or a king to complete his straight, or a seven to give him a fluky four of a kind.

The first time I spot him doing it, I have to stop myself standing up and yelling 'Cheat'. He deals a pair of jacks to Rabih, a pair of queens to Dr Death and the flop gives them both three of a kind. The betting is escalating out of control, but Balloon Boy is calling instead of raising. He wants them to make all the running. He wants them to think he's chasing a wild piece of luck, that he's just going along for the ride. But it's not luck. The final card brings him a full house, just like he always knew it would.

At this point I close down my own play completely. I can't concentrate on watching and play well at the same time, so I try to look like I'm just sitting tight for a while. The other players presume my nerve's gone and Big Louie goes back to calling me 'the idiot'. It doesn't bother me. I need to see if he'll do it again. I need to know for sure that it wasn't a fluke.

I'm careful about observing him, and I only glance up when I don't think he can see me. When he's looking at his cards or taking a sip of his drink, or blowing air into another of his long red balloons. He takes his time – moulding the rubber into stumpy, distorted creatures – and I notice that he repositions them right before he deals. It's classic misdirection – magicians do it all the time. The others are shaking their heads and grinning at his latest lunatic creation and nobody is watching him deal. Except for me: I'm watching every move he makes.

The second time he does it, it's more obvious. I spot the crimp in the deck when he offers it up to be cut and I notice a telltale hanging card protruding from the pack when he deals off the bottom. His hands let him down; they don't move quickly enough. When you're engaged in sleight of hand it has to be instinctive, fluid, second nature; he's clearly thinking about it too much.

And just like that, he mucks it up. He meant to deal a tempting hand to Patrick and another to Keith Sharp and an even better one to himself. And now he's furious because he's messed up the shuffle. He's given Patrick and Keith two pairs but he planned to win the hand himself with three eights.

I know what he's thinking. He's wondering where that four of clubs came from. He's wondering where he put his third eight. It should have been the next card out. He made a two-hundred-pound bet and now he's lost it all, just because his fingers were too slow.

'You mind if we take a minute?' he says, tossing his cards across the table. 'I've got to take a big shit.'

No one minds. Keith and Patrick battle it out over their pairs and Big Louie sighs heavily in his seat.

He's beginning to look uncomfortable. He's fiddling with his plasters and counting his chips, and his eyes are glued to the debris around the table. Mostly when we play, he doesn't seem to mind the mess, but tonight he's clearly bothered by it. He pulls an antibacterial wash cloth out of his pocket, runs it over his blistered palms and arranges the empty glasses into wobbly stacks. He rearranges them twice more – in size order – before getting fed up, and taking them to the kitchen to be cleaned.

I excuse myself, and go in after him. I ask whether I can

clean some more cups or cut some more sandwiches and he glares back at me like he wishes I'd just go home.

'You want to be useful?' he says, heading towards the taps.

'Yes. I'm just trying to help.'

'Well don't,' he says, staring at me, all bug eyed. 'Your kind of help I don't need. Do you hear me? Stop trying to be so goddam helpful all the time.'

I take the hint. I settle at the table while we wait for Balloon Boy to come back, and the moment I hear the toilet flush I reach over for the deck.

'Anyone mind? I say, riffling the cards gently in my hand. 'Thought it might help to change my luck.'

The others smirk to themselves, like there's no hope of that, but no one objects to me dealing. Except for Balloon Boy, who looks sullen and tense and squeezes one of his creations until it bursts.

I don't do anything for a while. I have to wait for the right moment and I don't want it to look too obvious. And I don't plan to cheat anyone else at the table, I only want to get back what I'm owed.

I wait until Balloon Boy has lost a couple of hands, and when I'm certain that he's beginning to get agitated I make my move. My hands move so fast that an eagle with a telescope wouldn't notice what I'm doing, and I don't even use the give-away grip. The length of my fingers means I can manipulate the pack without covering it, and that way not even Balloon Boy's likely to spot what's going on. It's a piece of cake. All of a sudden I'm back in Frank's front room with Margi's colander fixed on top of my head, and the twins waving their magic wands on either side of me. The image relaxes me. It makes me smile, which is good, because the worst thing I can do is look nervous.

I've already collected the cards I want from the last hand's discards and now I'm ready to stack them. I have them exactly where I want them. All I have to do now is shuffle them in such a way that none of them shifts position. This is where I use the classic Faro: the shuffle it took me so long to learn. I shuffle once, then shuffle again and, just like magic, the cards are exactly where I put them in the first place. I probably shouldn't have offered them to Balloon Boy to cut, but somehow I couldn't resist it. I've already noticed that he cuts deep when he's offered the pack, so that's where I place the crimp. A subtle one. Far less noticeable than his. And he can't help himself. He cuts the pack exactly where I want him to, just like I'd done it myself.

I deal poor hands to everyone apart from myself and my mark, and each one of them folds, just like clockwork. Except for Balloon Boy. He likes what he sees: a pair of red aces burning in the palm of his hand like lit torpedoes.

In my own hand I'm holding an innocent pair of threes, and I make a cautious bet, like I've got nothing special. Balloon Boy thinks for a moment and calls. He could have raised me, but he doesn't want to give away the strength of his hand. He doesn't want to scare me off too soon. He wants to take as much from me as he can.

I deal the next three cards, the flop, face up on the table. These are the first three 'community' cards, the cards each of us can use to complete the best five-card hand. They come down slowly – ace of spades, two of spades, two of diamonds – giving a full house to Balloon Boy. It's interesting to see his face – knowing what he's holding – and he doesn't hide his excitement very well. He flicks his balloon animals and shifts in his seat, and he's already reaching for his chips before I've checked.

He does exactly what I expect him to do. He makes a small raise, hoping to trap me, and I sigh and reluctantly call him back. This makes him happy. He's happy that I've stayed in the hand, and happy that I've called him, because he's utterly convinced he has me nailed. Perhaps I've got the fourth ace;

perhaps I've found myself two pairs. More likely I'm looking for spades; hoping to beat him with a flush, the same way he beat me last week.

The next card, the turn card or fourth street, is the three of hearts, and he can't keep the flicker of delight from his face. Again I just check, indicating that the three hasn't helped me much, and this time he raises me three hundred pounds: the maximum amount. I take a long time deciding what to do. I fidget with my cards and run my fingers through my hair, like I haven't already made up my mind.

'Raise,' I say, pushing my chips into the centre. 'I raise you a hundred and fifty more.'

Everyone around the table thinks I'm making a mistake. Big Louie is eyeballing me, Dr Death is picking the soap scum out of his nails, and Hamish is shifting about in his seat. Only Patrick is willing me on. I'm clearly the underdog, and there's nothing Patrick likes better than an underdog.

I deal up the last card – the river card or fifth street – as calmly and carefully as I can. It's the three of spades, giving me a winning four of a kind. Balloon Boy doesn't even suspect it. As far as he's concerned, the best I can have is a flush or a lesser full house and either way he thinks he has me beaten.

'Check,' I say, quietly. 'I check.'

He actually starts to smile. In his head he's already collecting up the money and buying himself a new lucky shirt.

'Three hundred,' he says, coldly, 'three hundred dead.'

He's grinning at me now, like a stoned Cheshire cat, his whole being expecting me to fold.

'Well,' I say, relaxing now the dealing's done, and stretching my arms out in front of me, 'I see your three hundred and I raise you three more, which pretty much puts me all-in.'

A gasp from Hamish and a snigger from Patrick next to Keith.

Balloon Boy taps his forehead. His mind is racing all of a sudden, wondering what I could possibly have. I couldn't have four threes, there's no way. I wouldn't have stayed in all this time chasing threes.

'You're bluffing, Audrey,' he says, calming down and reaching for his chips. 'Nice try. Bit desperate maybe, but I happen to know that you're bluffing. You want to toss in that last bit of change you've got in front of you? What is it, a hundred, a hundred and fifty?'

'Two fifty,' I say, brightly. 'I brought a little extra tonight.'

'OK. You want to bet it? I don't mind if nobody else does.'

I don't hesitate. Not for a moment.

Another giggle from Hamish, a head-shake from Dr Death and a long low whistle from Patrick.

Balloon Boy shows his cards first, and the whole table nods in appreciation when he turns over the two aces that I gave to him. It's exactly what they thought he had. A full house. How could I not know? How could I not realise I was beaten? Patrick's already reaching over to commiserate and Balloon Boy is reaching for the pot. He's almost there. His fingers are hovering millimetres above the chips when calmly, carefully, I tip over my pair of threes.

Patrick is the first one to react.

'Four of a kind. Fuck. You little diamond, Audrey. You beat him. What a fluke. You fucking beat him.'

Balloon Boy looks like he's in shock. He can't believe what's just happened. Every law, every rule, every statistic he's ever trusted, has been wilfully and ruefully disobeyed. His shock bleeds quickly into anger and disbelief, and he stands up and calls me a 'little bitch'.

I don't react. I reach out my hands and gather up the chips and turn to Patrick and say, 'Phew, that was lucky.'

Balloon Boy knows this isn't true. He knows that I'm lying but he's not sure what's just happened, and when he watches me pick up the deck again he almost chokes. I've changed my grip now. I'm holding the deck like a mechanic. Everyone else is watching his face instead of my fingers so I deal an ace off the bottom of the pack and flash it to him. So he knows.

There's nothing he can do. He can't say anything more without giving himself away, so he sits down, red faced and puffing, knowing that he hasn't got any outs. I can't help smiling. My eyes spin round the table, soaking up the approval and congratulations, until they come to a sudden stop on Big Louie.

He's the only one apart from Balloon Boy who's not happy. He doesn't even return my gaze. That's because his eyes are still firmly fixed on the table. On the deck, on my fingers, on my hands.

41

The game packs up early. Balloon Boy's mood doesn't improve and Big Louie has taken to wiping down the card table after every deal. Patrick congratulates me once more and offers to walk me to my car, and Rabih asks me whether I want to come to the casino with him next week. There's a poker tournament that he and Hamish are planning to enter, and they think I might like to have a go. I can't help feeling flattered that they want me to tag along.

I let Patrick go without me and wait around in the lounge to talk to Louie. I'm not sure how he's going to take it; finding out that the one great player in his game is a pathological con man: a cheat.

The last of the stragglers shuts the door and I loiter in the centre of the room, awkwardly shuffling my feet. I'm not sure why I'm feeling so uncomfortable. It might be the difficulty of what I've got to say, or it might be the way Big Louie is looking at me. He has his hands behind his back, his head tilted to one side and his eyes glued to mine like heat-seeking missiles. He reaches into his pocket for a handkerchief and begins mopping perspiration from his brow. His feet are tapping together like castanets and there's a touch of pure madness about him.

'I've got something to tell you,' I say, standing firm, and trying not to be intimidated by his stare.

'No shit,' he says, sarcastically.

'Yes. And . . . the thing is, it's about Balloon Boy.'

'His name's Karl. The kid has a name.'

'OK. Karl, then. I have something to tell you. About Karl.'

'You're sure you want to say this?'

'Yes.'

'You're sure you don't want to forget about it and go home?'

'No . . . why . . . what do you mean?'

Big Louie sighs like I'm one of the stupidest people he's ever come across. He gives me another chance.

'Listen to me,' he says, taking a step forward, 'I'll tell you one more time. You can leave now, turn around, walk away. We don't have to discuss this. We don't have to mention this ever again.'

It takes me a moment before I get it.

'You know, don't you?' I say, looking straight at him. 'You already know he's a cheat.'

Big Louie doesn't waste any more time. He flies towards me like a charging ball, with his hands held wide in front of him. He puts one hand on my shoulder and another behind my back and slides me forcibly towards the door. He's so angry that he doesn't even flinch when he pulls it open and throws me out. He stands there wheezing at me from the doorway, watching me stumble on to the landing, and throws my squirrel jacket out after me.

'He didn't cheat, Ungar. You hear me? He didn't play one card out of turn.'

'Yes he *did*, I saw him. He's a card mechanic . . . and . . . and he's not even a very good one, at that.'

For some reason this upsets him even more, and he lets out another of his wounded groans.

'He crimps the pack before he offers up the cut, he holds the pack like an arthritic monkey and sometimes . . . sometimes he messes it up. He can stack OK, but he can't shuffle. He messes it up on the shuffle.'

'What are you saying, *what* are you saying?'

He's coming closer to me now, he's almost out of the door. The wind is ruffling his hair and the air is swamping his face and he's having difficulty catching his breath.

'How do you know this shit? How do you know any of this stuff? Crimps and mechanics and culling and stacking. Where did you hear this kind of shit?'

'I read about it,' I say, picking my jacket up off the floor. 'I guessed last week. When he beat me with that lucky flush. But he wasn't lucky, was he? He cheated. He stole that money right out of my hand.'

'You knew about this last week?' he says, easing his toe over the threshold and sliding it back.

'Yes,' I say, trying not to panic. 'I knew last week.'

'Have you told anyone?'

'No.'

'Have you *told* anyone?'

He's bellowing at me now, his words flying past me like a gale. Curtains are fluttering in the windows next door and someone is hovering out on the landing next to the lift.

'Louie, I swear to you. I didn't tell anyone. I wanted to come back and make sure. I wanted to tell you first. I was trying to help you ... I was worried about you getting ripped off.'

'Get out,' he says, pushing the door towards me. 'Get out and don't you come back. You hear me? I don't want you coming round here no more. No e-mails, no surprise visits, no window boxes, no plants. Don't ever try and contact me again.'

'Louie, please—'

'Never, you understand me? You're a problem to me. That's all you've ever been. From the moment you walked through this door, you been nothing but trouble. You're nosy, you're aggravating, you're a lousy student, and above all ... above *all*, you're rotten company. You hear me? There's nothing good about having you around.'

246

I'm almost in tears. I don't know why it's hurting me so much, but every word feels like he's punching me in the stomach.

'You're deluded,' he says, breathlessly. 'You're totally out of your depth. You want to understand your father? Well, I'll tell you something, you already understand him plenty. You're just like him, Audrey. You're just like your dad.'

He slams the door hard towards me and I reach out and stop it with my foot. The wood crashes into my shin as he pushes it, but I can't leave now, I just can't.

'Wait, please. You said you had something to tell me. It was about my father, wasn't it? You promised. You said it was important.'

'Well, it ain't important now. You get me? Fuck you, Audrey, coz it ain't important now.'

My leg collapses as the door connects with the frame, unbalancing me and knocking me to the floor. And I rest there, collapsed on the freezing-cold concrete; dirty rainwater seeping into my skirt, while tears slide down the sides of my reddened cheeks.

I right myself as quickly as I can. I wipe myself down, pull my coat tight round my shoulders and make my way down the landing towards the lift. All I can think about is getting out of here, getting home, and about how stupid I've been. Joe was right. I should never have come over here tonight. It's the stupidest thing I've ever done.

The lift takes an age to come and I flinch from the smell as I step inside. My hip and shins are bruised from where I fell, I have mascara running into my salt-filled eyes, and now I'm engulfed by the scent of stale piss. I stumble out with my eyes closed – rubbing my lids and pulling at my lashes, and wishing I had something to wipe away the sting. My hands dig frantically through my bag for a tissue and my car keys and I don't hear the footsteps until they're right behind me.

I want to scream. Louder than I've ever screamed in my life. I want to cry out and yell and struggle and run away, but I can't. Because there's an arm around my waist and it's holding me tight and there's a hand that stinks of rubber, pressing into my mouth.

42

My eyes race into focus and I manage to turn my head just a fraction. I can feel the sharpness of his fingertips on my cheek and the squeeze of his forearm pressing into my kidneys but I still can't make out who it is. Not until he opens his lips to speak.

'You're not going to scream, OK? If I let go of you, you're not going to scream?'

I shake my head. And slowly, carefully, Balloon Boy lowers his hands and steps away.

Adrenalin has swollen my veins to the size of arteries, my heart is knocking hard against my ribs, but somehow I manage to steady myself and concentrate. He might want his money back, he might want to teach me a lesson, but my instincts tell me that first he wants to know. He needs to know how I sussed him out: how I discovered that he was cheating.

'You think you're a smartarse. Don't you?' he says, bitterly. 'You think you're better than me?'

'No,' I say, attempting to placate him. 'I don't think that at all.'

'You were trying to humiliate me up there. You were trying to make me look like an idiot.'

'No. I wasn't. I was just trying to get my money back.'

Mention of the money makes him angry again and he starts forward, like he's going to hit me.

'Don't you dare,' I say, snatching my hand in front of my face. 'Do you hear me? Don't you fucking dare.'

He moves back, slightly startled, and I don't waste any more time. I dig into my bag, pull out a small atomiser and wrap my hand tightly round its middle.

'You see this?' I say, holding it out to him. 'It's pepper spray. You come an inch closer and I'll blind you. Do you understand me?'

He shrugs.

'Do you *understand*?'

'Yeah, I get it,' he says, holding his hands up. 'I'm not moving anywhere. Alright?'

It takes him a while but he gradually begins to calm down. He takes a deep breath, rubs his hands over his forehead and lights himself a cigarette. I don't take my eyes off him. I glare straight at him; clutching the tiny canister tightly in my hand and calculating the running distance to my car.

'So?' he says, begrudgingly. 'You going to tell me or not? What was it? What gave me away?'

I don't go into any detail. I don't mention his shoddy hand-work or how nervous he looks when he deals. I just tell him that I was lucky. That I guessed. He's still not happy to hear it. He bends his sunglasses back and forth, back and forth in his hand, until the plastic gives out and they snap in half. He wants to know how I'm so good at it. Where I learnt, who taught me, how I get away with using the standard grip. I don't have any inclination to tell him: there's something I need confirming first.

'He knows, doesn't he?'

'Who?'

'Louie. He already knows that you're a cheat.'

At this, he starts to laugh. Deep and hard, like I've been had. Like I'm some sort of an idiot.

'Yeah, you could say that. Given that it's him that taught me how to do it in the first place.'

I falter for a second and exhale.

'What do you mean, he taught you? What are you talking about?'

'For the last two years. He's been coaching me every week. That's what he used to do, didn't he tell you? He was a hustler himself, a card-sharp.'

'I don't believe you.'

'Yeah you do,' he says, stamping out his cigarette. 'It all makes sense, right? That's how he lost all his money, that's how he ended up living like a fucking tramp. He got caught cheating in some high-stakes private card game out in the desert and they beat the shit out of him, took everything he had. He had to get out of the country or they would have killed him. Once word got around, there wasn't a card player in the whole of Nevada who didn't have some kind of a claim on him.'

I drift for a second and close my eyes. I don't want to believe it.

'What? He didn't tell you any of that? He told you he was a big-shot, I suppose? That he played in the World Series, that he played in the big league, took down Stu Ungar and Johnny Chan.'

I shake my head. Keep shaking it, back and forth.

'I'm right, aren't I? He got to you. You thought he was one of them big-time tournament players, some kind of high-roller or something? What did he tell you about me? Did he tell you he was training me to play in the World Series too?'

I don't answer. Balloon Boy's face shines with delight.

'Looks like he played you too, then,' he says, beaming at me. 'Just like he plays everyone he's ever met. He's a crook, that's all. An arsehole, a fuckin' thief.'

I straighten up. I push my hair out of my face and try not to look like I mind.

'What about his accident?' I say, squaring up to him. 'What about him being a basketball champion and him being in hospital . . . and what about his wife dying? I suppose that's all lies as well, is it?'

Balloon Boy shrugs.

'Is that what he told you, that she died? Christ almighty. His wife *left* him. She went off with his best friend. She'd been fuckin' him for years right under his nose, right there in his own house. I can't believe you bought it,' he says, smirking at me. 'You must be the most gullible person I've ever met.'

It seems that I am.

'What about the rest of it? His accident, the basketball?'

'No,' he says, running his eyes over me, 'I don't know anything about that. But what do you think? Does he look like the kind of man that played sports?'

My whole body deflates, and I must have visibly slumped in some way, because his confidence suddenly grows and he lurches toward me.

'What?' he says, reaching for my bag. 'You actually thought I was going to let you keep it?'

I struggle away as he grabs for the purse and he digs his fingers hard into my arm. I don't care about the money but my father's matchbook is in that purse and the chance that I might lose it makes me fight. I don't even think about it. I jerk the atomiser towards his face and squirt it directly into his eyes. It's only Evian water but he doesn't know it yet, and it gives me a window to take him down. He splutters for a second and coughs before he realises, and I kick him just as he opens his eyes. My foot meets his groin hard enough for him to double up and sink to the ground, and I turn on my heels and run.

I belt through the puddles and piles of litter towards my car, and I'm halfway to having it open when I hear the smack. Flesh connecting with flesh; a tight hard fist, slumping into a wide bony jaw.

*   *   *

'Jesus, where did you come from?'

'Upstairs. Heard a bit of a racket from outside Fatty's flat, so I went up to check it out.'

It's Cigarette Kid. He has blood dripping from his knuckles and his victim is laid flat out across the tarmac like a punctured balloon skin.

'Is he . . . dead?'

'No way. He's just havin' himself a little rest. Needed a bit of a lie-down, I reckon. What about you?' he says, nodding at me. 'You OK?'

'Thanks. I'm . . . yeah . . . I'm OK.'

Cigarette Kid opens his hand and shakes the tension out of his fingers. Blood flies off his knuckles like spittle, and I offer him a tissue to wipe it clean.

'Well, that's good,' he says, dabbing at his hand. 'Because Fatty was really worked up. Shouting at me through his letter box like he was going to have himself a heart attack or something.'

'What did he want?'

'Wanted to give me a tenner to come down here and check on you. Which is cool, because he usually only gives me five.'

'Usually?'

'Yeah, when you leave the flat. He doesn't like you walking out to your car on your own, so he pays me a fiver to follow you down. Gave me a tenner this time coz he was extra worried. Does he teach you cards? He's gonna teach me one day. He reckons I could be really good.'

I rub my face, take a deep breath and ask him for a cigarette. I take a couple of juicy drags, wipe my fringe out of my swollen eyes and reach into the front pocket of my bag.

'Well,' I say, 'let me give you something to get you started, then. That was . . . you know . . . quite a punch.'

'Cheers,' he says, swelling at the compliment. 'Me knuckles

is gonna kill me tomorrow, but not as much as his jaw. Fucker's made of glass. Wouldn't be surprised if it was broken.'

I keep back what I'm owed, peel off a tight bundle of twenties and press them into his bruised hand.

'Christ. How much is that?'

'Five hundred.'

'Shit. I mean . . . you know, nice one . . . but you don't have to . . . it's a bit much. You don't have to give me all your money.'

'Don't worry,' I say, dropping my cigarette stub on the floor and grinding it out on Balloon Boy's coat. 'It's not my money, it's his.'

43

It's been almost a week now, and I still haven't heard from Big Louie. I'd expected him to send me an e-mail at the very least. I thought he might call, or send a letter, or ask someone to get a message to me, but it's almost as if nothing happened. He's clearly not sorry about throwing me out of his flat and he obviously doesn't care how I am.

I've tried not to dwell on the attack, but I'm dreaming about it almost every night. I see a figure creeping up behind me and grabbing my waist, and sometimes I don't manage to get away. I wake up palpitating and sweaty and lie awake for the rest of the night, reciting logarithms and doing equations in my head. And dealing mock poker hands to myself. And losing.

Perhaps it's because I don't know what's become of Balloon Boy. I've phoned all the local hospitals – twice – but they've not admitted anyone matching his description. Admittedly, I didn't give them much to go on. You try wrapping a hanky round the phone, putting on a fake German accent, and enquiring about a tall man with a broken jaw, who may or may not have been carrying balloon animals in his pocket at the time he was admitted. It could be that they're just not telling me – my not knowing his surname and claiming to be his long-lost cousin from the Black Forest may have put them off – but it still gives me the creeps. Knowing that he's still out there somewhere.

The poker games have been cancelled until further notice. Patrick and Rabih both called to let me know, but neither of them can get hold of Big Louie. He's not answering his phone or coming to his door and it seems like he's completely gone to ground. At least Joe's happy. He thinks I've finally come to my senses. He doesn't know anything about the cheating or the fight; he just thinks I've stopped playing poker. I told him Big Louie was pissed off with me when I won my money back, and that he's banned me from going over there again. He's decided I'm too good for the group. He'd prefer it if I didn't play with them any more.

It wasn't easy. It took me a long while to calm down after I got home last week, and I drank my way through most of a bottle of wine before I stopped shaking. Joe just thought I was angry, that I'd had a row; that I was upset about the way I'd been treated. He tried to be sympathetic but I could tell a part of him was relieved it was over. At least he never said I told you so. It's simply not his way.

I think about calling the hospitals one more time, and I wince as I reach over for the phone. My shoulder's still sore from the struggle and I have bruises running up and down my shins from where Big Louie's door crashed into my legs. They've come up deeper and darker than I expected, and I've had to keep them covered with pale make-up. I can't afford to let Joe see them. If he knew the truth about what happened to me that night, he'd definitely want to call the police. And that would be the end of it. I'd never find out what Big Louie had to tell me.

'Audrey?'

'Yes.'

'Were you just talking in a German accent?'

'No. What do you mean?'

'Just now, when you were on the phone. I'm sure you were talking in a German accent.'

'Well, you know. Just practising.'

'For what?'

'For if I ever want to become a spy.'

'Right. I see. And is there something wrong with your legs? They look a bit strange. Sort of *pale*. And powdery.'

'Well, um, that'll probably be the fake tan.'

'Isn't that meant to make you go brown?'

'Not always. The cheap stuff can make you turn paler.'

'Well, what about the rest of you? Didn't you put fake tan anywhere else?'

'No.'

'Just your shins then?'

'Yep. Just my shins.'

Joe narrows his eyes, and I escape to my computer before he has time to ask me any more awkward questions. I've spent a lot of time on the Internet this week. I told Joe I had a ton of business accounts to finish, but I've spent most of the time doing fresh missing-person searches, and checking out what I can about Big Louie. It seems he was telling the truth about some things. I discovered a website for his old school in New Jersey, and there is mention of a Louie Bloom playing basketball for the college team in the early seventies. He's described as one of the most promising young basketball players they ever had. His scoring averages were way up there with the very best, and he's even written up in their Hall of Fame. He's remembered as being a good-natured and determined player – hugely competitive and controlled – and as having an excellent team spirit. I'm not sure what surprises me more – the idea of Big Louie being a team player or the suggestion that he was ever good natured.

After browsing through the college sites, I spent a couple of afternoons trawling through the local newspaper archives. His accident happened exactly like he said it did. I even found a picture of the exact street corner where he was hit. On one side is a dry cleaner's called Spotaway, on the other is a deli called Number One Subs. Perhaps he was on his way to buy a sandwich that day. Perhaps he'd stopped in on his way home.

But he never got there, not for months. Because there's too much blood on the pavement and far too much debris on the road, and the wayward Pontiac that crashed into him like a steam train looks like it's already been crushed up for scrap. Bent and splayed and practically sawn in half, it's engine hanging out like animal innards.

Further down the article is an obituary of the dead driver, a fifty-five-year-old man called Albert Sale. The journalist is careful about how he says it, but he seems to suggest that the driver was inebriated at the time of the accident. He'd argued with his wife, he was tearing along at twice the legal speed limit, and while results were yet to be announced, it was expected they'd find high levels of alcohol in his blood.

And somehow the two of them found one another. At that precise moment, on that precise day. The bitter drunk with the time bomb sizzling in his chest, and the star player with his whole life ahead of him.

Saturday night at a Chinese restaurant in Gerrard Street. Joe and I are munching our way through a complimentary bowl of prawn crackers and Lorna and Pete are on their way over. I try not to look preoccupied. I try not to look restless and bored.

'What's the matter?'
'Me? Nothing.'
'You look restless. And bored.'
'No. Not at all . . . I'm just, you know . . . thinking.'
'About what?'
'Oh, nothing much.'
Joe goes back to studying the menu and I fiddle with my rice crackers, trying to resist the urge to count them. Except I sense there's an odd number in the bowl, so I eat another one, just to make them even.
'Hey, sorry we're late. Traffic's shit. Have you two ordered yet?'

We order hot soups and crispy duck and things that come in lemon sauce and garlic. We talk about Meg's sports day and Pete's film script and Lorna says I look like I could use a holiday. Joe offers to give her some extra running lessons next month and orders us a second bottle of wine. He wants this to be a good evening. Just the two of us, with our two best friends, having a laugh together like we used to.

'Hey,' says Pete, dipping his hand in the bowl and messing up my crackers, 'did you know that Elton John's brother lives in a shed? The guy's got, like, a billion pounds or something, and he lets his own brother live in a shed.'

'No way.'

'It's true. I saw a programme about it last night.'

'He's only his half-brother.'

'So what?'

'Well, maybe he doesn't like him. You don't like your brother very much.'

'Yeah, but I wouldn't let him live in a shed.'

'Whitney Houston's bald.'

'She's not. That's rubbish. Where did you hear that?'

'She is. She's as bald as a coot.'

'What's a coot?'

'Something like a raccoon, probably. Or a rat.'

'It's a bird. A water bird, in fact.'

Everyone turns round to look at me. It's only the third time I've spoken since the soup.

'What? Like a duck or something?' says Pete, rolling up another crispy pancake.

'Yeah,' I say, 'something like a duck.'

They're being much nicer to me than I deserve. I'm lousy company and I'm miles away, but they're my friends so they take me as I come. They know it's been a difficult month. They know I'm preoccupied and maudlin and that every time they try to talk to me a part of me is thinking about my dad.

Except that's not the whole story. I'm thinking about Big Louie as well. I'm wondering how he is and what he's doing, and whether I should swallow my pride and go round to see him. I'm wondering if he's found a new crowd to play poker with yet, and if he has, then I'm wishing I was with them. Because I liked it. I liked the challenge and the order and the symmetry, and the prospect of finding the perfect play. That one great moment when you read it all right and every law bends into place. Things that are possible become likely. Things that are probable become sure. Perhaps that's why my father grew to love it so much. In a strange way, it made him feel optimistic.

I've been hogging the rest of the wine. I must have drunk most of the bottle of red on my own, because now everyone's talking about getting another one. Lorna looks tense, Joe looks desperate for another glass, and Pete has just started moping. All because Lorna said she didn't like Huey Lewis and the News. Pete tried to explain that he only liked them in a nostalgic, teen party, so bad they're good kind of way, but Lorna still wouldn't have it. It crushes him. Every time she rejects him like this it crushes him.

A black cab heading home, stuck in traffic outside King's Cross station. Joe is reading a tea-stained tabloid that someone's left behind and I'm staring out of the window like a trapped cat.

'Is that where he lives?'

I turn round suddenly. I hadn't realised Joe was watching me.

'Yes. He, er . . . it's back there. See the three blocks in a row? It's the second one along.'

Joe goes back to his paper. He's been wondering where I was all night, and now he knows.

44

When the envelope flashes at the bottom of my screen I'm not prepared for it. I'm in the middle of writing a cheque to Ryan's mum, and I'd almost given up hope. I hesitate over the mouse for a second, wondering whether I should open it or not. What if it's more insults? What if he's spent the last eight days sitting in his armchair getting more and more cross; eating extra-vinegary pickles and thinking up new ways to make me feel bad. He must have known I'd feel like this because he's headed his e-mail accordingly: 'You'd better open this, Ungar,' it says. So I do.

The message is short and sweet.

    How are ya? Let me know. Big Louie.

I'm in two minds. I could mail him back and tell him what a shit he is or I could get in the car and drive over there. Who am I kidding? I've always known that if he contacted me again I'd go round to see him straight away.

I know exactly what I'm going to say. I'm going to tell him that I know everything. About how he lied to me, about how he's been ripping off the other players for months on end, and about how he nearly got me beaten up and mugged. I'm keen to make him feel as guilty as I can. Because it's all his fault. He's a useless, no-good, thieving piece of crap, and he didn't even have the courtesy to find out if I was OK or not. I'm only going over there to give him a piece of my mind. I'm only going back to find out what he knows about my dad.

It takes me a while to pluck up the courage. I sit in the car, watching people trek back and forth from the lift, and keep an eye out for Balloon Boy in my rear-view mirror. When I'm sure there are enough people milling about, I lock the car and march purposefully towards the tired metal doors. The lift is out of order – that's why there were so many people walking away – so it looks like I'll have to take the stairs.

I thought I might feel safer walking up, but I don't. Each new level opens out on to a concrete balcony more decrepit than the last, and I keep imagining myself tripping and falling over the low iron balustrade. I imagine what it would feel like to free-fall towards the waiting concrete, and I attempt to calm myself down by working out how long it would take. Oddly enough, this only makes me feel worse, and by the time I reach Big Louie's floor I'm nervous and exhausted and cursing myself for coming over here on my own. What if he's in there? What if he's waiting for me? What if Balloon Boy's with him right now?

The front door is on the latch – as usual – so somehow he knew I was on my way. I don't ring the buzzer or knock on the blistered wood, I just steel myself and push it open a fraction. It swings forward on its rusty spring, squeaking and begging out for oil, and I call out a small hello. No answer. Now I'm really spooked, and I'm about to turn on my heels and run when I hear the unmistakable growl.

'Come in,' he says. 'I'm over here. What the hell took you so long?'

I bite my lip and count to ten but nothing prepares me for what's in there.

The flat looks like it's been tipped on its side. Every ornament, every lamp, every paper, every plant pot is lying creased or broken on the floor. Soil has spilt out on to the carpets, splinters of wood are embedded in the split lino; and poker chips, cards, food and dirty plates are scattered around the room like junkyard debris. He's sat in his favourite armchair, opposite the window, and he's wearing the same clothes he had on at our last poker game: the coral shirt with mother-of-pearl buttons, and the jogging trousers with wide elastic at the top. His skin is dirty with sweat, his grey hair is weighed down with sebum, and the plasters he was wearing on his fingertips have curled up like layers of peeling skin.

Surrounding him, stretching out in all directions for a metre or so, is what looks like an exclusion zone. No debris, no dirt, no plates, no playing cards: just a circle of pristine, licked-clean carpet. Its limits are sealed off by a tidy white line, and from the smell I think he must have marked it out with bleach. I'm edging backwards from the shock of it and he must have seen the look on my face, because he stares straight at me and tells me not to be scared.

'Don't worry,' he says gloomily. 'I ain't gonna hurt you. I ain't gonna charge at you or nothin'.'

He lowers his eyes, pulls in his knees, and tucks his feet further underneath his chair. I don't think I've seen anything quite so sad.

He's lost weight. He could lose half a dozen stone without it showing, but I'm sure I can see it in his face. His eyes look more bulbous than ever, and I wonder if he's eaten anything at all: if starving himself is all he has left.

I take another cautionary step and he grimaces and tuts at me disapprovingly.

'What you worried about? I told you, I ain't gonna pounce.'

I proceed with caution – in case he changes his mind and springs out of his chair like a jack-in-the-box – and he tells me once again that he's feeling OK. He doesn't look it. He has a small bag clutched on his knees – khaki canvas with chipped plastic buckles – and as I walk towards him, he drags it further up his lap, hugging it tightly to his chest.

'You look sick,' I say. 'Have you been eating?'

He shrugs and fingers the straps of his bag.

'Can I get you a drink? A cup of tea maybe?'

'Yes,' he says, 'I'd like that. I'd like a cup of tea.'

There's no fresh milk or clean cups but I find some tea bags and half a soggy lemon and I wash up a couple of dirty mugs. The sink is still full of beer glasses from the last game and I clean them and pack them away in the cupboard.

'You made quite a mess of this place,' I say, handing him his tea.

'Yeah, well. I was pissed.'

'At me?'

'At everything. At the whole friggin' world.'

He doesn't want to elaborate, and because I'm still feeling uncomfortable I look around for something else to do.

'Do you mind if I tidy up a bit?'

'No,' he says, as if the idea had never previously occurred to him. 'That would be good. I think this place would look a whole lot better tidy.'

I clean solidly for the next hour and a half, and Big Louie stares out of the window the whole time. Glaring at the outside world as if it's taunting him, cursing him; daring him to go out there and face it. And he's staring right back. Like something inside of him has broken.

I leave him to it. I sweep up the loose soil, pack the broken limbs of furniture into plastic bags and scrub every single plate, glass and cup. At least he still has all of his cleaning products. There's bleach and Fairy Liquid and cases of 'spring fresh' Glade and enough dusters, sponges and scourers to spruce up the entire block.

I do it all. I brush, polish, tidy and scrub and finish everything off with a thorough hoover. He likes the sound of it. He closes his eyes and listens contentedly to its gravelly hum and lets me come as close to him as I like. I sweep it right up to the edges of his exclusion zone and he lifts up his feet so I can clean underneath them.

I'm perspiring by the time I've finished, and I fetch a glass of water and wipe my forehead clean before I sit down. And now my mind is racing. The cleaning stopped me having to think, but now I have to work out what to do. Perhaps he needs to see a doctor. Maybe I should call an ambulance or contact the local authorities. Or perhaps I should sit here and talk to him for a while, work out whether it's safe to leave him on his own.

'Thanks,' he says, looking up at me. 'You did a good job. You missed a bit there by the radiator, but, you know, it looks sort of OK.'

He's complaining. He's actually complaining. I take this to be a good sign.

'How long have you been like this?' I say, carefully. 'Have you been sitting here like this since I left?'

'Afternoons mostly,' he says, shifting in his seat. 'Rest of the time I've been in bed.'

'Sleeping?'

'Yeah. You know. Trying to. But I've had a lot of stuff on my mind.'

'Have you been eating?'

'No. Not so much.'

'Well, do you want me to make you something? There's some peanut butter and crackers in the cupboard.'

'You don't mind?'

'No,' I say. 'I don't mind.'

By the time I get back he's cleaned himself up a little. He's been to the bathroom, changed his shirt and wrapped his fingers in fresh plasters. He's put his baseball cap back on his head to cover up his messy hair and he's turned his chair away from the window.

'You look better,' I say, putting down the crackers.

'Yeah,' he says. 'I feel better. I'm glad you came.'

'Are you?'

'Sure. But you might have thought to bring me somethin'.

Some pickles or chocolate or somethin'. I mean, it's not enough that I'm stuck up here in this crap-hole feeling sorry for myself all week. Now I got to starve to death as well.'

I'm speechless. I'm almost speechless.

'Serve you right if you did starve,' I say, practically throwing his plate at him. 'Have you any idea what you did? You threw me out. You sent me out there after that lunatic. I almost got myself mugged because of you.'

Big Louie shrugs his shoulders.

'I didn't ask you to steal from him, did I? Wasn't me who made you play the friggin' hero.'

'I wasn't playing the hero . . . I was trying to help. You didn't even phone me. You didn't even call to find out if I was OK.'

He shrugs again.

'Yeah, well, so what? Doesn't mean you can't bring me some decent food, does it? Doesn't mean you couldn't have stopped off at a decent deli and bought me some meat. Jeez, some people only ever think of themselves.'

He smiles at me sheepishly and digs into his crackers, and I sit down like I've run out of things to say. It's like arguing with a child. None of it makes any sense.

'Look,' he says, 'I'm sorry I didn't call you, OK? I didn't know exactly what had happened. I only just found out this morning.'

'I don't believe you,' I say, bitterly. 'How could you not have known?'

'Because,' he says, lowering his cracker, 'the shit-head who tried to rob you is in the hospital. His jaw is broke in three whole places and it's wired up so tight that he can't even speak. He only wanted his money back. You didn't have to break his goddam jaw.'

'It wasn't *me*. I didn't punch him, it was the—'

'I know, I know,' he says, batting his hand in front of his face. 'It was the kid who lives downstairs. Who'd

266

have thought he had it in him, huh? A scrawny little thing like that.'

'Well, how come he didn't tell you, then? How come he didn't tell you what he'd done?'

'He took off straight after it happened. Took himself on a nice little holiday with all that money you gave him. Got back this morning with dick-ache, a sombrero, a suntan and a chronic dose of the shits, and ran up here to tell me all about it. Fight sounded pretty bad from the way he told it, so I phoned round a few of the local hospitals. Said I was worried about my nephew, that he'd missed both of his bi-weekly visits.'

'So . . . did you find him?'

'Yeah. He's in the Royal Free. Nurse wanted to know if I was coming to visit him any time soon, so I told her, you know, that was highly unlikely. Also wanted to know if he had relations in Germany. Seems like some unhinged Bavarian lady's been trying to track him down for days. You know anything about that?'

'No. Not at all. Fancy that.'

'Well, anyway,' he says, pointing his half-eaten cracker at me, 'you're pretty lucky that kid was around. You're lucky someone had the good sense to send him racing down the stairwell to check up on you.'

'Wait, let me get this straight. Now you're asking me to *thank* you?'

'Well,' he says, holding up his hands, 'it couldn't hurt.'

That's it. He's gone too far. I've come all the way over here, cleaned up his disgusting flat, fed him, watered him, and listened to him moan and curse, and now he wants me to thank him for looking out for me. He should be on his knees begging my forgiveness. He should be thanking me for everything I've done. And pleading with me not to leave him up here to rot.

I stand up and roll down my sleeves.

'I'm going,' I say. 'That's it. I'm going home.'

'So soon?'

'For fuck's sake, Louie, there's nothing wrong with you. You're just the same as you always are. I was worried about you. How stupid is that? I was worried about *you*.'

'Wait. You can't leave yet.'

'Why not? You got some washing you want doing? Something else you want me to clean?'

'No. But still, I'm telling you. You can't leave yet.'

'Yes. I can. Just watch me. You haven't even apologised. You haven't even said sorry for what you did.'

Big Louie sighs like a whale.

'What about me?' he says, growling at me. 'You don't know what this week's been like for me. You've absolutely no friggin' idea.'

'For *you*? You're the one who threw me out. I've got . . . shit . . . I've still got bruises all over my legs . . . and I thought . . . I thought he'd killed the guy. I did. For a minute I thought he was dead.'

'Well he ain't dead, is he?'

'No. He's not. But he's still out there. He'll be out of the hospital soon enough, and then what? He'll probably come looking for me or something.'

'No. He won't.'

'How do you know?'

'I just do. I'm telling you. He won't bother you again.'

'And all of this,' I say, heading towards him and gritting my teeth, 'all of this is because I was trying to help you. I've listened to your lies and your sob stories and built you a sodding window box and . . . and you didn't have to treat me like that. I didn't deserve it.'

Big Louie thinks for a while, grinding his temples with his fingertips.

'You're right,' he says, putting down his plate and looking up at me. 'I should apologise. I'm sorry the place was such a mess and I'm sorry about throwing you out and I'm sorry you had to see me like this. But Jesus, Ungar, you still don't get it, do you? You ruined everything. You took it all away, don't you see? I know you didn't mean to but you did. You stole my one last chance of getting out of here.'

I hover in the middle of the carpet, hugging my coat round me like a blanket.

'I don't understand. I don't know what you're trying to say.'

'Well,' he says, unclipping his canvas bag, 'I would have thought that was obvious. You're all I have left now. You're my last hope, Audrey. It's down to you.'

45

The bag is stuffed full of money. Fat wads rolled up as tight as Havana cigars and thick bunches of notes bound with coils of fraying string. There are grubby fivers held together with sticky tape and rotted elastic bands, and loose coins bulging hard against the well-worn seams.

'What is all this?' I say, trying not to stare. 'Where did you get it? How much is in there?'

'Twenty odd thousand and some change,' he says, proudly. 'Had to play it real careful, but I did it. Between the two of us we built up a pretty healthy bank roll.'

'You and Balloon Boy?'

'Well, me mainly. I've only had him working for me the last few months. He was a quick learner but it took him the best part of two years to get it right.'

'So it's true then? You've been ripping off everyone you played with? You're just a common cheat?'

'Nothing common about it,' he says, with chagrin. 'It's hard to be a good cheat. Damned hard. Takes a lifetime of practice and balls as big as oranges, and what the hell? It's not like they didn't learn anything.

'Christ, Ungar,' he says, leaning over and smacking his hands together. 'How did you figure it out? He wasn't the best mechanic I ever taught, but he seemed like he was doing OK.'

'He's too rigid,' I say, shaking my head. 'I saw him – his hands aren't nearly quick enough.'

Big Louie rubs his neck dejectedly. Like I'm telling him something he already knew.

'Not like yours, huh?'

'No,' I say, 'not like mine.'

'Well,' he says, brightening slightly, 'that's quite a skill you got there. How did you learn to do it? How come you can manipulate the deck like that?'

'My stepbrothers were into magic when we were kids. I've been doing it since I was little. Card tricks, palming, false deals . . . I don't know. It's natural to me. It just feels . . . *natural*.'

Big Louie nods appreciatively.

'Well,' he says, 'it's quite a thing. And you're brave too. You didn't even raise a sweat. Not even when you handed the pack over to him for the cut. That was a pretty stylish move, Ungar. Little dumb maybe, but it showed you got balls.'

'As big as oranges?'

'Almost.'

I hadn't thought I was in the mood for flattery, but it seems that I am. I like it that he noticed how good I was and I like it that he's praising me now. Of course, it's a classic manoeuvre. And like an idiot, I fall right into his trap.

'So how did you learn, then?' I say, sitting back and feeding him his line.

'Not much else to do when you're all crippled up like I was,' he says, sadly. 'Needed something to occupy my mind. Friend bought me a book on poker when I was in the hospital, and you know, I sort of got hooked. Read every card book I could get my hands on. Guess I must have picked it up quick, coz pretty soon the entire night staff were lining up to play me. I think that's how come they finally got around to discharging me. Couldn't stand to lose to me no more.

'Anyhow, one day I'm reading this newspaper article about some card cheat that they arrested over in Atlantic City, and I sort of became obsessed by it. Fancied myself as going out to Vegas to become a pro player when I got back on my feet, but I wanted to take away the element of chance. You know what I mean, Audrey? I wanted to control it. Dictate it. Fix the odds in my favour a little bit. After the accident, I was suddenly real keen to know how things were going to turn out.'

'So you learnt how to stack the deck?'

'Yep. After I got home that's pretty much all I did. Morning, noon and night. Seemed to take for ever to get it right but I was determined to master it. Was the nearest thing I had to learning another sport. When I thought I had it down pat I played a few hands against some of my dad's friends and slipped in a couple of fake deals and shuffles.'

'And they didn't notice?'

'No,' he says, solemnly. 'I sometimes wish they had.' He talks at me solidly for the next hour. About how he got on his feet again and went off to Atlantic City and started playing poker in the casinos and private card rooms. He tried to play it straight and learn the hard way but he couldn't resist cheating when he got the chance. He says it was too easy. That there really is a sucker born every minute. That he toured the country from coast to coast, hustling and grifting and filling his pockets with easy money. He lost contact with his family, slept with whoever would give him bed space, and pretended to anyone who asked that he was a champ. He even had a canine partner: Little Louie. He'd trained him to sit up and beg and pant and bark, and it was just enough to distract the other players from his hands. That dog made him seem more trustworthy, more honest somehow.

'Did you ever play it straight?' I say, interrupting him. 'Did you ever compete in those big games, like you said?'

'Sure. Every time I got a decent enough bank roll I'd head out to Vegas to play in the tournaments. I wanted to win for real. I was ambitious, I wanted to be one of the greats.'

'But you weren't good enough?'

272

He edges backwards in his chair. The answer clearly troubles him.

'I tried, Audrey,' he says, attempting to get comfortable. 'I tried real hard. I'd play it straight for six months at a time and, you know, I was pretty hot, but I'd always end up losing it in the end. I couldn't stand not to win. I was so used to calling the shots, that I couldn't bear it when the cards gave up and went against me. Made me play loose and stupid. Made me play out of my depth. Just coz I could take these players down when I was dealing dirty, I convinced myself I could beat them playing clean. I'd build up just enough so as I could afford a house and something approaching a real life, and then I'd throw it all away after a whim. Drove my wife away from me. The one woman that could ever stand to love me. That's how come she left like she did.'

'You told me your wife died. You told me she choked to death.'

'Yeah, well,' he says, scuffing his shoe on the floor, 'would have served her right if she had. But it was me that got fat, not her. It was me that got sweaty and mean and obsessive and started scrubbing the guilt off my hands like it was dirt. I hated what I'd turned into. Every time I lost I felt a little worse about myself, and every time I cheated I hated myself more. Must have loathed myself almost as much as she did.'

Big Louie turns towards the window for a moment, shielding his eyes from the sun.

'There were times when she aggravated all hell out of me,' he says, picking at one of his plasters, 'but there wasn't a day went by that I didn't love her. It's not like she was beautiful or nothin', but she was kind and smart and decent enough to put up with someone like me. And she smelled so good. So clean. Sweet . . . like freshly cut lavender.'

Big Louie closes his eyes and sniffs the air gently. He has me right where he wants me and he knows it. I'm on the edge of my seat, sucking in every word, desperate to know how it ends. He tells me how he didn't go out for a week after she left him. How he stayed in all day staring at the walls. Until he found out that she'd been sleeping with someone else. Right under his nose. For months.

'That's when I made my worst mistake,' he says, gravely. I was so shaken up, I took the last ten thousand I had in the world and gambled it all away to a bowl of nickels. Committed suicide right there at the table. Bet after bet after lousy freakin' bet, until I'd nothing lining my pockets but pipe tobacco.'

He starts smoothing down his plasters, staring at his hands like he hates them.

'After that it got pretty desperate. I needed to get back on my feet real quick, so I borrowed five thousand off a good friend of mine – he even fixed me up with a game. Couldn't wait to help me, as a matter of fact. I was too far gone to realise I was being set up, so I walked right into it. He'd tipped everyone off before I got there. They were real polite about it, though. They waited until I took one of them down with four of a kind, then they piled in an' beat the living shit out of me. Damn near crippled me all over again. He paid them extra, can you believe it? Paid them extra just so as they'd kick into my legs. By the end of it they were so swollen up I could barely stand.'

Big Louie winces and tucks his feet underneath him, and I try hard not to picture them doing it.

'It was him, wasn't it?' I say, quietly. 'The man that tipped them off. He was the one who'd been sleeping with your wife.'

'Who else?' he says, bitterly. 'He wasn't content with lying to me all those months, he had to make sure he ruined me as well. I was back on crutches, I had no place to live, and my nerves were shot all to pieces. By the time they'd finished with me I couldn't have bet for pennies, let alone a bag of dollar bills.'

274

'So what did you do?'

'Wife felt sort of guilty, so she said I could recuperate over here. Place was so run down she'd never gotten around to selling it after her mom died. I guess it was her way of paying me off. Another friend of mine, Eddie, lent me money for the flight and a few expenses. Eddie was the one person who stood by me after I got caught. Ran a fair few scams of his own over the years, so he sort of knew where I was at.'

'And you ended up staying?'

'That's right. Was only meant to be for a couple of months, just until things cooled off and I got myself straight. But the longer I stayed, the harder it was for me to leave. After a week I could barely stand to leave the apartment. After a month I could barely stand to open the door. Coz I got scared. Of everything. I'm so scared of the world I don't dare live in it any more. You want to know why that is?'

I nod my head.

'It's because I can't control it,' he says, wringing his hands together. 'Coz I never know when I'm going to lose it all over again. If I'm gonna be hit by a car or lose the woman I love or find out my best friend just wants to stick it to me. Time was when I could have sat down in a poker game and played for everything I was worth without raising a single bead of sweat. I could shoot a hoop from the three-point line with my eyes closed, and know the trajectory was perfect before the ball left my hands. And look at me now. I can't even leave the room. I can't open a window to get a breath of air. I can't even control my own body. It's rebelling against me so hard it's halfway to killing itself already.'

'But you can stay clean?'

'That's right,' he says, defiantly, 'I can. I can keep everything real clean and organised. I've shrunk my world to a size where I can handle it and it's getting smaller every single day. But look at me now,' he repeats, tugging angrily at his shirtsleeves. '*Look* at me. I haven't washed or cleaned or tidied for more than a week. I'm living in my own filth, in a circle I've drawn on the floor with a can of bleach, with only my own misery for company. And if you don't get me out of here soon . . . if you don't get me out of here . . . I'm going to die.'

He says it coldly. Plainly. Like it's simply a matter of time.

'I don't need much,' he says, reaching for his bag again. 'Just a patch of my own, back on the coast. That was the thing about that last game I played. The thing I told you about, that beautiful smell. Happened a little differently than I said it did. Happened right there when I was lying passed out on the ground, all bruised up and covered in blood. Was the one thing that brought me back to life. It showed me a glimpse of the whole damn world, right before I shut myself away from it for good. So I got to have myself a garden. A place where I can tend plants and smell the ocean and make my own world grow over again. Slowly. Bit by bit. I got to have a place where I can go outside into the world, to look at the sky and feel safe.'

A thick tear slides down his face and he stares at me right from his bones.

'Please, Audrey,' he says, reaching for my sleeve, 'I'm begging you. You got to help me get out of here. You've got to play this game for me. There's two hundred grand riding on it, just enough to see me right. And I know you can do it, I'm certain. I never seen anything like you in all my life.'

'What game? What are you talking about?'

'The game Balloon Boy was going to play for me. Before you got him beat up so bad he can barely part his lips to speak or raise his arms up to deal no more. We'd worked it out between us, me and Eddie. It's the sweetest thing on the planet. It's all set up. A table full of suckers with more money than sense and the shit-head who stole my life out from under me for the second time.'

'The man who had you beaten up? You're going to cheat him at a game of poker?'

'Not me, Audrey, *you*. I've been working on Balloon Boy like crazy all this time, but deep down I always knew he wasn't right. So maybe it's a good thing that he's out of action. Makes what I have to ask you . . . that bit easier.'

He pauses for a moment, swallowing hard and running his eyes over my face.

'Every single night since I planned this, I've dreamt about finding someone better. A player who could go out there and beat this game for me, the kind who could engineer the perfect match. The point is,' he says, edging towards me, 'I haven't had that dream in over a week now. No matter how much I slept, or how hard I tried, I just couldn't make it come back.

'I saw the way you dealt up the cards that night and I've tried to stop thinking about it . . . but I can't. So you're going to take this bag of money to Vegas and play it for me. You're going to win with it, because you're my last chance. Because you're a genius, Ungar, a magician. You got a special kind of gift.'

46

'No. There's no way. You're absolutely crazy. You're madder than I thought you were and, to be honest . . . you know . . . I've always thought you were pretty fucking mad.'

Nothing. He's not saying anything at all. I can't stand the silence so I just keep talking.

'Look, see, have you got any idea what you're saying? Have you any idea what you're asking me to do? I've never even been to Las Vegas. I've never even played in a professional game. You want me to sit down with a bunch of thugs and cheats and con them out of their money, just so you can go back to New Jersey and spend the rest of your life sitting in the sun, and wondering about which type of watering can you want to use?'

He keeps eerily still. Eerily focused. Waits a few more seconds before he speaks.

'You're going to do it, Audrey. I know you are.'

'No. No, I'm not,' I say, backing away. 'In fact, I'm going to leave right now. I'm going to walk back the way I came, get into my car, drive home and pretend that I never even met you. I'm going to sit down with my boyfriend, ask him about his day, cook dinner for the both of us, watch a few hours of TV and go to bed.'

'No. You're going to help me. Just like I said. You're going to play that game for me, there's no question.'

'Why? Why do you keep saying that. *Why* do you keep saying that I'm going to do it?'

Big Louie huffs and puffs, like he's fighting a battle with himself.

'Look,' he says, getting aggravated, 'I'd prefer it if you said yes now, that's all. Before—'

'Before what?'

'Before I make you do it. I'd like you to say yes before I make you. From my point of view I'd feel a whole lot better about the *whole* damn thing if you'd just agree to it right here and now. Because you like me. Because you owe me. Because we're friends now and . . . well . . . because I'm fond of you.'

'You want me to go out there and risk my life? Just because you're *fond* of me?'

'You wouldn't be risking your life,' he says, dismissively. 'There's no reason to go getting all dramatic. But . . . yes, that's what I want.'

'Otherwise you're going to *make* me do it?'

'Yes.'

'How? What level of craziness exists in your head that makes you think you could force me to do a thing like this?'

He doesn't answer. He shakes his head like he's furious with himself, like he hates himself now, worse than ever. He rubs his hands up and down his neck, like he's looking for a way out, and all of a sudden he appears to have found one.

'Because that's what you want, isn't it?' he says, punching the side of his chair. 'To save me? I knew it the first time you walked into the apartment. Most people who walk through that door, they're so repulsed at the sight of me they can't even speak to me like I'm human. But you weren't like that. You treated me like I was normal . . . right from the moment you came in.'

'Yeah, well, see. That's because I'm decent . . . that's because I'm a decent person.'

'That's true. You are. But that's not all of it. Part of you wanted to rescue me. Why else would you have come back here week after week? Why else would a woman like you come and sit up here in this shitty apartment with a freak-show like me, night after night?'

'I told you. I wanted to learn how to play poker. It's no big deal, I just wanted to learn how to *play*.'

'You could have read about it. You're bright enough. You could have studied it for yourself, on your own. Truth is you wanted to help me. Because you couldn't help your mom or your dad. You couldn't stop her getting sick and you couldn't stop him going away. Could you, Ungar? You couldn't stop him. You ran around in circles entertaining him and learning all that math shit and listening to him and becoming his confessor. You did everything a kid your age could hope to do, but you still couldn't keep him from running away.'

'Stop it,' I say, standing up. '*Stop it*. You've got absolutely no right to comment about this. You don't even know what you're talking about.'

'And he's been out there all this time, hasn't he? Gambling his life away – Christ knows where – too proud, or too poor, or too stupid to come home and get you. And you've never stopped feeling guilty about it. If you'd only loved him more, he might have stayed. If you'd only treated him better he might have come back. If you'd been prettier or cleverer or brighter or kinder, he might have come back home to get you, instead of dumping you on a family you barely knew. You want to save everyone you've ever met. And right now, you want to save me.'

He's wrong. Utterly. Right now, at this precise second, I want to kill him.

'And it gets worse, doesn't it?' he says, struggling to stand up. 'Coz you recognise yourself when you look at me. You look at me living up here in this insane circle that I've drawn on the ground, and you recognise something of yourself.'

'In *you*? You think I recognise myself in someone . . . in someone like *you*?'

'Sure you do. You're only one click away. I seen you

counting and scratching and obsessing about the world: you like cleaning it up almost as much as I do. You can't stand to be late, you can't stand to be wrong, and you want to master every single thing that you touch. You lost control of your own world way back when you were a little kid, and you've been trying to get it back ever since. Because you never know when the next person is going to leave, do you? You never know when your world'll be ripped in half.

'What about that boyfriend of yours, huh? How long you been together now – four years, five? He wants to marry you, I bet. Have a couple of kids with you maybe? But you're too scared, aren't you? Too scared to let him know just how much you need him, in case he up and leaves you one day, just like your dad?'

I start to cry. It's as much as I can do not to vomit. I turn around, grab a chair-back to steady myself and head towards the safety of the door. Big Louie calls after me.

'Wait up. I'm sorry. Please. I'm sorry. I didn't know what else to do. Damn it,' he says, thumping the chair again, 'I'm no good at this shit. I don't know how to say it . . . please, Audrey . . . wait . . . wait a moment . . . I know where he is.'

I keep my back to him, my feet frozen solid to the floor. I hear the rustling of an envelope and Big Louie shifting in his seat, and slowly I turn around to look at him.

'Who?'

'Your dad,' he says, softly. 'I know where he is. That picture you gave me, the one of the guy in the white fedora. No one recognised your dad from the photograph but someone recognised the guy in the hat. Jimmy Joyce. The name Jimmy Joyce mean anything to you?'

I have to fight to keep myself upright. If I let go of the chair I might fall through the floorboards, through fifteen solid storeys, to the ground. I can't believe it. That the very person who took him away from me is the one person who might point the way back.

'I got a picture. You wanna see it? He don't go by the name Ungar any more, was too much to share his name with a world champion. He's pretty good though, gave up blackjack and craps and all that shit; he's a pretty hot Omaha player now, so I hear. You want to know what they call him?'

'What do they call him?' I hear myself saying.

'They call him the Prof, the Professor. Always doodling and telling stories to the other players to distract them. Facts and figures and funny little equations, and stories about the moon and the tides. He plays like you, Audrey, tight and clean. Always waiting for the good cards and adding up the right percentage move. Player like that don't get rich all that often, but it seems like he does alright.'

I hold the picture in my hands and look at my father's body clothed in a stranger's skin. The stranger is older and stockier than my dad and his facial lines make an unfamiliar map. The colour of his eyes has diluted with age and he's wider and fuller of face. But it's him. Beyond doubt, it's definitely him.

'Where was this taken? Are you going to tell me where this is?'

Big Louie stares at me, as still and silent as fog. He doesn't appear to be breathing.

'Are you going to help me?' he says, finally.

'Why are you asking?' I say, barely looking at him. 'You always knew that I would.'

47

It's a long way home. I drive through the shabby streets on autopilot with my dad's photograph propped up on the dashboard where I can see it. I pray for the traffic lights to be red so I can stare at it a little longer, and I curse at them every time they turn green. At some point I get paranoid and start to believe he can see me looking at him, and I have to put it away. A moment later I realise I'm being stupid, and position it back where it was.

It thrills me but it also upsets me. It saddens me to see his face so aged and so altered and to have no idea what events helped to shape it. The loves, the losses, the fears, the mistakes; I've no way of knowing about any one of them. A part of me hoped he'd look exactly the same. Like he might have had the decency to remain completely unchanged right up until the moment I found him. This photo is the evidence, the final proof, of more than half a life lived without me.

I arrive home faster than I wanted to and park the car on the opposite side of the road. I sit there for the best part of an hour, running things over in my head. Wondering how my life became so awkward and unkempt, wondering how best to fix it back together. One way or another my life has turned on its head again, but this time it isn't me that flipped it over. So I don't know what to do. I don't know how best to control it.

I scan the photo one more time before going inside, and by now I've committed every millimetre to memory. I know the precise colour of his skin, the exact width of his face, and I've detected the faint beginnings of a smile. It's not fully formed but it's there, nevertheless, waiting to spill out of his face. The lines around his eyes are about to soften and crease, and his eyelids are falling down towards his cheekbones. He still looks intelligent and handsome. He's not what he was but, considering what he must have been through, he's fought a decent battle with the years.

But there on his forehead, carved into it like chalk lines on a pavement, is an expression that says he's ill at ease. Perhaps he doesn't know the photographer, perhaps he's just lost an important game. Or perhaps he's not quite as comfortable as he appears to be. Maybe he's missing something from his life. Something that leaves him restless and wanting; that makes him feel as incomplete as me.

Joe is reading on the sofa and he jumps up as I walk into the room.

'Where have you been? I've been worried about you. Do you know what time it is? It's almost eight.'

'I'm sorry,' I say. 'I lost track.'

'Well, where were you? I saved you some food. Have you eaten?'

'I had a lot of lessons today. The last couple ran over. I should have phoned you. I'm sorry.'

He seems glad. He's glad that I'm back, glad that I'm alright, and he's happy when I tell him that I'm hungry. He warms up the food that he's made, pours me a glass of wine and comes to sit next to me while I eat. It takes all my effort to force it down. The photograph is burning a hole right through my pocket and I'm desperate to take it out and show it to him. But I don't. If he had the slightest inkling about what I was planning to do, he'd probably arrange to have me committed. And he'd be right. It'd be the only sane thing to do.

I wait until he's watching TV before I clear my throat, cough hard and say it.

'Joe?'

'Yeah?'

'I've been thinking that Lorna might be right.'

'Lorna? About what?'

'You know, what she said the other day about me taking a break. I mean, it's been a difficult few weeks and I need . . . maybe I should go away for a few days.'

'Well, where?' he says, turning round to face me. 'It's a good idea, but where do you want to go?'

'I'm not sure yet. I haven't decided.'

'What about waiting until next month? It'll have warmed up a little by then. We could get a cheap flight down to Nice or something.'

'I was thinking about going sooner . . . maybe next week.'

'Next week?'

'Yes.'

'But I can't. I've still got this project to finish.'

'The ornamental lake. I know.'

It takes him a moment, but he finally gets it.

'You want to go away on your *own*?'

'Just for a little while. A weekend, maybe. Definitely no longer than five days.'

He doesn't say anything. He turns away and starts pounding through the channels with the remote control.

'OK,' he says, finally. 'If you're sure that's what you want, then you should do it. Maybe you're right, perhaps we could do with a break from each other.'

He frowns and turns back to the TV. He looks hurt and vulnerable but he's trying not to let it show, so he pretends to be interested in a gardening programme that I know he hates. I want to tell him that he's got it all wrong. A break from Joe is the last thing I need. I want to curl up on the sofa and finish this bottle of wine and tell him about everything that's happened. About the poker games and the cheating and the kid with the cracked glass jaw, and all about Big

Louie's crazy scheme. But I can't. Because I'm certain that he'd try and stop me.

And I've already made up my mind. I have things to do. I have a flight to book and a stranger to find, and a bona fide giant to save.

48

I cancel all of my maths lessons and spend the whole of the next week round at Big Louie's flat. We go over it a thousand times. He takes me through my moves and watches me stack the deck, over and over and over again, until even he can't spot me doing it any longer. We practise until my fingers are stiff and sore like his, until I've blisters on my thumbs the size of pennies. We work at the bubble peek, the Greek deal, the base deal and the Hindu shuffle, and a range of other complex cuts and card transfers. I deal great hands to him and a better one to myself (the double duke) and I even centre-deal from the middle of the pack. I collect up the discards and place them anywhere I want, and when I get it right – which is pretty much all the time – he looks at me like he still can't believe it. As hard as he tried, he could never master dealing out of the centre; for a long time he didn't believe it was possible. But here I am, living proof. Sitting at his card table, sipping cold milk and cracking my knuckles, spinning aces out of midair like it was as easy as breathing.

We go at it non-stop. We only break to eat a mouthful of sandwich or suck down a pickle or two, and he sighs at me whenever I say I have to take a pee. We work on our pick-up culls and our discard culls and our crimps, hops and over-hand run-ups. When I'm sure I can't concentrate a second longer he makes a pot of coffee and tells me some more of his stories. About the cards that he marked and the giant hands that he won, and the dozen other ways of hustling dumb people out of their money. His favourite method when he started out was switching decks: swapping the honest deck with a pre-stacked one (a cooler) that he had pre-prepared in his pocket.

'The key to misdirection is to be subtle about it,' he says, explaining to me how he used to make the switch. 'Mostly I'd signal Little Louie to bark at somethin' out the window, but sometimes I'd work it out a little different. I might hide a spare chip on the floor early on in the game, and just before I planned to make the switch I'd point it out and ask which player dropped it. While everybody's looking at the chip and wondering if it's theirs or not, that's the moment you plant the cooler.

'A lot of mechanics operate in pairs,' he says, pouring me more coffee. 'Hell of a lot easier to work in pairs. One of you takes care of the sleight-of-hand, the other takes care of playing the winning cards. That way there's less chance you'll get caught. Not me, though. Always liked to do things on my own. Never found a partner who was as good as I was. Never found anyone I could really trust.'

'Until now?'

'What do you mean, until now?'

'Well, me. I'm your partner now, aren't I?'

He sighs, like he knew this was coming.

'Right,' he says, shuffling forward in his chair. 'Let's get this over with. I was wondering when you'd get around to asking about your cut.'

'My cut? No, that's not what I meant. I was onl—'

'Balloon Boy wanted half to begin with, but like I said to him then and I'll say to you now, half seems way, *way* too much. Seeing as it's me that's set up the game. Seeing as it's me that's provided all the stake. How would a flat fee suit you?

'How much?'

'Three thousand.'

'Dollars or pounds?'

'Dollars.'

'I see. That's not very much.'

'What are you talkin' about?' he says, faintly appalled. 'I'd say three thousand was plenty. I mean, you might screw it up. You might panic like a girl and get all teary eyed. You might sweat it and collapse under the pressure. It's all very well you flashing your magician's moves when you're up here safe with me, but in the real game you'll just as likely blow it. You might not have the courage, Ungar. The *heart*. The way I look at it, I'm being pretty generous. I'm taking quite a gamble with someone like you.'

He leans back from the table, pats the elastic round his middle and tries to work out what I'm thinking.

'OK,' I say, shrugging my shoulders. 'Three grand sounds fine.'

'It does?' he says, all suspicious.

'Yes. As long as you pay for the flights.'

'Done.'

'And the hotel.'

'Done.'

'And I want to stay somewhere nice.'

'What you worried about? I already said I'd book you somewhere with an en suite.'

'Nope.'

'What do you mean, nope?'

'I want to stay somewhere flash. With a bed the size of a snooker table and a view of the mountains, and a pool and a spa and—'

'Jeez, you're not going to Vegas to get your toes waxed. You're going there to win me back my dough. Ain't nothing a spa could do for you now anyways. I already told you, your best years are long behind you.'

I grimace at him, hard. He shrugs his shoulders.

'OK, then. OK. What about the Riviera or somethin'?'

'I was thinking more like the Mirage or the Bellagio.'

'The *Bellagio*? What, you think you're George Clooney now?'

'And I've been thinking, we ought to have ourselves a little side bet.'

'On what?' he says, already working out what odds he wants to give me.

'On whether or not I'll pull it off. On whether I'll cheat you or not. What odds did you give Balloon Boy of taking off with your winnings?'

He sighs loudly and rubs his chins.

'Wasn't even worth the bet. There's no way in the world he'd have double-crossed me.'

'How do you know?'

'Well,' he says, winking sharply and leaning back across the table, 'was more than his life was worth, if you know what I mean.'

'You threatened him?'

'I might have said something or other.'

'Something or other?'

'This or that.'

'This or that?'

'Yeah, you know. Suggested like I was connected; like I might've had him roughed up a little bit.'

'Roughed up?'

'Yeah, you know. Like I might have had him whacked or somethin'.'

'What about me?' I say, pretending to be alarmed. 'What about if I run off with the winnings? You going to have me killed as well?'

'Sure,' he says, quick as a flash. 'Absolutely. No doubt about it.'

I grimace and pick at my blisters. And then I start to smile.

'Well, no wonder you lost when you were playing straight, then. Because I'll tell you something, you can't bluff for shit.'

He frowns and rises up in his chair. All seven feet of him.

'Fine. You think I'm bluffing, do you?'

'Yes.'

'Well, I'm not. Truth is I wouldn't think twice about it. A red-haired, smart-alec, can't shuffle for shit woman like you. If you screwed me over, I'd have you whacked in a New York minute.'

He's gone too far and he knows it. He can't hold it together any more. His frown breaks out into a foot-wide grin and he lets out a resonant chuckle.

'Yeah, well,' he says, shaking his head from side to side and sitting himself back down, 'I guess you're right. Because I don't need to have you whacked, do I? Only way you're going to find out where your dad's at is if you wire me that money as soon as you win it. I'm only offering you a cut in the first place so you can afford to go get your toes waxed and stop looking like a monkey . . .'

He stops short when he sees the look on my face, but he knows it's already too late. I stand up, push back my chair and tell him that I have to use the loo. It happens like this every so often. Amid the banter and the chatter and the practice and the precision, it all comes back to one thing. I wouldn't be doing this if he wasn't making me: if he wasn't holding out on me about where my father is. I've kept his picture with me every day this week, and barely an hour's passed when I haven't looked at it. Every time I perfect another shuffle or pull off another deal I know that I'm doing it for him.

We try not to mention it unless we have to, but both of us know exactly where we stand. It means he's using me, manipulating me, controlling me. It means we're not really friends any more.

By the time I get back from the bathroom, Big Louie's left the card table and settled himself into his favourite chair. The flat is as tidy as I've ever seen it, but he still likes to sit in his bleached-clean circle from time to time. He has a brown paper package clutched firmly in his hand: the size and the shape of a large brick. He's running his fingers over the crisp, tight creases, handling it like it was made of solid gold.

'Here,' he says, handing it to me to look at. 'This is everything that you're gonna need.'

'The money?'

'Yep. Stayed up most of last night ironing it. Got it real flat. Nice and smooth, so it made a neat, clean pile for me to wrap.'

I pick it up. It's dense. And heavy.

'Can I take it with me?' I say, turning the package over in my hand.

'Not yet. Was just showing it to you so as you'd know it was for real. I'll let you have it to take home with you on Sunday night.'

Sunday is our last day together. I fly out to Vegas first thing Monday morning.

'And remember to bring your outfit the next time you come over. I know it's gonna be hard for you, but you're gonna have to at least try and look attractive. Wear something sexy. Somethin' low cut, maybe? They won't be expecting a good-looking woman to cheat them, and if you dress up nice you won't catch so much steam.'

'Steam?'

'Surveillance. They're less likely to be scrutinising your play if they're looking at . . . you know . . . something else.'

I start to look nervous but he chides me and tells me I'm not to worry.

'Look, it's all part of the hustle, that's all. You're a talented mechanic, Audrey. You could be one of the greats. A living legend. You should be proud of your skills.'

'Of being a cheat? You want me to feel proud of cheating?'

292

'Everyone's cheating, Ungar,' he says, solemnly. 'The whole world's at it. Ain't no one playing it clean, only the suckers. It's simply a question of degrees.'

Big Louie shifts in his seat. He wouldn't think to say it out loud, but I know a part of him feels uneasy about what he's asking me to do.

He does his usual trick. He waits until I'm almost through the door before he finds a way to make me feel better.

'Hey, Ungar?'

'What?'

'We never finished working out our side bet. I never gave you your odds on winning the game.'

'OK,' I say, turning round and looking at him. 'What do you give me? What are my chances of pulling it off?'

He hums and hahs like he's still deciding, then he smiles straight at me and nods his head.

'Honestly?' he says, gazing over at me.

'Honestly. Yes, I want to know.'

'Truth is I already closed the book on you. There's not a shred of doubt in my mind.'

'You really think I can do it?'

'Sure,' he says, 'I know you can.'

49

'Casablanca?'

'Yes.'

'In Morocco?'

'Yes.'

'That's where you've decided to go?'

Why did I say Casablanca? It doesn't sound remotely plausible. Of all the places, in all the world, I had to choose sodding Casablanca.

'Any reason?'

'What do you mean?'

'Well, why did you choose to go there?'

'I don't know. It's . . . well, it sounded romantic.'

'Romantic?'

Bad answer. Very bad answer. I'm going away for a week's holiday, on my own, without my boyfriend, and I'm justifying my choice of destination on the grounds that it sounds romantic.

'OK, no. I don't mean romantic in that way.'

'What way?'

'The sex way.'

'You think Casablanca is sexy?'

'Look, it's just . . . well, I've never been to North Africa, that's all. And I could take a trip to Marrakesh, or a trek up the Atlas mountains. I could rent a camel or buy a donkey and live with some crazy Berbers, up in the hills.'

'Yeah, or you could pretend you're Ingrid Bergman and run off to Gibraltar with Humphrey Bogart.'

'She didn't run off with Humphrey Bogart. She left him at the airfield and came home with the boring one.'

'The boring one?'

'Yes, what was his name? See, I can't even remember what he was called.'

Joe looks troubled. If only I'd chosen somewhere ordinary like Nimes. Or Trieste. I should have picked somewhere cultural like Prague. I should have said I wanted to look at old buildings and visit museums and take long moody walks round ancient monuments. Now he thinks I want to spend the whole week sitting in a smoky nightclub on the edge of the Sahara, fantasising about being Ingrid Bergman.

'So you've booked your flight then?'

'Yes, Monday morning. Moroccan Air.'

'Air Maroc?'

'That's what I said.'

'And where are you staying?'

'Um . . . I'm not sure. I thought I might wait until I got there. You know, sometimes you can get a cheaper deal that way.'

'You haven't booked a hotel? You always book. You never go anywhere without knowing where you're going to stay.'

'Well, if I get desperate there's always a Hilton, isn't there? I mean, as long as I've got my credit card, I'll be fine.'

'So you're just going to chance it?'

'Yes, exactly,' I say, seizing on his explanation. 'That's exactly what I'm going to do. I'm going to chance it.'

Christ, why did I say that? It's not in my nature to chance things. I don't chance, I *plan*. When Joe and I go away on holiday together, I research our destination with such dedication that I know precisely what it's going to smell like before we get there. I cross-reference our selected location in six different guidebooks and two dozen brochures and spend hours looking up facts about it on the Internet.

I spend an inordinate amount of time comparing and

contrasting. I check out facilities, restaurants, day trips and accommodation, and pay particular attention to researching the hotel pools. The moment we arrive I insist that Joe come with me to look at all the other hotel pools in the area, just so as I can prove to him that I made the right choice. It's insane. We spend half our time looking at places where we're never going to stay, just so I can prove that I was right. But I have to know. I can't enjoy myself otherwise.

Joe doesn't have any more questions. He looks at me strangely, opens a bottle of beer and wanders into the kitchen to phone Pete. I head straight back to the bedroom. I open the drawer, pull out a fresh deck of cards and shut the door tight behind me: something that I never usually do. But I need to practise in private. I can't let him catch me perfecting my moves.

I work out my escape route before I start. I've calculated that I have precisely four point five seconds between hearing his footsteps at the door and him seeing me with the deck, and I'm pretty sure I can cover things in less than three. I can put away the cards, get myself on to the bed and open a copy of *The Guinness Book of World Records* in one slick move. I try it a couple of times and end up face down on the floor looking at a picture of the world's biggest bogie, but the third time I do it I get it right. In fact, the pressure of being discovered is helping me concentrate.

I loosen my hands, dab surgical spirit on my blisters to harden them, and begin repeating the most difficult deals. I do it with my eyes closed. It actually helps not to look. It has to be about feel, intuition; about developing a sure sense of where each of the fifty-two cards sits in the pack. The more I think about the shuffles, the slower they are, but when I relax everything falls into place. I lay out a hand for six players, pick them up and lay out another for three. Each time I deal I lay out a winning hand for myself and weak hands for all the others. Except for one person. The person

I want to bet against me. And next week they're all going to take their turn. One by one, piece by piece, I'm going to take down each and every one of them.

'Why have you got a six of clubs up your sleeve?'

'I . . . oh . . . um . . . bookmark.'

'Up your sleeve?'

'I'm keeping it safe.'

'Why are you reading a chapter on bogies?'

'Oh, er . . . well, they're pretty amazing. This one's nearly six inches tip to tip.'

'I see.'

'Hey, how was Pete?'

'I didn't speak to Pete. I was talking to Lorna.'

'Oh. Didn't she want to speak to me?'

'You had the door closed. I thought you wanted to be left alone.'

Joe gets ready for bed and, without even asking me, he reaches over to turn out the light. I lie next to him listening to his breathing, and it irritates me that he's fallen asleep so quickly. I doubt I'll ever fall asleep again. My head is grinding like an engine, and I can't believe the noise isn't keeping Joe awake. I try to relax. I stretch all my muscles, contract them hard and let them go again, but I just end up giving myself a stitch. I resort to a tried-and-tested method; reciting the Periodic Table in my head. It takes me longer than usual and I get right to the end of transitional elements and halfway through the noble gases before my brain finally gives up and falls asleep.

I dream about Pete and his aliens, and Louie and his magic circle, and about Joe and Lorna and my dad. It's the moment after that marble match and he's waiting for me outside the school gate. I'm trying to explain to him how unfair it was that the teacher confiscated my whole collection and he kneels down and says he has something to ask me. He's wearing his thin leather coat and a long woollen scarf and there are flakes of sand falling out of the sky instead of snow. His face is the way it looks now, saggy and mottled, and I'm confused as to why he looks so old.

'Did you win it, Ginger-nut?'

'Yes. I did.'

'Did you win it fair and square?'

'Yes.'

'That's good, then. It doesn't matter what the other kids say. As long as you and I know the truth.'

'The truth?'

'That you didn't cheat. That you didn't con that boy out of his marbles.'

I think for a while and then I smile at him. Because I know the answer to this question. I definitely, positively didn't cheat.

50

'This is it then?'

'I guess so.'

'You want me to go over any of it again?'

'No. I think I've got it.'

'You *think* you got it?'

'I *know*. I know I have. I'm sure.'

Big Louie nods at me like he's satisfied.

'You bring your outfit?'

'Yes. Do you want to see it?'

'Sure. You can change in the bathroom.'

I slip out of my jeans and jumper and step into the new dress that I've bought. It's red and clingy and more low cut than I'm used to, and I've bought high heels and fishnets to go with it. And false eyelashes. And a new lipstick. And just so as I can get into character, I've topped the whole thing off with something perfect: my fake fur jacket.

'Jeez. I thought I told you to dress up a little more sexy. I didn't say you should try an' look like a low-rent hooker. And what's with the squirrel fur jacket? I thought you were taking that thing back to the shop?'

My face falls but I try not to let him see it.

'I meant to, but I didn't have time. I thought it went with the dress. Shit, do I really look like a hooker?'

'You look OK,' he says, grudgingly.

'OK?'

'Yeah, I mean, you know . . . if I was playing against you I might feel a little distracted.'

'Why, because I look attractive?'

'Nah,' he says, turning his face away. 'Because you look like a transvestite.'

I change back into my jeans and we run through the moves one last time. Louie says the dealing duties are going to move round the table and that he's expecting ten players to start. Eddie's going to meet me at the airport and he'll confirm the final set-up when I arrive.

'You know not to overdo it, right?'
'Yes.'
'You know to play tight for the rest of the time?'
'Yes. We've been over this a dozen times. I'll play extra tight but I'll lose on a couple of small hands, just so it doesn't look too clean.'
'And you don't win every time you deal.'
'No, you told me. Sometimes I should deal cards that'll provoke showdowns between the other players. I should let them fight it out among themselves once in a while. The more players I can eliminate the better. The fewer players there are, the bigger my edge.'
'And when you hustle them for real—?'
'I know, I'm not to do anything obvious like win with four of a kind all the time. I should win with small hands that are just a bit better than the ones that I've set up against me. A hand big enough to attract plenty of action but not big enough—'
'—to arouse suspicion. That's right. I'm glad you got it.'
We play a few more hands but neither one of us is concentrating very hard. It's like that time at the end of a party when you're waiting for a cab and you know your conversation is likely to be curtailed at any moment.
'Louie?'
'What?'
'Do you think I'd ever make a decent poker player?'

'Playing clean?'

'Yes. Without the shuffles and the fake deals and all this mechanic stuff. Do you think I could ever get good at it?'

He shrugs his shoulders.

'Who knows? You already turned out better that I thought you would. When you walked through that door and asked me to teach you, I figured you wouldn't be able to play for shit.'

'Because I'm a woman?'

'Hell, no. Plenty of great woman players out there. Only a matter of time before one of them shows the guys what's what and walks away with the World Series bracelet.'

'But you said—'

'I know what I said, but it ain't true. I didn't think you'd be lousy because you were a woman. I thought you'd be lousy because you're afraid. Because you don't trust yourself enough, or know yourself enough; because you haven't got the courage to use what you know. You ain't got enough gamble left in you.'

'You could tell all that? Right away?'

'From the moment you walked through the door. It's my job to know people. I'm well trained, and I'm always one hundred per cent on the button.'

I shift in my chair. Both of us know what's coming next.

'So . . . well . . . were you right?'

'Sure,' he says, nodding at me. 'Almost.'

'Almost?'

He thinks for a moment, lacing his fingers behind his head and working out the best way to say it.

'The thing is, Audrey, you're desperate to gamble. More desperate than almost anyone I ever seen. You got all this potential locked inside you, but you still can't stand to let go. You always got to do the right thing. You're always working out the best play, the best move, always adding everything up.'

'But that's what you told me to do. You told me that it's a game of discipline. That poker is life as it really is. No fate, no favouritism, just patience, hard work and calculation. A case of the best play wins.'

'Sure,' he says, leaning in to me. 'And that's all true. Don't get nowhere in this world without appreciating its logic, without viewing it with a rational eye. But you gotta know how to use it. In three years, maybe five, if you worked at it every day, if you practised real hard, a person like you could make a decent living. You'd grind away playing for small stakes and the occasional big win, but you'd never be a truly great player. The greats are the ones who're prepared to take a risk, to go the extra mile when they're under pressure. They call it *heart*, Audrey, it's something that all the legends have. The courage to take their life in their hands and trust their judgement. The strength to throw everything they have into the pot, the moment they sense the odds are in their favour.'

'So that's it, then. You think I play it too safe?'

He tuts at me and shakes his head.

'What you askin' me for? You know you do. The second you're not sure how a thing is gonna end, you get up from the table and walk away. And the funny thing is, it's the last thing on earth you really want. But I been there, Audrey. I know how it feels. It's the only way you know how to live.'

We both pause for a moment and then I say:

'What about you? What kind of player would you have been? If you hadn't been a hustler. If you'd played it straight every single game.'

'Well,' he says, closing his eyes for a second, 'there's no doubt about it. I would have been one of the all-time greats. Would have had Johnny Chan running scared at the sight of me, had Amarillo Slim shaking in his pants. If somewhere along the line I hadn't got a little scared. If some freak wind hadn't knocked me off my feet.

'But like I said, the odds don't always go your way in this world. It's how you handle the bad beats that counts. And whatever happens, however bad it gets, you can't afford to let it stop you livin'. It don't mean you gotta lose control and throw it all away; it don't mean you gotta wind up like your dad. I know that's what you been afraid of all these years, but you're much too clever for that. It's just that living so careful, it's liable to kill you. You gotta promise me something, Audrey. I mean it. You gotta promise that you won't end up like me.'

It's seven o'clock and our time's nearly up, but neither of us wants me to leave. I need to pack up my things and have dinner with Joe, but I'm worried about leaving him on his own.

'Sure, don't sweat it. I'll be fine.'

'You promise?'

'Yeah, I've organised a couple of games with the old Rat Pack boys. Marilyn's bringing me up a packet of salt beef and Dean Martin's seeing me right for pickles.'

'And you're not going to cheat them?'

'Hell no. What'd be the point? I could beat them with my eyes shut as it is.'

I smile and zip up my jacket and promise to call him the minute I know. He stops me as I walk towards the door. He has something for me: a small box wrapped up in tissue paper and tied with a navy blue ribbon.

'Should I open it now?'

'Sure,' he says, fidgeting and pulling at his hands. 'Why not?'

I pull off the tissue paper piece by piece and squeeze the lid off the box. It's a flower. A perfect, creamy white flower.

'Where did you get this?'

'Bloomed late last night,' he says, nodding over at the window box. 'It's a desert lily. Guess your fella must've thrown it in as extra. Anyways, I thought I oughta pick it for you. You know . . . to say thanks or somethin'.'

'You went out . . . on to the balcony?'

'Yeah, for a second I did. Thought maybe you could press it and take it with you. Maybe it'll bring you good luck.'

'But it's not about luck, though, is it?' I say, looking up at him.

'Yeah,' he says, 'a little bit it is.'

He turns away like he's embarrassed, waits until I'm almost through the door, and then he says:

'By the way, you looked real pretty in your red dress.'

'Really?'

'Yeah, you know, sort of classy.'

He swings round to look at me one more time.

'I think it was the jacket that did it, but the truth is, Ungar, you looked kinda glamorous.'

51

It's 5.30 in the morning and there's a light fog sleeping over London. We drive up the Euston Road towards the Westway and I can just make out the top of Big Louie's tower block saluting me from behind the station. The mist makes it look crooked – like it's leaning to one side – and I'm worried that it might collapse before I get back. I wonder if he's out of bed yet. I wonder if he's managed to get some rest. I don't think I closed my eyes for more than an hour last night; I was far too excited to sleep.

Joe has the radio on – I made him switch over for the traffic bulletins – and already I'm fretting about being late. The flight doesn't take off for another three hours, but I've got to negotiate the tricky business of changing terminals. Royal Air Maroc operates from Terminal 2, but my flight to Vegas leaves from Terminal 4. I'll have to pretend Joe is dropping me off at the right place, then catch the train over to the other terminal after he's gone.

We don't speak much during the journey. Joe asks if I've packed sunblock and Imodium and I tell him that I'll buy some at the airport. He asks me if I've got any travel insurance and I tell him I'll get some later when I buy my currency.

'You haven't bought your currency yet?'

'What? No. I'll buy some dollars at the Travelex when we get there.'

'Dollars?'

'Yeah, um . . . Moroccan dollars.'

'I don't think they use dollars in Morocco.'

'Don't they?'

'No. I think it's the dirham.'

'Right. Dirham. I'll get some of those then.'

Now I'm really anxious. All this talk of currency is making me worry about Big Louie's brown paper package. I have it packed at the bottom of my suitcase underneath my skimpiest knickers, and I'm hoping that if they search my bag they'll be too embarrassed to look through them. I've made a special effort and dressed up as smartly as I can. I've decided that they're less likely to search me if I look like a businesswoman so I'm wearing the grey flannel trouser suit that I keep for interviews and funerals.

'Aren't you going to be a bit uncomfortable?'

'How do you mean?'

'Wearing that suit on a four-hour flight.'

'Well, you know, I don't wear it very often. I thought it could do with a bit of an outing.'

'You think your interview suit needs a holiday?'

'Well, it's been stuck in the wardrobe for ages. I mean, it's not like it gets out much. I don't go to that many interviews.'

He stares at me. Like I've gone mad.

It's 7.35, I'm still in Terminal 2, and my flight takes off in under an hour. My elbows are itching, I've just burst the blisters on my thumbs, and I've only just managed to shake him off. He wanted to help me check in. He wanted to make sure I was at the right place. There was only one thing for it. I had to pretend the check-in desk wasn't open yet and drag him off to Garfunkels for a cup of coffee. I think he was trying to delay me on purpose. Why else would he have ordered the all-you-can-eat breakfast? How long does it take to eat a sausage? How can anyone make a strip of bacon last that long? I thought he'd never leave. I thought he'd hang around here all day. In the end, I had to yank him away from his hash browns and forcibly bundle him out of the terminal building, on the pretext that I don't like long goodbyes. He looked a bit hurt. I think he was hoping for one of those cinematic farewells where I wave back at him with tear-stained cheeks, just as I disappear through the departure gate.

The rest of it goes off like clockwork. I check in with fifteen minutes to spare, no one searches my bag, and for the first time ever I get upgraded. Something about my wearing an expensive suit and being last to check in, and I'm already beginning to feel much better. The other business travellers are eschewing the free champagne and waving away their complimentary slippers, but I'm taking everything that I'm offered. By the time we taxi out to the runway, I'm three drinks down, I've had two shoulder massages and I'm wearing a fleecy romper suit and a double layer of support socks. I've ordered six DVDs and a couple of cocktails with my fillet steak dinner, and I'm particularly looking forward to trying the eighteen-year-old vintage port. I have my father's photograph clutched tightly in my hand and I can barely wait to leave the ground.

The take-off is settled and graceful but as soon as we're up we hit turbulence. The plane lurches awkwardly from side to side – a few of the other passengers grimace and tighten their seat belts – but I've never felt happier in my life. The harder it bumps, the more I relax, and somewhere over Dublin I fall asleep. I miss the cocktails and the steak and the oak-aged port, and don't stir again for the next ten hours. Not until we've crossed the Atlantic and carved through the Midwest, and we're circling high above the dry Mojave Desert.

Las Vegas is made out of sunlight. It might be the alcohol or the jet lag or the fact that I haven't eaten, but I can barely open my eyes. There's something about six months buried away under a British winter sky that makes you feel a bit like a pit pony: starved of colour and sunshine. Everything looks so bright. The desert stretches out towards a door-stop of tawny mountains and the heat is already burrowing its way under my skin. The whole journey feels something like time travel; one moment I'm eating sausages in a grotty airport canteen, listening to the rain; the next I'm crossing a tarmac in 92 degrees of heat and munching fajitas in front of a ten-foot plastic cactus.

'Miss? Please put down your sandwich.'

'It's not a sandwich. It's a fajita.'

'Miss, you're going to have to put that away.'

'But the stewardess saved it for me. I slept right through lunch and dinner. I didn't even get to watch *Mrs Doubtfire*.'

'*Mrs Doubtfire*?'

'With Robin Williams. I wouldn't have ordered it – I mean, Robin Williams is probably my least favourite actor of all time – but I've never flown business class before, and I sort of got carried away with having so much choice.'

'You didn't like *The Fisher King*?'

'No.'

'Or *Dead Poets Society*?'

'God, no. It was awful.'

I thought we were getting along OK. We were having a fine old time discussing the ins and outs of Mr Williams's rocky career path when suddenly the immigration officer asked me a tricky question. He wanted to know whether I was in Vegas on business or for pleasure, and I thought for a second and said *both*. For some reason he didn't like my answer. According to him I couldn't be in Vegas for business *and* pleasure, and now he wants to know why I filled in my form wrong.

'Says here you've been a member of the Communist Party.'

'No. I haven't. I ticked the wrong box. I'd only just woken up. I haven't taken drugs or been arrested either.'

'What about being a Nazi?'

'Do I look like a Nazi?'

'What are you then, Australian?'

'No, look. Its says here on my passport. I'm British.'

'Hmmm. Then how come you sound like an Australian?'

'Um . . . did I mention that I liked Robin Williams in *Mork and Mindy*?'

'Yeah, well . . . I didn't care for *Mork and Mindy*.'

It's no good. He makes me go right to the back of the queue and fill in my immigration form all over again. By the time I've finished, two more flights have touched down and it takes me another forty minutes to claim my baggage and reach the arrivals hall.

People are already gambling. The corridors are lined with coffee shops and slot machines, and clusters of luck-starved tourists, pouring away the last of their pennies. I stop for a moment and shove a couple of quarters into a machine called the Wheel of Fortune. It spins, clicks, gurgles and whines and spits out five dollars in change. I take this to be a good sign. It's the first and the last time I'm going to gamble in this town; I didn't come here to play a game of chance.

I pocket my winnings and squeeze my way out towards the crowded exit. Hotel reps are picking up tired travellers, nervous husbands are waiting for their wives, bored chauffeurs are milling around smoking cigarettes and reading newspapers and some of them are holding up signs. They say 'Bally's' or 'The Venetian' or 'Good Luck from Harrah's', and one of them says 'Ungar from London'. The man waving it above his head is short and rosy cheeked with a black Stetson pulled low over his eyes. He's wearing cowboy boots and shorts made out of cut-down sweat pants, and has the name Eddie embroidered across the breast pocket of his shirt. I walk over and introduce myself.

Eddie shakes my hand and takes my suitcase. He's polite

enough – he enquires about my flight and asks after Big Louie – but he's clearly not much of a talker. When I ask about the final set-up for tomorrow's game, he shrugs and says we'll talk back at the hotel. He strides towards the exit, marching briskly ahead of me, and I follow him out into the scorching sunlight. I smile like a kid when I see it. A white stretch limousine with blacked-out windows, the length of a small suburban street.

'You ever been in a stretch before?' he says, opening the door for me.

'No,' I say. 'I haven't.'

'Yeah, well,' he says, turning up his lip, 'it's a little flashy for my tastes, but the Big Man thought you might get a kick out of it.'

52

A few minutes later we're parked at the southern end of the Strip, in front of a vast black pyramid made out of glass.

'The Luxor,' says Eddie, nodding towards it. 'That's where you'll be staying tonight. You want me to show you the rest of the Strip before you check in?'

I do. I definitely want him to show me.

I settle into the butter-soft leather, roll up my sleeves and push my face right up to the limousine's tinted window. We take it slowly, cruising the three and a half miles from one end of the Strip to the other, past giant roller-coasters, exploding volcanoes, dancing water fountains and life-size galleons overrun by marauding pirates. We drive through Paris, New York, Venice and the South Sea Islands, and at one point I spot the Guinness World of Records Museum, and point it out excitedly to Eddie. He doesn't seem all that impressed. He rolls down the window, lights a cigarette and nods in the direction of a lap-dancing club called Hooters. Hooters is Eddie's favourite place in the whole of Las Vegas, apart from Cheetahs and Lee's Discount Liquor, and a tattoo parlour called Absolute Ink.

At the north end of the Strip, after a quick peek at Fremont Street, Eddie swings the limousine back around. The sun is going down and the lights are coming on, and now the skyline is fizzing with rainbow-coloured neon. It's gorgeous and grotesque; like it was designed by porn stars, clowns and circus midgets and the ghost of Gianni Versace.

By the time we get back to the Luxor I'm worn out. I'm nauseous from the pulsing and the flashing and gawping at all the Elvises, and I'm beginning to feel like I've just eaten a bag of magic mushrooms. Eddie wants to meet me in an hour. I should have told him I needed longer to freshen up, but he seems disappointed in me as it is. Perhaps it was my unhealthy interest in the Guinness World of Records Museum, perhaps it's the way I look in my dowdy grey suit. Perhaps it's the fact that he was expecting a man, instead of a nosy-arsed, can't-shuffle-for-shit woman.

By the time I've queued up at the check-in and located my room, our hour is almost up. I've spent the last forty minutes getting lost in a casino the size of an aircraft hangar, pleading with someone to direct me to the elevators. There are no arrows or signs or directions and it's hard to make yourself heard over the shrill notes of two thousand clanging slots. Gangs of people are plugged into them like saline drips – buckets of quarters bleeding into the machines. Some of them play in groups; crossing themselves before they press the button, and holding hands while they wait for the wheels to stop. Some of them are still and silent like they've been hypnotised, and others are chattering all the time. They sigh and growl and curse when they lose, and shriek like hyperactive children when they win.

I can't help scanning their faces. I look for tall men with bent arms that don't straighten properly any more, and goofy men wearing white fedora hats. I look for thin leather coats and conker-coloured eyes and glimpses of a past that's been lost to me. I even looked out for him at the airport. I know it's ridiculous, but a tiny fraction of me half hoped that my father would be waiting.

By the time I reach my room I'm already running late and I change as quickly as I can. I tie up my hair, dab on a slick of lipstick and prop my father's photo on the bedside table. I throw on a clean skirt and, just so I can practise how to walk in them, I dig out my fishnet tights and heels. Eddie is waiting for me in the Nefertiti Lounge; he's already bought me a drink.

'What is it?'

'White Russian.'

'What's in it?'

'How should I know? White Russian's a woman's drink.'

I eat the cherry, fold up the umbrella and take a sip of the thin milky liquid.

'How is it?' he says. 'Sweet enough for you?'

I grimace and put it down and order myself a beer from a passing Cleopatra. Eddie has obviously trained at the same charm school as Big Louie, and it's pretty obvious that he's taken a dislike to me.

'How's your room?'

'It's fine.'

'You got a Jacuzzi?'

'No.'

'The best rooms have got a Jacuzzi. You can watch the sunset from the tub.'

'Really?' I say, tipping back my beer. 'That must be nice.'

'It's nice if you've got some of the Hooters girls in there with you. Otherwise, you know . . . it's just a sunset.'

I nod like I know what he means, and he starts to shift about in his seat. He's clearly gearing up to something important but he kindly waits until I've got a mouthful of peanuts before he says it.

'Look . . . uh . . . Audrey. Would you mind if I spoke frankly for a second?'

'Shoot,' I say, trying not to spit out my peanuts. 'You go right ahead.'

'Well, thing is . . . uh, I mean, I don't want to upset you or nothing, but you weren't exactly what I was expecting. I was sort of expecting—'

'A man?'

'Yeah. That's right. See, this game's been finalised almost

six months now, and the point is, well, I don't like last-minute changes. They don't sit too easy with me, you know what I'm saying?'

'They make you nervous?'

'That's right,' he says, rubbing his belly. 'Give me a nervous stomach. And if there's one thing I sure don't appreciate in life, it's a nervous stomach.'

'I see.'

'Don't get me wrong. I gotta whole lot of respect for the Big Man, we go back a long way, but it's been a good while since he was out here. I'm thinking that maybe—'

'He's lost his touch?'

'Exactly. I'm glad you can see what I'm saying.'

Eddie leans back in his chair, satisfied that I've understood his point. He wants to offer me a pay-off. My three thousand dollars – right here, right now – if I'll take a rain check, turn round and go home again. He has another card mechanic that he trusts. Someone that might better take my place. He'd need a bigger cut than me – of course he would – but he's one hundred and ten per cent reliable.

'You can't have a hundred and ten per cent.'

'Say what?'

'You can't have a hundred and ten per cent. The most you can have is a hundred.'

Eddie smacks his lips. He doesn't appreciate me trying to be clever.

'Look,' he says, patting the side of his shorts, 'I got it in my pocket right now. Three thousand in cash, no strings attached. You wouldn't even have to get your hands dirty. All you have to do is give me the package, and the two of us can forget this ever happened. You can have yourself a little holiday, get yourself a fancy tan, visit the Guinness museums or whatever.'

'I don't tan.'

'Say what?'

'It's the red hair. I don't tan. I just burn.'

Eddie lets out a disgruntled sigh and I fill the ensuing silence by ordering myself a neat Bourbon. I wait until the waitress brings it over before I continue. I imagine Eddie is Humphrey Bogart and that I'm the real Lauren Bacall, and I lower my voice a couple of notches, until it's as strong and husky as I can make it.

'Listen to me,' I say, holding up my glass and leaning towards him. 'I want to thank you for picking me up today and giving me that little sightseeing tour of the Strip. I appreciate it, I really do, but there's a couple of things we ought to get straight.'

He nods his head. I cross my legs.

'First of all it'll be me playing that game tomorrow evening, and second of all I don't want your lousy money. Thirdly, and you might want to make a little note of this, Eddie, I don't really care for White Russians.'

'I see.'

'Good. Because the point is . . . the thing you need to know, is that I'm the best card mechanic you've ever seen. I've got fingers as sharp as knitting needles and a brain that can add up faster than you can speak, and I've been training for a game like this since I was eleven years old. Nothing is going to push me off it. Do you understand? Not you, not your money, not your "hundred and ten per cent" weasel-boy, and certainly not . . . certainly not you.'

'You said me already.'

'OK. Good. Just testing. I'm glad you were paying attention there, Eddie. But . . . well, fuck it, you know what I mean.'

He starts to laugh. He drains the rest of his beer, orders us both another Bourbon and raises his hand so I can give him a high-five.

'Sheesh,' he says, slapping his palm into mine. 'The Big Man was right on the button. I bet him two hundred dollars you'd take the money and run the minute I offered it to you.

I mean, you don't even look like you got it in you. Don't look like any card mechanic I've ever seen, that's for sure.'

I smile into my drink, happy that Eddie approves of me at last and glad that Big Louie had enough faith to place his bet on me. I reach into the peanut bowl, flick a salty nut into my mouth and take a celebratory glug of my Jack Daniel's.

'That whisky a little strong for you?'

'No, ahem, it's fine.'

'Why you coughing so hard, then?'

'It's not the drink. It's the nut. I think it went down the wrong way.'

'You want me to order you up another one of them drinks with the cherries on the top?'

'Instead of the Bourbon?'

'Uhuh.'

'Ahem . . . yes please. That'd be very nice.'

53

'You sleep OK?'

It's Eddie with my lunch-time wake-up call.

'Shit, what time is it?'

'Almost twelve. Don't worry, you're on Vegas time now, honey.'

The pair of us stayed up pretty late last night. We spent hours going over the ins and outs of this evening's game, discussing the exact way it should breathe and unfold. We talked about the venue and the timing and the background of all the other players, and only when he was one hundred and fifteen per cent certain I had it covered did Eddie relax and offer up another of his little tours. We drank more cocktails and cased the other casinos, and wandered into a few of the poker rooms along the Strip. We joined in a $5/$10 Hold'em game at the Mirage and Eddie won two hundred dollars in his second hand. I played cautiously and tight and left the game about even, but I don't think I played too badly. It wasn't exactly the big league but Eddie seemed content enough with my performance. I looked confident, I knew what I was doing and, most importantly, I didn't slow up the game.

After that he decided it would be a good idea for me to let my hair down. Tonight I'm going to have to concentrate harder than I ever have in my life, and Eddie wanted the gamble drained right out of me. I tried to persuade him that I didn't have that much gamble in me to drain, but he was oddly and uniquely insistent. We spent the rest of the night squandering his poker winnings: playing low-limit blackjack; circling numbers on sheets of losing Keno tickets; and feeding fistfuls of coins to the gurgling slots. We zigzagged back and forth – through the crowds and the newly-weds and the blood-thickening heat – from the Venetian to Caesar's Palace, to the shark tanks at Mandalay Bay.

We finished off the night downtown at the El Cortez: breathing in the scent of swollen ashtrays and weeks-old perspiration, and walking fresh bald spots into the faded carpets. The pair of us played low-stakes roulette with old men dressed in jogging suits and women with fingernails as long as knives. We drank coffee in circular leather booths and ordered tequila from waitresses in hot pink dresses, with beehive hairdos as solid as Russian concrete. We ordered ice cream covered in syrup and sprinkles and ate hotdogs at four in the morning. I was just wondering what kind of tattoo I should get when Eddie said we ought to think about getting back.

By the time we reached the Luxor the sun was almost up; filling the sky with broad bands of rose-coloured light, and warming the cold desert back to life. The serious gamblers and high-rollers were just heading for their beds, and I stopped by the elevator to scan their weary faces. I could imagine my dad doing the same thing on the first night he got here. Jet-lagged and elated and far away from home, preparing to risk it all to be one of them.

I found my way back to my room, quickly this time, and fell into a deep, easy sleep. I dreamt of jackpots and poker chips and wheels with double zeros, and of playing a Saturday afternoon game of cribbage with my dad. My mum was playing along with us. Crossing her elegant fingers before the turn of every card, while my dad smiled at her and gently rolled his eyes. It was always his job to keep track of the scores and he'd jot down the numbers in three neat columns. If my mum was losing too badly he'd sometimes shoot me a wink, and nudge up her scores so she did better. I think she always knew that he'd helped her along, but none of us ever thought to break the secret.

I miss those games we shared more than anything. It's been a long time since life felt that playful. A good while since it felt quite so free.

On Eddie's advice, I set myself up with an all-you-can-eat breakfast and take some fresh air out on the Strip. I have bacon slathered in maple syrup and a mountain of scrambled eggs and toast, all for $1.99. I don't stay out for long. It's too hot to breathe this afternoon, let alone walk, and I still haven't managed to catch up with Joe. He was out when I tried to get hold of him last night, but the time difference means he should just be getting home from work.

I try several times but the answerphone keeps picking up and I end up leaving him a short message. Just to let him know that I'm safe. And that he's not to worry about me. And that Casablanca's more fun than I could ever have imagined.

For the next three hours I work on my card-handling skills and concentrate on getting myself into character. I'm meant to be a wealthy businesswoman who runs a cosmetics company in London, and Eddie thinks I should play it dumb and pretty. All the other players are of a similar background. Businessmen, oil men, bonds salesmen, importer/exporters, all lured here by private invitation. He's been working on the guest list for the last six months. Scouring the card rooms for rich people with more money than sense, who think they know more about poker than they do. They've come to play for high stakes, in a club that smells of tobacco and risk, with a man who's supposed to be a world champion.

That man is Ray Cleaver, the person who stole Louie's wife out from under his nose and almost crippled him all over again. He's here to separate the wealthy losers from their money, but he doesn't realise that he's the real mark.

He doesn't realise that Eddie and Big Louie have stayed in touch these last two years, or that the pair of them have been planning to set him up. When Eddie visited his house and offered him a place in this game he thought he was coming as a friend. When Eddie asked for a ten per cent share of anything he wins, he didn't debate it for a second. It seems Ray's a little short of cash right now. Because his second-hand wife turned out to be quite high-maintenance. Some people might even call her aggravating.

At seven o'clock sharp Eddie calls my room and I try one more time to reach Joe. He's not at home and his mobile's switched to voicemail and I'm beginning to get a little nervous. I want to touch base before I set off, to know there's somewhere real to go home to after I'm done. I just want to know that he's there; that he still loves me; that one day he might understand what I'm about to do.

I take one last look at myself in the mirror and head down to the foyer to meet Eddie. I think I have it about right. I've dispensed with the false eyelashes and the heavy lipstick and I look simple and sexy and classy. People glance up from their games as I walk past and some fat men in shorts start to whistle.

Eddie whistles louder than all the rest.

'Goddam,' he says, running his eyes over my dress. 'I'll tell you something, if you don't make it big as a card shark in this town, you could always get yourself a spot over at Hooters.'

We're parked outside a dingy topless bar a few blocks from the Strip and my heart is hammering right through my chest. I'm trying to keep it in check but I'm sure Eddie can sense that I'm nervous. He tells me once more that it'll be fine. That it doesn't matter if I blow it, that I should just try to do my very best. I nod gently and wipe my palms on the upholstery. Eddie reaches into his pocket.

'Here,' he says, handing me a note. 'This is for you.'

'What is it?'

'Well, why don't you look?'

It's a scrap of paper with a phone number inside, scratched out faintly in pencil.

'I don't get it,' I say, shaking my head at Eddie. 'Whose number is this?'

'Number of the man who knows where your dad's at. Big Louie wanted me to give it to you before you went in.'

I shake my head. I still don't get it.

'Look,' says Eddie, taking hold of my hand, 'he wanted to give you the chance to back out. He knows how much he's asking of you, and I know you're nervous an' all, but the point is you can walk away now. You can get out of the car, walk to the nearest phone box and find out exactly where he's at. The Big Man wanted you to have the choice. He wanted you to do this out of your own free will. He respects you too much to play it any other way.'

I don't know what to say. I turn the scrap of paper over in my hand until I've memorised every single digit.

'Well?' says Eddie, after a while. 'Are we still going inside or ain't we?'

'Yes,' I say, quietly. 'We are.'

'Good,' he says, 'I'm glad. That's what he thought you'd say.'

'What about you, Eddie? What did you think?'

'The Big Man's got the best instincts I've ever seen, kid. If he has faith in you, then so do I.'

54

The card room is set back behind the strip club and it's the grottiest space I've been in since I arrived. Dark walls, low ceilings and a floor scattered with G-strings and broken sequins; evidence that it was once used as a dressing room. The other players seem to be loving it – tanned men in Italian silk shirts and expensive suits, with gold Rolexes glinting brightly on their arms. They're enjoying the sleaze and the mess and the sweet odour of risk, and they all feel this is exactly as it should be. They've left their suites and their chauffeurs and their Jacuzzis and their wives, to come and play hardball with the low-lifes. No fancy cocktails, no vintage malt, just a keg of cold beer and a half empty bowl of stale potato chips. And now they have a moll to play with too. A woman in a red dress with a cute English accent who doesn't know her flops from her four flush.

The nine of us mill around making polite conversation, waiting for the game to get under-way. They ask me about London and quiz me about my business, but everyone seems fairly relaxed. Maybe it's because it doesn't matter if they win or lose. A thirty-thousand-dollar stake is a piss in the ocean to each and every one of them, and it's mostly their pride that's at stake. What they've come for is an evening of light entertainment: a chance to prove something to themselves, and to show each other that they can hold their own against a champ.

I chat and nod and smile at their stupid jokes, and every now and again I ask one of them to fill me in on a couple of the rules. They circle like vultures and chide me for drinking milk, and I should feel uneasy, but I don't. Tonight I feel just like Jimmy Silk Socks, the night he came to our winter kitchen and claimed that he couldn't play, and walked away with a piece of my father's soul.

When Eddie walks into the room, the pair of us act like we've never met. He greets everybody warmly, thanks them for coming and asks if they've got everything that they need. This question is met with hoots of laughter. Back at the casinos, high-rollers like them are treated to five-star hookers, lavish dinners and private jets, but Eddie thinks he knows what they really want. They want to feel dangerous. They want to feel like they're starring in a film. Tonight they're the Man, and any moment now Eddie's going to introduce them to the Cincinnati Kid. For a small share of the winnings and a nominal fee, he's endeavoured not to disappoint them.

'This here is my good buddy Ray,' says Eddie, introducing him. 'One of the finest poker players in the state. Top ten in the whole country come to that. Prefers the cash games to the tournaments, so you might not've heard his name all that much. But what the hell. You lightweights ready to take him on or not?'

The others nod and grin and try not to stare, but I can tell they're excited by the way he looks. He's lean and hollow cheeked with skin the colour of lard and has a narrow scar branded into his left eyebrow. He's wearing a torn denim jacket and a stained cotton T-shirt and a needle of contempt in his eyes. He's the kind of man their wives would secretly like to sleep with, and they know it. The kind of man they'd all love to beat.

We take our places at the poker table and I position myself directly opposite Ray. He glances up at me from time to time, checking me out, but he has no plans to take it easy on me because I'm a woman. Eddie stands next to the makeshift bar; pouring beer and making coffee and adjudicating any hands that go awry. Some of the players aren't sure of the betting structure and they want to know how much they can raise. Eddie says the same thing every time. Any amount. You can raise it up as high as you like.

All of these men have expensively educated brains but it's clear none of them really knows poker. They babble incoherently when they're chasing weak hands and they're frighteningly composed when they've found their cards. They play loose and aggressive with big raises and bigger reraises and some of them bet every single pot. It feels like a sign of weakness for them to fold, when in fact just the opposite is true.

The mathematicians among them work through the pot odds from time to time, but eventually their impatience gets the better of them. They're hard players to bluff and it's difficult to bully them off a hand, because they can't bear not to know whether they would have won or not. In contrast, Ray is the essence of control. He plays tight and hard and doesn't say too much and never looks like he's under any pressure. The other men have 'tells' as bright as neon billboards advertising their hands, but Ray barely fidgets or seems to move. He's one of those mental athletes that Big Louie talked about, and as far as he's concerned this is the Saturday morning 'little league'.

The first time the cards come to me to deal, I'm pretty sure they can see my fingers shaking. A Hollywood agent named Sonny asks if I want him to take over, and I smile and tell him I'm OK. I can see Eddie watching me from the back of the room. He's trying to look composed but he's shifting from foot to foot, nervously rubbing the crown of his Stetson.

I calm myself and take the cards in my palm. I gather up the discards from the last hand and mix them into the pack – neat and fast – so I know exactly where each of them is. The two queens that Rolex Man threw away after the flop, the ace ten of clubs that lost the last hand for Sonny. The nine, ten, jack that almost made a straight, and the pair of kings that I threw away as soon as they were dealt to me. Because I wanted them exactly where I could see them. And right now I can see the whole pack. All fifty-two cards shining brightly in my palm, as clearly as if they were all turned face up.

The second before I offer the cards up to be cut, I run through the digits of my father's phone number in my head. I need to remember why I'm doing this, I need to feel centred and alert. It does the job. I crimp the pack and offer it up to the man in the blue silk shirt, and he separates the pack exactly how I want him to. I riffle them one more time, until each card is back in its place, breathe deeply and serve up the deal. Two kings to Sonny, two queens to the sky-blue shirt, and to myself I deal the beginnings of a high-end straight.

When the flop comes out, the kings and queens both make two pairs and I pick up the ten that I need. The two of them bet big and I call all the way to the last card: to fifth street. Their hands didn't improve, this much I know, but I've filled up the straight I was looking for. I mixed it all up like a gourmet cook, and now I add a little extra seasoning just to convince them. I shuffle up my chips, one-handed as usual, but this time I spill them like a goon. To my own amazement I even manage to blush, and now my opponents are sure I've got nothing. The kings win or the queens win, but one thing's for sure; the girl in the red dress has lost.

There are five thousand dollars' worth of chips on the table when the target starts shooting back and I come out raising. The pair of them bet into me like starving dogs, reading my reraise for a bluff. Seconds later it's all done. I sigh and apologise and turn over my high-end straight: nine through king. A short silence from the table, followed by groans of disbelief.

And so it begins.

Rolex Man and the sky-blue shirt burn out fairly quickly after that. They didn't appreciate being beaten by a woman and they were too eager to prove it was a fluke. I let Ray finish them off and lose a couple of small hands myself, so he doesn't get edgy or suspicious. The plan is to leave Ray in all the way to the end; that way it'll hurt him all the more when he loses.

I quickly settle into a pattern. I cheat at random intervals – no more than three or four times in every hour – but it's enough to give me a sizeable edge. I make an effort to win a small proportion of games I don't deal, but I'm careful not to take any risks. Occasionally I set strong players up against one another, so they'll knock each other out and narrow the field. Now and then a player comments on my 'good fortune', but they're too bound up with their own play to detect a lasting pattern in mine.

By midnight everyone is getting a little fraught and the stakes are growing bigger and wilder. I have to stay centred and composed. I finger the piece of paper in my pocket and count cards to keep myself alert. I run through old Rat Pack hands and work out life stories for my opponents and try not to think about Joe. I think about Big Louie's flower, pressed inside the copy *Super/System* that he gave me, and my father's matchbook still tucked inside my purse.

By three o'clock I've taken down four more players. I have a pile of chips in front of me as wide as a birthday cake, and Eddie is staring at my hands like he's fallen in love with them. The cards slide out like they're on rails. From the middle, from the base, from the depths of the pack, never sticking or protruding or going astray. I'm rigorous and patient and I time it just right, ensuring that I always keep it simple. Just when they think I'm betting into nothing I frustrate them by turning over a marginal winning hand. Just when they think I'm getting cocky, I soothe their egos by messing up a couple of bets and letting them glance down the cleavage of my dress.

An hour later there's only three of us left. Ray and I have nearly three-quarters of the chips between us and an oil man from Nebraska is limping along behind us like an injured horse. It's my deal again and I'm riffling the cards, preparing to finish the oil man off. I hold queens full of tens, he has jacks full of tens, and this time he's sure he has me beaten. He smiles and pushes the remainder of his chips into the centre. 'All-in,' he says. 'I got you. I'm all-in.'

I call and shrug my shoulders and he immediately knows the way this is going to go. He stands up before I turn over my winning hand.

'Well done,' he says, graciously, reaching over to shake my hand. 'You found good cards, no doubt about it, but I congratulate you, miss, you're quite a player.'

I thank him and rake in his remainder of his chips, but for the first time tonight I feel guilty. I know he can afford to lose it, but it troubles me to be congratulated for cheating. I feel ashamed suddenly, and weak, like I've taken the easy way out. Maybe that's what Big Louie used to feel like all that time. Knowing he could do better if he gave himself the chance, but unable to resist stacking the odds in his favour. The truth is, I can see how it might become irresistible. To sacrifice the challenge and the beauty of the game, for the safety of knowing you can never lose.

I stretch my arms, shift in my seat and try to switch my attention back to the table. Eddie is gearing up for the finale. He's taken off his hat and he's wiping his brow and fixing the remaining pair a fresh pot of coffee.

'Just you and me then?' says Ray, quietly.

'Yes,' I say. 'Just you and me.'

He waits until Eddie brings the coffee before he drops the bombshell. A few of the losing players have stayed around to see how it ends, and Ray suggests one of them take over dealing duty until it's over. They've come all this way, they've contributed a lot of money to the pot, it's only fair that they get to feel included. He's been concentrating all night, and to be honest it would help him if he didn't have to take his turn at dealing. I'm not sure if he suspects me or if he's just being cautious, but it's already too late to protest. The guy in the blue silk shirt is reaching eagerly for the pack. He wants to serve up the showdown between the sexy English girl and the trailer-trash punk, and he can't wait to get himself started.

My stomach sinks, my mouth fills with saliva and I try to keep the fear out of my eyes. Eddie can't bear to look at me, but there's no way I can walk away from the table now. This game goes all the way to the end. Until one of us has every single chip.

I do what I can for the next twenty minutes or so, but one on one gives you no place to hide. Ray doesn't make it easy. He never takes his eyes off me. He pulls me around by a lead while I grow weaker and weaker, and it's clear from his face that he's enjoying it. I can imagine him arranging to have Big Louie beaten up, and I can see him enjoying the sound of every blow. I can imagine him watching Louie's plane take off from the airport; never once worrying that his bad deed would come back to haunt him.

By dawn, it's clear that I'm almost done for. I have less than twenty per cent of the chips left in front of me and Ray is sitting on a multi-coloured chip mountain. The oil man has taken over as dealer and I'm praying that he might bring me some luck. I tip up the corners of my cards and stare down at two bright red queens. It's the best hand I've seen in the last hour of play and I know I'm going to have to make it count.

I make a tentative bet like I've got nothing much and Ray comes steaming in with a twenty-thousand-dollar raise. I hesitate for a moment and call him, knowing that if he bets any more I'll be all-in.

The flop comes down seven of spades, jack of spades, queen of clubs, and my heart leaps when I see the third queen. I'm sure Ray can hear the rush of blood steaming through my veins, but amazingly it seems that he can't.

I try to work out what he has. The size of his original raise made me think he had an ace, but I'm pretty sure the flop hasn't helped him. I check my three queens, hoping to trap him and he checks along with me, indicating that I'm right. We wait solemnly for the next card to come down. A king this time. The king of spades.

Ray's eyes flicker almost imperceptibly and I notice his fingers edging forward towards his chips. He wants me to think that last king helped him. That he's holding another two in his hand. I don't think he has them. He might be holding one, which won't stand up against my queens, but his eyes look greedy for something else. I'm not sure what makes me sense it, but all of a sudden I know exactly what he wants. Ray is on a flush draw – he's praying for another spade on the final card.

And that's the moment Eddie opens the window. A blush of wind sweeps through the curtains, cooling the stagnant air and fighting with the cigarette smoke and sweat. It takes a moment before it reaches me, but when it does it almost knocks me off my chair. It's the sweetest thing I've ever smelt. A scent like ice and mountain flowers and limes and English roses, topped off with a glassy top note of the Pacific Ocean. It has the whole world wrapped up inside of it, the fragrance of deserts and wheat fields and palm trees and clematis and a lost soul who's forgotten how to live.

I breath the salt-laced air deep into my lungs and prepare myself to let go. Ray's tapping his foot and waiting for me to act, and I turn round to grab the oil man's wrist.

'How much is it worth? That gold watch on your arm. How much did you pay for that watch?'

He shrugs and runs his hand over the tiny diamonds and says, 'It's about fifty thousand dollars' worth of watch.'

'OK,' I say, 'now take it off.'

'What for? What you gonna do with it?'

'I need it,' I say. 'I want to bet with it.'

Oil Man can't believe his luck. He can't wait to rip it off his hand. He slips it off his chubby fingers and tosses it towards me, and I catch it in my outstretched hand.

'Go ahead,' he says, 'but if you lose it, you ought to understand that you're going to owe me.'

'That's my problem,' I say, not even glancing at him, 'and while you're at it, I'll take a couple of your rings.'

'My rings?'

'You heard me. Take off your rings.'

Oil Man duly obliges and tosses another twenty thousand dollars' worth of gold into the pot. The atmosphere in the room is crackling with heat, and Ray looks nervous for the first time since he walked in. I don't even bother looking up at Eddie. I know he's about to piss his pants.

'You sure you want to do that?'

'Yes,' I say. 'No doubt about it.'

Ray thinks for a while and I reach for my glass of milk, think better of it and put it back down. Ray closes his eyes and comes back smiling; he thinks he's worked out my tell.

'This isn't what you wanted, is it?' he says, sourly. 'You were hoping to bluff me off the pot. With your baubles and your rich friends and your shitty rings. You only sip that milk when you're winning, so right now it seems to me like you've lost.'

I don't say anything. Not a word.

'How much is in there? A hundred and eighty?'

'Two hundred. Two hundred thousand dollars in the pot.'

'Well I'll meet it then. And I'll raise you all-in. That's another fifty to you. Now what do you say?'

This is the only second when I doubt it. Maybe he does have two kings in his hand after all. Maybe I'm wrong and he's set me up. For a second I think about bailing out and handing back the rings, and then he makes the most beautiful move. He rubs his hand down to his ankles, reaches for his socks and gives a little tug on the fabric. In that moment I know he doesn't have it. He ought to give it up but his pride won't let him fold, and I smile and glance over at Rolex Man's wrist. He doesn't wait to be asked. His watch is bigger and shinier and more expensive than the oil man's and he's already taking it off.

Eddie walks calmly towards the table and asks if he can deal up the final card. No one raises an objection. He discards the top one and reaches for the next, and I know that if it's a spade or another king then I'm done for. Ray and I both lean forward to watch it fall and the whole room is hushed to a frozen silence. The card hits the table in slow motion and I'm more excited than I've been in my entire life. I feel elated, high, abandoned; like I'm skiing down a mountain on a single ski with only my arms held out for balance. For a moment I'm actually living in this world, instead of sitting around on the edge of it waiting to die.

'Ace of clubs,' says Eddie, quietly. 'It's an ace.'

The other players stare at the table, waiting for one of us to react. A pale smile spreads across Ray's lips, and for a second he thinks he must have won. I called it right. He missed the spade flush he was looking for, but he hit two pairs on the last card.

He's almost out of his seat. He tips his ace of spades, king of clubs face up on the felt and raises his arms in the air.

'Aces,' he says, looking straight at me. 'I beat you with aces and kings.'

'No,' I say, standing up to face him. 'Not good enough. Not this time.'

I turn over my queens one by one. Three queens beats his two pairs hands down. I win and the whole place erupts.

I don't know where it came from but somebody found some

champagne. They're pouring it into cups and forcing it into my hand, and the oil man has just asked me to marry him. They've taken back their watches but he wants me to keep his rings because he thinks they brought me good luck. Eddie's shaking his head, trying to hide his delight, but he looks like he might be close to tears. Rolex Man is hugging me and telling me that he can't believe it, and Oil Man is swapping my chips for money. It's beautiful. A pile of crisp green dollar bills as high as a tower block, tall enough to buy the finest, widest garden.

Ray is staring at me like he's been run over by a truck. He looks dazed, like he's not sure what just happened. I decide to make it clear for him. I peel fifty dollars off the top of my new fortune and toss it to him across the table.

'Here,' I say, 'take this. Why don't you treat yourself to a taxi home?'

He stands up as if he's about to hit me and the oil man steps forward and holds him back. I walk over and tuck the crushed notes into his pocket and lean forward to whisper in his ear.

'Keep it,' I say. 'It's a gift from the Big Man. He says to buy your wife something nice.'

55

The sun is boiling up over the mountains, but I have to wrap my coat tight around me to keep warm. The champagne and the lack of sleep, and the shock of what I've just done, have left me feeling chilled and alone. I risked everything. Money I couldn't afford, things I didn't own, on the turn of a plastic-coated card. I keep expecting my elbows to itch or my brain to start counting, but all I feel now is empty.

The city looks tired through the dim tint of the limousine windows, like I've surprised it and caught it unawares. It's not up yet, not fully dressed, like a city caught without its make-up.

Eddie is busy making plans. He wants to train me and manage me, and he only wants ten per cent, but he's pretty sure we could become multimillionaires by the end of the year. He wants to mould me into a champion and buy me a Stetson of my very own, and he can't understand why I'm not more excited.

'Eddie?'

'Yeah.'

'Aren't we going the wrong way?'

'Nope, don't think so.'

'But we just passed the hotel. I'm sure we did, it's right back there.'

'No, see, we're not going to the hotel. You and me, we're going to the airport.'

'Why?'

'Well,' he says, 'we got to meet someone. We got someone important to pick up.'

He doesn't explain anything more until we get over to the arrivals hall. He pulls me by the hand, leads me through the early-morning crowds, and I ask him what I'm meant to be looking out for.

'Over there,' he says, 'by the slots. Looks like he's been playing for quite some time.'

It's Joe. Sitting on his suitcase with a worried smile on his face, a half-spent bucket of quarters clutched tightly in his hand. I can't believe it. He looks damaged and beautiful and exhausted, and I just want to reach out and hold him. I clutch my winnings to my chest and slowly, carefully, I walk towards him.

'How's your luck been?' I say, putting my arm through his.

'Not bad,' he says, gently. 'How was yours?'

'Good,' I say. 'My luck was good.'

We park up in one of the coffee shops behind the slots, and talk for the next couple of hours. He's jet-lagged and tired and almost as drained as me, and he still can't get over what I've done. He hasn't slept since I left; not since he caught up with Big Louie.

'He sent you out here?'

'Yeah, he did. I went over to his flat after I left you at the airport. After I watched you change terminals and check in for the Vegas flight. I guessed he'd be the only one who could explain it.'

'What did you think?'

'About you lying to me?'

'Well . . .'

'About you breaking someone's jaw?'

'Well, it wasn't actually me it—'

'About you coming over here to con people out of their money?'

'Yes . . . well . . . I mean, all of that, of course. But what did you make of him?'

'Louie? He was great. He made me a sandwich, showed me his photo albums and tried to force-feed me giant pickles.'

'Anything else?'

'Plenty. He told me that you were a bigger screw-up than he was, that you need me far more than I realise, and after that he sat me down and told me I was an idiot.'

'Really? He said that?'

'Yeah. He wanted to know what kind of a man would let his girlfriend give him the run-around like this. Let her fly halfway across the globe to gamble a fortune.'

I start to smile.

'What did you tell him?'

'I told him the truth. The kind of man whose girlfriend won't let him help her. The kind with a girlfriend who's tired of him, the kind who won't ever let him in.'

I fidget and gulp down some of my cold coffee.

'Please,' I say, 'you can't think that. I'm not tired of you . . . you've read it all wrong.'

He frowns hard, like he's not sure he believes me.

'Then why didn't you tell me what you were planning? You know I would have helped.'

'I'm not sure. I just thought . . . I suppose I thought you might try and stop me.'

He shakes his head.

'That's not true,' he says. 'You'd have done it anyway. You've never needed my advice for as long as I've known you.'

Joe looks confused. He rubs his fingers over the return portion of his plane ticket and runs his eyes longingly over the departure board. Perhaps there are things he's already missing. Things that he wants to get back for.

'Look. It's OK. I'll understand if you want to go home.'

'To what?'

'To the flat, to the business, to our friends. I'll understand if you want to get back . . . to Lorna.'

'To Lorna? What are you talking about?'

'I don't know. I mean, I've seen the way you two look at each other. I've seen how well you get on with Meg. You can't tell me you haven't thought about it. And you've been spending so much time together. You've been speaking to her almost every day.'

Joe stares at his drink like he's ashamed of me.

'Why do you think that is? Why do you think I've seen so much of her?'

I shake my head. I'm not sure I want to hear the answer.

'Because I had to talk to someone. Because you've turned into a brick wall these last few weeks and you keep on cutting me out. I didn't know what else to do. I thought she might have some answers, but Lorna's as worried as I am. You cut your friends out too, Audrey. Did you know that? You cut your friends out too.'

He lowers his head gloomily. Running his fingers over his cup.

'I'm sorry,' I say, 'I didn't realise. Really, I had no idea.'

He thinks for a long moment and then he sighs. He glances up at the departure board one more time, thinks better of it, then leans over to kiss me.

'Audrey,' he says, pushing my hair off my face, 'I love you to death, but you're the most infuriating person I've ever met. For once in your life you have to let someone in. The world won't stop turning if you take your eyes off it for a second. You're not the only one holding it up.'

'That's easy for you to say.'

'Is it?'

'Yes. You wander around the place without a care in the world, content to take everything as it comes. You don't even use a map. I mean, what kind of a person are you? Who gets into a car and drives all the way to the countryside without even consulting a map.'

He starts to smile.

'And anyway, how do you know?'

'Know what?'

'That the world won't fall down if I stop watching it.'

'I don't,' he says, gently. 'I'm just saying that I'll be there if it does.'

I reach over and take hold of his hand and squeeze his fingers so tightly it hurts.

'Louie was right,' he says, carefully. 'You're more deluded than he is. You're not the only one who's scared of the future. You're not the only one who's worried about being left on their own, of seeing everything they care about fall apart.'

I close my eyes for a second. Grab on to his hand even more tightly.

'I know that. I do. It's just that everything always has done in the past.'

'Well it won't this time. I promise you.'

'You promise?'

'Let's just say the odds are in our favour.'

I smile and loosen my grip.

'And besides,' he says, 'I can't afford to let you go now, can I?'

'Why not?'

'Because Eddie says you're going to earn us a small fortune, and because you look incredibly fucking sexy in that red dress.'

'You lovebirds ready to go to the hotel yet?'

It's Eddie. He's been waiting all this time.

'Yes,' I say, 'but I need to use the phone first. I need to call that number that you gave me.'

Eddie takes off his hat and runs his hand over his head.

'Ah, well, I meant to tell you about that. Uhm . . . it might not be quite what you was expecting.'

'What do you mean?'

'You hungry?'

'Eddie, what's that got to do with it? Who gives a shit if I'm hungry or not.'

'Well, see, that number I gave you . . . it's not exactly a contact for your dad . . . It's more like . . . something else.'

'What else, exactly?'

'Local Dunkin' Donuts.'

'Dunkin' Donuts?'

'Yep.'

'I don't understand. You said you were giving me the chance to walk away. You said Louie wanted me to have that number so I'd play the game of my own free will.'

'You're right, uh-huh, I did. But it sure helped your play though, didn't it? It sure helped you concentrate when you was mixing it up and shuffling out all those cards. And besides, kid. What did you expect? Once a hustler . . .'

I stare into my drink, wondering what to do next, and Eddie reaches over and puts his arm round my shoulder.

'Don't worry,' he says, cheerfully. 'We haven't double crossed you none. Your boyfriend knows where he's at, don't you?'

'Yes. Louie wrote it all down for me.'

Joe reaches into his pocket for his notes.

'He asked me to tell you something,' he says, unfolding the sheet of paper and handing it over.

'What was it?'

'He wanted you to know that he'd always have told you. Whichever way it would have ended.'

56

'The Anaconda Club?'

'Yeah. Big Louie thinks he's either there or out at some place called the Bicycle in LA. He goes to one or other of them every year around this time, to put in some practice for the World Series.'

'But he might not be? He could just as easily be somewhere else?'

'If he's not there, we'll try some other card rooms and casinos.'

'Like where?'

'I don't know. There's a whole list. We'll go through all of them if we have to. We could tour the circuit for a while, take a holiday. Do some travelling together, just the two of us.'

'What about the ornamental lake?'

'Pete can take care of it.'

'You're sure?'

'Why not? He's capable enough. Who knows, if I let him look after the business for a couple of months, Lorna might even start to take him seriously.'

'Well, what about moving to the countryside? What about us settling down and having kids?'

'Bollocks to the countryside. I don't care where we live. Like I said, it was only a suggestion. As far as having kids goes . . . well, I think we'll both know when it's right.'

'Then I should do what Eddie said. I should play a little bit. I'd be crazy not to.'

'Play?'

'*Poker*. A woman's never won the World Series . . . in two

years time, maybe three . . . if I studied hard, and worked on my people-reading skills . . . and I've got a pretty healthy bankroll to start us off. I've got twenty thousand dollars' worth of gold rings that I won.'

'That you *hustled.*'

'Well, technically, yes. But I like to think of them as a graduation gift.'

'So that's it? You're not going to cheat again?'

'What'd be the point? It's too easy. And it would be exciting. A challenge. To take everything I've learned and play for real. It's good to take a chance once in a while.'

'Is it?'

'Yes,' I say, reaching over to kiss him. 'It sort of lets you know you're alive.'

'This is it. This is the place. You want me to go in and check it out for you?'

Eddie offers to go inside and see whether anyone is at the tables yet, while Joe and I find some shade away from the sun.

'What time is it?'

'Almost twelve.'

'What time in London?'

'Around seven.'

'There's someone we need to call then. I have to let him know how it finished.'

I let the phone ring for as long as I can stand it, before setting the receiver back down. I so badly wanted to speak to him, to thank him for everything he did. For teaching me and guiding me and pointing me in the direction of my father, and for telling Joe everything that I couldn't. I wanted to hear him call me an idiot one more time, even though I know he'd be proud. That I managed to take the risk and play it straight; for all of the times he wasn't able to.

It's not to be. I'm pretty sure Eddie beat me to it, but

right now I couldn't feel any happier. I walk back from the payphone like I'm floating on air, with a foot-wide grin on my face.

'How is he? What did he say?'

'Nothing, he didn't say anything at all. He didn't answer the phone.'

'Right. Maybe he was asleep.'

'No, he wasn't asleep.'

'How do you know?'

'I just do. I'm certain. He isn't sleeping any more, Joe. He was out.'

Eddie emerges from the dimly lit card room and waves for us both to come over.

'What does he look like, this father of yours? He ever wear a thin leather coat?'

'Sometimes, yes. Big Louie says he has a poker name. They call him the Professor.'

'Well, I don't know anything about that, but there's an English guy in there driving everyone half crazy. Telling them all kinds of goofy stories.'

'What kind of stories?'

'Some shit about the moon and the tides, and somethin' about some whacko polar bird.'

'A bird?'

'Yep, some bird than can never seem to settle. That likes to scoot around all over the damned place. Flies twenty thousand miles every winter, which is quite some distance when you come to think about it.

57

I'm not sure what part of me he recognises but his eyes flicker the moment I walk in. Perhaps it's the length of my fingers, or the colour of my hair, or the matchbook that I'm clutching in my hand.

He's halfway through his story when he stops. Some of the players think he's finished, but a couple want to find out how it ends.

'So, what kind of a bird is it?' says one of them. 'What kind of a dumb-assed bird flies halfway round the world, from one pole to another, every winter?'

My father shakes his head. For a second he can't seem to remember.

'The Arctic tern,' I say, gently, watching the tears spill on to his cheeks. 'The bird is an Arctic tern.'

Acknowledgments

For their talent, advice and generous encouragement a heart-felt thank you to the following: Carolyn Mays, Claire Wachtel, Jonny Geller, Jane Gelfman and the fabulous Hannah Griffiths. Also join me in raising your glasses to the entire Morrow team. My thanks to Geoff for introducing me to poker and getting me hooked, to Andy for putting up with my burgeoning obsession, and a special mention to those who stayed up long into the night; betting, drinking and telling stories and providing such excellent company. To those who took money off me (that includes you Hyde, Chappell, Morgan and Johnny Pesto), I ought to warn you, I've been practicing.